Jus.
Beyond
the **EDGE**

2011

Gene,
THANKS for
your support

Just Beyond the **EDGE**

Michael Hager

Mill City Press
Minneapolis, MN

Mill City Press, Inc.

212 3rd Avenue North, Suite 290

Minneapolis, MN 55401

612.455.2294

www.millcitypublishing.com

ISBN - 978-1-936400-38-6

ISBN - 1-936400-38-3

LCCN - 2010935607

Cover Design and Typeset by Melanie Shellito

Printed in the United States of America

www.michaelhager.net

To Tyson,
who has taught me that finding courage
far outweighs the acceptance of failure.

ACKNOWLEDGEMENTS

Gratitude to my friends Bonnie Gordon, Carol Wheeler and Minerva Neiditz for their suggestions and editorial comments. I will be eternally grateful to Alexis White for editing my book. Thanks to Joan Columbus for providing a safety net with her proofreading and advice.

I could not complete this acknowledgement without lifting up the wonderful work of Christina, my wife for over thirty-five years. Her encouragement, patience, and dedication in helping me complete this labor of love are unfathomable.

Nothing goes untouched just beyond the edge,
in that sacred space between life and death.
Where the survivor is seldom mistaken for the winner.
Where the splendor of love is overshadowed by its frailties.
Where the truth is obscured by the compassion of lies.
And where all things we hold precious, can vanish instantly.

MDH

CHAPTER 1

The late spring of 1983 was already rendering its vengeance on the high desert of central Mexico. The tormented landscape lay scorched and dying outside the window of the slow moving passenger train. Chase Chandler squirmed around in the broken down seat trying to find a more comfortable position. Resting on his elbow, with his open palm tucked under his chin, Chase struggled not to dose off from the stifling heat. His eyes strained to track the fleeting scene of half-starving cattle wandering aimlessly through the saguaro cactus. These pathetic animals, their rib bones protruding with a grotesque transparency, were only a shadow of their relatives north of the border on his family's ranch in west Texas.

Through the half-open window, Chase could smell the faint aroma of blooming sagebrush intermingled with the acrid odor of the coal-fed engine as it drifted past and into the over-crowded passenger car. His thoughts were stationary, holding every frame, trying not to let go of this momentary distraction. He fought off the temptation to answer the pestering questions that kept crisscrossing his mind.

"Where you headed, friend?" an unfamiliar voice repeated for the second time.

The coarse sound was originating from the pock-faced man sitting in the aisle seat across from him. Chase was one of only two gringos who had crowded onto the train headed for the interior of colonial Mexico. They had left the border town of Nuevo Laredo the day before yesterday, but as usual, the lumbering procession of steel and wood stopped often and for long unexplained stopovers. Chase knew before he departed that it would be a small miracle if he arrived on time at his final destination in Queretaro.

Once again, the persistent stranger inquired, "Down here on business or pleasure?"

Chase remained lost somewhere between the rhythmic cadence of the train wheels and his crowded thoughts. He struggled to ignore the call to conversation. Chase had more pressing problems to solve than entertaining another lonely traveler looking for idle conversation. He was all too familiar with these conversations spurred by long hours of boredom, which invariably started with the same curious question, "What's it like doing business in a foreign country? It must be really exciting." Unfortunately, this was far from the truth. Chase's experience over the past five years of managing a business in the southern hemisphere could be characterized as more frustrating than "exciting". It required a determined patience, an unyielding ability to adapt to the "mañana" mentality of the Latin culture. Patience was a quality Chase prided himself on, having learned it at a very early age while waiting for his mother to get ready for Sunday church. Still, there were times even for Chase when confronted with such mundane questions that it challenged him beyond his own boundaries of tolerance.

Somewhere on the outskirts of Chase's consciousness, the stranger's signal finally eked through. "I'm sorry....I didn't mean to be rude. Trains have a way of dulling the senses." Chase turned to face the man peering at him.

"You were saying?" Chase asked, still resisting the invitation to fully engage.

The flaccid-jawed man wiped his sweaty brow with a yellow-stained handkerchief and responded in a slow curling southern drawl, "Yeah, these old trains have a cadence as comforting as an old rocking chair." He twisted sideways for better eye contact. "So...are you down here on business or pleasure?"

"Business, mixed with a very little pleasure," Chase reluctantly offered as he returned his attention to the endless panorama of sand and tumbleweeds. The scene outside his window was similar to the dry west Texas landscape Chase had been raised in. He knew the hardships of this wide open country demanded a certain resiliency, an ability to coexist with nature's angry stepchild. As his Uncle Chas often quoted, "*You don't ever beat this god-forsaken land; you just try to survive it.*" This time-honored tenet for staying alive in the badlands of the Lone Star state applied to plants, animals, and even small children. After all, this part of Texas was home to the notorious hanging judge, Roy Bean; bolts of sheet lighting that could knock a cowboy off his horse, and black tornadoes that could swallow up a man's life in a heartbeat.

Undeterred, his seatmate persisted in his attempt to garner Chase's full attention. He held out his stubby-fingered hand hoping for a reciprocating handshake.

"Frank Evans is my name, but most people just call me Frankie E. Alabama, born and bred."

"Chase Walker Chandler..... Pecos, Texas," he said, firmly gripping Frankie E's sweaty palm. Chase didn't actually live in the town of Pecos, but resided on a thirty-thousand-acre family-owned ranch about twenty miles outside the city limits.

"Wow.... that's a mouthful. Sounds like a lot of tradition comes with that handle," Frankie E. chuckled, having found a clever way to extend the conversation beyond just introductions.

If he only knew how much *tradition*, Chase thought. Chase, even at the age of thirty-two, still cringed at the thought of explaining his name to strangers. Being from Texas, he never had a chance to get used to one simple name like most folks he had met. His mother, Rebecca, called him by his first and middle name, Chase Walker, except when he had broken one of her many rules. Then it was Chase Walker Chandler, with sharp biting emphasis on his middle name. His father and most of his uncles called him C. W., pronounced "C. Dub." This was his "good old boy" name, and one he seldom shared outside of his close friends and family. Proud as he was of his Texas heritage, he wasn't about to have his future dictated by two simple initials that sounded more like a radio station call sign than a proper name. It was just before he headed off to attend the University of Texas that he made it known to old and new acquaintances that he preferred to be called Chase Walker Chandler. He chose the name because it was the closest he could come to his paternal grandfather's name, Charles Walker Chandler.

Chase tried to calm his mind before answering Frankie E., "You're right, being from Texas, tradition *is* everything. And I guess that even applies to how we hand out our names," said Chase, intent on changing the subject. "What kind of business keeps you busy?" Chase flinched at his question, knowing even before the last word rolled off his slightly chapped lips that he had made the classic mistake of asking a complete stranger such a loaded question. He could already see the long horizon of the ensuing conversation rolling out of Frankie E's mouth. Fortunately, in this particular case, Chase was only traveling as far as Querétaro, about a five-hour train ride from San Luis Potosí, where he had started his day.

"Well....." Frankie E. took a deep breath, as if preparing for takeoff, "like most businessmen down this way, I'm in the import business. Ironwork. Not just any ironwork.....but ornate designs for classic old homes and buildings. Fancy gates, garden arbors, stairways, and such." Without taking a breath, he continued, "Hell, I ship wrought iron from all over Mexico to the U.S. Three years ago in '80, I had my best year, almost $425,000 in gross sales. Not bad for an old fart like me. How about you? What business are you in?"

Chase, after a long pause, responded, "Transport. We lease railcars to foreign governments and private corporations transporting materials in and out of Mexico. My family has been in the same business for over seventy-five years..... I guess you could say I'm carrying on the legacy."

"Leasing railcars, well, that's a new one on me. You ride these old trains long enough and you run into every type. Heck, I've probably shipped materials on your railcars." He cleared his throat, spitting into his handkerchief. "It's a small world after all, wouldn't you say? Where you headed to, Chase?"

Frankie E. didn't give Chase a chance to answer before resuming. "I'm on my way to Puebla, just outside of Mexico City. It's a great old colonial town, with all the trappings; bars that stay open all night, willing señoritas, and an unlimited amount of what I call *mis amigos*. Everyone in town is your "friend" and has something they want to sell you. From drugs to high-end silver jewelry to selling their sister for a night on the town, they got it all. It took me a couple of trips to figure out how to get them off my back. I just tell them I'm a bounty hunter looking for criminals south of the border, and that's the end of the conversation. No more hassles." Frankie E. stopped talking to wheeze out a reflective chuckle.

Chase had to restrain himself from laughing out loud at Frankie E's colorful ruse to fend off unwanted attention. Chase struggled to imagine this pot-bellied, balding salesman from Alabama pawning himself off as a hardened bounty hunter. He knew something about the business of capturing fugitives south of the border. Chase had lied to Frankie E. about being in Mexico solely on behalf of Lone Star Leasing. He was actually here to fulfill a contract he had as an extraction specialist with the Federal Bureau of Investigation. Chase had been working for the Bureau as an independent contract agent for several years. His specialty was to track down fugitives who had fled to Mexico and bring them back to the U.S. for prosecution. The FBI had no legal jurisdiction in Mexico, so when they lost the trail of the bad guys south of the border they relied on *"outside"* help. That's where Chase came into the picture. The Bureau had a long-standing policy of maintaining covert activities outside of the U.S. borders. The FBI of the 1980's was not about to be bound by legal jurisdictions or international boundaries in hunting down their quarry.

Chase had started working for the Bureau almost immediately after the Vietnam War. His assignments were generally located in Mexico and Central America. More recently the Bureau had wanted to expand his territory to Southeast Asia due to his high success rate, but Chase declined, wanting to stay close to home. He still had a commitment to his family to run Lone Star Leasing and try to expand their operations in the southern hemisphere. Even though he had only worked for the Bureau for eight years, Chase was one of the Bureau's most highly respected independent agents. Because of his reputation, he only took on assignments that interested him and warranted risking his life. Of course, he expected to be well compensated, but it was not all about the money for Chase. If he wasn't living on the edge, he was miserable. The tedious work of the leasing business wasn't enough to satisfy his need for the occasional adrenaline rush he got from working on assignments for the FBI.

Chase's relationship with covert government agencies had a long history. It all started for him right after he graduated *cum laude* from the University of Texas in 1969 as a pre-law student. He was twenty-three years old. Vietnam was just starting to really heat up and Chase wanted to be a part of the action. He enlisted in the Army Officer Corps and immediately demonstrated an ability and serious interest in undercover work, especially given his facility with foreign languages. Chase was totally fluent in Spanish, having worked with migrant workers since he was a kid on his family's ranch. He had taken a double major in Chinese and business law in college, and his fluency in Chinese made him invaluable as a candidate for infiltration activities behind enemy lines in North Vietnam.

During the early part of the war, Army intelligence had a complex network of secret agents who operated out of Singapore. Singapore was a haven for all kinds of clandestine activities, both legal and illegal. On any given day, the streets of Singapore were bustling with drug traffickers, jewel thieves, and special agents operating on the Asian front. Chase's specific expertise was the extraction of captured U.S soldiers and fellow agents. Army Intelligence used his skills only for the most sensitive missions which generally meant that his life and the lives of his targets were on the line. Although he primarily operated out of Singapore, his assignments often required that he cross into enemy territory. Occasionally, he was forced to venture deep into North Vietnam to rescue captured pilots. Chase was particularly known for his patience, his strict attention to detail, and above all, his reputation for being relentless in completing his assignments without any injuries or casualties. During his entire tenure in Army intelligence, he never failed to extract his intended targets and bring them safely back to freedom. Like all agents, he was trained not to take his assignments personally, but this was just not part of his make-up. Getting those guys out was *very* personal to him. His dedication to his compatriots was legendary, even to the point of personally sacrificing himself. On two different occasions he took bullets for them, one in the chest that passed through his rib cage just inches from his heart, almost ending his life. It was a tough recovery period but he refused to be shipped back home until after the war was over. Although honored several times for his valor, Chase remained the quiet hero who kept to himself and avoided the glory of the praise as if it was the plague. He just wanted to get home in one piece, to hell with all the shiny medals.

Two months after the war ended, he resigned his commission and resumed working for Lone Star Leasing. He enjoyed the extra challenge of working in the foreign business environment, but soon became bored with the day-to-day grind. When he was contacted eight months after the war by the FBI, he jumped at the opportunity to re-engage in covert activities. The Bureau and he worked out an arrangement allowing him to act as a contract independent agent, which kept the Bureau out of trouble when and if foreign governments started asking questions about their covert operations. Chase knew, if push came to shove, the

FBI would categorically deny any knowledge of his activities on their behalf. He gratefully accepted the risk that came with this kind of arrangement rather than face the complacency of his monotonous job a Lone Star Leasing.

At first, the FBI assigned him to low profile cases, but with each assignment the Bureau realized how thorough and dedicated Chase was in his work. It wasn't long before he moved up on the list of top independent operatives. In a slick, efficient fashion, he proved there was no one better at taking on and successfully completing extraction missions. Realizing the significance of having a resource like Chase available to them, the Bureau only assigned him to the most sensitive, high profile cases. His targets ranged from terrorists trying to make their way to safer havens in South America to U.S. fugitives crossing over into Mexico. In his most recent assignment, he had just brought in a Federal agent who had decided to trade sensitive information with the Russians. It was a major coup for the Bureau and proved once again how valuable Chase was to their operations. The Bureau Chief wanted to bring Chase in-house but Chase politely declined. He valued his independence more than the prestige of promotional opportunities inside the Bureau. Chase knew he was in control of his own destiny, and that was right where wanted to keep it.

Even though he was at the top of his game, working for the Bureau had its challenges. Keeping his clandestine life secret from his friends and family was one of them. With the exception of his international underground contacts, he kept his work for the Bureau totally confidential. It sometimes made for a lonely existence, but he wouldn't have it any other way. He liked being a loner and making decisions without having to consider other people's feelings. Living this double life allotted him very little time for a personal life which, for now, fit his lifestyle perfectly. Yes, he had the occasional affairs with young Texas socialites that his mother conveniently arranged, but they were all short lived, much to his mother's constant disappointment. It was clear to Chase from her relentless matchmaking efforts on his behalf that she would never give up her hopes that her only son might someday marry and grant her the grace of grandchildren. To date though, Chase had won out over her efforts, knowing he was far from being ready to settle down into the idyllic existence of family life she so much wanted for him.

For the next hour and half, Chase politely listened to the rattle of Frankie E.'s chatter as it was infused with the constant clanking of the railcar wheel. Occasionally, he would glance out the window in the hope of seeing familiar landmarks that would signal his final destination. He couldn't stop himself from slipping into thoughts about getting to his home base in the quiet surroundings of Ciudad Hidalgo and working out the details of his current case for the Bureau. Not unlike most assignments he took on, once he started, it consumed all aspects of his life. This trip to Mexico was no exception. He was in pursuit of an embezzler named John Wallace, who had raked off over half a million dollars from a federal loan agency in Iowa. The difference with this guy was that he had killed his devoted wife to run off with a young blonde bombshell, hoping to start a new life south of the border. Why was it always the middle-aged accountant fighting off the doldrums of life, who somehow convinced himself he could pull off the crime of the century? Chase had seen this so many times, it almost bored him.

Chase glanced over at his seatmate and resisted laughing out loud at the thought of enlisting Frankie E. to assist him in his current assignment. Looking over at the sagging figure of the man facing him, he realized Frankie E. would have trouble catching an old lady shoplifting at the local five and dime, much less capturing a murderer.

About an hour after Frankie E. followed him to the club car for a drink, they pulled into the station at Querétaro. Chase politely said good-bye to Frankie E. and wished him a safe journey. Frankie E. told Chase that hopefully they would run into each other some other time, so they could continue their conversation. Chase chuckled under his breath and mumbled a faint acknowledgement of Frankie E's hopeful prediction. Chase grabbed his bag from the overhead rack and moved quickly down the aisle, anxious to get on with the serious business of tracking down John Wallace, who was still at large, hiding out somewhere in the highlands of Mexico.

CHAPTER 2

Chase stepped off onto the well-worn wooden planks of the Querétaro station platform, thankful to have escaped from the constant babble of Frankie E. He glanced over his shoulder to make sure Frankie E. wasn't following him. When he turned back around, two well-dressed Mexican men who had been waiting for him for over two hours in the hot sun, approached to greet him. Chase towered over his Latin counterparts. At six foot two he still felt somewhat out of place when he traveled south of the border. He bore the typical rugged features of his Scottish heritage, mixed with some Cherokee from his great-grandmother's side. His skin was a deep shade of bronze from long hours of working in the Pecos River Valley sun. His smile was friendly, but not overly enthusiastic. He carried himself with imposing confidence that left a lasting impression on anyone who met him. There was no question on the faces of the two men approaching him that this was a man they deeply respected.

The first to shake Chase's hand was Eduardo Munez, a dark, slightly built man with a razor-thin mustache. His somewhat flat features proudly represented his Mayan heritage. Eduardo was always reserved in his manner, but never cold. He was in charge of Chase's leasing operations in Mexico. Eduardo was well-educated and more importantly had studied in the United States, which was one of the major reasons Chase had chosen him for such a critical position in his company. Eduardo took his responsibilities seriously, sometimes a little too much for Chase's style but relationship worked for both of them. Eduardo was grateful to Chase for giving him such a high-ranking position in Lone Star Leasing. His salary, by Mexican standards, was more than sufficient to provide a luxurious lifestyle for his wife and new baby girl.

Eduardo reached for Chase's bag and asked, "Long ride but enjoyable, I hope."

Chase gave a hint of a cynical smile and said, "You can only imagine how long."

Eduardo understood exactly what his boss meant. He had heard the horror stories from Chase from past trips about meeting long-winded strangers.

Politely, Eduardo inquired, "Why don't you use one of those planes your father keeps on his ranch?"

"You know very well why I don't fly," he offered emphatically. Chase was referring to a hair-raising trip he had made a couple of years ago from Pecos to San Antonio on a single engine plane.

Chase and his pilot, Dutch Evans, ran into a storm front that tossed them around like fishing bobbers going over Niagara Falls. The plane was forced to land out in the middle of a small ranch, barely dodging grazing cattle and fallen oak trees. As they touched down on the hard-packed earth, the landing gear snapped. The nose of the plane dug into the field, sending the plane and its passengers head over heels. He could distinctly remember the metallic grating of the propeller tearing at the top-layer of sand and throwing it skyward in a smothering cloud of dust. Chase walked away from the experience with only minor bruises but a lifetime commitment to avoid, whenever possible, using a small plane as his major means of transportation. Dying suddenly in the line of duty was one thing; falling helplessly out of the sky was another.

Chase stepped forward and held out his hand to the man standing next to Eduardo, Emiliano Fuentes.

"Emiliano, it's great to see you again. How is your family?"

Chase was genuinely glad to see his most trusted contact in Mexico. He was one of the few people who knew about Chase's "other job." Emiliano had worked with Chase for the past five years on some of his most dangerous missions. He ran a small network of informants and amateur detectives who assisted Chase in gathering information on the possible whereabouts of fugitives in Mexico. Since Chase was a foreign operative, he could ill afford to get involved in this type of hands-on-work. Emiliano was also Chase's liaison to the Mexican government. When Chase needed inside information from the Federales, Emiliano was his man. The very people who were responsible for upholding the laws of Mexico were often being paid off to help hide the same desperados Chase was pursuing. Emiliano, unquestionably, was part of the reason Chase had been so successful in completing his assignments. Not only was Emiliano critical to his covert operations in Mexico, but he was also a respected friend.

Emiliano was a slightly pudgy, gregarious man with an engaging smile. There were few people who could ignore his charming ways. He knew how to have a good time but was serious about his work and his commitment to Chase. In addition to his dedication, Emiliano had two characteristics Chase highly valued. Emiliano Fuentes, above all, was trustworthy and discreet when it came to business matters, both with Lone Star and with the FBI. Chase couldn't count the times Emiliano had rescued him from touchy situations with the Mexican government, even at the risk of going to jail and leaving his wife and children abandoned. And for anyone familiar with the reputation of Mexican prisons, the prospect of landing in one of those rat-infested hellholes was something one avoided at all cost. Emiliano was willing to take this chance, knowing full well that Chase would personally go to any lengths to get him out of a jam. It was this commitment to each other that sealed the closeness of the relationship.

"Bienvenido, Chase." Emiliano reached out and gave Chase a firm, warm handshake. His smile beamed across his dark, round face. "Yes, the family is well and no, my beautiful wife, Gabriella, has not thrown me out of the house yet," he laughed, fending off the inevitable question from Chase whenever they reacquainted themselves after a long period apart.

"You're a lucky man, Emiliano. How she puts up with you is beyond me." Chase smiled back at him.

Eduardo interrupted their bantering. "The driver is waiting for us, and if I know you two, you'll want to get down to business as soon as possible."

Eduardo knew Chase and Emiliano had a special relationship. As far as Eduardo could discern, their unusual relationship was purely business-related. He never suspected the two men were working together to extract dangerous criminals from Mexico.

"As usual, you're right. We have a lot to work to do. Did you receive the contract from our lawyers on the leasing arrangements for Tencore Corporation?"

Tencore was one of the largest export businesses in Mexico, and Lone Star Leasing had a long-standing relationship with the company. Highly respected companies such as Tencore provided a legitimate cover for Chase's covert operation without raising suspicion regarding the frequency of his visits to Mexico.

"It's in my briefcase. I thought we could go over the terms of the new contract on our drive to Ciudad Hidalgo," Eduardo responded, hoping he wasn't rushing to business too quickly.

"That works for me. I also want to discuss how we are going to work with new governor of Guanajuato," Chase replied as he motioned toward the car.

Chase looked directly at Emiliano and asked, "How are we progressing on setting up a meeting with our new contact in Mexico City? Remind me of his name again." Chase phrased his question in a secret code only Emiliano understood. Chase was anxious to know what kind of progress Emiliano had made in acquiring information from his informants regarding the whereabouts of John Wallace.

"We're almost there. I have one more call to make and it should be all locked up," Emiliano reassured Chase. "The contact's name is Rolando Gomez. From what my associates tell me, he is a reasonable man. He understands the relationship with American companies like Lone Star and their importance in bringing new revenue to Mexico. I don't think we'll have any problems with him or his people."

Chase expected a significant payoff would be required to obtain the needed information, but Emiliano had given him assurance everything was being taken care of and headed in the right direction.

"Good work."

He turned to Eduardo, as they continued toward the car.

"I may want you in on this one. There may be some follow-up issues I'll want you to run down."

"No problem. I've cleared my calendar."

Chase didn't like lying to Eduardo, but it was all part of a diversion to keep Eduardo's curiosity in check. He could ill afford suspicion by anyone, including Eduardo. Chase knew the Mexican government did not appreciate any type of U.S. intervention on their soil, particularly the FBI, which had a bad reputation in Mexico for overstepping its legal boundaries over the past few years.

The driver stood patiently holding the door of the brand new 1983 Lincoln

Continental. Chase had purchased the "boat" because it provided the prestige he needed when dealing with Mexican dignitaries and important clients. It reinforced that he was a successful gringo businessman trying to make an honest buck. It was just another one of his diversionary tactics to keep suspicion away from his covert operations.

Emiliano climbed in the front seat next to the driver, while Chase and Eduardo slid into the luxury of the rear seat.

They resumed discussing the details of a potential meeting with the new governor of Guanajuato. Chase wanted as much insight as possible about the governor before their meeting next week. He was a perfectionist when it came to knowing every nuance, every detail associated with his business endeavors. Nothing about this aspect of his personality had changed since his military days. Negotiating a government contract might not be the same as the life and death situation in war, but he was not about to allow anyone to have the upper hand, including the new governor.

It was difficult for Chase to stay focused on their conversations about Lone Star business when all he really wanted to do was get to the business of bagging John Wallace. Chase knew the longer Wallace was on the run, the better chance he had of slipping away and getting lost in the teeming masses of Mexico.

The two hour drive from Querétaro to Ciudad Hidalgo that wound over the ridgeline of the mountains between two of the most important agricultural valleys of central Mexico, would give them more than ample time to conclude the business at hand. The ribbon-thin, two-lane highway to Ciudad Hidalgo was typical of Mexican roads, filled with deep potholes and barely wide enough for two cars to maneuver safely. God forbid if anyone ran into an old Mexican bus along these roads. Chase couldn't count the times he had seen his driver discreetly make the sign of the cross when oncoming trucks approached.

They finished their discussion on the new contract just as the car turned down the road into the historic village of Ciudad Hidalgo. Chase had recently purchased a home near the central plaza. The remodeled 19th century hacienda was understated but had all the features Chase was looking for as a quiet retreat from the chaos of Mexico City, where he conducted most of his work on behalf of Lone Star. Whenever he could arrange it, he preferred to work in the tranquility of Ciudad Hidalgo. Aside from the peace and quiet it offered him, it allowed Chase to keep a low profile while working for the Bureau. The small village had a good size population of expatriates which allowed Chase to move around freely without standing out.

Chase seldom took full advantage of the city's beauty and busy nightlife. From the fine restaurants to the exotic bars, Ciudad Hidalgo had it all. On most occasions, Chase was so consumed with getting business completed that he left the nightlife for the tourists and the hardcore partygoers from nearby Mexico City.

Chase concluded their conversation just as the chauffeur eased the Lincoln through a private gate and into a large circular driveway whose center was accented with a large stone fountain. The walls of the courtyard were draped in magenta and orange bougainvilleas that were in full bloom.

An impeccably dressed older Mexican man stood at the intricately carved wooden entrance doors to the house.

As Chase exited the car, the elderly gentleman stepped toward him.

"Buenas tardes, Señor. Bienvenido. Como esta usted?" the man asked, bowing his head slightly.

"Bien....gracias," Chase graciously offered. "Fernando, as always it's a pleasure to see you again. I hope all is well with you and your family."

"Si Señor and your family, they are well?" Fernando said, returning the courtesy.

"Yes, and as always, my father thanks you for watching out for his son."

"My pleasure, Señor," Fernando said with a slight smile.

Eduardo and Emiliano followed Chase into the house politely greeting Fernando as they passed by.

The interior of the house was bright and airy with stone archways throughout. The downstairs had a sizeable great room decorated with over-stuffed sofas and chairs arranged in a semi-circle in front of a river-stone fireplace. Opposite the fireplace were two oversized French doors accented by beveled glass windows, all of which was framed in polished mesquite. Outside the French doors was a tiled patio with a walkway that led to a spacious garden of tropical plants and flowers. The adjoining archway on the left led to a spacious kitchen, which looked out over another small interior courtyard. Through another archway at the opposite end of the living room was the hall leading to a large library, which Chase also used for his office. All four walls of the library had floor-to-ceiling, built-in mahogany bookcases. An avid reader since childhood, it was Chase's favorite room in the house.

Chase showed his guests to the living room and got right down to business.

He turned to Eduardo and asked, "What are the latest numbers on the inventory of railcars in the southern region?"

Eduardo was prepared for his boss's question, having done his homework in anticipation of Chase's visit. Comprehensive in his presentation, he gave Chase a rundown on the status of all the business issues affecting Lone Star. It was this kind of detailed report Chase relied on to make sure that his business continued to prosper. They discussed the logistics of acquiring more railcars for the upcoming quarter, and when Chase was sure they had sufficiently covered all the critical questions, he concluded the meeting.

"Well, gentlemen, I think we've earned our money for today. Let's reconvene tomorrow at eight." Chase turned to Emiliano and asked, "Could you stay for a few minutes longer? I have something I want to discuss with you in private." Emiliano nodded.

Eduardo stood up and said without hesitating, "I've made arrangements for dinner at Tauromaquia at nine. The food is fantastic and they have great entertainment. One of the best flamenco dance groups in all of Mexico is performing tonight." He paused momentarily to see what kind of reaction he was getting from Chase.

Chase didn't immediately respond. "Well... do I really have a choice?"

Emiliano and Eduardo were nervously eyeing at each other, hoping their spontaneous invitation might be a breakthrough with their boss who never went out for an evening on the town.

"OK, gentlemen you're on. Let's meet downstairs at 8:30. I'm assuming there is no special attire required for this evening of frivolity."

"No....no sir. We'll be here promptly at 8:30," Eduardo responded.

"Emiliano, let's meet in the library," Chase said, as he glanced in direction of the library.

Eduardo was aware that Chase's request to speak with Emiliano privately was his cue to exit. It wasn't the first time he had heard this request coming from his boss.

Chase gathered his papers and packed up his briefcase. He told Fernando that he would not be eating at home tonight. Fernando was as shocked as anyone else on the household staff. Chase's upcoming night on the town would be a point of gossip among the staff for the next couple of hours.

Chase closed the door behind him as they entered the library. Chase sat directly across from Emiliano, their knees almost touching. Chase spoke first. "What do you have for me?"

"Well, for starters, this guy could be major trouble. Wallace has put up a lot of cash to keep his whereabouts secret. Rumor has it he has hired one of the top drug lords to assure his safety. These guys are not going to be your average thugs trying to make a quick buck. They're heavily armed and well organized." Emiliano paused, hoping for a reaction from Chase.

There was no response. Emiliano didn't hesitate. "If you don't mind, why have you been asked to track this guy down? We generally don't work on low-profile embezzlers cases."

"I wish it were simple, but Wallace is on the Bureau's Top Ten Wanted list. He not only embezzled over a half million dollars from the government, but he also faked the accidental death of his wife. They found her at the bottom of a ravine in her new Chevy convertible. The initial report from the police was that her brakes went out, but it turned out his wife just had a maintenance check on her brakes done a week before she decided to take flying lessons off the side of a mountain. Mysteriously, two weeks later Wallace and his blonde bimbo girlfriend disappeared and they haven't been seen since."

"We'll have to be careful with this one. This guy's got enough cash to make it dangerous. I'll turn the heat up; we should have what we need by the end of next week." Emiliano was unusually sober, and Chase could tell that his partner was genuinely concerned about the risk of this mission.

"Thanks. Sounds like we're on track. I think we're done for now. See you at 8:30."

Chase met his two colleagues downstairs promptly at 8:30. He was dressed in cream-colored linen slacks and a matching coat. He wore a black open collar shirt, which perfectly complimented his polished black alligator boots. It was obvious Chase had put some serious effort into looking his best. Eduardo and Emiliano had always wondered why such a handsome man was not constantly accompanied by beautiful women. Neither one of them could recall Chase ever mentioning any woman in his life.

Emiliano cautiously greeted him, "Well.... are you ready for an evening of good food and some great entertainment?" It was apparent Emiliano was still surprised Chase had agreed to join them for a night on the town.

"As ready as one could be in the hands of you two," Chase joked.

He was in an exceptionally good mood. It had been a long week, and he was looking forward to a little diversion from all the serious work. Tomorrow he knew he would be back to the grind of trying to track down Wallace.

"I've arranged for the driver to drop us off at the restaurant. I thought we could take a taxi back if that's all right with you," Eduardo said, knowing Chase, like everything else in his life, would want to know as much about the arrangements for tonight's outing as possible.

"That's fine, but isn't the restaurant only a short walk from here? If you wouldn't mind, I need the exercise." He hesitated long enough for both men to shake their heads in agreement, "Let's get on our way, before I change my mind."

The two men followed Chase as he walked through the outer courtyard and onto the cobblestone streets. Initially there was a moment of tense silence among them. This was new territory for everyone. In the past, all their dinner engagements had centered on Lone Star business, always serious, never for idle socializing.

Sensing their uneasiness, Chase finally let them off the hook. "Gentlemen, if at all possible, I would like to avoid discussing any business tonight. I realize this is asking a lot, but I think we could all use a break. Agreed?"

Eduardo surprised, stuttered slightly, "Of... course, no problem."

During the short walk to the restaurant, the men shared casual conversation about what was happening this weekend in town, including a discussion about a major fencing exhibition on Sunday. Chase showed some interest in attending, and Eduardo told his boss he would check into the details.

After meandering through the main plaza, they arrived at Tauromaquia, a noted hangout for celebrities and fans. The building, dating to the mid-1800's, was a classic colonial design with its high brick *boveda* ceilings and Romanesque stone pillars. As Chase entered through the louvered wooden doors, he could see the long mahogany bar stretched on the left side of the restaurant from which patrons could view the entire "happening" scene. It was reminiscent of some of the old cowboy bars he had visited with his Uncle Frank when he turned legal drinking age. Just in front of the bar was a large open dining area with several colorfully arranged tables, each with a clear view of the raised wooden stage, which was adorned on both sides with red satin curtains.

As they stood waiting to be seated, Chase could see a large, festive crowd gathering inside. Tonight was particularly important for the owner of the Tauromaquia because one of Mexico's most noted flamenco dancers was going to be on stage. The electricity was palpable in anticipation of her performance. Chase glanced over Emiliano's shoulder, noticing a trio comprising a guitarist, a violinist, and a drummer who had wooden boxes for drums. Their music had a strong gypsy flavor as the guitar moaned out guttural sounds. It reminded Chase of the *fado* he had heard in the bars of Portugal.

When the gregarious owner spotted Chase and his companions, he immediately greeted them, shaking hands with all three men. He escorted them to a table directly in front of center stage. Eduardo had made sure that they would have the best seats in the house for what hopefully would be a memorable evening of entertainment for his boss.

"This should be the perfect place to enjoy the show," the owner offered, nodding at Eduardo. "If you need anything, please don't hesitate to ask." He retreated to greet his other guests. It was obvious to Chase that there wasn't going to be an empty seat in the place before the night was over.

"This seems like a colorful place," Chase teased with a hint of cynicism as he peered over at Eduardo.

Eduardo didn't know exactly how to react to the comment, but he took it as a question.

"Yes, it's known for being one of the more spirited places in town. It has a long history as a gathering place for some of city's more eccentric characters. As you can see from the crowd, sometimes the entertainment doesn't necessarily always happen on the stage."

"Great recommendation, Eduardo. My first night out on the town, and you're telling me I might get into fisticuffs with one of the locals. I can see it now—drunken gringo arrested for assault and battery!" Chase frowned, hoping to get a rise out of Eduardo.

Eduardo's forehead scrunched up in obvious concern over Chase's remarks.

"Relax. I was just joking. I haven't lived a sheltered existence all my life. Don't forget, we've got our fair share of lively places in Texas."

The waiter approached their table, waiting politely for Chase and his companions to finish the conversation before asking for their order.

"Good evening. Can I take your drink orders?"

Before Chase could respond, Emiliano ordered for all of them, "We'll have *La Bandera Mexicana*, por favor."

"I'll be right back with your drinks," the waiter responded, smiling directly at Chase.

"OK, you've got my attention now. What's a *La Bandera Mexicana?*" Chase asked.

"It's a traditional Mexican drink—a shot of some of our finest *anejo* tequila, a shot of sangrita, and a slice of lime," Emiliano explained.

"Sounds like it has some kick to it. You two wouldn't be trying to get me drunk would you?"

"No sir!" Emiliano quickly renounced. "I promise you will enjoy this; and best of all, it won't leave you with a hangover."

The waiter returned with their drinks, advising, "We have your order for paella. It should be ready in a few minutes."

Their dinner conversation was relaxed and sociable, as Chase had requested. Most of their discussion revolved around the curious patrons crowding into the restaurant and this Sunday's upcoming international fencing tournament.

At one point in their conversation, Eduardo pointed out one of Mexico's rising Olympic fencing hopefuls, Lolo Nieto, sitting at a table near the stage. All the ladies at nearby tables were attempting to make eye contact with Lolo Nieto, hoping for an invitation to his table. It was apparent from the young man's unruffled behavior that all the attention he was receiving demonstrated that he was used to being in the limelight.

Emiliano, seeing Chase's interest in learning more about the obscure sport, walked over to a nearby table and invited a charming looking middle-aged man to join them for a drink.

Emiliano introduced Chase to the former Mexican fencing champion, Señor Alfonso Fernando. He had retired ten years ago from the court of honor but still commanded respect in important social gatherings.

Señor Fernando gave Chase a crash course on the recent history of his sport, pointing out the brilliant young swordsman, Lolo Nieto, sitting at the corner table near the stage. Señor Fernando told Chase that Lolo was one of Mexico's up and coming talents but Chase immediately sensed some resentment in the ex-champion's reluctant compliment. Before Señor Fernando returned to his own table, he invited Chase to be his guest at Sunday's upcoming fencing exhibition. Chase gladly accepted his offer, and they agreed on a time and place to meet.

Emiliano ordered another round of La Bandera, and all three men were starting to feel the warm, careless feeling that comes with Mexico's national drink. Chase was taking it all in, from the overweight caballero flirting with a waitress half his age to the two sinister looking companions sitting at the bar dickering over some kind of illegal activity. Chase caught himself observing these two as they nervously fidgeted on their barstools while they tried to figure out why this strange gringo was staring at them. Chase laughed to himself, knowing even when he was off duty, his mind was on duty.

The waiter had just finished clearing their table, when the owner ascended to the stage. He requested the audience's attention, then exuberantly proclaimed, "I hope you all enjoyed your meals, but as they say, "*One does not live by food alone, one must also feed the soul.*" To that end, in a few moments you're going to be entertained by one of Mexico's most beautiful and talented flamenco dancers, Lorena Santoya!"

The crowd interrupted him, bursting into raucous applause. He waited for the applause to subside and continued, "As you know, she has been raising eyebrows all across Mexico with her stunning interpretations and flawless performances. Of course, we are very proud that she is a native of our own hometown—born and raised here in Ciudad Hidalgo."

The crowd burst into another flurry of thunderous applause.

The proud owner continued, "I need not say more. Her dancing speaks for her great talent. She will be accompanied tonight by Jorge Diaz, one of the finest guitarists in all of Mexico. Please enjoy." He was obviously excited to have such an important star in his establishment. From what Emiliano had told Chase, Lorena Santoya would not normally perform in such a small venue, but she was given her start here at the Tauromaquia, and she was returning the favor to the owner.

"Chase, you're in for quite a treat. She is one of the great beauties of Mexico. Señorita Santoya is said to be able to warm the icy heart's of even the most stoic men," Emiliano announced confidently.

As Chase looked around, he could see there was standing room only. There were even people clamoring outside the doorway of the restaurant, vying for a good viewing spot. They waited for another twenty minutes before the lights dimmed. The stage was pitch-black directly in front of Chase, but he could hear a slight commotion onstage. Suddenly, a single beam of silver-white light shown down on the stage, and in the middle of the brilliant glow stood a tall, slender woman. She was turned sideways to the audience, with her face looking over her left shoulder toward the back of the stage.

Lorena wore an iridescent crimson silk blouse, which fit her upper torso perfectly. The bottom edge of the blouse cut a fine seam around the middle of her belly. The rest of her midriff was exposed, including her navel, from which a small silver ring dangled. Lorena wore a matching crimson pleated skirt that hugged her small waistline, the silken edge descending from her exposed mid-thigh to the hemline that stopped just above her right ankle. Her partially exposed back was rippled with taut muscles. Her long, dark auburn hair gently cascaded down her perfectly proportioned body. Her skin was cocoa brown and appeared soft to the touch even from a distance. Her high-heeled polished shoes were identical in color to her dress.

Lorena held the crowd in suspense, not revealing her face for at least a full minute to the audience. Her arms formed an elongated pyramid above her head, stretching upward into her elegantly entwined fingers, which were holding two black ebony castanets. It was as if everyone in the establishment had slowed down their breathing to ease the tension.

Seductively, out of the shadows, the guitarist began plucking the guitar, one chord, then another, each melodic vibration resonating into the hearts of the mesmerized patrons. All the while Lorena stood motionless, petrified. Slowly, with a deliberate glance, she gradually pivoted her head until she faced the crowd. There was a collective hush as everyone peered at the fullness of her beauty.

Chase was mesmerized by her commanding presence. He seldom believed the rhetoric of boastful promoters, but in this case, every word the owner had spoken was etched with truth.

The first thing that struck him was her piercing eyes. Her thick, dark eyebrows perfectly accented almond-shaped chocolate eyes that radiated poise and confidence. Her elongated angular facial features reminded him of the elegant beauty of women he had seen in the Far East. A slight dimple on her chin drew attention to her full lips that were highlighted with translucent ruby lipstick.

Lorena stood center stage, motionless, her face holding the classical mystical allure of a gypsy dancer, her eyes seeming to peer into each set of eyes transfixed on her. Chase was no exception. He thought her beauty bore a strong resemblance to a young Jane Russell. What healthy man could ever forget the famous movie poster from the film *The Outlaw*, depicting Miss Russell stretched out in the straw, her seductive pose inviting every man to be her lover?

Without warning, the sharp clacking of her castanets broke the silence. Lorena's body remained completely still but for the motion of her elongated fingers snapping the castanets together. Almost cautiously, she began to lift her heels and to strike the scarred wooden floor in a slow, rhythmic cadence. She was anticipating every note that flowed from the sound hole of the guitar. She reached down and seductively raised the hem of her dress, pulling it to her waist until it exposed her thighs. She snapped her head back as if pulled by a set of horse rein and all at once her entire body was in motion. Her heels began to tap out a rapid, syncopated beat on the scarred oak stage, increasing in intensity with each slap of the percussionist's hand on his wooden box drums. She held onto her hemline and began to make slow, fluid turns; all the while keeping her eyes on the audience. Her hands gracefully stroked the air and spoke a language everyone seemed to understand. Her hips swayed from side to side in a sensual, raking motion. Her back arched in a long curve, as her full, round breasts lifted elegantly toward the ceiling. As the music started to become more frantic, so did the intensity of her moves. She was taking the crowd along with her on a journey of body and soul. Her fingers and hands twirled through the air in an elegant ballet. As her movements became more kinetic, everything unexpectedly seemed to slow down for Chase. Her dress began to float out like lily pads on a rippled pond, exposing her black silk panties. Her hair shimmered as it hovered around her face. Her arms were stretched above her head as if a marionette were gently controlling their every movement. Her hips rotated in a hypnotizing motion, clockwise, then counter clockwise, thrusting forward without inhibition. Chase could sense his whole body becoming tense with each slow, deliberate movement she made. He felt as though he was alone with her, as if she was dancing exclusively for him. He was sure at one point that her fiery expression transformed into an invitingly submissive smile meant solely for him. If he had not been paralyzed by the effect of the whole experience, he surely would have been tempted to stand up and sweep her off the stage and in the process make a complete fool of himself. Chase realized he was slowly succumbing to a set of emotions beyond his always-reliable logical mind. It was not just her sensuality he was drawn to but also some indescribable attraction and it left him grasping for answers.

Lorena, in one last erotic flurry of movement, arched her body, furiously tapped her high heels onto the floor, and drove the beat deep into the conscious of the audience. She threw her hands vigorously above her head and froze in a lifeless, statuesque pose. Her final resting position was a perfect replica of how she had started her performance.

Chase was catapulted out of his trance by the audience's riotous applause. The patrons leapt to their feet and gave her a rousing ovation. Lorena turned, faced them, and graciously bowed. Several loyal patrons threw roses at her feet until the stage was almost completed covered in red.

Emiliano turned to Chase, "Pretty remarkable, wouldn't you say?"

Chase hesitated, not ready to reveal his true feelings for what he had just witnessed. He struggled to regain his composure before answering Emiliano. "I have to admit she's pretty amazing. She definitely puts her heart into her performance."

Chase continued to stare in the direction of the stage, while Lorena gathered up the last of the roses from the appreciative crowd. He was still curious as to whether her inviting smile during her performance was intended just for him or was something he had imagined.

Lorena handed the large bouquet of roses to a nearby stagehand and started down the stairway to the right of the stage. As she approached the first table where Lolo Nieto sat, he stood up and made an attempt to pull her in his direction. She gracefully smiled and started to walk away, but Lolo persisted. Chase could not hear what transpired next, but Lorena's body language made it clear she was irritated by his inappropriate advances. Undeterred, Lolo grabbed Lorena's arm and pulled her onto his lap and kissed her cheek.

Lorena never hesitating, slapped Lolo's face, stood up, and stepped away from the awkward scene. Lolo made another swipe at her in an attempt to pull her back into his lap but was unsuccessful. Lolo's companions doubled-up with laughter at Lorena's angry reply to Lolo's unwanted advances.

Chase, no more than fifteen feet away, could no longer hold himself back. He stood up, and snarled, "Excuse me!" and took one step in the direction of the commotion surrounding the two combatants.

Emiliano quickly snagged Chase's arm. He knew Chase could take Lolo out in a few violent swipes but a scuffle with this well-known celebrity might jeopardize his cover. A few testy questions from the police and his boss might be deported on the next train out of Mexico.

"Chase, this is not the time," Emiliano sternly pleaded, leaning closer to Chase so he could whisper. "I know it is part of your wild-West code of honor to come to the aid of a maiden in distress, but let this one alone." He continued to hold tightly onto Chase's sleeve. Eduardo sat stunned, having never seen Chase react so irrationally.

Chase angrily proclaimed, "I don't care what part of the world you're from; no woman deserves to be treated like that." Chase looked down at Emiliano, who gave him that recognizable, peculiar nod they used to signal each other when trouble was imminent.

Emiliano continued, "Chase, they're ex-lovers. I know he's an asshole, but they've got a history." He could feel Chase's arm relax, so Emiliano cautiously released him from his grip.

Several people had seen Chase stand up and move toward Lolo's table, including Lorena. She thought to herself, "*Ah yes...a knight in shining armor willing to come to my rescue. How old fashioned.*" She could see Emiliano was still holding Chase back and was thankful to see the gringo had finally regained his composure. She surely did not want to spoil what was an almost-perfect evening by inciting an altercation between her ex-lover and a complete stranger. She could see from across the room that Chase was the stereotypical ruggedly handsome man she had seen in so many spaghetti westerns as a child. He had actually caught her attention more than once during her performance. What was even more surprising to her was the fact that she was not generally attracted to American men. She was curious whether he had caught the sly smile she intended just for his eyes during her final undulating movements on the dance floor.

Lorena continued to sneak a peak in Chase's direction as she moved among the tables thanking her fans for their support. At one point, their eyes locked, and it was obvious he was embarrassed at having been caught in the blatant act of staring. Not wanting to embarrass him, Lorena cautiously smiled back.

Chase acknowledged her smile and then reluctantly turned back to the conversation at his table.

Emiliano leaned over to whisper something to Chase, "Guess who is coming our way?"

Before Chase could react, Eduardo and Emiliano were on their feet.

"Gentlemen, I hope you enjoyed the performance," Lorena offered as she held her hand out to Emiliano, who responded by bowing his head and lightly kissing the back of her hand.

Chase stood up to greet Lorena, still unsure of how he was going to respond to the woman who had just captivated his attention. Before he had a chance to complete his thought, she turned in his direction, held out her hand and offered, "I believe that you already know my name?"

"Chase Walker Chandler," he said, feeling somewhat foolish for being so formal.

"Well, that's a mouthful! I'm not so sure I can remember all that," she teased, as her smile broadened.

Looking at her at this close range affirmed Chase's suspicion that she was a woman of rare beauty. She was somewhat younger than he would have originally guessed. He guessed her age to be around twenty-five. What surprised him even more was her command of the English language. Except for a very slight Latino accent, it was almost perfect.

"Actually, I would prefer you call me by my first name," Chase said, still captured by her intense gaze. "Would you consider joining us for a drink?"

"I would be glad to join you but I'd like to change into something more comfortable." She reached up and brushed her slightly dampened hair away from her face. "It shouldn't take me more than ten minutes. I hope you don't mind waiting."

"Of course not," Emiliano anxiously responded. "No amount of time would be too much to wait for a woman of your talent."

Chase turned and looked at Emiliano in stunned disbelief. He was aware that Mexican men were known for being the consummate romantics, but this was almost too much to take.

"Oh, we have a poet among us," Lorena proclaimed, acknowledging Emiliano's over-exuberant compliment. "I'll see you gentlemen in a few minutes." Lorena glanced over once more at Chase, tilting her head in a polite gesture of acknowledgement.

As soon as she was out of earshot, Chase turned to Emiliano and growled, "And what the hell was that all about, Señor Don Quixote?"

Emiliano could sense Chase wasn't serious. "I was just trying to help you out. It's obvious she is interested in you."

"Who said I needed any help? And what makes you think that she is interested in me?"

Emiliano did not hesitate, "First of all, the very fact that she came over to our table. I've attended her performances before and I have seen many a brave fool attempt to invite her for a drink. I can't remember ever seeing her accept an offer. Secondly, you might have thought I didn't notice, but she clearly smiled directly at you during her performance. You're not the worst looking guy in the room, so why wouldn't she be attracted to you?"

Chase refused to listen to Emiliano's back-alley reasoning and continued to try to deny his attraction to Lorena.

"I would have to agree with Emiliano. I haven't seen sparks fly like that since our last Independence Day celebration," Eduardo boldly stated. It was unusual for him to cross over the boss-subordinate boundary with such an overt comment.

"OK.... you two have made your point," Chase conceded.

Emiliano turned to Eduardo and winked, making sure it was out of Chase's view, and casually offered, "I don't know about you, but I'm pretty tired, and it's been a long day."

Eduardo picked up on his friend's hint. "I agree." His eyes avoided Chase's, as he turned to Emiliano. "I've got a lot of work to do on those contracts. I'll go call us a cab."

"I can recognize a setup when I see one," Chase accused.

"Sorry, but we're family men. We have reputations to uphold. We can't be caught carousing around all night with one of Mexico's most beautiful women. What would our wives think?" Emiliano charged.

"Our cab is here," Eduardo calling out across the room, waving in Emiliano's direction.

"Don't call if you get into any trouble," Emiliano joked.

"Very funny," Chase scolded in a sarcastic tone, watching his companions disappear to the other side of the swinging louvered doors.

Chase nervously waited for Lorena to join him. She promptly arrived in ten minutes, immediately impressing him with her punctuality. It was a trait he appreciated, given his lifelong obsession with always being on time.

She was dressed in a simple, lime-green cotton dress that plunged down in a sweeping arch from her shoulders, exposing the thin crease between her breasts. Her hair was pulled back in a long ponytail and tied with a matching green silk ribbon. Most of the makeup she had on during her performance had been removed, and the natural beauty of her skin shone through. She was taller than he remembered, even though she had traded her high-heel shoes for comfortable leather sandals.

Chase stood as Lorena approached.

"I hope I didn't keep you waiting?" she politely asked.

"No, not at all. I may not be the poet my friend is, but it was well worth the wait. Can I order you a drink?"

"Yes, thank you. What are you drinking?" She could see from the line of shot glasses that they had been drinking their fair share of tequila.

"Well, my compadres got me started on *La Bandera Mexicana*, and I have to admit they're pretty addicting," Chase proclaimed, realizing the effects from all the tequila had been wiped away by the sobering experience of meeting Lorena.

"They have an old saying here in Mexico, '*Once you have kissed the devil, you have made your bed for the night.*' I'll have the same, thank you."

The waiter took their order, and Chase turned to Lorena and confessed, "I must apologize for my behavior earlier. I almost rudely interrupted what was obviously a private matter between you and another gentleman. I hope I didn't cause you any embarrassment."

"No, I appreciated your concern. Lolo had too much to drink and was out of line. He is known as "El Macho" in fencing circles, and sometimes it carries over into his private life." She calmly folded her hands in her lap. "We had a brief affair a few years ago. We were originally just friends and then I made the mistake of thinking I was in love with him. It's over now, but sometimes he still thinks of me as his personal property."

Chase was shocked by her frankness. It was a quality he greatly admired. He had known only two other people who were so candid: his late grandfather, and, of course, his mother. Although Lorena freely disclosed her regret over having an affair with Lolo, he could see from her slightly pained expression that there was still discomfort in her admission.

Sensing her uneasiness, Chase immediately changed the subject. "How long have you been dancing professionally?"

"It seems like my whole life. I started when I was four years old. My mother was one of the great flamenco dancers of her era. My father accompanied her on guitar. We were a family act until my mother retired a few years ago."

"Well, it is apparent that you've dedicated a lot of time to your profession. I've never seen anyone dance with such passion."

"Thank you," she said, turning her eyes downward, slightly embarrassed by his compliment.

"I admire anyone who has the fortitude to sacrifice so much for their art. I suppose it is because I'm one of those people without a creative bone in my body; I have to admit....I'm a little envious."

"I'm sorry you feel that way, but I have to disagree with you. Everyone has some artistic talent; I believe its part of the soul. It is just a matter of discovering it."

"I would like to believe you, but I can't even get on the dance floor without tripping over my own two feet."

The waiter arrived with their drinks, and Lorena lifted her glass of tequila and toasted, "Here's to art and finding its soul. Salud!" She beamed at him, raised her shot glass, and emptied it.

Lorena asked him why he was in Mexico. Chase explained that he was here on business for Lone Star and in negotiations with the governor of Guanajuato. He was relieved to be talking about something he knew about. He still felt apprehensive that at any moment, he might stumble like a tongue-tied schoolboy and make a complete fool of himself. He gave her a brief history of how his grandfather had started Lone Star in Bolivia in the late 1890's. He told her he'd taken over as president of the company when his father's health started to fail a couple of years ago.

Lorena asked him whether he would rather have done something else with his life, and Chase reluctantly told her that just before going to college he had thought about studying to be an architect, but he put those dreams aside when the war started. There was a true sense of loss in his tone of voice.

"See, you do have a hidden talent. You must have been able to draw at one point in your life or you would never have considered architecture as a career."

"OK, you win. Yes, at one time, I did do some doodling, but I wouldn't exactly call it art."

She reached over and placed her hand on the top of his hand and purred, "I have a feeling someday you'll get back to your artistic talents, Mr. Chase Walker Chandler; and when you do…. please let me know; I'll be glad to be your first model." She left her hand gently resting on his.

"I may have to start looking for a good art supply store tomorrow." Chase waited to see if she hesitated regarding her promise to pose for him.

"It would be my pleasure."

Chase was starting to sense that Emiliano's premonition about him and Lorena connecting might be true; maybe she was genuinely attracted to him. Chase decided to seize the opportunity. "Would you be interested in joining me on Sunday for the fencing tournament? I've been invited by Señor Alfonso Fernando to be his guest. Perhaps you know him?"

"Yes, I know the gentleman very well. He is a very generous and kind man. Señor Fernando was very influential in helping to introduce me to several important people during the early part of my career." She paused to catch her breath. "Yes, I'd love to go. Are you a fan of fencing?"

"Actually, I have to admit I know nothing about the sport. I'm a complete novice."

"I'm not an expert but I would be glad to share what little I do know. Why don't we meet around four o'clock on Sunday before the event?"

"Four o'clock it is."

Lorena unexpectedly stood up. "I hate to say goodnight, but I have two more performances tomorrow, and unfortunately, I need to get my rest. I hope you understand." It was clear she was reticent to end their evening together.

Chase rose to his feet. "Thank you again for such a wonderful performance. I look forward to Sunday." His last words were a gross understatement of his genuine excitement at the prospect of seeing her again.

Lorena reached out to shake his hand, but instead Chase leaned over and kissed her hand. "See, I'm starting to learn," he said, releasing her hand.

"Yes, I can see that." She bowed her head slightly and grinned affectionately.

Chase watched her until she disappeared into a doorway just right of the stage. He could already sense it was going to be a long two days before Sunday rolled around.

Chase kept busy with Lone Star business most of Saturday. Eduardo and Emiliano laid out their strategy for their meeting with the governor next week. Several times during their meeting Emiliano could sense Chase was not fully engaged in their discussions. They concluded their workday early. Chase checked with Emiliano to see if everything was progressing in their hunt to locate information about the whereabouts of John Wallace. Emiliano told him that he expected to have a location by no later than Monday. As much as Chase tried to concentrate on the details of the case, he could feel himself distracted with thoughts of Lorena Santoya. Emiliano asked Chase if everything was all right. Chase lied, telling him he was just a little tired from the long train ride from Texas.

He had a restless night on Saturday and woke up several times thinking about his "date" with Lorena. He was positive no woman had ever had such a lingering effect on him. He tried to get her out of his mind, but it was a hopeless exercise. As he stared up at the revolving ceiling fan, he tried to slow his breathing but his mind kept betraying him. Unlike his relationships in the past, Chase was intent on letting Lorena know that he was capable of letting someone into his private world, of opening up the dark, empty spaces in his life. The last thought he had before he finally drifted off to sleep rattled him to the core. Chase realized if he were going to get seriously involved with Lorena, he would at some point have to tell her about his work for the Bureau. The prospect of having to reveal his secret was unsettling. He convinced himself for now that his secret would have to remain just that, a secret. He wasn't about to jeopardize his burgeoning relationship with Lorena even if it meant hiding the truth from her against his own better judgment.

CHAPTER 3

Chase awoke on Sunday morning after a restless night. He struggled to fight off the grogginess as he sipped his first cup of coffee. He was anxious to get his day started. He tried to focus on the Wallace case, but was unsuccessful. Thoughts of Lorena kept inserting themselves in his mind like pins in a voodoo doll.

He spent the early hours of the day doing busy work, hoping it would hurtle him into the afternoon and closer to his reunion with her. He organized and reorganized his favorite books in the library, reviewed the contract he already knew by heart—doing anything to keep his mind off of today's rendezvous with Lorena.

Chase spent longer than normal grooming himself but he was out the door of his hacienda an hour and a half earlier than necessary to keep his appointment with Señor Fernando outside the *salle d'armes*. He wandered through the streets of Ciudad Hidalgo for almost an hour, hoping it would satisfy his need to feel like he was moving a direction closer to seeing Lorena. He arrived at the *salle d'armes* forty-five minutes early, pacing constantly, checking for any sign of Lorena. On more than one occasion a friendly passersby asked him whether he needed directions. Chase politely declined their offers and was just about to leave when Señor Fernando arrived.

Señor Fernando was dressed entirely in black with the exception of his pressed dark red shirt and a white Panama hat. For a middle-aged man on the down side of his physical prowess, he was still an impressive figure. He had that distinctive air of aristocracy, while at the same time emanating genuine warmth.

The older gentleman cordially greeted Chase, telling his guest to expect a great exhibition of swordsmanship today. Chase thanked him again for his gracious invitation and told him he had asked Lorena to join them. He hoped it was not inappropriate to have invited her. Fernando laughed aloud and seemed to be very pleased with Chase's surprise announcement.

While they waited for Lorena, Fernando told Chase that many of the best fencers of Mexico would be in attendance. Chase asked his host several questions about his former career. Señor Fernando answered every one of Chase's questions in excruciating detail. One particular piece of information that totally surprised Chase was the assumption that modern fencing was not a dangerous sport. Chase was under the impression that with all the protective gear and modern technology it had become a completely safe sport. Señor Fernando explained that one of fencing's greatest stars, Vladimir Smirnov, had been mortally injured in a tournament the previous year in Italy. Fernando explained that during an encounter at the World Championships in Rome, a blade broke and penetrated Smirnov's mask, mortally wounding him through the eye socket. Chase winced at hearing the old master's graphic description. He had heard of a lot of ways to die but a jagged steel blade through the eye had to top the list.

"It happens rarely." The former champion's eyes squinted as if he were in pain. "But sometimes when these thin blades of steel are defective, serious injuries do occur."

As Chase continued to listen intently to Fernando's tutorial, out of the corner of his eye he suddenly saw Lorena approaching. He tried to focus his attention on Señor Fernando, but his mind completely shifted to Lorena. Chase tried futilely to compose himself, but he could feel his apprehension rising with each approaching step she took. When Lorena was twenty yards from Chase, she waved and exuberantly smiled. Chase could only hope her alluring smile was for him and not for her old friend, Señor Fernando.

Lorena wore a white, embroidered peasant blouse with a finely gathered waistband caressing her midriff. Her pleated turquoise skirt accentuated her hips that swayed with the natural, graceful cadence one would expect from a dancer. The delicate light of the late afternoon enhanced the innate features of her classic looks, and the bright sheen highlighted her auburn hair flowing out from under a large-brimmed woven straw hat.

When Lorena finally reached them, out of respect for both his age and status, she greeted Señor Fernando first. "Señor Fernando, what a wonderful pleasure to see you again." She leaned over and kissed him lightly on both cheeks.

"As always Lorena, you're a ray of sunlight." Señor Fernando boasted, as he returned her kiss. "I hear you've been getting rave reviews for your performances." Lorena blushed slightly and said, "You're very gracious. I'm sure you've been filling Señor Chandler's mind with grand stories of your exploits with the sword."

She turned to Chase, "Believe only half of what you hear from this cagey old man. Retired swordsmen are notorious for painting their accomplishments with a very broad brush."

"I'm not the romantic Señor Fernando is, but he captured my sentiments exactly," Chase said, as he nervously smiled in her direction. "As we say in Texas, you're a real eyeful."

Señor Fernando raised his eyebrows, tilted his head, and sheepishly smiled at Lorena.

"I see you've been taking lessons from my wily old friend. Watch out, Chase Walker Chandler, or you might sweep this defenseless girl off her feet." Lorena slipped Chase a wink as they headed for the ticket booth.

Señor Fernando insisted on paying for his guests. He purchased three tickets in the front row of the *salle d'armes*.

As Señor Fernando escorted his guests to their seats, several fans affectionately greeted him. He moved through the appreciative crowd, obviously enjoying having Lorena Santoya by his side. His face beamed with pride, and Chase was sure the old man's blood pressure was rising with each backslapping acknowledgement. The trio's seats were perfectly positioned to see the matches up close. Lorena sat between Chase and Señor Fernando. It was apparent to Chase and everyone around them that Lorena was attracting a great deal of attention. Chase normally tried to avoid being in the spotlight, but today he was content to be in the presence of such a noted personality.

The first contest presented a novice swordsman, Joaquin Ortiz, in his first tournament. The somewhat overwhelmed young man looked to be no more that sixteen years of age. He fought bravely but showed all the signs of a neophyte. The fledging swordsman's main problem, as Señor Fernando explained, was his footwork. Señor Fernando told Chase that one of the first signs of a well-trained fencer was whether he had "busy feet" as his opponent counter-attacked.

"I can see there is a lot I have to learn if I'm going to have an appreciation for this sport," Chase said. He turned to Lorena and continued. "I imagine the footwork of a fencer is similar to the same discipline required to be a flamenco dancer."

"Very observant, Chase. I struggled for years thinking I would never be an accomplished dancer. It wasn't until I developed the patience for the exactness of every move, of every step, that I finally came to appreciate my own art form. Since then, I've been obsessed with practically nothing else."

"I find that hard to believe. I'm sure you have a busy social schedule to contend with. It's a wonder you have any free time at all," Chase suggested, keenly interested in her answer.

"Oh, I wish it were true, but by the time that I've met all my professional obligations and done three shows a week, I barely have time to relax in the quiet of my dressing room. It is a much lonelier life than you can imagine."

She explained to Chase how being raised in a family in which her mother and father were major stars on the dancing circuit made for a very difficult childhood. Lorena said her parents placed huge expectations on her to become the next great star of Mexico. Her family traveled constantly, and she never knew what it was like to stay in one place long enough to call it home. She started performing professionally at the age of eight and had never stopped. As she concluded, Lorena turned to Chase and in a very endearing tone said, "You're my first real *date* in a long time."

"I would have never suspected that someone like you would have such a problem. I feel privileged you accepted my offer to join us today.......I hope I've not disappointed you."

"Not so far, but the day is young." Her eyes twinkled mischievously.

The entire time they were engaged in their conversation, the spectacle of the tournament continued. The second contest was as inconsequential as the first battle, but everyone in the *salle d'armes* perked up when the next contestant entered the room.

The brash, handsome fencer, decked out in full fencing garb, entered the room and made his obligatory acknowledgement by doffing his protective mask to the jury of judges and other dignitaries.

It was Lolo Nieto, nicknamed "El Macho," the same man with whom Chase had almost gotten into fisticuffs two nights before in defense of Lorena. Chase did not immediately recognize the lone figure standing at the edge of the fighting strip.

Lolo walked over until he was standing directly in front of where Lorena was seated. Chase still did not recognize Lolo, but as he looked at the annoyed expression on Lorena's face, it all came back to him. Lolo's smile was lifted and replaced with a disapproving scowl. Lolo's sandy-blond, medium-long hair was twisted in a tight bun on the back of his head. He had the perfect body for a swordsman, and it was evident that every fiber was well toned from long hours of training. He stood totally erect except for the smooth curve of his spine, bowed into the shape of an ascending crescent moon. There was no mistaking his prowess inside and outside of the *salle d'armes*. The crowd buzzed with anticipation.

Lolo looked unswervingly in Lorena's direction and slowly bent over, making sure he kept eye contact with her the entire time. In the time-honored tradition Lolo bowed at the waist, tucked his head gear gracefully under his torso, and raised his foil in Lorena's direction.

The crowd cheered at Lolo's grand gesture.

Lolo was the only one who knew that there was a hidden meaning in his grandstanding gesture. His impish expression implied that he was asking for forgiveness for his rude behavior toward her the other night. Lorena politely acknowledged his gesture but did not smile. It would have been inappropriate for her to rebuff him in front of the crowd, no matter what the circumstances. As Lolo returned to the upright position, he grinned at her as though everything had been reconciled between them. It was a mistake he would regret.

Lorena, all too familiar with his arrogant posture, decided to toss tradition to the wind. She was not about to let him think he was off the hook for his rude behavior at the Tauromaquia. Just as Lolo was about to turn from her, she leaned over and affectionately kissed an unsuspecting Chase on the cheek.

Lolo froze in his tracks, obviously annoyed by her blatant snubbing of his public gesture. He was clearly insulted.

Lorena had subtly but purposely embarrassed him in front of the crowd by showing affection to another man after he had dedicated the bout to her. Chase, shocked by Lorena's show of affection, turned to face her. He knew he was being used as a pawn in their game, but he was glad to be on the receiving end of her affection.

Lorena, after watching Lolo angrily walk off, leaned over and whispered regretfully to Chase, "Please, forgive me. I'll explain later."

Chase nodded, not wanting to press the matter any further. He returned his attention to the action at the center of the *piste*. Lolo was forcing his opponent backwards with several aggressive moves, scoring three quick points in the process.

Lorena seemed distracted by what had just occurred with Lolo. It was apparent she could care less about the outcome of the ensuing battle. It was clear, even to a novice fan like Chase, that the quality of Lolo's performance was superior to that of his fellow combatants. His dazzling work with the foil was beyond anything he had seen displayed to this point of the day's festivities. Lolo performed several complex moves, defending skillfully as his opponent lunged forward in a futile attempt to score a touch. As Lolo became more confident, so did the boldness of his moves. Lorena squirmed in her seat, and uttered something unintelligible. Chase tried to catch what she had said, but it was muffled by the crowd's applause. Chase sensed that something about watching her former lover compete was making her uncomfortable.

Lorena leaned over to Chase and murmured, "Would you mind terribly if we left now?"

Chase did not hesitate. "Of course not; I've seen enough." Chase turned to their host and discreetly explained Lorena was not feeling well, and that he was going to escort her home.

Señor Fernando politely excused his guests. Chase thanked him for his hospitality and returned his attention to Lorena.

The crowd continued to cheer Lolo on as Chase and Lorena managed their way through the congested stands. Chase turned and looked back at the action just before they reached the exit. He saw Lolo poised with his foil held high in preparation for his last dramatic move. Lolo turned his head to look in Chase's direction. He rapidly twisted his foil as if skewering a victim and nodded at

Chase with a disdainful glare. Chase did not know whether Lolo's gesture was due to the insult of their early departure or jealousy over Lorena's affections. Chase raised his hand to his brow and tipped his hand invitingly, making sure Lolo understood he was not dealing with a man who was used to backing down. Chase turned his back on Lolo and walked Lorena out of the *salle d'armes*.

As they walked down the shaded avenue, Lorena again caught Chase off guard by reaching over and gently taking hold of his hand. They strolled in silence toward the center of town, unceremoniously accepting the fact that something was changing in their relationship. As they approached the central plaza, Chase could see Lorena was still troubled by what had happened between her and Lolo.

Lorena finally turned toward him and apologetically said, "Thank for going along with my antics in there. I guess I owe you an explanation."

"There is no need to explain."

Lorena was relieved that Chase was letting her off the hook so easily.

"Can I buy you a drink? La Cava is just a few blocks from here," she offered, trying not to be too bold in her invitation. "It has great atmosphere, and it's a quiet place where we can talk."

"Sounds perfect," Chase agreed, hardly able to contain his enthusiasm. Finally, he was going to have the chance to be alone with her.

When they arrived at La Cava, the early evening was in full bloom, casting its diffused shadow over the amber lights of the main plaza. They had to step down a small flight of stairs before reaching the stained glass doorway. As they entered the restaurant, Chase noticed the place was practically empty, which was fine with him; the fewer distractions, the better.

They were escorted to a table by the maitre d' and immediately ordered margaritas on the rocks.

As an icebreaker, Chase commented on the unusual constructions of the walls in the restaurant, which were made entirely of river stone; from the floor to the low-arched ceilings. It reminded him of the dank catacombs of Italy. The spacious room had no windows, and if it were not for the scattered array of candles around the room, they would have been sitting in complete darkness.

Lorena explained, "In its earlier days, this building was used for underground grain storage. Legend also has it that it was a hiding place for Benito Juarez during the revolution. Before it was recently remodeled, it was a hangout for banditos." Lorena seemed to have regained her cheerful disposition from earlier in the day.

"Ciudad Hidalgo seems to have its fair share of colorful places," Chase said, as the waiter set down their drinks. "My turn for a toast. Here's to the hinges of friendship: may they never rust."

"To friendship. Salud!" She returned his smile.

"Chase, I know you said I don't owe you an explanation, but I want to apologize. It was rude of me to have kissed you to get back at Lolo. I hope you can forgive me." Her tone of voice was submissive as her eyes avoided Chase.

"I was thinking about making a formal complaint to the local police," he said with a deep, serious frown on his face.

"Very cute. Are you enjoying yourself?"

"Well, as long as it isn't the last time....I suppose I can forgive you." Chase was delighted with the direction of their conversation but knew that he had to control his eagerness. He could sense there was still a slight wedge of tension between them.

"So tell me more about your family," he inquired hoping the conversation would lead to lighter conversation.

They soon discovered they had a lot in common regarding their upbringing. They both had doting parents who were intent on controlling the destiny of their offspring. Even though they were not the same age, nor reared in the same culture, the similarities in their upbringing were apparent. They laughed out loud at their rebellious teenage years, which had nearly driven their respective parents to the brink of insanity. The earlier tension in the conversation had transformed into a relaxed exchange about all the trouble they had caused their parents.

It was almost ten o'clock when they left the restaurant. They headed in the direction of the central plaza and the main gathering place on the weekends for locals and tourists. When they arrived at the Jardín, Chase noticed that it was filled with teenage girls and boys. There was some kind of procession going on around the perimeter of the large gazebo in the center of the Jardín. Chase was curious and asked Lorena if she knew what was going on.

"It's an old courting tradition that takes place in most Mexican towns and villages on weekends. The boys go in one direction and the girls go in another. After they've made a few passes around the perimeter of the Jardín, and having eyed potential partners and flirting appropriately, they all turn in the same direction and join up with their selected partners. It's quite the scene to watch. Just when you think you've figured out who will go with whom, you're totally surprised by their final selections. Of course, the mothers of the daughters are sitting nearby to make sure everything is done in the proper manner."

"Have you ever participated in one of these?"

"What do you think?" Lorena stepped right in the middle of the girls' procession. She looked back, waiting to see how Chase would react.

He hesitated momentarily then joined in the procession with the teenage boys. The fact that he stood a foot and half taller than any of his fellow marchers made it all the more amusing to everyone watching, including Lorena. Chase tried to keep track of Lorena as she passed behind the large trees lining the Jardín, but he lost sight of her. Finally, as they rounded the square just in front of the tawny lights of the cathedral, he spotted her. He called out to her, "How long does this last?"

She just shrugged her shoulders, smiled, and kept walking with the giggling young ladies.

The third time around, and just before they were going to pass each other again, the boys suddenly switched direction, and the whole procession began moving in the same direction as the girls.

Chase was amazed at the accuracy and politeness demonstrated by the boys' maneuvering to acquire their selected partner. In a few instances, there was some minor confusion when two boys wanted the same girl, but to his amazement, it all seemed to resolve itself. Having chosen partners, the couples held hands and marched off to nearby benches to continue the courting process. And so, the selection process proceeded, while Chase waited patiently for his turn.

He turned and quickly caught up with Lorena. As they came into close proximity, she jokingly rebuffed his attempt to hold her hand. Chase thought for a moment that maybe his expectations were too high, but then Lorena relinquished and firmly took hold of his hand. She led him over to the ornate gazebo and, under the gauzy light of a street lamp she waited to see what Chase would do next. Having waited for what seemed like forever, she looked up at him and demurely inquired, "I thought you said earlier you hoped it was not the last time?"

"Last time?" He cocked his head to the side, trying to recall their earlier conversation.

"You've forgotten so soon?"

At first, Chase failed to make the connection to her earlier reference about another kiss. Finally, he reached down, put his arm around her waist, pulled her tightly to him, and kissed her. At first, his kiss felt slightly reluctant, but as her lips encouraged his, he pulled her even closer, and kissed her more passionately.

Lorena had never kissed any man other than a Mexican before but she found herself eager to linger in his affection. She was not sure what attracted her to this charming American, but she sensed something special was happening. On one hand, she wanted to take her time to get to know him better, while on the other, she felt an intense attraction to him. The intensity of what she was feeling for him drew her back to memories of the only two sustained love affairs in her life; one with Lolo Nieto and the other with her first sexual partner, a young, talented guitarist who was part of the traveling flamenco troupe. She had met her first love while touring with her parents in southern Mexico. Her tryst with the guitarist lasted only three months but was filled with passionate nights of learning about her body's potential for satisfying a man. She was broken-hearted when the tour ended, though she knew from the beginning it was a doomed relationship. He simply wanted to live a gypsy life, while she wanted to be a serious performer.

Her affair with Lolo, as she had told Chase, was a big mistake. She knew he was immature but thought with patience he would eventually grow out of it. They were together for six months when she caught him in bed with one of his overzealous fans. Lolo had no will power when it came to refusing the attention of an attractive woman, but his ego was severely bruised when Lorena left him, and he harassed her for almost two more years, insisting that they belonged together.

Neither relationship had been what she would call true love. Lorena was determined that if and when she ever made a lifelong commitment to another human being, their love would have to have a foundation at the deepest spiritual level, an uncompromising sense of uniqueness. She wasn't talking about being swept off her feet by a brief sexual infatuation but a relationship that could sustain itself through the most difficult of times. Strangely, she wondered if Chase might be the one as he held her in his arms.

"Aren't we a little old to be making out in the park?" Chase inquired.

They both laughed at their indiscretion.

Lorena leaned over and whispered to him, "I know a quieter place.....if you're a little adventuresome."

Chase was intrigued and willing to risk just about anything to be with Lorena.

"I could use a little adventure in my life. I haven't been exactly living on the edge lately," Chase said, scolding himself for having been so self-absorbed with the business side of his life.

They stepped out into the street, and Lorena flagged a cab. As they climbed in, she leaned over the front seat and told the cab driver something Chase couldn't completely understand. They drove for twenty minutes through the *campos* in the surrounding hilly countryside. Eventually, the driver turned up a corrugated dirt road and headed out into the deserted landscape. Just over the horizon, Chase could see the flicker of dim lights in the distance.

Arriving at a small dirt parking area, Lorena got out of the car and headed toward a small casita.

In a few minutes, she returned to retrieve Chase but it was obvious she was not about to reveal her secret plans for the rest of the evening.

Chase couldn't stand the suspense longer.

"What's with all the intrigue?" he asked, as he followed her along a gravel pathway leading to a group of small buildings.

"Be patient; you will see soon enough."

They walked up to what looked like a small casita, and a young woman happily greeted them. She said something to Lorena and pointed in the direction of a set of smaller buildings. Lorena thanked her and kissed her on both cheeks.

"She is a childhood friend of mine, and she says we can have the place to ourselves."

"That's great, but what is this *place*?"

"Follow me...."

Lorena led him to a line of small adobe buildings.

"You'll find everything you need inside. I'll meet you back here in a few minutes," she said with a hint of secrecy in her voice.

"Talk about a mystery. I'm starting to wonder what I've gotten myself into." He looked at her, hoping she would explain.

"See you in a few minutes." She seductively waved at him and disappeared into one of the small dressing rooms.

He entered the dimly lit room where two candles were set on the edge of a windowsill. A white terry cloth robe hung on a hook. He was a little uncomfortable, but he wasn't about to refuse her invitation. He stripped off all of his clothes, hoping he was not about to find himself in an embarrassing situation. He put on the soft robe and tied the belt, stood for a moment trying to calm his pounding heart, then took a deep breath, and exited the changing room.

Chase stood, staring at the star-filled night sky, waiting for Lorena to reappear. She sneaked up behind him and tapped him on the shoulder. She was wearing the same white robe he was wearing. He noticed immediately that her whole disposition seemed to have changed. She had a certain serenity about her as she stood in the sifted moonlight. She reached over, took his hand, and led him down a short path toward what looked like three interconnected geometric domes. As they neared the buildings, he could see steam venting through an opening in the oval roofline.

Lorena led him down a set of stairs and through a small opening. He could hear the sound of running water and could almost touch the balmy wave of humidity as they entered the room. They stepped onto a flat, tiled platform. The room was dark and there was barely enough light to see the interior walls.

Lorena walked over to an arched brick tunnel entrance, removed her robe, and hung it on a nearby hook.

Chase's gaze froze in place, his eyes transfixed on Lorena's naked outline. Even though there was barely enough light to make out her full form, the light was sufficient enough for him to appreciate her athletic body. She reached up with her long arms, bundled her thick hair on top of her head and placed a tortoise shell hair pick firmly to hold it in place. Slowly, she stretched her limber neck from side to side. Chase felt the sensation that he might have momentarily stopped breathing. He quietly exhaled and tried not to continue to stare but it was at best a futile attempt. Lorena turned toward him and smiled at him seductively and then turned back around, disappearing beyond the small archway.

Chase could hear the soft splash of her footsteps as she stepped through the passageway leading into another steam-filled room. Chase removed his robe and hung it next to Lorena's. As he approached the archway, he could see water was cascading over a set of brick stairs. Stepping onto the first step and feeling the soothing sensation of the hot mineral water for the first time slightly calmed his nervousness. He followed the steps up and over into another vaulted room. The rectangular room was lit with candles that were strung along the perimeter of the room on a thin ledge. He called out to Lorena but there no response.

All he could hear was the sound of rippling water. He could see ahead of him that there was another archway similar to the one through which he had just passed. There was a glow of soft light emanating from the other side. He made his way to the passageway and crossed the steps into a much larger oval room. The lighting in the room was dimmer and certain portions were painted in complete darkness. He looked up and saw the *boveda* ceiling with a huge brick crown that seemed to defy gravity. The room itself was at least twenty-five feet in diameter and the ceiling was of a similar height. At the top of the *boveda* a large, round opening perfectly framed the star-laden heavens. All of Chase's senses were alive as he tried to control his eagerness to find Lorena.

Standing at the entrance of the room, he saw that there was a sizeable pipe opposite him that was throwing a thick fountain of hot mineral water into the pool.

"Over here, Chase," her faint, wisp of a voice called out.

His eyes searched into the mosaic of shadows until he finally saw the soft form of her outline. As he gingerly moved toward her, the amber glow of the candlelight illuminated the soft features of her face. She reached out with both hands, gently pulling him next to her body. Chase wrapped his arms around her torso as she lifted her legs off the floor of the pool and wrapped her thighs around his waist. She put her arms around him and laid her face softly into the crook of his neck.

Chase was a well-built man and it was apparent to Lorena that he kept himself in excellent physical shape. His arms felt powerful as she relaxed into his embrace. She felt weightless, resting on the buoyancy of the turquoise-blue waters. She kissed him as they slowly swirled around the large pool. Chase realized it had been too long since he had held a woman. Lorena sensed this yearning in him, so she was willing to let him take his time. Chase laid her body out on the warm water, and watched her float like a scattered leaf on a still lake. Everything around Lorena seemed to be evaporating. She surrendered herself to the rippling action of the water flowing around her. She clasped her hands behind her head and stretched out until her body lay fully extended. Time stood still as she yielded to his tender caress; her rising and falling whispers reverberating around the room in syncopated tones of gratitude.

Chase began to massage her lower torso. He felt her whole body starting to go limp in his hands. They both seemed to know intuitively what each other needed. Chase carefully guided them under the steaming water pouring from the waterspout. The fountain's soothing water pounded down on them as they shared in each other's bliss. They lingered in a long embrace, waiting for the storm to subside. Finally, they collapsed, letting themselves flow out into the center of the pool. They held each other like two intertwining pieces of silk, not wanting to let go.

They soaked in silence for a while longer, then made their way back to the changing rooms and dressed. Lorena asked her friend to call a cab.

Their conversation during the drive back into town was lighthearted; they talked about their plans for getting together the next evening for dinner. They avoided the subject of what had just happened and what the future might hold.

When they arrived in front of Lorena's house it was 3:00 a.m. She started to exit the cab when Chase reached out and pulled her back toward him.

"This is not going to be simple, is it?" Chase asked, as his eyes intensely focused on hers.

She laid her head on his shoulder and said, "No, it's not, but let's not complicate things for now. I just want to be with you and not think about everything that could get in our way."

Chase turned toward her and lightly kissed her on the forehead, wishing somehow he could tell her about his complicated double life. He hated the thought of having to deceive her about his work with the F.B.I. Lorena was the first woman with whom he had ever felt like sharing his secret, but he knew this wasn't the right time.

They kissed each other passionately; unaware the driver was getting an eyeful in his rearview mirror. After one last, lingering kiss, Lorena reluctantly exited the cab determined to not look back at him, fearing she would rush back into his waiting arms.

Chase watched her disappear into her house, already feeling lonely.

As the cab drove though the winding streets of Ciudad Hidalgo, he tried to convince himself that he couldn't be falling in love with a woman he had known for only a few days but he knew it was true.

When he arrived home, Chase was so keyed up that he went to his library and started rearranging the same books he had rearranged earlier that very morning. There were so many possibilities of where their relationship might lead. He knew what direction he wanted it to go, but was Lorena feeling the same?

When Chase finally forced himself to go to bed, it was just before dawn. He was just starting to fade off when Fernando unexpectedly awakened him with an urgent message from Emiliano.

CHAPTER 4

Chase sat out on the veranda waiting for Emiliano to arrive, trying to shake off the cobwebs. He was dreading the news regarding Wallace. Chase knew he would have to get busy with the case once Wallace's location was known, and that would take him away from Lorena.

Emiliano arrived thirty minutes after Fernando had woken Chase. He told Chase that his contacts had a possible location on Wallace. Wallace had, in fact, hired some thugs to protect him, and had moved into a small hacienda outside of Morelia, about a seven-hour drive over rough mountain roads from Ciudad Hidalgo. The bad news was that Wallace was on the move and would only be in that location for the next forty-eight hours.

"We'll have to leave later today if we are going to have any chance of catching him. I've got a driver ready to pick us up in two hours. I hope it gives you enough time to get ready," Emiliano said, making sure Chase understood the gravity of the situation.

"I'll be packed and ready to go within the hour. I need to make one quick stop on our way out of town."

"I wonder where that could be. I thought you looked a little ragged this morning," Emiliano said, goading Chase into a response.

"Let's keep our focus on the task at hand, OK?" Chase answered as he headed upstairs to start packing.

His scolding remark to Emiliano about staying focused was really more of a reminder to himself. Chase was consumed with trying to come up with a legitimate excuse to give Lorena for canceling their dinner engagement this evening. He was concerned that no matter how hard he tried to explain his hasty departure, Lorena would surely think he was just another gringo who had fulfilled his fantasy of bedding down a local Latin beauty. Chase wanted to make sure Lorena knew he was not that stereotypical, ugly American and, more importantly, that what had happened between them last night was not a one-night stand for him.

Chase met Emiliano in the courtyard. They threw their bags into the trunk and headed in the direction of Lorena's house.

When they arrived, Chase knocked on her front door, but there was no answer. He knocked again, and there was still no answer. Chase peered through the windows, trying to see if there was anyone around with whom he could leave a message.

Emiliano could see the aggravation building up in Chase. He rolled down the window and called out to him.

"Chase, why don't we stop by Tauromaquia on the way out of town? You can leave a message for Lorena with the owner."

"I guess I don't have a choice."

They drove to Tauromaquia, and Chase went in hoping to find the owner. Unfortunately, the owner was out running errands. Chase quickly scribbled a note to Lorena, explaining he had been called out of town on urgent business. He apologized for canceling their dinner plans and explained that he hoped to be back in town in a couple of days. He would call her as soon as he returned. Chase gave the note to the bartender and handed him a hundred peso note to emphasize the importance of making sure Lorena received his message. The bartender assured Chase he would personally give it to her.

As Chase jumped in on the passenger's side, Emiliano knew this was not a time to make light of Chase's frustration. He tried to reassure him, but he could tell Chase was still unhappy about the circumstances of leaving so suddenly.

Lorena was hard at work in her studio while Chase was making his attempt to contact her. She had a very busy day ahead of her. After she worked out some changes to her dance routine, she had to meet with her manager to discuss the upcoming national tour, which was starting in two weeks. Then she would lunch with her mother and father at their home, leaving her just enough time to get ready for her dinner date with Chase.

Not unlike Chase, she was also distracted most of the morning with thoughts of the previous night. She was exhausted from lack of sleep but still felt exhilarated by the memories of their lovemaking. Not since her brief affair with Lolo had she felt such intense feelings towards a man. She knew it would be complicated, but she was willing to put in the effort and she hoped Chase felt the same way. She planned on using tonight's dinner to test the waters regarding his commitment to moving their relationship forward. Despite her fears that Chase's response might disappointment her, Lorena could hardly wait to see him.

Chase and Emiliano arrived in Morelia at 10 o'clock and went directly to a small café, El Pato, to meet their local contact, Antonio Blanca. Antonio was a gruff-looking man in his late fifties with sagging jowls that hung from his face like melting wax. His eyes were bloodshot from lack of sleep. He had been working on the case nonstop for the last twenty-four hours. Antonio had worked with Chase on tough assignments several times in the past. He was not as close to Chase as Emiliano, but Chase considered him a trusted colleague.

The two men entered the smoky bar and found Antonio sitting at a table in the back room. Chase sat down across from Antonio. The grim figure staring across at Chase had once had a promising career in the police department until his affair with a local official's wife had came to light and sidetracked his career.

The three men quickly got down to the business at hand.

Chase started with a barrage of questions.

"Do you know how long he has been holed up here?"

Antonio promptly answered, "Yes. He arrived three weeks ago. He snuck across the border in Nogales with his traveling companion. Some young blonde bimbo with tits that could stop a runaway freight train."

"Who owns the house?"

"A local drug dealer hoping to cash in on Wallace's troubles."

"Does Wallace suspect anything?"

"No. He's more interested in banging his lady friend and buying her fancy clothes."

"What kind of protection has he hired?"

"Three local hoodlums. Word on the streets is they have no limits. These are the kind of guys you don't want to meet in a dark alley."

Chase, turning to Emiliano, asked, "If we have to take them out to acquire

Wallace, what kind of flack are we going to catch from the local cops?"

"No problem. We might get a medal for getting rid of some of the local garbage. We need to be careful though. One of the guards is the brother of a powerful drug kingpin, Fermin Lorca; if we can avoid taking him out, we'd be better off."

Chase turned back to Antonio. "Why the change in locale if Wallace has all the protection he needs and has a comfortable place to settle down with his sex kitten?"

"She wants to be on the beach. I guess even crooks on the run can be pussy-whipped."

"Do we know when they're leaving?"

"My people tell me they've been packing up for the last couple of days, and they could be on the move any time."

"Do we know where they are headed?"

"I've still got my people working on it. They are pretty hush-hush about it. We suspect it is near Puerto Vallarta. Lots of gringos make it easier for them to blend in."

Chase asked about the logistics and whether Antonio had a layout of the hacienda. Antonio had done his homework and already had someone working on the inside. He handed Chase a rough sketch of the hacienda. Chase asked Antonio where he thought the best entrance point to the compound would be. Antonio told him that from the information he had gotten from his informant, the east side of the compound provided the best access. It had a lot of thick brush they could use for cover. Cover or not, it looked daunting. There was way too much open space from the twelve-foot high walls to the house for Chase's comfort level. Combined with the fact that the house was guarded around the clock by Wallace's hired guns, Chase knew this was not going to be a simple grab-Wallace-and-go scenario. This job would take some real planning.

It was clear to everyone that getting into the compound would have to be done under the cover of darkness. It would be too risky to attempt anything in broad daylight. Aside from the obvious reasons, there was also a greater chance someone would find out an American was involved in the plot. It wasn't hard to identify a gringo of Chase's stature in a crowd of Mexicans. Chase was always extremely cautious on all of his operations in Mexico to stay as inconspicuous as possible. The Federales wouldn't hesitate to pounce on anyone overstepping their legal boundaries, especially someone working for the FBI.

Chase asked, "Is there any chance we could hit them on the move as they are leaving?"

Emiliano jumped into the conversation. "Antonio and I discussed that option before we headed down here. We think it would draw too much attention. Besides, they are likely to have an escort, and they'll all be well armed. The less attention, the better, wouldn't you agree?"

"All right, but any plan I come up with will require all three of us," Chase said, staring directly at Antonio. "Are you in?"

Antonio moved his head slowly in an up and down motion. Chase had used him twice before in touchy situations. He knew Antonio was always ready for action.

"We'll hit them tomorrow night. Have you got twenty-four hour surveillance on them?" Chase asked Antonio.

"Yes. If they start to make a move, I'll let you know," Antonio responded confidently.

Chase turned to Emiliano, "Are you feeling all right about this? I usually don't like to involve you at this level, but I don't have time to recruit anyone else without losing this guy."

Emiliano didn't hesitate. "I'm in."

Emiliano trusted Chase's ability to put together the safest plan for extracting his target. He had seen him in action before and knew Chase wouldn't ask if he weren't in desperate need of help. He also knew if things didn't go according to plan, they would all be in trouble. Even though Emiliano was an accomplished marksman, he always tried to avoid the blood and guts aspects of this kind of operation. The proposition of facing Fermin Lorca's gang scared the hell out of him, but he wasn't about to leave Chase high and dry.

Chase told them he needed the rest of the night to put together the plan. They had a good arsenal of weapons already, but Chase asked Antonio if he could get some diversionary weapons, such as smoke bombs. He also wanted some short-range weapons for close-up action; sawed-off shotguns would do just fine. Antonio assured Chase there wouldn't be any problem in acquiring what he needed.

Chase could see that both of his colleagues were concerned about the mission, but he had no choice other than to enlist their help. He reassured Emiliano and Antonio that he wanted to avoid gunfire at all cost, but better safe than sorry. He also was aware that any plan that included taking out their adversaries would make their exit from the country extremely complicated. It didn't matter that the thugs protecting Wallace were wanted by the Mexican government. The Federales would tolerate a lot of things when it came to gringos, but an American operative who killed Mexicans on their home soil was not included. It was a line no one in this business ever wanted to cross.

They agreed to meet the next day for breakfast and go over the final plans. Chase thanked Antonio for his hard work and reinforced the necessity for complete discretion regarding the operation. He and Emiliano stood, shook hands with Antonio, and headed off in the direction of their hotel.

Chase went directly to his room and started working on the details of the plan. He spent hours reviewing the diagrams of the compound that Antonio had given him. There were only two major entrances to the compound. The first was a small entrance on the left side used by the hired help to come and go. The other was the main entrance. Two heavy, wooden double doors guarded the front entrance, which allowed vehicles in and out of the compound. The hacienda was surrounded by a ten-foot rock wall that protected the inner sanctuary of the manicured grounds. The top of the stone wall was covered with broken shards of bottles, typical of low-cost security systems in Mexico. Regardless of this flimsy attempt at security, Chase wanted to avoid having any plan that required scaling the wall. He knew he was physically capable of making it over the wall if need be, but he wasn't sure that Emiliano or Antonio was in any shape to accomplish such a feat. The plan might have to include some kind of diversion tactic to make a clean entrance.

Chase scribbled down several alternatives and then began the painstaking task of eliminating all but one. He didn't finish the final details until four o'clock in the morning. After mulling it over one more time, he was satisfied that, given the short period of time, he had developed the best possible plan for getting Wallace out without any collateral damage.

Chase didn't lay his head down on the pillow until almost five o'clock. Although he was exhausted, he still had a hard time falling asleep. He was not only worried about tomorrow night's operation, but his mind kept flashing back to Lorena. Had she received his note? Would she understand? Even if she had, would it still appear as if he had taken advantage of her? His mind was whirling with the possibilities, and it took well over an hour for him to finally drift off.

Lorena arrived at the restaurant early and eagerly waited for Chase. They were supposed to meet at eight o'clock. It was now almost nine, and he was still nowhere to be seen. She wracked her brain over the possible reasons why he was so late. Was she confused about the time? She tried to convince herself that maybe there was a misunderstanding. Lorena turned her head toward the entrance every few minutes, hoping Chase would appear. Uncertainty was starting to creep into her thoughts, and it left her with a restless, aching feeling.

Her waiter inquired several times if she would like to order. It was starting to become embarrassing. The other patrons in the restaurant recognized her and were beginning to stare in curiosity at her obvious predicament. At one point, she asked the owner whether anyone had left a message for her. The owner checked with his staff, but reported that there were no messages for her.

Lorena could feel her anger welling up, but it was tempered by her concern about Chase's whereabouts. *Had he been in a serious accident and unable to contact her?* As quickly as these thoughts of alarm raced into her mind, they were replaced with an intense suspicion that maybe she was just the victim of a smooth-talking gringo looking for a one-night stand. She found it hard to believe that Chase was the kind of man who would treat anyone so callously. He seemed sincere in everything he said to her at the hot springs last night. She couldn't convince herself that the time they had spent together was just another one of those passing flings for a traveling businessman.

She finally gave up hope around 9:30. She gave the owner a description of

Chase and left her phone number in case he showed up later.

She stepped out onto the street and flagged a cab. Not yet ready to give up, she asked the cab to take her to Chase's home. When they arrived, Lorena asked the driver to wait for her. She knocked on the front door and Fernando answered.

"Good evening Señorita," Fernando said somewhat surprised by Lorena's presence.

Lorena spoke in an apologetic voice, "I'm sorry to bother you at such a late hour, but I was supposed to meet Señor Chandler for dinner this evening. Do you happen to know where he might be?"

Fernando was head of the household, but Chase never informed him of the details regarding his business trips. The only information Fernando had in this particular instance was that Chase was going to be gone for two to three days working on some urgent business issues for Lone Star.

Fernando suspected the beautiful young lady standing before him was the reason why Chase had returned home so late the night before. "I'm sorry Señorita, but unfortunately I do not know the exact whereabouts of Señor Chandler. He left this morning with one of his business associates and is not expected to return for a couple of days."

"Did he possibly leave any messages?"

"Not that I'm aware of."

"Does he often leave so unexpectedly on business?" Lorena inquired, knowing that she was probably overstepping the boundaries of his boss's privacy.

Fernando would have normally refused to answer such a question, but he felt sorry for Lorena, who was noticeably disturbed by Chase's absence. "Señor Chandler is often called out on pressing business matters but is almost always explicit in his instructions regarding any important messages or tasks he wishes for me to take care of on his behalf," Fernando gently emphasized.

Lorena silently assessed what she had just been told. It was obvious Fernando would be of no help to her regarding Chase's whereabouts. She asked Fernando to let Señor Chandler know that she had inquired about him and to have him call her when he returned to Ciudad Hidalgo.

"Is there anything other message you would like me to give to Señor

Chandler?" Fernando inquired, hoping that she might reveal a hint of her feelings for his employer.

"No, no. That's all." Her voice trailed off into quiet submission. "Thank you very much."

Lorena returned to the waiting cab and instructed him to take her home. By the time she arrived, her curiosity had transformed into genuine anger. She paid the cab driver, ignoring the fact that she gave him an unusually large tip. She could understand if Chase had to leave town on urgent business, but not to have left a message was unforgivable. She was already starting to expect the common courtesies of being a "couple."

Lorena's frustration was percolating, slowly bubbling up from deep inside the nucleus of her disbelief that anyone could be so coldhearted. *Where the hell are you, Chase Chandler?*

What Lorena didn't know was that Chase had left a message, but the bartender to whom he had entrusted the note had a family emergency. Chase's note was still in the bartender's pocket when he rushed to catch the next bus out of town to help his sister who had fallen ill.

Unbeknownst to Chase, who was finalizing his plan in a hotel room in Morelia, Lorena was sulking in despair over what had happened between them at the hot springs. She started to become angry with herself for being so naïve, for trusting a man she barely knew. What was she thinking when she invited him into her complicated life?

She lay down in a futile attempt to go to sleep and found her mind still wandering off to thoughts of Chase. She could almost hear him telling her how much he cared about her. She couldn't believe everything he shared with her was just the superficial musings of a hard-up gringo. Lorena tried to ignore her mounting anxiety, but her mind was clouded with so many questions. She knew she was no closer to resolving the mystery of Chase's desertion than when she had started. How was she going to respond to him when and if he ever returned? She cried herself to sleep thinking about how close she had come to having found a man with whom she might have fallen in love.

Chase met Emiliano and Antonio at El Pato at noon. He had gotten very little sleep and was anxious to share the details of his plan. He badly needed the distraction to stop thinking about Lorena. He thought earlier that morning about calling her, but he knew it would be a breach of security. It would be almost impossible to explain why he had left so abruptly. He had to tell her in person, and still, he knew he would have to lie to her about where he had been for the last couple of days. He knew it was foolish for him to worry about Lorena right now; he had put all of his focus on the task at hand. Not only was his life on the line, but also the lives of two other men; he never took that responsibility lightly.

The three men sat at a corner table overlooking the central plaza. Chase first turned to Antonio and asked about the weapons Antonio was to acquire.

"Everything we discussed is taken care of," Antonio proudly responded.

"I may need a few more items added to the list." Chase reached into a folder and handed Antonio a short list. Antonio quickly glanced over the list: a fifty-foot length of heavy-duty rope, a ten-foot square of black canvas tarpaulin, two nightsticks, and a large vial of chloroform.

Antonio looked at Chase suspiciously, "This is an unusual list of items. What kind of party are we having?"

"We'll go into that in a couple of minutes. Any problem with this list?"

Antonio could see by Chase's expression he was in no mood for levity. "No, I'll have it all taken care of before we meet tonight."

Chase turned to Emiliano and asked, "Is the car ready and our route set?"

"Yes, but we need to make sure we meet our friends at the agreed upon time, or our arrangement will be off," Emiliano said, referring to the transportation he had lined up for their escape.

Emiliano had arranged for them to meet outside of Morelia with a convoy of three trucks that would transport them and their captive to the border. He had instructed the truckers to construct a false compartment in the back of one of the trucks, a common practice *coyotes* used in getting illegal aliens across the U.S. border. Once they crossed, FBI agents would be waiting for them on the other side, and they could transfer Wallace into their custody. Chase had been successful with a similar plan in one of his previous operations, but it was still a tricky process to get through both Mexican and U.S. borders. Customs was always on the lookout for illegal aliens, and they knew all the tricks of the trade. Although Chase worked for the FBI, the Bureau did not involve U.S. Customs in their plans due to possible leaks. Chase knew he wouldn't get any help if his operation were exposed during the border crossing. Besides, U.S. Customs had to constantly tiptoe around their Mexican counterparts given some past FBI operations that had left a bad taste in their mouths.

During their entire conversation Emiliano could tell Chase was uneasy. Something was up. Chase confessed a minute later that he was uncomfortable sharing the details of his plan in such a public place. He suggested they find a place that would be more discreet.

Antonio volunteered his brother's printing office, just down the street. His brother was out of town on business, so they could have it all to themselves. Chase paid their bill, and they resumed their discussion at the printing office.

Chase pulled out the sketch of the compound Antonio had given him the night before. For the next two hours, he meticulously went over the plan, making sure everyone understood their individual roles. He told them that if anything went south in the execution of the plan, they would immediately abandon it and make another attempt later.

During the entire discussion, Chase never cracked a smile. Experience told him that if something broke down during the mission, someone could easily end up dead. He wasn't about to spoil his perfect record on a scumbag like Wallace. Chase was confident the men who were guarding Wallace would shoot a man as easily as they would a mangy Mexican dog. Whenever this kind of money was involved, these hired guns would do anything to protect a paying customer. Chase also knew his adversaries had a reputation to uphold for the sake of acquiring future business, and there was never a shortage of gringos on the run looking for hired help.

Chase asked Antonio and Emiliano if they had any questions. Both men shook their heads. Chase could sense they still had concerns but were too proud to reveal them. They synchronized their watches and agreed to meet at eleven o'clock. The compound was thirty minutes outside of Morelia, so they would arrive sometime around eleven thirty. Chase wanted to make sure Wallace and his lady friend were quietly asleep in their bed.

Chase eyed both men closely, giving them one last gut check, making sure there were no lingering questions. "If anyone changes his mind before tonight's rendezvous, no hard feelings. I know this is out of the normal scope of things."

His comment was aimed more at Emiliano, who had only limited experience in hazardous field operations. He had no worries about Antonio, a battle-worn warrior who had been in a lot tough scrapes as an ex-military sergeant and local policeman. Chase knew if push came to shove, he would likely have to rely on Antonio's experience to get them out of a jam.

The three men parted company outside of the print shop. Chase and Emiliano met up at the hotel, and Chase suggested they get some rest. Both men knew they would need to be sharp to pull this operation off. Emiliano took Chase's advice, and went straight to his room to grab some much-needed shuteye.

Chase, on the other hand, was too keyed up to sleep, even though he was exhausted. He would have to wait until he got back to Ciudad Hidalgo and, hopefully, into the arms of Lorena before he could let down his guard.

Chase met Antonio and Emiliano at the prescribed time in front of his hotel. It was a Tuesday night, and the streets were empty. Antonio loaded the gear into the car, taking extra precaution with the bottle of chloroform. He had a tough time acquiring it, but was able to finally convince a local pharmacist that he needed it to put down an ailing horse. Everything was set; it was just a matter of executing the plan.

Emiliano got behind the wheel while Antonio and Chase jumped in the back seat. They drove out through the back roads of the hilly countryside until they spotted the lone hacienda perched on the crest of a hill. They turned out the lights and slowly drove up the heavily rutted road toward the hacienda. They were fortunate it was a cloudless night and there was a three-quarter moon to help guide their way. When they were about a quarter mile from the compound, they parked the car on an adjoining dirt road.

Antonio had checked out the road during his initial surveillance to make sure it was the closest access to their target. From here it was a short hike through the sandy hummocks to the secluded hacienda and Wallace. Chase peered through his binoculars and saw there were only a few lights on. He took it as a good sign that the occupants were down for the night. He knew from the information Antonio had gathered that there was only one guard on duty for the nightshift. The other two hired hands slept in a casita adjoining the main house occupied by Wallace and his girlfriend.

It took them ten minutes to load up all the gear, each man carrying his allotted share of the equipment. Chase carried the heavy rope he had cut into appropriate lengths, one of the sawed-off, twelve-gauge shotguns, and a .45 caliber Colt in a shoulder holster. He also carried the vial of chloroform, a handkerchief in his back pocket, and a small lock cutter. Emiliano was equipped with a .44 caliber pistol slung from his left side and a nightstick that dangled from the other. He carried the canvas tarpaulin and a backup vial of chloroform. Antonio looked like a perfect replica of Pancho Villa. He carried a menacing-looking, ten-inch skinning knife around his bulging gut. Across his chest were two crisscrossing gun belts fully outfitted with .44 caliber shells. Chase was glad to have him by his side. Antonio was an expert with his knife at short distances. He could take a man out as fast as Chase could draw his pistol.

Chase handed Antonio a pouch containing plastic explosives and a remote detonating switch. "I probably don't need to tell you this, but go light with this stuff. I don't want more attention than necessary," Chase cautioned, anxious about having given the responsibility for the explosives to someone else other than himself.

Chase did a quick once-over to make sure that they had not forgotten anything. He turned to Antonio and Emiliano and made sure that they were set to go.

"Are you gentlemen ready to take down the bad guys?" Chase said.

Both men smiled and nodded affirmatively.

From here on, most of their communication would be by hand signals. Out in the desert night air, noise could easily travel unimpeded to the ears of their awaiting enemies. Chase took the lead as they made their way over the sage-covered mounds leading to the hacienda. It took them twenty minutes to creep their way to the stone wall surrounding the compound. Having reached their first checkpoint, they rested against its cold, rough face. They were about thirty feet downwind from the entrance they were planning to use. They tried pushing the old wooden door open, but as they expected, it was locked from the inside.

Chase knew his first chore was to get over the imposing wall without alerting the guard. He had memorized the entire layout of the compound and interior of the house. Chase had chosen this position knowing that the two-story hacienda would throw a dark shadow across the compound to the stone wall. He had calculated how he could easily slip over the wall and drop into the darkness of shadow without being discovered by the guard. Chase had even consulted the star charts, making sure the position of the moon at that time of night would not cast its light onto his intended landing area. This kind of attention to detail was why Chase seldom failed and had complete confidence in the plan he had designed.

Chase removed his leather jacket. His shirt was soaked in sweat.

Emiliano wondered why he had lugged such a heavy jacket all the way from the car when the outside temperatures were in the mid-seventies. Emiliano was about to find out the method to his companion's madness. Chase signaled to his compadres to get ready to give him a boost over the wall. Emiliano and Antonio stood a few feet apart, forming a foot harness with four sections of rope. Chase stepped gingerly onto the strands of rope. At first, he struggled to gain his balance but eventually steadied himself, using the shoulders of Antonio and Emiliano as crutches. He was fortunate both were sturdily built men or they would not have been able to lift his large frame. Chase slung his leather coat over the top edge of the wall to protect himself from getting sliced to pieces by the razor-sharp shards of glass fixed in cement to the top of the wall. With his arms outstretched, he would need a sizeable boost to reach the top of the wall and hoist himself over. Chase held out his hand with three fingers outstretched. One by one he closed them into his fist. As the third finger disappeared, Emiliano and Antonio gathered up their combined strength and hoisted Chase into the air.

Chase immediately became airborne as he reached for the top of the wall. He extended his arms high above his head, as far as he could physically muster, but he still had the sense he was going to fall short of his target. In one sweeping motion he slapped his hands forward, barely grasping the top edge of the stone wall. He immediately felt a searing pain in his left hand. Somehow, one of the ragged pieces of glass had penetrated his heavy leather coat and cut a deep gash in his palm. A two-inch shard of glass protruded into his hand. It was everything he could do not to scream or let go of his grip. He quickly hoisted himself up and over the wall and dropped lightly into the freshly cultivated ground of the inner compound. He was in!

The several small flowering bushes made for good cover as he dived behind them. His hand was bleeding profusely. He grabbed his handkerchief out of his back pocket and he wrapped it tightly around the deep gash. He knew didn't have time right now to worry about the severity of his wound. Chase scanned over the top of the bushes to make sure the guard on watch had not heard him. He hoped he hadn't let out some kind of wounded animal sound when his hand hit the top of the wall.

When he peeked over the brush he could see the guard on duty was half-asleep in a rocking chair on the front porch of the main house—an unexpected advantage that would work in their favor.

Chase started to creep along the inner wall toward the small opening where Antonio and Emiliano were waiting on the other side. When Chase got to the door, to his surprise, there was only a steel rod inserted through a rusty horizontal lock hinge. He carefully removed the rod and inched opened the door to avoid any squeaking from the rusted hinges. As he slowly cracked the door open, Chase peered through to see Antonio and Emiliano braced with their guns pointing straight at him. Once they realized it was Chase, they lowered their weapons and breathed a deep sigh of relief.

Chase could see Emiliano's hand shaking, but he purposely didn't acknowledge it. The last thing he needed to do was make his friend more nervous.

Chase signaled for his colleagues to join him and closed the door behind them. Both men had grim looks of concern as they stared at the splattered blood on Chase's shirt and the crimson soaked handkerchief around his hand. He didn't have time to explain his wound as he motioned them to follow.

The three men scrambled for the back entrance of the house. Emiliano kept turning his head in the direction of the guard on duty to make sure their passage continued unnoticed.

When they reached the corner of the hacienda, Chase did one more silent gut check with his colleagues and formed his right hand in a tight fist, symbolizing "keep it together, no mistakes." It was a symbol Chase had used since his war years and both Emiliano and Antonio instantly recognized it. If everything went on schedule, they would have Wallace in their hands and be out of the compound in less than fifteen minutes. They checked their watches one more time, making sure they were still synchronized.

Chase and Emiliano headed for the back entrance of the house. As Chase departed, he gave Antonio a nod, as if to say, "See you on the other side."

Antonio headed off in the direction of the car parked alongside of the house. As Antonio was securing the plastic explosives to the underside of the 1968 Impala and setting the timing device for thirty seconds, Chase and Emiliano were picking the lock that led into the rear entrance of the house. Wallace and his girlfriend were sleeping down the hall in the master bedroom.

Once the back door was open, they slithered in and maneuvered their way through the cluttered kitchen. It was like walking through a minefield of culinary bombs. The pots and pans hanging from the ceiling were particularly dangerous for a man of Chase's stature.

As Chase and Emiliano made their way down the long hallway to the master bedroom, Antonio had perfectly positioned himself to take out the attending guard, who was still dozing in the rocking chair on the front porch. The guard's hand was lightly draped on a Remington rifle sitting in his lap. Antonio, with cat-like moves, maneuvered his way behind the unsuspecting guard. He was so close he could hear the slow rhythmic breathing of his intended victim. Antonio reached down, raised the butt of his pistol and, in one smooth motion, slammed it into the guard's skull. The guard whimpered one deep low grunt and slouched forward. Antonio tied his hands to the back of the rocking chair and found a comfortable position to stand watch over the other sleeping guards in the nearby casita.

While Antonio was completing the crucial details of his assignment, Chase and Emiliano had safely made their way to the door of the master bedroom. Chase gripped the glass doorknob and slowly turned it until he heard a dull steel click. He opened the door as if he was peeling the back page of a rare, 14th Century Bible. Chase peered in through the crack and was relieved to see Wallace and his girlfriend fast asleep. He pivoted his head around to look at Emiliano and make sure he was ready for the next stage of the plan. Emiliano nodded and they dropped to their knees and slid along the polished, wooden floor. When they reached the foot of the bed, Chase took the left side where Wallace was sleeping, and Emiliano took the right.

Each man held a handkerchief soaked in chloroform. Their timing had to be perfect in seizing their victims simultaneously. One scream from their victims could alert the guards and then all hell would break lose.

When Chase reached his side of the bed, he cautiously peeked over at Emiliano. He signaled he was ready and once again held up three fingers and counted them down. As the last finger dropped, both men firmly placed the saturated cloths over the mouths of the two sleeping victims.

The woman's eyes rattled open with a panicked grimace. Emiliano could see the intense fear in her dilated pupils. She kicked hysterically at the bed sheets, trying to escape from the strange horror pinning her down. As Emiliano looked down at the woman's flailing nude body, he could tell why Wallace had chosen to take her along. Her rock-hard nipples were pointing up at Emiliano like two finely cut pieces of pink soapstone. Momentarily, Emiliano lost his concentration until he was shaken back to reality by Chase's icy glare.

Slowly, the chloroform started taking effect on the struggling woman. Her eyes fluttered momentarily, and then all fear poured out of them as they closed. Emiliano could feel the tension drain from her entire body until she lay limp beneath the weight of his body.

Meanwhile, Wallace was much stronger and thrashed about like a wild animal, making it almost impossible for Chase to subdue him. Chase could feel his grip starting to loosen, so he applied more pressure to the rag over Wallace's face. He slung the full weight of his body on top of Wallace.

He could feel the stabbing pain in his left hand, which had started bleeding again. The scattered drops of blood on the sheets were starting to resemble a Jackson Pollack painting. Chase knew if he released Wallace from his grip for even a second, the whole operation would be compromised. Fortunately, Wallace was an older man of small stature and not much of a match for the overpowering strength of Chase.

At one point in the struggle, Wallace got his arms out from under the covers and began flailing at Chase's upper torso, slamming his fist into Chase's chest and trying desperately to free himself. After what seemed to be several minutes, Wallace succumbed to the effects of the sedative, and his arms fell limp onto the bed.

Chase whispered to Emiliano, "How are we doing?"

"She's down for the count." Emiliano's eyes were the size of cue balls.

"Tape her mouth shut and tie her to the bedpost," Chase ordered, panting from his efforts to subdue Wallace.

Emiliano followed Chase's instruction, ripping off strips of duct tape and binding her hands to the bedpost. While Emiliano finished the final touches on Wallace's girlfriend, Chase was laying out the square of canvas. He threw back the covers and felt fortunate Wallace wore pajamas. He wasn't looking forward to having to dress him.

Chase motioned to Emiliano, asking for help with moving Wallace onto the stretched out canvas. They gingerly lifted his limp body onto the floor and began to loosely turn him as if they were making a Chinese egg roll. When Wallace was completely enclosed in the canvas, Chase tied each end with a strand of rope. Emiliano carefully cut a small slit in the canvas as a breathing hole so Wallace wouldn't suffocate during transport.

Once Wallace was secure, they checked on his girlfriend, making sure she was still out. Chase lifted her eyelids and wondered what her first thoughts would be when she finally awoke, realizing that her meal ticket was gone. He felt a small twinge of sympathy for her, but it lasted only long enough for him to know that she was getting everything she deserved. She had rolled the dice and they had come up snake eyes.

For a split second, Chase thought about taking her along for the trip as a material witness but decided against it. He knew it would be much more dicey and time-consuming trying to get two bodies out of the compound. She just wasn't worth the risk. Besides, Chase had already arranged to have the border patrol waiting to greet her when she tried to return to the U.S. He knew from the file on Wallace that she was not in on Wallace's murder or embezzling schemes. At best, she was just an accomplice to his escape across the Mexican border. Chase was pretty sure she would fold up like a cheap tent and turn state's evidence against Wallace once the pressure was put on her.

Chase turned to Emiliano and whispered, "Are you ready to get this bag of shit out of here?"

Emiliano smiled and gripped one end of the canvas roll that encased Wallace. Chase checked his watch, making sure that they were still on schedule. Ten minutes had passed since they had parted company with Antonio. They were right on schedule.

Chase picked up the other end of the canvas, and they made their way out into the hallway and headed toward the kitchen door.

Antonio continued to watch the casita where the other guards lay fast asleep. He held his breath, hoping Chase and Emiliano would be successful in getting Wallace safely out of the house without waking the guards. Antonio nervously looked at his watch, knowing at any moment he should see Chase and Emiliano scrambling across the inner courtyard with their payload. He kept glancing in the direction of where he expected to see them appear.

Unexpectedly, he heard a loud clanging noise from inside the house; the sound disappeared as quickly as it came. He stopped breathing momentarily and waited to see if the sleeping guards had been awakened. Thirty seconds passed. The casita remained dark. He was starting to relax, sure his partners had escaped a major calamity, when he heard a loud rustling of men yelling at each other. Suddenly, a light came on in the casita, and two half-dressed men rushed out of the small building, each brandishing a shotgun.

At the same moment, Chase and Emiliano appeared in the pale moonlight carrying Wallace. They were hurriedly beating a path for the exit door. Fortunately for Chase and Emiliano, the two guards were disoriented and didn't notice the two men struggling with their package to reach the safe confines of the high brush bordering the stone wall.

The two guards were trying to put their clothes on as they frantically stumbled in the direction of the main house. Antonio crept back from his position next to the guard who was still out cold from his vicious blow. He peered from the corner of the building to make sure the other guards were still heading in his direction and not toward his partners.

As the two guards approached the porch, they yelled at their unconscious comrade but received no response.

Antonio could see that Chase and Emiliano were making good progress on their escape route. The ex-policeman decided it was time for him to get the hell out of there, and he headed for the back of the house. He held the detonating switch in his right hand. As the guards approached their slouched comrade, they angrily called out to him again; still no answer. They lifted his drooping head and it fell back onto his chest as if his neck vertebra were made of Jell-O. One of the guards screamed out a barrage of "fucking assholes." With hardly a mournful thought for the dead cohort, they ran toward the front entrance of the main house and entered. As they approached Wallace's bedroom, they could see the door was wide open and there was only a single outline of a body in the bed. They rushed over and threw back the covers to expose the limp, nude body of Wallace's girlfriend. They could see she was bound to the bedpost and her mouth had been taped.

One of the guards rushed to the bedroom window throwing back the shade just as Antonio's shadow disappeared around the other side of the house. The other guard yelled at his partner, who was still staring at the voluptuous body stretched out before him. "Vamanos!" Both guards scrambled in the direction of the back entrance to the house.

As Antonio was skirting across the open courtyard, he could see his partners disappearing through the small doorway and out into the open desert. He felt relieved his friends were safely out of harm's way. Just before Antonio reached the cover of the garden area that led to the doorway and safety, he heard a loud, angry shout.

"Stop, you son of a bitch!"

Antonio kept moving in the direction of the small opening. He could see Chase waiting for him on the other side of the gate. Chase could see that the two guards were gaining on Antonio, and he yelled at him to pick up the pace. He raised his pistol hoping to get a shot off at the approaching guards but Antonio was blocking his line of sight.

Antonio glanced back just in time to see one of the guards stop to shoulder his twelve-gauge shotgun and take aim at him. As he reached the doorway, he heard the thundering sound of the shotgun and for a split second thought he had escaped the rapidly approaching buckshot. Then he felt the unmistakable searing pain of the copper pellets striking him violently in the lower back.

The force of the surging pellets threw Antonio forward into Chase's arms, knocking both men to the ground. Emiliano quickly rushed to their aid, slamming the door shut to stop the onrushing guards. Chase gently rolled Antonio off him and knelt beside the mortally wounded man. His hands were covered with warm blood. Antonio was still breathing, but his breath was labored.

Chase could hear the angry guards banging on the door and cursing in frustration. Emiliano continued to brace the thick wooden door with his body as he looked desperately for something to hold the door.

Chase returned his attention to Antonio and could see from the pained looked in Antonio's eyes that he was in serious trouble. Antonio was gasping for air with each deep breath. Chase bent over close to his wounded friend and promised, "We're going to get you out of here, so just hang on."

Antonio gripped Chase's bloody hand as he gasped for air. "What about Wallace?"

"To hell with Wallace. Another time, another place," Chase anxiously replied as he peered over at the canvas roll containing Wallace.

"No, my friend, I'm not going to die for nothing. I want you to promise me you'll get that son of a bitch out of here." He looked up at Chase with an expression that left no doubt about what he was saying.

"We're not leaving you here! I made a promise, and I'm going to get you out of here."

"Chase, this is my call." Antonio heaved, gasping for breath. "Prop me up against the door and get the hell out of here before it's too late for all of us." His breathing was becoming more labored as each second passed. Even Antonio's normally dark face was starting to turn an ashen-gray from the loss of blood.

Chase looked at Emiliano, who reluctantly nodded his head in agreement with Antonio's request.

Chase looked down at Antonio and realized he was fighting a losing battle. Antonio could see Chase was still resisting the idea of leaving him.

Antonio burst out with what little energy he had left in him, "Dammit, Chase, do it! We're running out of time." His eyelids began to flutter.

Chase placed his hands under Antonio's shoulders and began to drag him toward the door. As Chase gingerly pulled Antonio, he could see a track of dirt and blood left from his mortal wound.

When they reached the door, Chase pulled the dead weight of Antonio's body into a sitting position against the wooden door. The guards were still attempting to burst through from the other side. They had even fired their shotguns at the impenetrable thick door, hoping to finish off their enemies.

Once Antonio was in place, Emiliano slowly moved away from the door, making sure that his friend's body weight was sufficient to keep their pursuers at bay. Antonio had barely enough strength to remain sitting upright, but it was just enough to hold the door secure.

Antonio whispered to Emiliano, "I'll need my gun."

Emiliano reached down and pulled the pistol out of Antonio's holster, placing it in his friend's right hand. Antonio's grip was so weak Emiliano had to wrap his fingers around the butt of the pistol. As he did so, he gave Antonio's hand a firm consolatory grip.

"I'm sorry, my friend. Don't worry about your family. They're taken care of," Emiliano said with a tear in his eyes knowing that he was the one who had accidentally knocked the skillet in the kitchen, awakening the sleeping guards.

Antonio had only enough energy to nod his head and smile in acknowledgment of Emiliano's promise.

Chase was standing at the foot of the canvas roll, waiting for Emiliano to join him. Emiliano patted Antonio on the shoulder and turned to help Chase. They each grabbed an end of the canvas bag and heaved Wallace's body off the sand. Neither man looked back, as they marched off into the darkness toward their stashed car. As they approached the car, they heard the distinct sound of gunfire, and then there was silence. Chase and Emiliano stared at each other knowing Antonio was making the ultimate sacrifice on their behalf.

Both men felt awkward for not stopping to acknowledge Antonio's sacrifice, but they knew if they hesitated any longer, their chances of escaping would quickly evaporate. They were not about to let Antonio's life be wasted on a botched mission. They owed it to Antonio and his family to make sure they made it out alive.

They removed Wallace from the canvas and placed his lifeless body in the back seat. It was a precaution, just in case cops stopped them *en route* to their rendezvous point with the truckers. They could always use the excuse that their friend had had a little too much tequila.

Emiliano jumped in behind the driver's seat and started the car. Chase took one quick look to make sure the guards were not hot on their heels. Just as he ducked into the passenger's side, he saw a bright orange and yellow ball of fire rising up from inside the compound. Seconds later, the thundering roar of the explosives Antonio had planted in Wallace's escape vehicle echoed across the emptiness. It was as if Antonio's last dying gesture was a message to his colleagues, wishing them a safe journey.

Emiliano, having heard the explosion, slammed the foot pedal to the floor and sped down the dirt road leading to the main highway. Chase turned around and glanced through the back window to see the plume of dark smoke billowing into the night sky. He relished the thought of the two guards being shaken to their very core by the explosion and knew Antonio would have had a good belly laugh from the chaotic scene of everyone scrambling for their lives. No better way for a tough, hard-nosed soldier to go out, he thought.

When the car reached the main road, they looked in both directions for any sign of their pursuers, but there was no one in sight. As they turned onto the main highway, Emiliano made the sign of the cross and looked at Chase, hoping for some kind of redemption from his sense of overwhelming guilt. He couldn't get over the thought of having caused Antonio's death. *Why couldn't he have been just a little more careful in the kitchen?*

Chase laid his hand on his friend's shoulder, trying to comfort him. "It comes with the territory. Antonio wouldn't blame anyone, especially you; he considered you a good friend."

While Chase was doing his best to reassure his partner, his own heart felt as though someone was squeezing the life out of it. He accused himself, thinking, "God dammit! It wasn't supposed to go down this way. What the hell did I do wrong?" He was already starting to blame himself for Antonio's death.

Two days later, following an uncomfortable ride in the back of a big rig, Chase turned Wallace over to FBI agents in Laredo, Texas. Chase was grateful to have completed the mission, but he was full of regret, knowing the price for Wallace's capture was Antonio's life. Chase knew his perfect record ended when Antonio heaved his last breath, but right now, he didn't give a damn about his almighty "reputation." Losing Antonio had a much more profound affect on him than he expected. He actually, for the first time, let the thought creep into his mind that maybe it was time to get out of this business. He wasn't ready to make the decision about his future with the Bureau right now, but this had definitely left a bad taste in his mouth. Right now, he had more important business to take care of.

Chase drove to a local branch of his bank in Laredo and transferred fifty thousand dollars into his account in Mexico. He was determined to make sure Antonio's family was taken care of as he had promised. After making the arrangements with the bank, Chase returned to his hotel room, took a badly needed shower, collapsed on the bed, and dropped off into a dead sleep.

The next morning he caught a train back to Ciudad Hidalgo. During the entire trip, his mind was ravaged with a sickening feeling that he had not only lost Antonio, but that he may also have sacrificed his relationship with Lorena. The last time Lorena had crossed his mind was just before they entered the compound to snag Wallace. He remembered having a slight moment of hesitation, a chilling sense of remorse that stopped him dead in his tracks. Chase knew for the first time in his life he had something he wanted to come back to, someone who mattered to him.

As Chase was making his way back to Ciudad Hidalgo, he had no idea that Lorena had left town two days before. She was starting a performance tour in northern Mexico. She had waited patiently for him and even considered delaying her trip in the hope that he might return. But after several days without any word from him, she decided chalk her night up with Chase as a bad decision on her part for falling in love with a complete stranger.

Lorena boarded a northbound train, wondering if she would ever unlock the mystery of Chase Chandler. As she listened to the familiar chug of the steam engine leaving the station, the same lingering thought crisscrossed her mind, *"Where the hell are you, Chase Chandler?"*

CHAPTER 5

Winter of 1963–Mexico City

His perfectly carved silhouette cut a solitary image in the sun-drenched *salle d'armes*. The absence of any sound seemed almost calculated. Only the slow, deliberate cadence of his breathing disturbed the intensity of his concentration. Diego Julio Sanchez was tired of behaving, of cautiously doling out his youthful energy. He so much wanted to be part of the legacy of the great fencing champions, to lift up Mexico's reputation in one of the oldest Olympic sports. Having begun his studies at the age of nine, and after ten years of relentless practice, Diego's patience was wearing thin. The long days of meticulously training every muscle in his body to follow his mental orders were evaporating as fast as the receding mist outside the practice facility where he had spent most of his life. From the crescent arch of his spine to the slight angle of his hand gripping the sixteen-ounce foil, every position required perfection, each deliberate lunge a dramatic purpose. Even outside the "court of honor," he found himself obsessed with his footwork. The simple task of making his way from his bedroom to the living room—heel to toe, toe to heel; falling to the floor, mimicking a cat's slow-curving arc as it stirred from its midday nap.

This morning was no different from any other. Obsessed with punctuality, Diego made a point of arriving before his fellow combatants. He stared intently at the small arched opening across the practice court, waiting for any sign of his opponent's arrival; waiting, always waiting. Through the paper-thin soles of his shoes, Diego could feel the coarse roughness of the 6' X 44' *piste* that would define his life; that would hopefully raise him above the less committed. Within this horizontal canvas strip, all the great heroes of his sport had slashed and parried their way into history. For Diego, this was not a choice; it was his chosen destiny.

Diego was checking the position of his defensive stance, when he caught a glimpse of a slightly pudgy man and his assistant entering the *salle d'armes*. His challenger for today's practice session was Edgar Vargas, a former national champion of Mexico who had agreed to come out of retirement at the behest of Diego's maestro, Juan Luis Alvarez. Alvarez was hoping Vargas could provide the kind of challenge that would bring some humility to his young protégé.

The two competitors greeted each other with a barely noticeable head nod. Neither man wasted time stepping onto the *piste,* having already donned the appropriate fencing garb and checked their equipment. As was tradition, each man posed in the classic *en garde* stance, politely saluted each other with a bow of his head and then the tipped his blade in the opponent's direction. Each man slipped on their small-meshed protective headgear and prepared for the intense dance of a fencing duel.

The bout started with what the French called the "deadly conversation," where each man tries to determine the strengths and weaknesses of his opponent skills. Vargas attempted a *feint,* a common ruse to get an opponent to expose his next move but Diego did not flinch. Vargas, in a whip-like fashion, flicked the end of his foil and thrust forward. Diego braced himself, watching the space between him and his opponent disappear in the burst of three syncopated heartbeats. As Vargas lunged, Diego could almost hear the rapid-fire slashing of his adversary's foil cut the air. Diego arched his back and prepared for the charge. He was going to hold his ground, against his own better judgment and the advice of his maestro, Señor Alvarez, who sat skulking in a small observation balcony evaluating the performance of his reckless student.

At nineteen, Diego Sanchez was one of the most talented *escrimeurs* in Mexico if not the world, but he had yet to learn when not to foolishly challenge a more experienced swordsman. Fortunately for Diego, Vargas had slowed with age and was not capable of handing out the humility Diego's arrogance deserved. Diego alertly defended with a swift parry, stepped slightly to his left, and with an almost immeasurable movement of his foil counterattacked and struck Vargas in the torso and scored the first "touch" of the bout.

"No!....... No!" Señor Alvarez's gravelly voice barked. "You must gently inch yourself forward while not revealing your next move. Fencing is an art, not a game!" he said, slamming his fist against the carved stone ledge on which his arms rested.

Diego winced from the full weight of his teacher's disdain.

Alvarez was more impatient than usual this morning. He was painfully aware that Diego's unbridled flamboyance was the only thing getting in the way of stepping up to the next level in international rankings. He knew better than anyone else that Diego could not wait to do battle with the great fencers of France and Italy. As much as Alvarez prayed Diego would realize his dreams, the old master was not about to have his reputation tarnished by an arrogant, immature swordsman. Diego was as much a product of Alvarez's dedicated tutelage as he was of his own natural talent.

Alvarez returned his attention to Diego. "You do intend to show me something of your skills today, I hope. Please tell me you're not here simply to waste my time."

Diego knew he had crossed over the thin line of his maestro's patience. He feigned a smile to no avail, momentarily forgetting about his opponent, who stood only a few feet away. Still anxious to do battle and embarrassed by the young upstart's rebuff, Vargas pivoted and lunged at Diego. Diego did not move from his spot as Vargas carved his way forward trying to gain the right of way, *raison*. When his adversary was only inches away, Diego raised his foil, knelt to the floor and managed a brilliant parry. Vargas's foil barely missed Diego's left shoulder by a millimeter. Diego slid his feet sideways scarcely avoiding a foul by breaching the lateral boundaries of the *piste*; he advanced toward Vargas, crossing one leg over the other, performing a *passé advent*. Without hesitating, he flicked his foil, avoiding Vargas's attempt at parry, and struck his opponent's *lamé* just above the abdomen, scoring another touch. Vargas in his over exuberance to score a point clumsily tried to reengage but missed his mark. Vargas tripped over his own feet and tumbled to the floor in a clumsy heap.

Diego turned, raised his protective mask and casually walked over to the edge of the court, leaving the bewildered Vargas wondering what happened to his once finely honed agility.

"What was it you said, Maestro?" Diego brazenly asked as he approached Alvarez. "I was concentrating so much on my form....I did not hear your instructions."

"You know very well what I said, young man....such foolishness! I won't sit here and take this kind of insolence." He peered directly into Diego's eyes, making sure the cocky fighter registered the full force of his anger. "There are so many young men who would trade places with you in a second. Have you forgotten the kind of financial and moral support your family provides just so you can amuse yourself? What should I report to them....that you're wasting my time, and their money?" His expression soured with each word.

"Maestro, I'm sorry but I didn't mean to insult you or my family," Diego offered, bowing his head in reverence. "Please forgive me," his words collapsing as they were swallowed up by his anxiety.

Without acknowledging Diego's apology, Alvarez growled, "That is enough for today. Tomorrow we will practice your footwork. I suggest you prepare yourself to demonstrate to the best of your ability when we see each other again." With that, Alvarez rose, laboring to stand erect, and rudely waved off his humiliated protégé.

Alvarez's gait had a distinctive limp from an old injury, favoring his left side. The years had taken their toll on the sixty-eight-year-old man, once one of the most respected swordsmen in Mexico—and one of the few who had fought in the Olympics against the notorious French and Italian champions. It was hard to believe from looking at his bulbous, twisted body that he was once a nimble opponent. His face had the character of a crinkled newspaper. The fact that he constantly puffed on a yellow stained ivory cigarette holder packed with rich Algerian rolled tobacco didn't help his haggard appearance.

Diego watched his maestro hobble toward the exit, knowing he was among a select corps of pupils who could tolerate Alvarez's harsh instructional style. Diego had seen many aspiring *escrimeurs* fold under the intensity of Alvarez's outbursts. Diego knew Alvarez, feeble as he was, could still be a force to be reckoned with. As much as Diego hated to admit it, he respected Alvarez, and more importantly, he knew how critical the old master was to his career. Without his sponsorship, he had little chance of entering the major tournaments scheduled for the upcoming season. The Committee for choosing the 1963 Mexican National Fencing Team was already in the middle of the selection process and Diego was at the top of their list. His dream was to debut this September in his hometown of Monterrey, where contestants would be gathering for the first major tournament of the year. Diego was intent on showing his family that all the sacrifices they had made for him were worthwhile. He particularly wanted to honor his father, Don Julio Sanchez, who had steadfastly supported him despite his mother's longstanding wishes that Diego pursue a more meaningful career.

As Diego stared up at the ornate frescos on the ceiling trying to regain his composure, he was interrupted by a familiar voice from the upper tier of the balcony.

"Brilliant my friend! Just brilliant. Once again you demonstrate your superb judgment," echoed a low-pitched voice.

Diego slowly spun around, trying to locate the unwelcome sarcasm.

On the top rung of the balcony sat his best friend, Ignacio Lento.

"At this rate, if you're lucky, you should fight your first bout by the ripe old age of forty," Ignacio scolded, as he began making his way down to the bottom rung of the balcony.

"Don't you have anything better to do with your time than harass me? What happened to studying at the University and becoming a famous poet?" Diego said, not wanting Ignacio to have the last word.

"Not everyone needs to have a formal education to be a great writer. The world is my classroom; I live my art!" he proclaimed with buoyant laughter.

Ignacio's family had a long heritage of successful lawyers who did support his foolhardy effort to become a poet. If and when he came to his senses, then of course, he could join the family law practice and live the life of drudgery he so much disdained.

Ignacio did not skip a beat, reciting a cutting piece of free verse,

"Oh to be a great swordsman was all that he dreamed
His heart was so brave, but his mind was so weak
His blade so brilliant, as he broke every rule
While his maestro scolded, "You fight like a fool."

Ignacio, finishing melodramatically, tucked his arm toward his waist, and bowed slowly.

"Very clever, my friend, but I don't think you'll win many writing awards for that piece of crap," Diego responded, laying his foil across his shoulder as he walked toward Ignacio. "You must have a better reason for coming here than to harass me. I can only imagine what you're cooking up in that devious mind of yours."

"Well, since you asked, there is a dinner party at Rafael's parents' house tonight and we're invited. It starts at eight. I assume you're free......or is the future great champion too busy with his studies?"

"I'll have to check my schedule. You know the demands on me ......"

Before Diego could finish, Ignacio interrupted.

"I guess I'll just have to go it alone. Just so you know....Rafael's cousin, Celaya Flores, is visiting, and she is supposed to be a real beauty. If you're too busy, then all the better for me," Ignacio teased, as he started to move in the direction of the exit.

Diego let him take a few steps before he responded. "I'll meet you at 7:30 in front of the Municipal Museum. Promise me one thing. Try not to fall all over yourself in front of the ladies."

"Based on what I just heard from Señor Alvarez, you're more likely to be the one to stumble and make a fool of yourself." Ignacio turned and waved goodbye. "See you at 7:30 sharp."

Diego still had several hours before his dinner engagement. He knew he would need to make good use of the remaining practice time if he was going to have any chance of redeeming himself. He signaled to another opponent waiting in the wings. Even though the Plaza Quitzal where the 1960 Olympics had been held was only a short distance from where he stood, it felt like an insurmountable abyss as he approached the center of the fighting strip. How would he ever get to compete in such an important venue if he couldn't control his impatience? Diego bit down hard on his upper lip until he drew blood. It was his way of refocusing his fierce determination, of awakening the discipline he needed to fulfill his destiny. Reluctantly, he positioned himself in front of his opponent and challenged him to charge. His opponent lunged forward, swiping his foil in rapid fashion. Diego bent his front knee forward, preparing for a parry, all the while mentally checking every fraction of his movement, every angle of his body.

"Practice, more practice," Diego whispered, scolding himself.

Diego and Ignacio met in front of the Municipal Museum and took a cab to one of the wealthier sections of Mexico City. As they pulled to a stop in front of the Castillo's imposing 18th century home, they could hear a mariachi band resounding from inside the mansion.

Stepping out of the cab, Ignacio exclaimed, "Sounds like they've started without us. We'll have to do some catching up."

Diego cringed at hearing Ignacio's proclamation. It wouldn't be the first time he had to help his somewhat intoxicated friend home after drinking too much of Don Castillo's homemade tequila.

Diego sent up a warning flare. "Take it easy. This is a formal dinner at the home of a respectable family."

Ignacio ignored Diego's warning as he continued walking up the steps, all the while readying himself with a last minute adjustment of his coat sleeves. Diego had to rush to keep pace with his over-anxious friend.

The two, ornately carved Italian marble columns guarding the entrance to the house were only a precursor to the true opulence of the Castillo home. The Castillo's were from old money and their home represented established wealth. As they approached the front door, their mutual friend Rafael Castillo stood just inside the foyer politely greeting his guests. Rafael shook Ignacio's hand, looking at Diego with surprise.

"Well, I see you managed to break your friend loose from his magnificent obsession."

"Oh yes, the great Diego Sanchez has decided to grace us with his presence," Ignacio proclaimed, resting the crook of his elbow on Diego's shoulder.

Before Diego could come to his own defense, Rafael turned to Ignacio, "He had no choice, once he found out that you would have all these ladies to yourself." Rafael paused only long enough to garner a reaction from Diego. "We all know Diego's reputation with the ladies is unsurpassed."

Rafael knew in truth that although strikingly good looking, Diego had little time between his studies and relentless practice schedule for romancing women.

"Okay, you two, you've had your fun. I'm sorry I've been a stranger lately, but my life has been crazy. Please don't tell me I've forgotten your birthday again."

Diego slowly walked past Rafael.

As he did, Rafael motioned as if he was a matador making a pass with a cape. "And no, you have not forgotten my birthday. It's my parents' thirtieth anniversary, and as usual, they've outdone themselves."

"Thirty years—that's a hell of an accomplishment," Diego offered, wondering how anyone could commit to such a long-term relationship. He had neither the inclination nor the chosen profession for such loyalty.

Diego glanced around looking for Ignacio. Never the shy one, Ignacio had already moved into the heart of the crowd and was introducing himself to a dark-haired beauty. Ignacio wasn't the handsomest man, but he always seemed to have his fair share of women. Maybe he was a better poet than Diego gave him credit for.

"Let me introduce you to some of our other guests," Rafael offered, motioning Diego over to a group of well-dressed guests standing near the bar.

As Diego approached the bar, he was struck by the stunning presence of a young woman having a conversation with Rafael's father, Don Roberto. He tried not to stare as he moved closer. His palms began to sweat, something he rarely experienced, even in the most threatening situations during a match.

"*Breathe you fool,*" he reprimanded himself.

It was hard for him to distinguish the single unique quality that caused him to have such a reaction. He had seen his fair share of beautiful women before, but it was the way she stood there with a confident grace that caught him off guard. It stirred something in him that was completely unfamiliar. She was taller than the average Mexican woman and stood gracefully erect. Her body was slender and fit, while still having a supple quality. A veil of coal-black hair flowed around her oval face and draped softly onto her shoulders. It was obvious she needed no makeup to capture the attention her beauty demanded. The maroon dress she wore was cut just low enough to expose the crease between her perfectly upturned breasts. A single, dark freckle adorned her right breast just above the edge of her descending cleavage. Even her long, delicate fingers seemed perfectly proportioned.

Awakening from his momentary stupor, Diego wondered how long he had been staring in her direction.

Fortunately, Don Roberto saved Diego from embarrassing himself any further. "Diego, my boy, how have you been? We have missed you." The older man gave Diego a warm gentleman's hug.

He had known the Castillo family since his boyhood. His father and Señor Castillo had attended the University of Mexico City together. The dashing elder Castillo was in his late fifties and carried his age with a youthful exuberance. Diego particularly admired his pencil-thin mustache, which was always perfectly trimmed and accented his engaging smile.

Still somewhat distracted by the presence of the mystery woman standing next to his host, Diego had to gather himself before replying, "Congratulations on thirty years of marriage. Señora Castillo is a lucky woman."

Don Castillo chuckled, "Actually, I'm the lucky one. How she has put up with me all these years is a miracle."

Don Castillo turned toward the older couple on his left. "I'd like to introduce one of Mexico's brightest new fencing talents, Diego Sanchez."

Diego stepped forward and shook hands with Señor Cervantes. "It's my pleasure but Señor Castillo is much too generous regarding my place in the sport of fencing," Diego admitted, impatiently awaiting his introduction to the young lady on the couple's right.

Don Castillo finally turned in her direction and boasted, "Diego, I'd like to introduce you to my beautiful niece, Celaya Anna Maria Flores. She is staying with us during her spring break from her studies at the University."

Celaya held out her hand, peering straight into Diego's eyes. Her green eyes sparkled with affability.

Diego took her hand in his and held it as if he was not going to let it go. "Your beauty is a perfect match for your name; a rare flower indeed."

Celaya retrieved her hand from his grasp. "Señor Sanchez, I've heard that swordsmen of past and present have a reputation for adorning the ladies with praise......but doubt there is much sincerity in it?" Celaya challenged with a confident smile.

"I can promise you.....I seldom squander such a compliment so easily."

"So....you've never told a lie to impress a lady?" Celaya said, folding her hands in front of her waist as if cupping a small bird.

"Touché," he responded with a crooked smile, "but you have to admit that there is a poetic nature to your name."

"So among your other talents, consider yourself a poet?"

"I guess..." Diego attempted to rejoin the battle of words, but Don Castillo politely interrupted.

"Well, Diego, it seems you've met your match. I hope you never have to contend with such a competitor in a tournament .....or I predict your career will be short lived." Diego's host was obviously enjoying their spirited banter.

"It would be a pleasure to be felled by such a beautiful foe." Diego shrugged, hoping to earn another smile from Celaya.

"I'll leave you two to resolve this battle of wits, but please take the time to enjoy the music and food. It would be a waste to spoil such a lovely evening," Don Castillo said, as he headed across the room to join his wife.

Diego glanced down and tugged at the tails of his vest.

"Please accept my apology. I get a little overzealous sometimes," said Diego, raising his eyes to meet hers.

"Accepted. I only hope we can redeem ourselves before the night is over," Celaya shamefully admitted. "And please call me by my first name. I'm not one for tradition." Her expression relaxed and seemed almost inviting as she changed the subject. "I understand from my uncle that you have hopes of joining the Mexico's National Team this upcoming year."

"Yes, it's been a lifelong dream, but I still have a lot to work on."

"That's not what I've heard."

Diego, wanting to deflect the focus from himself changed the subject. "Your uncle said that you're attending the University. What are you studying?"

"I'm a second year psychology student. I'm particularly interested in uncovering the motivation behind the foolishness of risk takers; something I'm sure you can strongly identify with."

They both smiled in chorus.

"Well, maybe I could be your first patient."

Celaya could not resist laughing, "From what I understand about men in your profession, looking for a cure would be a hopeless cause."

"I'm just a little curious....what have you learned so far about us.....foolish risk takers?"

"If I thought for a moment you were serious, I would be glad to tell you."

"I'm serious."

Celaya could see from his intense expression that he was genuine in his request. She proceeded to give Diego a litany of findings from her research project, and was pleasantly surprised that Diego knew something about her field of study. It was obvious he was well educated. She had long believed sports figures were endowed with natural physical talents but had little to no intellect. To her even greater surprise, Diego also seemed to be much more sincere than her initial impression. Along with his good manners and quick wit, he had strikingly handsome features that fit the prototype of a young swordsman she had seen so often in Saturday afternoon movie matinees. Considering his age, which she guessed to be his late teens, he had a surprisingly rugged attractiveness. His tall, muscular body obviously had benefited from his years of training. His shoulders were broad, which accented his slim waistline. His light brown hair was meticulously groomed. His olive complexion was unlike the typical dark brown of most Mexican men, suggesting the strong Spanish influence of his heritage.

His face was his most appealing feature, with its strong angular jaw and piercing sapphire eyes. He was scrupulously attired, as one would expect from a young man of such distinction. He wore tight black slacks, a pressed white silk shirt and a black embroidered vest. The gleam of his brightly polished boots completed the impressive figure of a man standing before her. Regardless of his reputation for being completely obsessed with his sport, Celaya guessed he would have no problem surrounding himself with attractive women.

The more she found herself trying to resist her physical attraction to him, the deeper she became enveloped by his natural magnetism. She could not recall having ever been so intrigued by a complete stranger, especially one who was obviously younger than she. After all, she was an intelligent, rational woman of twenty-one! How could she possibly be infatuated with this young, brash swordsman?

Fortunately for Celaya, Diego interrupted, saving her from having to answer her own question.

"Would you like to dance? As our host suggested, it would be a waste to miss out on the music."

She hesitated and then accepted his outstretched hand.

The music was festive but traditional. Since they had both been well trained in the art of Mexican folk dancing, they moved skillfully across the dance floor. Even though the only parts of their bodies that touched were their hands, there was a sensual fluidity in each step they took. It became readily apparent to everyone on the sidelines watching them dance that there was an undeniable chemistry brewing between the striking couple.

As the last note fluttered across the room, Diego gracefully bowed, and started to escort Celaya off the dance floor. The bandleader quickly introduced the next song, a new Argentinean piece appropriate for the tango. Out of the corner of his eye, Diego noticed his friend Ignacio standing next to the bandstand, whispering to the bandleader. He was obviously up to one of his old tricks.

Ironically, Diego had learned the intricate steps of the tango as a way of improving his footwork. At least, this was the excuse Ignacio had used to cajole him into taking lessons at a local tango bar last year. Besides, Ignacio had told him at the time, "Where else can you meet older, more *experienced* women?" Even Señor Alvarez had commented on the improved grace of his footwork after only a couple of lessons. Diego knew Ignacio was laying down a challenge by asking the band to play the tango, hoping Diego would embarrass himself in front of the large crowd gathering around the dance floor. He was aware of the risk involved but was not about to be upstaged by his conniving friend.

Diego reached over for Celaya's hand as she motioned to exit the empty dance floor.

"Please don't tell me a modern-day woman with your interests has never danced the tango," Diego challenged, confident Celaya would not refuse his offer.

Celaya didn't hesitate. "In fact, I love the tango, but the question is—are your moves on the dance floor as good as those on the fencing floor?" She extended her other hand toward him, as the staccato notes began to slowly float across the dance floor.

He gently brought her body to his. They folded into each other like origami paper. Within a few beats, they became enveloped in the pulsating rhythm. Her right hand softly interlocked with his left as he confidently led her around the dance floor. He perched his right hand on the curve of her waist, as he pulled her hips tightly to his body. As their bodies dissolved into one another, they gracefully wove their way through each sensuous twist and turn of the provocative dance, swaying, arching backward, and then falling forward in a slow, rocking motion. Every seductive move brought whispers from the crowd. Their eyes were locked in a firm stare, oblivious to everything and everyone. They did not notice that they had the entire dance floor to themselves. As the last feverish pulse of the music ended, Diego tenderly leaned Celaya over his left knee in one last grand gesture. Her spine was arched so dramatically that her long black hair touched the dance floor. She balanced herself in his fully extended left arm, and then Diego snapped her toward him in one powerful fluid motion until their flushed cheeks lightly brushed together. They hesitated in this pose momentarily, heaving gently against each other's breasts; two perfect bookends of grace entombed in their own private world.

Reluctantly they were awakened from their trance by the clattering applause of the other guests. They bowed in acknowledgment of the crowd's approval, obviously embarrassed by all the attention.

Don Castillo approached them from behind and teasingly proclaimed, "I see you two have managed to put your differences aside."

The whispers of the crowd darted across the room as they prattled about the young couple's daring interpretation of the tango. Celaya's girlfriends were already entangled in rumors about what they had just witnessed and where it might lead.

Diego and Celaya hurriedly escaped the dance floor and headed in the direction of the bar.

"I hope I wasn't too clumsy on the dance floor," Diego offered apologetically, knowing full well they had both danced to perfection.

"No, and if your skill on the dance floor is any indication of your talent on the fencing court, I'm sure you will have a long, successful career," Celaya replied, accepting a glass of champagne from the bartender.

"I could use some fresh air," Diego said, motioning toward the two large open French doors, hoping she would accept his invitation.

"We've already raised enough eyebrows; I guess another indiscretion will only add to our failing reputations."

They strolled through the finely manicured garden along the crushed gravel pathways. The bougainvilleas were in full bloom, and the strong, pervasive fragrance of honeysuckle surrounded them. They walked in silence, enjoying the warm night air and the privacy of the garden. A towering jacaranda tree accented the far end of the garden, its branches cloaked in iridescent purple blossoms. They stopped under the thick canopy and stood looking at the half-crescent moon, almost afraid to let their eyes meet.

Diego turned to Celaya and put his hand under her chin, raising it ever so slightly in the direction of his face. She did not resist his advances. Diego stared into her eyes as he leaned to kiss her, but just before their lips touched, she reached up, pulled him toward her and kissed him passionately. At first, Diego was taken aback by her boldness, but he suddenly found himself absorbed in her eagerness. Their kisses became as kinetic as their steps on the dance floor. They held each other tightly, not wanting to surrender each other's touch.

Celaya could not believe how overwhelmed she felt as she tried to satisfy her hunger for Diego's affection. She wanted to be swallowed up by the raging storm of emotions overtaking her normally guarded behavior. She didn't care if onlookers might see their moment of indiscretion or that she might have to explain her permissive behavior to her mortified aunt and uncle.

When they finally untangled themselves, Diego whispered in a prayerful tone, "Can you get away from the party? I've got to see you alone."

Celaya tensed at his suggestion.

"I can't just leave. I'm a guest at my aunt and uncle's home. What would they think if I suddenly disappeared?" She struggled to be convincing, but her feeble tone of resistance begged for an appropriate excuse to accept his offer.

"Just have one of your girlfriend's say that she is not feeling well and that you need to take her home. Meet me on the corner of Hernandez and Zacatecas."

"I'll try, but I can't make any promises."

Diego escorted Celaya back to the party. They both felt as if a theater spotlight was drowning their every movement as several onlookers watched them re-enter the room.

Diego casually walked up to his hosts and announced, "I want to thank you for a lovely evening. Unfortunately, I have an early practice session tomorrow." His eyes purposely avoided direct contact with Don Castillo.

"I'm glad you enjoyed yourself and I would like to take all the credit, but I'm sure my niece had something to do with it," his host jokingly said, waiting for a reaction from Diego. "Please try and make yourself a more frequent guest. Give my fondest regards to your father when you see him." Don Castillo reached out and shook Diego's hand, then escorted him to the door.

As Diego turned to leave, he half bowed toward Celaya, beckoning her with his eyes.

"Are you sure you're not leaving something behind?" Don Castillo teased, slyly hinting in Celaya's direction.

"No, sir. Your niece was quite a gracious partner, but I'm afraid she is too much for me to handle," Diego said, not wanting to raise any suspicion of his true feelings.

Diego stepped out into the fresh night air, his thoughts weighted with the anticipation of having Celaya to himself.

Diego stood on the corner beneath the dimly lit street lamp. He had been waiting for over thirty minutes without any sign of Celaya.

"She has to come," he whispered to himself, feeling his anxiety building with every passing minute.

Suddenly, out of the darkness, he heard a faint but distinctive voice.

"Diego, over here," Celaya called out, hiding in the shadows of a banyan tree.

He stepped rapidly in her direction. When he reached her, they embraced and kissed as if they were lovers reuniting after a long, painful separation.

"Diego, I only have a few hours," she said, trying to catch her breath.

Diego, not wanting to waste a moment, led her to the busy intersection and flagged a cab.

"Where are we going?"

"You'll see soon enough. Just trust me." He leaned over to the cab driver and whispered a destination.

The driver drove through the well-lit boulevards of Mexico City until he reached the Plaza Quitzal. This was holy ground to Diego, the place where great duels had been fought between Mexico's very best swordsmen. It was within these hallowed walls that throngs of devoted aficionados soaked up the artistry of the ancient sport of fencing, where selfless determination was sometimes exchanged for honor and glory.

"That'll be ten pesos. A fair price for some privacy, wouldn't you say?" the cab driver joked, unable to count the number of times he had dropped anxious lovers off in out-of-the ordinary places. The grounds surrounding Plaza Quitzal were noted for being a weekend hangout where young people came to "make out."

The driver continued, "Are you sure you want to get out here? This isn't exactly the safest place in town."

Diego ignored his warning and paid the driver as he opened the door for Celaya.

"What are we doing here at this time of night?" Celaya asked, hoping her question would not blemish the moment.

He turned toward her, making his face calm. "Please, trust me. I have something important I want to show you." He gently took her hand and guided her toward the right side of the circular building. They disappeared into the shadows of the looming edifice, creeping along the perimeter of the stone archways.

Celaya could feel the fringes of fear starting to nip at her faith in Diego. She knew this place had a reputation as a haunt for the homeless. She had read the newspaper accounts of how thugs would lie in wait for unsuspecting couples to rob them of their money and jewelry. On rare occasions, it had been reported that certain young ladies had been molested for their foolishness.

Her nerves began to tingle with each advancing step. On the edge of her vision she could see tattered pant legs extending from the dark alcoves. Sinister, muffled voices echoed vulgar taunts as they passed by. The stench of evil wafted like the smoldering fumes of sulfuric acid, slowly burning through her normally steadfast courage. Celaya was sure at any moment some grotesque, hulking figure would spring from the darkness. She gripped Diego's hand more tightly. He turned his eyes toward her to reassure her that they were in no danger. For some uncanny reason, she was willing to trust Diego even though it was against her better judgment. When they reached a large locked wooden gate bordered by two marble reclining lions, Diego reached his hand deep into the opening of one lion's mouth and retrieved an old brass key.

"What are you doing? Are you trying to get us arrested?" she pleaded, stumbling over her words.

"Relax. I've been coming in here since I was a kid. The night watchman is an old family friend, and he lets me sneak in here at night," Diego boldly proclaimed, trying to reassure Celaya he wasn't totally insane.

He unlocked the gate and they crossed the threshold into a nearby passageway.

Diego paused momentarily, opened a large metal cabinet and retrieved a kerosene lantern. The creak of the rusty door opening reverberated down the dank passageway. He lit the lantern and took hold of her sweating palm.

"Please don't tell me you've dragged me from my uncle's party so that I can be arrested for trespassing."

"Please, just bear with me. I know this seems crazy, but I have my reasons," he said, glancing back to make sure her patience had not been exhausted.

They cautiously walked deeper into the heart of the aging building. All the time, Celaya was questioning what she had gotten herself into by following someone she hardly knew into the bowels of this damp catacomb. After meandering past several small rooms, they came to another passageway. Diego's hand searched along the face of the door until he found the old iron handle. The clank of the handle's turning shot a menacing tone down the empty space, as if he had opened some musty dungeon.

He slowly opened the door and held the lantern high in an attempt to light the long corridor. The lantern's amber glow barely extended halfway down the stone corridor, on each side of the corridor hung a long line of black and white photographs.

Celaya turned to face Diego, her voice wavering, "Where are we?"

"It's the passageway where challengers enter the court of honor," Diego whispered as he escorted her into his inner sanctuary. "It is sacred ground only a few champions have had the privilege of walking down."

He stopped after a few steps and held up the lantern to a framed picture of two swordsmen engaged in combat.

"Along these walls are photographs of all the great swordsmen of the past fifty years. All my heroes are here," Diego avowed with the same awe a younger brother might have toward the exploits an older brother.

They edged their way down the corridor, Diego stopping at each photograph, explaining the story behind each photo.

When they reached the last dusty frame, Celaya noted there was no photograph.

"Why is this frame empty?"

Diego spoke with an absolute reverence, as he stared at the empty frame, "It's reserved for the next fencing champion of Mexico. I hope to have my photograph placed in this frame some day. I've lived my entire life for that dream. I haven't cared about anything else........ until tonight."

He studied Celaya, hoping she might somehow understand the magnitude of his declaration. He continued, "I know this may sound crazy, but I found something more important than fencing."

Celaya was struck by the strength of his conviction.

Diego persisted, "To be a master swordsman requires total selfishness. I was taught from the very beginning that my career must *always* come first."

Celaya purposely interrupted him. "Do you actually believe that?"

"I hate to admit it, but yes, I did." His eyes glanced downward then he confessed, "Every part of my life has been about precision, about me. Celaya, what I feel for you...." He paused, waiting for her reaction, almost afraid to complete his thought.

Before he could resume, Celaya cut him off, "I thought I was the only one losing my mind. I almost didn't come tonight because I was afraid of myself, afraid of what I might say."

She could barely expel the words from her lips fast enough. "I can't stop thinking about you. I tried to push you out of my mind but it's impossible." Her eyes sparkled as a small teardrop cascaded down her cheek. She laid her head on his chest. Diego felt a sense of fulfillment he had never felt before. It was as if his heart had temporarily stopped and she was gently massaging him back to life.

Before Diego could respond, they were startled by the soft shuffle of footsteps echoing down an adjoining passageway. Diego took hold of her hand and whispered, "Follow me!"

He led her across the corridor to an arched opening. They entered a cramped room barely lit by a small window that faced the street. He carefully shut the heavy wooden door behind them, leaving it slightly ajar so that he could still hear the approaching sound. As Diego placed the lantern on a nearby shelf, it shone down on a pile of loosely stacked white fencing garb. Just to the right and above the pile of clothing was a set of heavy menacing sabers firmly attached to the stone wall with metal anchors.

Diego dimmed the lantern to a soft, golden glow, barely leaving enough light for him to see Celaya, who was frozen in the middle of the room.

Diego reached over, took her by the hand and slowly drew her to him. He could feel her warm breath pouring onto his chest. They stood in the silence, poised, listening for any further sign of the intruder. The cadence of footsteps had a discomforting scraping hobble to them. Just before Diego was about to confront the intruder, the footsteps suddenly curved around the corner and began to fade, evaporating into a still calm.

Celaya exhaled a sigh of relief but was unwilling to abandon Diego's embrace. They both nervously giggled at their predicament, as if they were children playing a game of hide and seek.

The air was dense and cool, but Diego could feel the heat of Celaya's flesh next to his. He sensed the eagerness of her body and started to caress her with his hands.

Celaya wanted to say something, to tell him that even though she prided herself on being a "modern woman," she was still an inexperienced lover. It was as though her voice had been stolen from her, leaving her a defenseless mute. She was suffocating from the intensity of her own eagerness. Although still fully clothed, she felt naked to his touch, stripped bare of any inhibitions.

They stared at each other in confirmation of their mutual desires, knowing that in this fleeting moment their lives were about to change forever. There was no need to explain why they were ready to end their years of adolescent anguish, it was etched in their eyes, carved in the collective sensuality of their aching bodies.

"Celaya, are you sure?" he questioned, exhaling anxiously.

She did not answer him, but nodded confidently, sliding the back of her cupped fingers gently over his cheek. Celaya rose up on her tiptoes and kissed him open mouthed, fearlessly.

Diego reached behind her and gingerly began to unbutton the clasp of her dress. In one fluid motion, Celaya reached back, unclasped her bra, and then stepped out of her black silk panties.

Diego took a step back, never releasing her from his gaze. He wanted to take in every crease, every angle of her body. He was almost embarrassed staring at her nakedness.

Celaya sensing his hesitation, reached up, and started kissing him. All the while her hands tore at Diego's clothes, doing everything she could to help him disrobe. Standing there completely nude, Diego felt a different sense of his adolescent inhibition, a sense of being totally exposed, physically and mentally. He made a futile attempt to speak.

"I may not be the lover you think...."

She placed her fingertips over his lips and murmured, "Make love to me like you danced with me."

They let their nakedness melt into each other's bodies, gliding over each other's damp skin. Celaya reached up behind him and gripped the handles of the two sabers tacked to the wall. As her body tightly rested on Diego, she couldn't tell where her body ended and his started. She felt a sense of completeness she had never expected to experience in all her adolescent imaginings.

Celaya, wanting to satisfy every dream Diego had of making love to a woman, let her body take over. She could hear herself moaning his name with each cautious movement. Diego responded, gingerly accepting the full weight of her body, slowly backing her away from the wall until her arms were stretched as taut as violin strings. Reluctantly, she let loose of the grips of the sabers and draped her arms around his neck. As her long black hair poured over his shoulders like a cool stream, he began to slowly parade them around the small room. They were dancing, gliding across the floor; letting the rhythm of their liberated bodies guide their every movement.

Diego muttered her name as his whole body began to shiver.

"It's all right...." Celaya trembled, sensing the wholeness of finally knowing the pleasure of being a woman.

They turned one last time and fell into the soft pile of clothing. Celaya moaned out something unintelligible, as if begging for redemption; her sense of space and time melding into a blur of touch and sound, of tempered insanity.

With an astounding suddenness, a shroud of exquisite silence enveloped them; they collapsed into each other, gracefully intertwining their bodies like two carved, ivory dolls. Their breath slowed to a calm cadence as they struggled to hold fast to their shared awakening.

Diego reluctantly broke the silence, whispering something he thought he would never say, "Celaya, I love you." He turned, lightly brushing his lips against her cheek.

"Mi amado," she answered him, using the Spanish term for loved one. It sounded so strange to hear such powerful words coming from her lips. She felt as though a great burden had been lifted, a freedom for which she had yearned for so long, but had been afraid to acknowledge.

The mirrored reflection of two nude bodies shone in the pupils of the intruder's eyes as the stranger spied through a crack in the door at the unsuspecting lovers. Pepe Robles, the night watchman at the Plaza Quitzal, had heard alarming noises as he was making his late night rounds. He had followed the rumblings, which grew louder with each step. At first, he thought they were just the ghostly echoes that sometimes haunted these empty halls. On any other night, walking these dark passageways alone would have left him standing frozen in a puddle of fear, but tonight, he recognized that the peculiar sounds were distinctly human, almost as if someone was in pain.

As he peered again through the crack of the door, he was stunned at the scene before him. He felt guilty for spying on Diego and his lady friend, especially having just overheard their tender words of devotion. The shock of hearing his young friend espouse such love seemed unreal to him. Pepe winced at the disappointment he felt in finding Diego in this discomforting situation. How could Diego break the trust they had developed over the years by bringing a woman to this sacred place? To have behaved so irresponsibly was inexcusable.

He knew he had no alternative but to report this incident to Diego's maestro, Señor Alvarez. Peering in at his unsuspecting victims, he knew it would only be in the boy's best interest. After all, he had an obligation to Diego's father, who had helped him get this job at the Plaza Quitzal. Pepe hated to betray his young friend but he could not risk that this secret might be found out later, and then where would he be? He would have to face the wrath of Señor Alvarez and Diego's father for not reporting Diego's recklessness.

Pepe sneaked one more peek at the resting lovers, slowly backed away into the cool confines of the adjoining passageway, and disappeared.

Diego and Celaya sat in the parked cab two blocks from her uncle's house. They had been gone longer than she could legitimately explain, but it was worth all the risk of potential embarrassment. They looked into each other eyes, both afraid to say what needed to be said. Celaya motioned to exit the cab, and Diego pulled her back into his arms.

"When I can see you again?"

"I'm leaving tomorrow night to visit my parents in Guadalajara. My train leaves from the station at seven o'clock. I can't leave my uncle's house again without raising suspicion, so meet me at the station at six," she said, trying to reassure him. "I'll be back here in a week." She paused trying to regain her composure. She could already feel the misery of their impending separation.

"A week? It already feels like a lifetime."

"I'm sure you will survive, mi amado," she teasingly declared.

"Mi amado?"

"You don't mind do you?"

"No, not at all, as long as you don't use it in front of my fellow competitors."

"Of course not, *mi amado*. We wouldn't want them to think that the macho Diego Julio Sanchez has a sensitive side, would we?" Celaya stepped away from the cab and started toward the house. She felt as though at any moment she would rush back into his arms and begin sobbing uncontrollably. It was everything she could do to continue her forward momentum.

Diego watched in agony as Celaya's image vanished before his eyes. He did not want to let her out of his sight. He stepped out of the cab, shadowing her footstep, watching her as she slowly ascended the stairs to the Castillo's home, praying she would turn around and look in his direction.

He was starting to lose hope when she pivoted and gestured to him. She placed her open palm on her heart, then raised it to her lips and blew him a kiss. He stood motionless for several seconds, not wanting to disturb the sanctity of the moment. This extraordinary evening was now complete, Diego thought as he strolled back to the waiting cab. He had found something he treasured even more than his devotion to fencing—Celaya Maria Flores.

CHAPTER 6

Señor Alvarez sat quietly listening to Pepe Robles describe in meticulous detail the distressing scene involving Diego Sanchez and a certain young lady at Plaza Quitzal. At first, he was suspicious of the night watchman's story, thinking maybe Pepe had some kind of hallucination from the long hours of working alone in the tunnels of the Plaza Quitzal. It was only after realizing Pepe's conviction was unwavering that Alvarez had no choice but to believe the night watchman's story.

When Pepe concluded his chronicle of events, he lowered his head and admitted, "Señor Alvarez, you know I love this boy, and I would not do anything to hurt him. All night long I was haunted by the thought of revealing the truth of what I saw."

"Pepe, you did the right thing by reporting this to me. Your loyalty to his family won't be forgotten. I must to insist that you never speak of this again....to Diego or anyone in his family. Is that clear?" His tone was considerate but stern.

"I understand, Señor Alvarez. I haven't told anyone but you." Pepe understood what he was being told and was relieved not to have to carry this burden any longer. It was better for a man of sophistication like Señor Alvarez to deal with such a touchy issue. He could only hope he might somehow benefit from the maestro's generosity.

"Pepe, I have only one question. Are you absolutely sure you heard Diego state his love for this young woman?"

"Yes, Maestro, there is no doubt in my mind. I heard it as clearly as my mother's name." He made sure his eyes did not waver from his interrogator's cold stare.

"Very well, I'll need to give this some serious consideration."

"You will keep my name out of this with Diego's family, won't you?"

"Yes....it will be our little secret," Alvarez said in assuring tone, knowing he had no intention of keeping any secrets from Diego's father. Alvarez had little respect for Pepe and could barely tolerate sitting in the same room with him. Pepe had a reputation for gambling and drinking too much for his own good.

Alvarez thanked Pepe again, showing him to the door of his office. Pepe was obviously disappointed he was leaving empty-handed, but he assumed he would be compensated at a future date.

As soon as Pepe was out of earshot, Alvarez picked up the phone and dialed Diego's father, Don Julio Sanchez. He not only had his own interest in Diego to protect, but he was also being highly compensated by Diego's father for his mentoring services.

"Don Julio, this is Señor Alvarez. I'm sorry to call you at this early hour," he said in a dour tone.

Don Julio hesitated, hoping it was not the news that families of aspiring swordsmen sometimes receive. Accidents did happen on occasions.

"Is everything all right?" he anxiously inquired.

"I'm afraid......I have a serious issue to discuss with you."

Alvarez was cautious as he began to relay to Don Julio the story the night watchman had conveyed to him. He purposely left out the more unsavory words Pepe had used in his description of the young couples tryst. There was no need to add insult to injury.

Don Julio listened without questioning Alvarez. He had entrusted his son's future to this man and had no reason to doubt his word. After Alvarez concluded, Don Julio asked the same question that Alvarez had asked Pepe regarding the exact words Diego had spoken to this mysterious woman.

"Yes, I'm afraid it's the truth," the old maestro stated reluctantly.

"I see.....what do you suggest we do?" Don Julio's voice registered both disappointment and concern.

Alvarez suggested that confronting Diego with their newfound secret could potentially start a conflict that was irreparable. They agreed the best plan of attack was to take immediate action to thwart Diego's foolish indiscretion with this young woman. Diego was much too talented a swordsman to have his career spoiled by such a reckless affair. Alvarez sympathetically argued that all the work and investment his family had made should not be thrown away over some brief infatuation.

"And what about the young lady in question?" Alvarez bitterly pointed out to his attentive listener. "What respectable woman would allow herself to be caught in such a compromising situation? She is to know nothing of our plan."

Alvarez, anxious to play the hero, suggested they send Diego to study in France under the guise that it would be an opportunity of a lifetime to work and perform with some of the most talented fencing champions in the sport. Alvarez told Don Julio that he had several close contacts in France who would, for the right amount of money, take on a gifted young man such as Diego.

Don Julio at first resisted the plan, but knew in his heart that it was the only reasonable alternative. He had seen too many lives destroyed over such youthful infatuations. After all, he once was a young man himself, and he understood how "love" could derail the goals of even the most deliberate men. They agreed Alvarez would travel with Diego to assure he arrived safely in France. Once Diego was in safe hands, Alvarez would return to Mexico to resume his teaching duties. Of course, he would continue to receive a hefty stipend from Diego's family for his loyalty. Alvarez suggested they leave on the first ship from Veracruz to the port city of Marseilles. He would have to check the schedule but was pretty sure there was a passenger ship leaving early next week. Don Julio was curious as to why Alvarez had chosen an ocean crossing instead of the convenience of flying. Alvarez told him he thought that a long cruise across the Atlantic would give Diego some time to "settle down" before starting his studies with the great masters of France. Don Julio agreed.

Having gained approval for his plan, it became apparent to Alvarez that Don Julio was tiring of their conversation. Before Don Julio concluded their conversation, he insisted, "I'll need your complete trust in this matter, Señor Alvarez. I do not want my wife to know of this plan. She has always tried to protect Diego and would never understand our motivation."

"I understand completely. You have my word."

Don Julio gripped the phone tightly and said, "I know this was difficult for you as well, and I cannot thank you enough for all that you've done for my son." He cleared his throat. "Please let me know what funds you will need, and I'll make sure they are wired to you immediately. Good day, sir." Don Julio winced at his words of betrayal, hating the thought of conspiring against his own son.

As soon as he hung up the phone, Alvarez started constructing the story he would tell Diego. Tomorrow's practice session would be a day of reckoning with his young prospect. He knew he had no time to waste. He looked at his pocket watch, knowing he had a lot of arrangements to make to set his plan into action. He grabbed his black felt hat, gave a quick glance at the cane standing in the corner, and stepped cautiously into the busy streets of Mexico City.

Diego showed up promptly at ten the next morning for his practice session. He still had a broad smile pasted on his unshaven face. He had not slept the entire night, consumed with thoughts of Celaya. He replayed the scene of the previous evening over and over in his head. He could still smell the fragrance of Celaya hanging over him like a comforting mantle. There was no question in his mind that amid the tattered costumes of his sport where they had made love, he had found his soul mate.

Diego's focus this morning seemed almost inspired to Alvarez. He had never seen Diego work so diligently. His blade work was fluid and graceful, and his footwork impeccable. The only noticeable difference in Diego's appearance was his jubilant disposition. Normally, his face was plastered with a contentious sneer....but not today.

Watching Diego, Alvarez was momentarily saddened knowing his best protégé was about to be shipped off to Mexico's fencing rival, France. There was a tremendous jealousy among Mexican swordsmen regarding the champions of France. Alvarez could only hope Diego would perform as brilliantly as he was capable, thus enhancing his own reputation as a great teacher.

Alvarez called out to his protégé. "Diego....that is enough for today. Please come here."

Diego was surprised that Alvarez cut the training session short. It was a rare occasion when his dogged maestro would make such a generous offer. He sauntered over to the observation balcony and waited politely for his maestro to bless him with words of wisdom or scold him for his mistakes.

Alvarez put a serious scowl on his wrinkled face as he began to speak. He did not want to take any chances that Diego might suspect a conspiracy was brewing against him.

"Diego, I have some very exciting news. I've been in correspondence with my contacts in Paris, France, regarding the possibility of your joining their esteemed fencing program. They've shown great interest in having you become part of their stable of young swordsmen. You're very fortunate to be afforded such an opportunity. I've already informed your father, and he is in full agreement."

Diego was shocked and overjoyed at the same time. There was no question that France was the most prestigious place in the world to train and compete in his sport. Many of the former Olympic champions of the past two centuries had come out of France. This would be his chance to learn from some of the best in the world.

"Maestro, I've had this dream for so long, I can hardly believe it's finally coming true. How can I ever thank you?" he said, his voice coursing with genuine excitement, momentarily forgetting about the previous night and his pledge of love to Celaya.

"How many months before I can be ready to leave?"

"You sail on Saturday. I've already purchased your ticket from Veracruz to Marseilles. I'll escort you there and introduce you to my colleagues in Marseilles, and then return to my duties here in Mexico." His face was composed, almost expressionless.

It was as though a bullet shattered Diego's brain when he realized the implications of Alvarez's words. Suddenly, a clear vision of Celaya appeared before his eyes. Saturday! There was no way he could be ready to sail across the Atlantic Ocean in four days. This was insane! How could he possibly be prepared to tell Celaya this development at the train station tonight? Celaya would never understand; she would never forgive him.

The blood drained from his face. He felt his knees start to buckle. Only after a long pause was he able to offer a response.

"Sir, I greatly appreciate your help, but I need more time to think about such an important decision."

"Young man, do you realize all the work that went into creating this opening for you? Do you know how rare it is for someone of your inexperience to be accepted into such a prestigious cadre of swordsmen?" he said emphatically, as he continued, "To be able to train and learn from such prestigious swordsmen is beyond anything I ever hoped for you."

"But, sir...." Diego started to reply, but Alvarez cut him off.

"It is already decided. Your father has asked me to take care of all the arrangements, and I have done so. You have a duty to your family, to me, and to yourself to fulfill your destiny. Besides, it is only for six months and then you can return home." He turned his eyes away from Diego, knowing that he could not hide such a blatant lie.

Diego was about to mount another protest when Alvarez sternly proclaimed, "You have very little time, so I suggest you make the best use of it. There is so much to do." Having completed the circle of deception, Alvarez stood up and headed for the exit.

Diego stood open-mouthed without moving, unable to fathom what had just transpired. *What was he going to tell Celaya? How was he going to explain his sudden departure without looking like a self-serving cad? Would she believe he had nothing to do with this insanity?*

He suddenly felt as though a chunk of his heart had been violently ripped from his chest. He struggled to catch his breath. He wondered if he could take a step without stumbling. Finally, Diego moved from the edge of the balcony and walked toward the exit. As he sluggishly ambled across the room, he thought back to the previous night, hoping the memory of their night together would carry him through the anxiety of the next few hours.

Diego felt wounded, painfully distracted, during the entire cab ride to the train station. His sole focus was to make sure Celaya understood that he had no control over his predicament. He had called his father after hearing the news and pleaded with him to give him more time. Don Julio was resolute in his decision. His father reinforced what Alvarez had said regarding Diego's duty to make the best of this great opportunity. Don Julio also made it clear to his son that there was also the matter of family pride. After all the time, money, and sacrifice put into Diego's lifelong calling, he surely would not embarrass his father by refusing such an offer. Having listened patiently to his father's discourse, he made one last desperate plea. Don Julio refused to listen to his son's request. Even though Diego knew his father had only the best intentions in mind for his future, he had hoped for more compassion. Diego was almost tempted to explain his need for more time was because he had fallen in love with a woman but knew using Celaya as an excuse would make matters even worse.

Having failed to slow down the events that were steamrolling over his life, Diego made his way to the Estacion Buenavista. He arrived at the station at 5:45 p.m., hoping Celaya would arrive early but there was no sign of her. Diego leaned against one of the marble columns lined up like soldiers in the garish interior of the station and waited. Over and over he replayed in his mind how he would explain to Celaya the circumstances of his immediate departure for France, and tried to imagine how she would react to the news. Every time he thought he had constructed the appropriate words of solace, he found himself panicking at their inadequacy, trapped, as if standing defenseless before an executioner's blade. He wished Ignacio could be there for moral support, to feed him poetic words of reconciliation, but he knew this was something he had to do on his own. His moment of reckoning had arrived, not unlike what he would eventually face in his first major tournament. This was the time he had to prove he was worthy of Celaya's respect, to tell the truth no matter how painful.

Suddenly, out of the corner of his eye, he saw Celaya approaching. She had a smile on her face that would make a saint envious. Diego could feel his resolve weakening with each hurried step she took in his direction.

Celaya, seeing Diego, raced toward him with open arms. The baggage carrier scrambled to keep up with her fleeting pace. When she finally reached Diego, she practically jumped into his arms. She drenched him in passionate kisses. He could not believe her lack of inhibition in such a public place. Diego overwhelmed, could do nothing but reciprocate, reluctantly sacrificing his normal self-restraint.

He was ecstatic to see and hold her again; nothing mattered, not even France.

For a split second, he had found a temporary sanctuary from the foreboding task of facing the bitter truth of their future together, from the sadness that was about to be spawned in both their lives. There was no hiding from the inevitable weight of the truth closing in on him.

"Mi amado, I waited all day to hold you." She could sense the tension in Diego's body language. She continued hugging him, hoping she was only imagining his reluctance. "Everyone kept asking all day why I was acting so scattered. It was so hard to pretend. I just wanted to shout out that I'd fallen madly in love with this crazy man!" She intertwined her arm in his and started walking toward the boarding area.

"Celaya, there is something I need to tell you."

He hesitated just long enough for her to interrupt.

"Diego, you look so serious. Please don't tell me you've had a change of heart about what happened last night." She stared at him with sincere concern, trying to read any sign of affirmation.

"No.......I just wanted to tell you....... how much I care for you."

With each corroded word he uttered, he felt as if the column of his spine was slowly collapsing one vertebra at a time. He had lost his nerve to tell her the truth! How could this have happened? He relied on nerves of steel to survive in his sport. Diego had crossed over into a territory into which he had never been. The thought of facing the truth choked his words. He tried desperately to convince himself he needed more time, but his lie hung in front of him like a noxious cloud.

"You had me worried for a second. I thought maybe I scared you away."

"No, you'll never get rid of me." Diego was falling deeper into the abyss of deception. He couldn't stop himself, he was freefalling. His feelings for Celaya far outweighed his ever-dependable strength of character.

"Diego, I have so much I want to share with you."

She escorted him over to a nearby bench and sat down. They snuggled close to each other, Celaya resting her head on Diego's shoulder. Celaya shared her plans with Diego on completing her degree next year and how she had already made some contacts for an apprenticeship at a local clinic in Mexico City. Her voice was passionate and excited as she told Diego about her future hope of creating her own research clinic. She wanted Diego to know everything about her, to share all her dreams, and her new-found passion for life.

The more Diego listened to her talk, the more he knew he had chosen the right woman to fall in love with. Regrettably during the entire conversation, he felt as though dull knives were being slowly, painfully inserted into his chest. With each supportive nod of his head, his lie deepened, solidified. His chance for redemption dissolved with each word she spoke. He was painfully aware that after a few hours he would not see her for six months. If last night had felt like forever, then how could they survive such a long separation, particularly after he had created such a deep chasm of deception? He could only hope Celaya's commitment to him was unwavering and that she would somehow forgive him when he returned.

The train inched into the station as scheduled. They both sensed the encroaching anguish of their parting. Celaya's expression turned from joy to instant gloom. Diego could see tears starting to well up in her eyes. Ignoring his own sorrow, he turned to her and in a consoling tone offered, "Let's not think about the future." He reached up and caught a single tear with the back of his hand. "In fact, I hope you will be able to stand all the attention I'm going to give when we see each other again." Diego forced a smile onto his face, knowing full well that he would not be here when she returned next week.

Her face broke into a wide smile. "You're such a romantic, but I'll hold you to your word. Promise me you will be careful," she said as the porter made the last call for passengers to board. As she stood up to board her train, she reached around her neck and removed a cream-colored cashmere scarf. She raised her arms above Diego's head and placed it around his neck.

"I want you to wear it until we see each other again. My grandmother swaddled me in this scarf when I was born. She told me it possessed magical powers, and it would always protect me. Now, I want it to protect you."

Diego lightly stroked the soft cloth, "I can't take this...."

Before he could finish she kissed him tenderly and said, "Promise me you won't let anything happen to it."

"I promise," Diego said, knowing anything he said to her right now had little truth to it.

Their eyes locked on each other. Only the clanking of the railroad cars stretching tight broke them from their trance. They held each one last time and Celaya hurriedly boarded the train, only letting go of Diego's hand at the very last moment.

Diego watched her take a seat through the train window. As the steam engine puffed and jolted forward, he walked along with the slow pace of the railcar, never breaking eye contact with her. As the train gained speed, Diego jogged alongside trying to keep up. In the last fleeting moment, before Celaya disappeared out of sight, she placed her hand over her heart, then to her lips and blew him a kiss, just as she had from her uncle's doorstep.

Diego momentarily disappeared in a cloud of steam as the train disappeared from the station. When he reappeared, he was sitting alone on the last bench at the end of the platform. He collapsed into a fetal position. He put his hands over his face and felt the tears wash through his fingertips. He sensed he was losing control of his future with Celaya, and not unlike the forward motion of the train's engine, there was no stopping its progress.

Diego marked the date indelibly in his mind—April 12, 1963—as he stood on the gangplank in Veracruz, staring out over the horizon and wondering if he was making the biggest mistake of his life. He knew going to France was the best thing for his career, but he wasn't sure he could stand the pain of being separated from Celaya.

His mother and father traveled from Monterrey to wish him a safe journey. Doña Maria was distraught that her only son was leaving and had to fight off her tears several times. He tried to forgive his father for his role in forcing him to leave on such short notice. He partially blamed his father for the guilt he felt for abandoning Celaya. It was only just before stepping onto the gangplank that Diego was finally able to fight through his anger long enough to thank his father for all his support.

As Diego stood waving to his parents from the starboard side of the massive passenger ship, he felt a genuine sense of isolation for the first time in his life. He was alone and afraid of what the future might hold for him. He had never experienced such a debilitating emotion, a helpless feeling that everyone he cared about was being ripped out of his life. He kept telling himself it was only six months, and with any luck he would return sooner than expected.

The trip across the Atlantic was uneventful. Diego used his time to compose his first letter to Celaya, knowing he had an obligation to explain the unusual circumstances of his sudden departure. Confronting this task left him feeling incapacitated at times, but he knew he somehow had to put onto paper what his heart was crying out to say to her. If he had only had the guts to face the truth at the train station, he wouldn't be sitting here in the throes of writer's block.

The moment Celaya's train disappeared from the station Diego knew he had made a terrible error in judgment. Having realized his mistake, he desperately tried to get word to her cousin Rafael, but Rafael and his parents had left on an extended vacation two days after their anniversary celebration. Diego had forgotten to get Celaya's family's address in Guadalajara before they parted. His only hope was to entrust Señor Alvarez with the task of contacting her family and delivering his plea for forgiveness.

Diego wrote and rewrote the letter. He questioned if he would ever be able to put down in words the sorrow and guilt he felt at abandoning her. He finished the letter just before they reached Marseilles. Now, all he had to do was make sure Celaya received his letter.

When they arrived in the bustling port city of Marseilles, Alvarez and his young protégé were greeted by Jacques Denot, one of the most important fencing masters in all of France. He was a very gracious man and Diego knew from Denot's reputation that he would be in very capable hands. Denot drove them to a local hotel, where Alvarez made the final arrangements for Diego's overland trip to Paris. Alvarez was scheduled to leave in two days on his return trip to Mexico.

Diego spent his spare time trying to prepare himself mentally for the task on which he was about to embark. He was already contemplating ways to accelerate his training and make his triumphant debut in a major tournament in

Paris. Once having accomplished this task, he would be free to return to Mexico, and Celaya.

On the day of Alvarez's departure, Diego went to his room to wish him a safe trip and to thank him for his support. He knocked on the maestro's door. Alvarez answered. "Diego....so glad to see you. Please come in," he said with a genuine tone of affection, as he waved Diego into his room.

Diego was somewhat taken aback by his maestro's sudden warmth. "I just wanted to stop by and thank you for all you've done for me. You've been very patient. I'm sorry I was so stubborn at times. Please forgive me."

"I'm proud of you, Diego. Promise me that you will try to be the best that you can." He sat down and continued, "You must be focused and mindful about your work or you will simply end up like so many other mediocre swordsmen. You must forget everything you're leaving behind and look toward the future. I have great expectations for you."

"Thank you, Maestro, but I have one more favor to ask of you. I've written a letter to a friend in Mexico. I would appreciate if you could deliver it for me. It is imperative my friend receive it," Diego said, leaving no doubt regarding the gravity of his request.

Diego made it abundantly clear to Alvarez he was not about to reveal the contents or the intended recipient of the letter. He had not told anyone of his affair with Celaya, not even his best friend Ignacio. Diego was particularly determined not to let Alvarez know about his new love interest. He knew Alvarez had a strong allegiance to his father and would not hesitate to reveal his secret. Diego had addressed the letter to Celaya's cousin, Rafael Castillo in Mexico City, thereby assuring that he would not be raising any suspicions.

Alvarez immediately recognized the seriousness of Diego's request. "Of course, you have my promise. I'll mail it as soon as I arrive in Mexico City. Your letter wouldn't happen to be to a young lady would it?" he inquired, already knowing the answer.

For a moment, Diego suspected Alvarez had found out about his affair with Celaya. *Was he just guessing or did he really know something?* Diego was sure he had not spoken to anyone about Celaya. Could Celaya have told a friend? And if she had, how would his old maestro have found out? Diego convinced himself that Alvarez was teasing him in the hope of finding out something about his personal life.

"No, I'm afraid not. It's just a letter of thanks to a close family friend," Diego said, and with that, he handed Alvarez the letter. He thanked his teacher once again and they parted company.

Alvarez sat perched in one of the cane deck chairs of the passenger ship, watching the last remnants of the rugged shoreline disappear. He was holding the letter Diego had written to Celaya Flores. He paused momentarily, staring at Diego's handwriting on the outside of the envelope, knowing the address was only a futile attempt by Diego to hide his message to the young woman in question. Alvarez reached into his pocket, retrieved a small pocketknife, and slit open the letter. He slowly unfolded it and started reading Diego's impassioned words:

My Dearest Celaya,

There is so much I want to say to you. So much I have to say to you. When I left you at the railway station, all the courage I had relied on in my whole life was stolen by the anguish of possibly losing you. I am so sorry; I was not brave enough to tell you I was leaving for France. Please believe me; I had no control over the circumstances of my abrupt departure. Refusal would have caused my family great distress. I can only pray you will somehow understand my predicament.

I will be in France for the next six months studying with the greatest masters in the world. I swear I will dedicate every ounce of my body and soul to come home to you as soon as possible. You must know if it had been up to me, I would have remained in Mexico and fulfilled my promise to you, but my obligation to my family left me no choice. No matter how hard I try to convince myself that I had legitimate reasons, I realize abandoning you without an explanation was the act of a coward. I can only hope when I return, that somehow you can somehow forgive me.

As I cross this vast ocean, I very often find myself staring into the deep blue waters and wondering if it is as infinite as the love I feel for you. I can still see you lying in the cool light of the moon at the Plaza Quitzal. I will never forget the gift you gave to me that glorious night. You opened up my heart and breathed life into its darkest corners. I swear by all the love pulsing through my veins that there is no distance that can stop me from coming back to you.

Forever yours,

Diego

Alvarez folded the letter, placing it carefully back into the envelope, knowing he would never fulfill his promise to Diego to deliver the letter.

Diego sat amongst his fellow competitors in a dressing room preparing to face his first battle in the major international tournament. It had been five months since he had arrived in France and all of his energy had been put toward this important day. But at this very moment, his thoughts were solely focused on Celaya. Under his lamé he wore the scarf Celaya had given him at the train station. As he bowed his head to say a final prayer before entering the *salle d'armes*, he quietly whispered her name as if it were the holiest of all prayers, and kissed the edge of the scarf.

The solemn but daring newcomer fought brilliantly. The usually conservative reporters boldly reported that Diego's flamboyant work with the foil was some of the finest ever displayed by a novice competitor. His undaunted boldness and grace was apparent to everyone from the moment he stepped into the arena. True aficionados knew they were seeing one of the next important talents in the sport. The newspapers gave him rave reviews and touted him as a benchmark for upcoming swordsmen. Every major team in France was clamoring to sign the gifted Mexican swordsman. His future was set, and he had all the glory he had always dreamed of, but Diego knew there was something missing in his life. As he sat alone in his room, the night after his brilliant premiere performance, he knew he had accomplished all that he set out to do in France. His mind filled with images of Celaya and how much he wanted so desperately to share his glory with her. She was his inspiration and all he could think of was getting back to her. But was there any reason to try and return to her? He had not heard a word from her since their emotional parting at the train station.

Diego had inquired several times through friends about Celaya but to no avail. In desperation, Diego asked Senor Alvarez whether Celaya had tried to contact him. Alvarez, wanting to end all of Diego's hopes of continuing the relationship, told Diego that he had spoken to the young woman in question and she indicated that she wanted nothing to do with him. Alvarez concocted a stream of vicious lies about Celaya, telling Diego how she had chosen to move on in her life. She wished Diego well and hoped he could do the same. At one point, Alvarez told Diego that Celaya was engaged to a prominent young doctor in Mexico City and had plans to marry him in the spring. The man Diego had entrusted with his life—his teacher and mentor—had betrayed him at the most fundamental level.

Diego could not fathom how his maestro's words could be true. Even though he was shattered by the agony of the truth, he held out hope for months that when he returned to his homeland, he would reconcile with Celaya and they would start a new life together. Diego tried relentlessly over the next six months to write Celaya, but never received a response to his desperate letters. It all made sense to Diego after he had so callously abandoned her. How could she ever forgive him? If the fans and critics who had heaped such acclaim onto him for his most recent performance knew of this despicable behavior, would they have been so supportive?

Still Diego persisted, hoping for any word from Celaya. For over two years, before every match, Diego would place his hand over his heart, kiss the scarf Celaya had so unselfishly given him, bow his head in reverence and swear his undying love to her. In this brief moment of solitude, Diego prayed that they would be joined together again. He let himself descend back to the memory of their brief time together, seeing himself dancing with her again, feeling her tender caress as they held each other at the Plaza Quitzal, holding fast to the love she had so openly given him.

CHAPTER 7

Spring 1983–Coast of France

Diego stood on the same docks in Marseilles where he had twenty years earlier. He gazed out over the great blue expanse of the Atlantic Ocean studying the passengers as they waved good-bye to loved ones. Diego was about to board the passenger ship to return to Mexico. He was still struggling with the fact that he was abandoning a very successful career as one of world's top fencing champions. A quiet absence of regret came over him for not taking more time to say the appropriate farewells to his fellow teammates and the few precious friends he was leaving behind in France. The bustling city of Paris had been his only home for most of his adult life, yet he never felt the same attachment to France that he had for his beloved Mexico. He knew he was going to be a stranger in the Mexico of 1983, but there was no doubt in his mind, it time to go home.

In all the years since he had waved his final farewell to his parents on the docks of Veracruz, he had only been home once, and that was for his mother's funeral shortly before the onset of the Vietnam War. With her death, Diego not only had lost his mother but his confidante and consoler. Doña Maria was the one person he felt comfortable talking to during the time he was recovering from the trauma of losing Celaya Flores. In Diego's early letters to his mother, he shared all of the disbelief and pain of what had transpired between him and Celaya. Doña Maria was sympathetic to her son's sorrow and suffered equally in his pain. At one point she even talked to her husband, Don Julio, and asked him if he would inquire about the whereabouts of Celaya and why she had so abruptly ended their relationship. Don Julio put on a good show for his distraught wife but returned with a grim report that everything Señor Alvarez had conveyed to Diego about Celaya was true. Don Julio told his wife that the young woman in question wanted nothing to do with their son.

Diego's own father was now a part of the conspiracy to hide the truth from his son. In fact, he never even made an attempt to contact Celaya Flores or her family. Doña Maria resisted for weeks before relaying the disheartening message about Celaya to her son. She was hoping Diego would get over his youthful infatuation with this woman realizing their relationship was destined to fail. But her son was persistent, and ultimately she told him the bitter truth about Celaya and how she had chosen to move on with her life without him.

Upon hearing this news, Diego became even more distraught and his performances in the tournaments suffered. He was often distracted during his matches and, on more than one occasion, considered giving up fencing for good. If it were not for Jacque Denot convincing him to take a break from tournament matches until he could solve his personal problems, there was no doubt that he would have destroyed any chance of competing at a high level.

It was only after weeks of anguishing over Celaya that Diego was able to crawl out of his inner darkness and return to his career. He immersed himself in his work and set about to become one of the most skilled and respected swordsman of modern times. He won the gold medal in the 1968 World Championship and fulfilled his dreams by winning the gold medal in the 1972 Olympics.

All through this gloomy period, Doña Maria was there to console her son. When he received notice of her unexpected death, he was in Italy preparing for a major tournament. Unfortunately, he did not arrive in Mexico until two days after his mother's funeral. He was furious at his father for not delaying the memorial service until his return. It wasn't until years later that he and his father were able to finally reconcile. The lingering friction between them was part of the reason why Diego did not feel a strong pull to return to Mexico earlier than the spring of 1983.

Aside from that one tragic trip home, Diego always had an excuse for not visiting his family. He had convinced himself and his family that he was too busy with his career to return home. But Diego knew the real reason he avoided going home, was there would be no avoiding the despair he felt in knowing Celaya had abandoned him for someone else.

Even as Diego stepped onto the gangplank of the ship, he could not shake the memories of Celaya that continued to haunt him. He wondered whether he might someday pass Celaya on a busy street and what he would say to her.

Would it be a polite hello and congratulations on all that she had accomplished in her life? Or would he scream out to her, shaking his fist in anger, *"Why the hell did you destroy my one chance at love?"*

"Are you boarding, sir?" asked the steward standing at the top of the gangplank.

Diego was momentarily confused by the sound of the stranger's voice. "Yes....yes, I am. I believe my berth number is twenty-four," he answered, as he climbed up the remainder of the gangplank, glancing back one last time at his adopted homeland.

When he reached the top of the gangplank, the steward politely instructed, "Sir, if you take the first door on your right, another steward will be glad to escort you to your stateroom."

He followed the steward's instructions and was met by a young man who escorted him to his room. His luggage was already was neatly stored in the corner. He had a large berth in the first class section. His longtime manager, Roberto Nunez, had taken care of all of his travel arrangements. After all, one of the world's most famous swordsmen could not be expected to travel in any other fashion than the very best. Diego looked around the glamorously decorated room and decided to unpack later. Right now he just wanted to rest. He felt as though he had been going nonstop for the last twenty years. Diego stretched out on the sofa and closed his eyes, but his mind kept going back to his concerns about concluding his career in Mexico.

Roberto Nunez had successfully promoted a highly touted, two-year schedule of exhibitions and tournaments as the grand finale to his outstanding career. Although Diego had never fought in any tournaments in his homeland, his illustrious career was followed closely by proud Mexican fans. Any Mexican fencer who had a successful career internationally was automatically put up on a higher pedestal than those who fought exclusively in Mexico. It was a bias that did not go unnoticed by many of the top aspiring fencers of Mexico.

The culmination of Diego's career was to be at Mexico's Fencing Championship in Mexico City. He would be joined by the most prominent swordsmen of the past and the present. The three-day event would take place during the Independence Day celebration in September, and already it was expected to draw the largest crowds ever to see a fencing match in Mexico.

Diego knew it would be a long two years, but he felt he owed it to the fans that he had abandoned when he was so abruptly sent to France. Nunez had already warned him to expect tremendous press coverage and demands on his time. Diego was not looking forward to all the chaos surrounding his return, but knew it came with the territory.

As an added pressure, there was a great deal of envy building among the up-and-coming competitors in Mexico regarding his return to Mexico. His aggrieved colleagues did not appreciate all the hoopla associated with someone who had never competed in Mexico. Diego was aware he was stepping into a lion's den of resentment, but he was determined to rise above the jealousy. He just wanted to finish his career, settle into his hacienda outside of Ciudad Hidalgo, and teach the next generation of Mexican swordsmen.

At almost forty years of age and a confirmed bachelor, he had no hopes of ever having a family life. It was something he had accepted, whatever chances he thought he had had for a family disappeared the day he stood on the train platform and watched Celaya pass out of sight.

Unable to sleep, Diego went up to the main deck, found a secluded spot to try and quiet his mind. Looking back toward land over the ship's railing he could barely recognize the fading shores of his former home. As each frame slowly flickered by, he was drawn back to the early years of his life in France.

After the rousing success of several major tournaments and his winning of the silver medal in the World Championships in 1964, it was not long before he was on the exhibition circuit, which led to more lucrative payoffs. After two years, when his first contract ended, Diego was in such demand that he was able to command a top salary. By the age of twenty-four, he was on the way to becoming a wealthy man.

With all the fame, he easily garnered the attention of beautiful women. His entourage never lacked in the area of glamorous starlets or socialites, every one of them seeking marriage to the reluctant fencing champion. It was a certainty that on any given night, he would have a stunning young lady at his side. Eventually, he warmed to their attention, but it was always superficial, never serious. None had the intensity or could compare to the promise of his brief relationship with Celaya. He was often reminded, during his numerous affairs, what his grandmother had told him when he was sixteen, "*Diego, remember, it is a man's destiny to have but one true love in life.*" As far as he was concerned, no truer words were ever spoken. He knew he had lost his chance when Celaya deserted him. From that day forth, his heart slammed shut, and he was convinced it would never open again.

Diego continued to make headlines over the years, for both his exploits in and out of tournaments. The newspapers were always trying to embellish his reputation as a ladies' man. The real truth was that Diego spent a great deal of time alone at his private estate on the outskirts of Paris. Diego was content, after competing in tournaments, to return to his sanctuary and escape from all the insanity that came with being a major star in a country that adored its fencing champions. He was more consumed with trying to understand every nuance of his sport than improving his reputation as a ladies' man. Diego spent hours looking at old black and white footage of the great fencers of France and Italy. He would study every detail of their footwork and their timing. After he was certain he could replicate the moves, he would go into his private training room and practice until he was satisfied that he was executing them to perfection. He wanted to be the best at every aspect of his sport. It was his way of rebalancing the world, of holding on to something he could count on.

Diego peered out at the moon as it crested the horizon, knowing his career as fencing champion was coming to a close. Even though he had no idea what the future held for him, he felt a sudden calmness come over him as he laid back in the wooden chaise lounge, feeling the cool ocean breeze wash over him. He closed his eyes and he let the gentle shifting of the ship, as it cut through the waves, lull him to sleep. He was finally going home.

CHAPTER 8

Hundreds of aficionados and fans were waiting to catch a glimpse of their national hero before he entered the Plaza Quitzal. The crowd had been standing out in the hot sun of Mexico City for over two hours waiting for Diego Sanchez to arrive. A black 82' Mercury appeared on a side street across from the Plaza Quitzal, and Diego exited the car. He was hoping to avoid the large crowds that had been showing up at all the exhibitions since he arrived in Mexico a few weeks ago, but several bystanders spotted him and a mad rush ensued. Diego backed up against the wall, trying to avoid being crushed. He felt a personal obligation to indulge his fans, but the intensity of their enthusiasm was getting outrageous of late.

While all the shoving and pushing was going on, his entourage tried to help maneuver him toward the opening that led into the side entrance of the *salle d'armes*. The throng started chanting his name. Diego attempted to appease the crowd by signing several autographs, but the horde of anxious fans was overwhelming. Finally, Diego pushed his way through the onslaught of writhing bodies and dived through the doorway that led to the dressing room.

The other contestants on the card for today's tournament had already arrived and clearly had heard all the commotion associated with his arrival. Two of them who had fought in a tournament with him a month ago were not surprised by all the attention he was receiving, but this was Lolo Nieto's first experience in confronting Diego Sanchez's enthusiastic fans.

Lolo stared curiously at the wide-eyed Diego, who was obviously embarrassed by all of the attention. No matter how hard Diego tried, he could not avoid creating some contempt in his colleagues. Lolo had yet to personally meet Diego, but he was already jealous of the older swordsman's stature in fencing circles. He could not fathom why a man who had only fought a few fights on his home soil was so revered by the people of Mexico. He had read all the accounts of Diego's accomplishments in the newspapers. He was keenly aware that the senior swordsman had won both the World Fencing Federation Championship and the gold medal in the Olympics. Lolo had asked himself several times over the past few months, "*Could this elder statesman of fencing still be that good?*" Lolo knew that if Diego was half as talented as television and the newspapers had reported, he was a direct threat to his own reputation as a rising star in the world of fencing.

Lolo would have his chance today to see in person the impressive talent of the noted master. Lolo was second-to-last on the card, fighting just before Diego, who drew the premiere spot on the program. This was another fact that irked Lolo, who had held this position several times before Sanchez arrived on the scene.

Lolo's plan to counteract Diego's reputation was to put on such a display for the crowd today that they would completely forget Diego Sanchez even existed. He had been practicing relentlessly ever since he heard Diego would be on the same card. His career had been on the upswing before Diego returned to steal his thunder. A few more spectacular performances and Lolo would be at the top of the rankings for Mexico. He knew his place in the rankings was at risk now that Diego had arrived on the scene. Lolo had worked too hard to let some worn-out, old man get in the way of his dream.

"*Diego Sanchez....we'll see how good you really are,*" mouthing the words to himself, as he peered over at Diego in complete disdain.

Diego was still somewhat ruffled by the scene outside as he made his way over to a bench in the corner of the dressing room. He acknowledged the other contestants with an apologetic nod, knowing it was also embarrassing for them to be so completely ignored. It was as though his fellow competitors were the supporting cast in a feature film starring Diego Sanchez. On every occasion possible, Diego had graciously made it a point with the press to acknowledge the performances of his fellow competitors on the program. Very often, in post tournament interviews, he would avoid talking about himself and try to focus on his colleague's accomplishments. He knew most of them were experienced, successful swordsmen. The last thing he wanted to do was insult them by taking all the glory.

At first, it was a tough pill to swallow for his colleagues, but once the other competitors had an opportunity to actually see Diego perform and get to know him personally, most of them developed genuine respect. They understood why Diego was so loved by fans and promoters. It was clear to most of them, having watched him over the past few months, that he was not a publicity seeker but simply a victim of over-zealous fans and the press.

As Diego made his way across the room, he approached Juan Gonzales. "Juan, good to see you again. I heard about your win in Morelia. Congratulations," Diego said.

Juan held out his hand to receive Diego's and cracked a big smile. "Thanks. We all get lucky once in awhile," Juan modestly confessed knowing full well that the reason he had won was because Diego did not participate in the tournament.

Diego walked over to shake hands with Pedro Mendez, one of the other contestants on the program, and warmly greeted him. He was glad to see two familiar faces, yet he could still sense an air of tension in the room and knew most of it was coming from Lolo, who had yet to acknowledge his presence.

Diego turned in Lolo's direction and joked, "I wish you all good luck today.....as long it is not against me."

Almost everyone in the room laughed. Lolo continued dressing, ignoring Diego's attempt at a joke. It was not unusual just before a contest for a competitor to want to be left alone, but Diego could tell something else was eating at Lolo. He knew Lolo was one of the bright new stars in the sport and was probably unhappy having to contend with all the attention he had been receiving.

Diego approached Lolo and held out his hand, "I don't believe we've met. Diego Sanchez."

Lolo ignored Diego's offer of a handshake and cynically replied, "It would be impossible not to know who you are. Everywhere we go all we hear about is the *great* Diego Sanchez." His voice trailed off with a bitter twist.

"Don't believe everything you hear," Diego offered, trying to make light of Lolo's cutting remark.

"Don't worry, I won't," Lolo replied in the tone of a snotty schoolboy, all the while staring straight at Diego. "Excuse me, but if you don't mind, I would like to be left alone."

"Of course," Diego said, as he turned to walk over to the corner of the room where Juan Gonzalez was completing his final preparation.

As Diego bent down to grab his bag, Juan whispered to him, "Ignore him. Lolo's had a hair up his ass ever since he came on the scene four years ago. He is about as cutthroat and arrogant as you can get."

"I probably haven't helped the situation."

"Don't blame yourself for the press's behavior, and by the way don't forget... I've seen you in action. I personally think you deserve all the acclaim and more."

"Thanks. You're very generous."

Each contestant prepared to do battle in his own way before entering the *salle d'armes*. Some would spend their last moments stretching or meditating on what moves they were planning to incorporate into their performance. Others would quietly sing to themselves in an attempt to relieve their tension. Diego was noted for meticulously checking the blade of his foil, delicately running his hand down the entire length of the blade until he was satisfied there were no flaws or potential areas where the blade could be defective. Even the slighted flaw could result in major injury. He was in Italy at the tournament when Vladimir Smirnov was killed.

While Diego continued to check the blade of his foil, he watched Lolo across the room, fascinated by this brash, young swordsman who was so much like him when he was coming up through the ranks. He wondered if Lolo was just putting on a show, or if he really was as bitter and arrogant as he appeared. He was curious what could cause someone who had the looks and talent to be so angry at the world?

Diego had read about Lolo, aware he had the reputation of being one of the most skilled fencers in Mexico, yet the fans had not accepted him into their hearts. It was obvious to Diego that Lolo hadn't figured out this important factor for success.

Diego had a reputation for helping out up and coming swordsmen. He felt it was part of his duty, his responsibility to help continue the long-standing legacy of his sport. A somewhat odd thought entered his mind as he studied Lolo, "Why not mentor Lolo?" Of course, there was the question as to whether Lolo would accept his advice; but for some inexplicable reason, Diego was determined to give it a try.

Lolo sat on a bench across from Diego, leaning up against the wall with his eyes shut, acting as though he was unaffected by all the pre-fight activity. Diego stared at Lolo's hands and saw that they were slightly trembling. He knew a man's hands never lied. This kid was as nervous as anyone else facing the stress of a major contest. Diego looked down at his own hands. They were stone quiet.

Diego was putting his foil back into its weathered leather carrying case when he saw the referee enter the dressing room to announce the beginning of the tournament. As Juan Gonzales led the way, the other competitors entered the *salle d'armes* of Plaza Quitzal. As expected, when Diego finally came into view, the decibels of cheering increased into a crescendo that resounded across the packed audience. Once again, the promoters of the tournament had done an excellent job, and the event was sold out. Each man raised his foil in acknowledgement of the crowd's applause. All the contestants slowly turned to recognize special members of the crowd who were friends or lifelong supporters. In looking at these striking swordsmen, it seemed as though they all had to be cut from the same extraordinary cloth. They carried themselves in a way that left no doubt that they were the elite of their sport.

As Diego was giving his obligatory acknowledgment of the crowd's appreciation, he momentarily paused. When his eyes caught a glimpse of a striking figure in the third row, a young woman in a lime green dress whose beauty was so compelling that Diego inexplicably caught himself bowing in her direction. The mystery woman acknowledged his gesture by returning a warm smile. As Diego turned to walk toward the edge of the sidelines, he leaned over to Juan and asked if he knew the woman in the green dress.

Juan laughed, "I sometimes forget you've only recently returned to Mexico. She's a noted flamenco dancer and one of the great beauties of our country. Her name is Lorena Santoya."

"I was just curious," Diego sheepishly replied, as he glanced once more in her direction.

Lolo noticed Diego's gesture toward his ex-lover, further fueling his resentment of Diego. How could an older man even think he had a chance with a woman of Lorena's stature? She was not one of those commonplace starlets looking to have an affair with a well-known swordsman in the hope it would improve her career. Lorena was from a respected family and not about to take up with an ex-champion on the downside of his career.

Lolo sneered at Diego, who was still mesmerized by Lorena's presence. Not since Celaya had Diego been so immediately captivated by a woman.

Juan Gonzales fought first and moved on to the next round of matches. Diego congratulated him as Juan joined him on the sidelines.

Lolo, on the other hand, stood off in a corner by himself, barely acknowledging Juan's effort. It was this rude behavior that alienated Lolo from his colleagues. Being a loner was one thing, insulting his fellow competitors was disrespectful.

Round by round the competitors were eliminated until there were only four: Juan Gonzales, Luis Montes, Lolo Nieto and of course, the favorite, Diego Sanchez.

Lolo was matched against Juan Gonzales in the next bout. He confidently strolled onto the *piste* directly in front of where Lorena was sitting with a noted flamenco promoter, and bowed in her direction. Unlike two weeks ago in Ciudad Hidalgo when she was with Chase, she totally ignored his gesture and acted as though she were engrossed in a conversation with her host. She was not in the mood for his games and was still reeling from her disappointment with Chase's abandonment. She was in Mexico City for her first appearance on her national tour. Today, she was the guest of Hector Leonardo, a prominent entertainment promoter. Although she would have preferred not to be at the tournament, it was impossible for her to refuse an offer by such an important backer.

Lolo gave Lorena one more chance to acknowledge his gesture dedicating his performance to her, but she continued her preoccupation with her host. Embarrassed by her total disregard, Lolo turned, gave the jury an obligatory tip of the sword, and returned to prepare for his bout.

When Lolo was sure he had the complete attention of the crowd, he stepped onto the *piste*, made one last adjustment to his grip on the foil, assumed the *en garde* position and edged forward toward Gonzales.

The first stage of the bout went just as Lolo had planned. His offensive work with the foil was exceptional, and defensive parries blocked every effort by Gonzales to score a touch.

At one point in the bout, Lolo glared at Diego and tipped his foil in Diego's direction; signifying a direct challenge to the older master. Although insulted by the young upstart's insult, Diego was impressed by Lolo's speed and technique with the foil. Whatever doubt he had about Lolo when they were in the dressing room vanished.

Unfortunately for Lolo, his grandstanding opened an opportunity for Gonzales to strike. As Gonzales rapidly lunged forward, Lolo was forced to retreat. In the process he tripped over his back foot and fell backwards toward the floor. In trying to brace his fall, Lolo's foil became trapped behind his back and the weight of his fall snapped the thin blade in two. Diego, along with several other competitors, motioned toward where Lolo lay. They knew from past history that whenever a foil breaks, a man could easily be injured. Diego stepped over to assist Lolo. Although Lolo was uninjured, his pride had been severely bruised. Lolo angrily waved Diego off and gave him a lightning stare filled with resentment. He placed his protective mask back on snapping at his assistant to replace his foil, and immediately resumed the bout.

Lolo easily won the bout 15 to 2, but it was still humiliating having taken a clumsy fall.

Amidst the audience's applause for his dominating performance, Lolo walked over to where his assistant was waiting and angrily slammed down his foil. He knew, but for one abrupt move, he had fought one of the best contests of his life.

The crowd continued to show appreciation for his performance as Lolo tried to prepare himself for the finals. He was still fuming over the fact that Diego had seen him stumble so ungracefully. Of all the people who could have come to his assistance, why did it have to be Diego Sanchez?

As Diego prepared for his semi-final match against Montes, Lolo turned toward Diego and bowed indignantly in his direction. There was no doubt in anyone's mind what he intended by his insulting gesture. Lolo had cast the bitter stone of confrontation, and the challenge was on. It was clear to Diego his counterpart did not appreciate his help. Both men knew it was Diego's obligation to check on a fellow competitor, but Lolo would have preferred the stinging pain of his own broken blade to the humiliation of Diego coming to his rescue.

Diego masterfully won his bout with Montes in a 15-1 rout. Montes unfortunately just happened to be the victim of Diego's fury from Lolo's affront. Diego rarely lost his composure, but Lolo's behavior was a direct insult and he was not about to let Lolo embarrass him in front of such a large crowd. It was time to teach the young upstart a lesson.

As Lolo prepared himself for the final match with Diego, Diego walked over until he was directly in front of where Lorena sat. He bowed and tipped his foil in her direction. Unlike her response to Lolo's gesture, Lorena stood up and placed her hand over her heart, signifying that her prayers were with him. As Diego rose to see her response, he smiled and turned toward Lolo to make sure he had seen her gesture of support. He sternly nodded at Lolo, making it clear that his rebuff had not gone unnoticed.

Diego returned to the *piste*, donned his protective mask and inched toward the awaiting Lolo. As brilliant as Lolo's work with the foil was in the earlier bouts, Diego's artful display left no doubt that he was the more accomplished fencer. It was as though Diego's every movement was a polished ballet step, and he was dancing with his angry combatant. Striking a touch with ease and blocking every offensive move Lolo made with his own *riposte*. Diego's first touches against his younger opponent were so dramatic and fearless it was as though they were manifestations from the hand of God. His foil seemed possessed as it elegantly fluttered around Lolo's foil.

The crowd was mesmerized into breathless wonderment. Except for occasional applause, they sat riveted in attentive silence. Before Lolo knew what happened, the bout was over. He had lost to Diego by an embarrassing margin of 15-5. It was his worst loss in four years of tournament play.

As Diego left the *salle d'armes*, he threw his head back, raised his right hand into the air with his foil, and marched defiantly to the sidelines. Lolo watched with gnashing resentment at the outpouring for Diego's magnificent performance from the crowd. Lolo's fiery glare was so intense his eyes could have burned a hole clean through Diego. If he hadn't despised Diego before today, there was no doubt now that he would do anything within his power to bring down this great master. He had never wished for a fellow competitor to be injured, but for a fleeting moment it crossed his mind. He knew it was the only thing that would stop Diego from dominating the rest of the tournament season. Any memory of Lolo's earlier performance today had been wiped out with the last single, flawless thrust of Diego's foil onto his chest.

Diego walked over until he was standing in front of the cheering fans. When he came into close proximity to where Lorena was sitting, he paused momentarily and placed his hand over his heart and bowed, returning the gesture she had bestowed on him prior to the contest. Lorena stood up, bowed slightly and returned a congratulatory smile. His eyes filled with a watery gleam as he held her eyes. Lorena was somewhat startled by Diego's emotional response to her earlier gesture. What Lorena didn't know was that her gesture at the beginning of Diego's battle had brought back lucid visions of Celaya gesturing with her hand over her heart at the train station over twenty years ago. All the glory of this victorious day was tempered by the painful memories Celaya.

Diego spent the next hour signing autographs and being interviewed by the press. By the time he reached the dressing room, all the other competitors had packed up and gone home. The difficult battle with Lolo and his brief interaction with Lorena had left him physically and emotionally drained. Diego collapsed on a bench and whispered to himself, *"You're getting too old for this, my friend."* His face crinkled into a smile, and he sighed in relief, knowing he had once again faithfully represented his lifelong passion.

CHAPTER 9

Lorena sat in her dressing room at the Grand Teatro Degollado of Mexico City, putting on makeup for the first performance. The room was filled with flowers from fans and well wishers. She always felt the distinct ratcheting up of her nerves before a big performance, but tonight there was even a sharper edge to her anxiety. No matter how hard she tried to forget about the recent events with Chase, she was unable to shake the relentless disillusionment with the way their affair had so abruptly ended. It had been less than a month since they had parted ways in front of the hotel and she was still smarting from the experience. Attending the fencing tournament earlier in the day had only enhanced the memories of their time together. She was familiar with this sense of loss from her failed relationships in the past but never had she felt remorse to this extent. She was hoping the demands of a busy tour schedule would eradicate any lingering regret for having gotten involved with Chase Chandler.

Her manager for the past three years, Luis Goya, entered her dressing room beaming a wide smile. "We are going to have a full house tonight. You should hear the buzz of excitement!"

"Thank you for all the hard work, Luis. I know I haven't exactly been myself lately, but I promise it won't affect my performance."

"Just go out there and have fun. You love to dance and they love you."

"How long before I go on?"

"Fifteen minutes. I'll make sure the rest of the troupe is ready."

Lorena was traveling with one of the best flamenco ensembles in Mexico. It was not a hard sell for Luis to convince a top musical troupe to grab onto Lorena's rising star. Her reputation was growing with each engagement. They had sold out most of the tour, and Luis was looking forward to huge crowds in every city.

Luis recognized Lorena's talent the first time he saw her dance in a little club in Veracruz and knew she was destined for stardom. Lorena had a provocative but yet an innocent quality about her. At the time he met Lorena, Luis was managing two other flamenco groups from Mexico City, but when he saw her phenomenal performance, he immediately dropped them and signed Lorena to a four-year contract. Luis was not only her manager, but also acted as her press agent, personal secretary, and on rare occasions a soft shoulder to cry on.

Luis was worried about Lorena. She seemed distracted and distant of late. Watching her during practice sessions over the past few weeks, he could see she was losing control of her emotions and often on the brink of tears. The last few days, Lorena's state of mind seemed to be improving; nonetheless, he was going to keep a close eye on her. He couldn't afford to let an important piece of property like Lorena incinerate right before his eyes.

Luis went down the hallway and informed the other members of the troupe they had ten minutes before they went on stage. It was traditional among flamenco troupes for all the members to go on stage at the same time, but in this case, it was clear Lorena was the star of the show and would have the privilege of making a grand entrance.

Lorena could hear the muffled sounds of her fellow performers getting ready on stage. She took one last glance in the mirror, inhaled a deep breath, and prepared herself for her entrance. She knew that no matter what was happening in her personal life, she owed it to herself and the audience to dance her heart out. Lorena stood at the edge of the curtain, peering out at the low-lit stage. She could see through a slit in the curtain that every seat in the house was filled. Lorena quickly glanced across the first few rows of seats, and she noticed a familiar face. It was Diego Sanchez. It was obvious he had come to the theater alone, which surprised Lorena. He was such a handsome man and a celebrated hero that she knew he could have his pick of beautiful companions to adorn his side.

Lorena was pleased to see such a prominent figure in her audience, but she knew she would have to perform her best to even come close to matching his performance in the tournament. She wanted him to know that she was just as dedicated to her art as he was to his.

Diego sat in the second row of the theater. He noted that the old theater was not unlike the sports pavilions that he performed in throughout Mexico, not necessarily in design, but in historical value and elegance. Diego looked around at the sold-out event, and could sense the excitement of the audience. It was not unlike what he experienced only hours earlier. He let go a smile, knowing it was another performer's turn to face the pressures of the limelight and not his.

Diego had to pull some strings to acquire such a prime ticket to an event that was already sold out. After he had recovered from his battle with Lolo, he had planned on going back to his hotel room and collapsing. Unfortunately, he could not get the "woman in the green dress" out of his head. He called an old friend who was well connected in Mexico City, and asked if there was any chance he could get a ticket for tonight's performance. At first, his friend told him there was little to no chance of getting a ticket at this late date, but he that would try. An hour later, his friend called him back and said he had to practically trade his first born, but he had acquired a second-row center stage seat for the performance. Diego rushed to get ready and barely made it to the theater before the front doors were closed. Diego had seen his fair share of great flamenco dancers while living in Europe, but tonight was different. It wasn't just another evening at the theater; he had a personal interest in learning more about its star performer.

The theater lights slowly began to dim, signaling his wait was finally over. The red velvet stage curtain slowly parted, revealing the statuesque figure of Lorena Santoya. She was dressed in a long, flowing maroon dress that billowed from her waist. Her long auburn hair was combed back tightly into a bun adorned with a mother-of-pearl hair comb. She stood facing the crowd with her head slightly bowed, her chin tucked against her chest. A bright, silver light illuminated her outline as she waited patiently for the guitarist's first strum to signify the beginning of the performance.

When Lorena heard the first notes echo from the guitar, she slowly raised her head to face the audience. Her expression had a hard, sensuous edge, as she stared into the eager crowd. At first she did not move any part of her body, but then from under the drape of her silk dress clamored one sharp sound of her shoe heel, then another, and another, until a syncopated cadence reverberated across the theater. She reached down, grabbed the hem of her dress and began parading across the wooden dance floor, never missing a beat as her tapping feet accelerated to a feverish pitch. Her delicate hands danced above her head in an intricate weaving motion, as if pushing the musical notes gently through the air.

The music and her engaging style of dance instantly carried Diego away. When he had first noticed her in the crowd at the tournament earlier today it was hard to discern her true beauty, but now sitting in such close proximity to her, he could see she was a striking woman.

The first part of her performance was balanced with dramatic gypsy songs and flamboyant interpretations of traditional dance. Twice, she incited the audience to leap to its feet in applause. It was obvious to everyone in the theater that she was enjoying herself and the crowd's reaction.

Lorena concluded the first half of her show with a powerful interpretation of Rodrigo's *Guitar Concerto* and left no question in the audience's mind that it was seeing one of the finest flamenco dancers in all of Mexico, if not the world. Diego joined the audience in sustained raucous applause as she exited the stage for a brief intermission.

Standing backstage, Luis Goya, had been concerned about Lorena's ability to get her act together given her recent behavior, but once he saw the look on her face on the dance floor, he knew everything would be all right. As Lorena stepped backstage and headed for her dressing room, he could almost hear the cash register ringing in his head. He knew it was one of the best performances of her career, and the critics were going to be all over it in tomorrow's newspaper.

"You were magnificent! You have them right in the palm of your hand," Luis proclaimed enthusiastically.

"Luis, calm down," Lorena said, seeing Luis was practically tripping over his own words.

"No, I mean it. You looked obsessed out there. What came over you?"

"Nothing special. I was just letting myself flow with the music."

"I've never seen you dance with such fire, such passion."

She ignored her manager's comments and continued in the direction of her dressing room.

As they reached the door to her dressing room, she turned to Luis and said,

"I only have a few minutes to change into a new costume, and I would like to have a little time by myself."

"Of course, of course, my dear," Luis said almost apologetically.

Lorena entered her dressing room, sat down in front of a large mirror and smiled. She knew everything Luis had told her was true. It was as though she was exorcising all of her frustration through the intense energy of her performance. The ferocity of her dance steps was more powerful than ever before. In fact, the heels of her feet were still burning from the heat she had generated from the intensity of her dancing.

Lorena didn't have a lot of time to enjoy the splendor of the moment. She had to be back on stage for her second act in fifteen minutes. She quickly checked her makeup and changed into a beautiful lavender silk dress. She let her hair down from its tight constraints and changed her shoes to match the dress. She was anxious and excited to get back on stage.

When she came out for the second half of her performance, she turned to the accompanying musicians and indicated she wanted to say something to the audience. They were somewhat surprised by her request. It was rare for a dancer to interrupt a performance to speak with the audience. Luis stood backstage curious as to what Lorena was up to. She stepped forward until she was standing on the edge of the stage. Lorena waited for the remaining members of the audience to take their seats before she spoke. It was obvious she wanted the full attention of the entire audience before talking.

"I want to thank you for all your kind applause. It's most appreciated," she said, as she put her hands together as if she were praying and bowed to the audience. She continued. "I would like to recognize someone in our audience, who put on the most astounding performance of skill and grace I've ever seen. He is a man of superb talent, and I know he is respected by so many. Would you please give a warm welcome to the esteemed fencing champion, Señor Diego Julio Sanchez!"

The crowd instantly broke into applause. Heads were craning from side to side, trying to get a glimpse of Diego. There were several people at tonight's performance who had attended the tournament and Diego's brilliant performance at Plaza Quitzal was already the talk of the town. The audience was persistent in its applause, wanting Diego to rise to his feet and acknowledge their appreciation for him as one of their national heroes. Lorena grinned widely and gestured for him to stand. Diego's reluctance only intensified the audience's determination. He finally rose to his feet, his head slightly bowed, as if he were a schoolboy being scolded and waved to the audience. As he acknowledged their praise, the applause increased twofold, and it was not until Diego signaled for them to sit back down, that they grudgingly returned to their seats.

Diego was caught off guard by Lorena's generosity. He turned to face her, placed his hand over his heart in the same gesture of gratitude he had signaled to her after winning the tournament, and bowed. Lorena teasingly smiled at him, knowing she had embarrassed the shy champion. He pointed his finger, waving it at her, implying that someday he would repay the favor.

Lorena returned to center stage and began the second half of her performance. She danced just as brilliantly as she had in the first half of her performance. The audience gave her several standing ovations at the conclusion of her show and demanded an encore. Lorena obliged their wishes, and again received a standing ovation. She graciously thanked them for their enthusiastic reception, exited the stage; satisfied she had given one of the best performances of her life. As she made her way to the dressing room, all the stagehands formed a line and were applauding. She thanked them for their support and walked directly to her dressing room.

Luis was waiting for her arrival. He rushed up and kissed her on both cheeks. "Wonderful! Absolutely wonderful!"

"Thank you, Luis. I thought the musicians played well tonight," she said, not wanting to take all the credit.

"All the newspapers are waiting to interview you. Introducing Diego Sanchez was a stroke of genius. This is going to make for great publicity." Luis was gushing with excitement.

"Luis, I didn't do it for publicity purposes. Señor Sanchez is such a respected and loved figure in our country.... I was just returning the favor from his kind gesture this afternoon at the tournament." She turned away from her manager so he couldn't see that she was lying. "I thought it was only appropriate for me to acknowledge him."

Luis could not stop himself. "We can't help it if the newspapers want to try and put their own spin on this story. Think of the headlines tomorrow:

"Famous Flamenco Dancer Flirts
With Mexico's Most Beloved Swordsman"

Luis continued, "This will be a national story in all the newspapers by tomorrow morning."

"Wait just a minute, Luis. If I find out that you're promoting this ridiculous idea with the newspapers, I'll have your hide for it. Do we understand each other?" Lorena demanded emphatically.

Luis reluctantly agreed, "Yes, I understand, but they still want to interview you about your performance and your comments about Diego Sanchez. Don't blame me if they take off and run with it."

"I'll agree to an interview, but if they ask me anything about Diego Sanchez, I'm going to politely decline to answer their questions. Is that clear?"

"You sure make my job tough sometimes." Luis understood her reluctance to talk about her personal life. He knew from past experience that offstage she was a very private person.

Lorena turned her back to face the mirror and said, "I'll meet you in the lobby in twenty minutes."

"Yes, that's fine. Would you like to join me for a late night cocktail at El Mirador?"

"Thank you for the offer, but I'm pretty exhausted so I'm going to pass," Lorena said as she reached up and raked her hands through her slightly damp hair.

Luis exited her dressing room and was heading in the direction of the lobby when Diego stopped him halfway up the aisle of the theater. Luis was so distracted that at first he didn't notice it was Diego Sanchez. Diego finally caught Luis's attention by stepping directly into his path.

"Señor, please excuse me. I was informed by the theater manager that you're Señorita Santoya's manager," Diego said, beckoning Luis. "I'm Señor Diego Sanchez, and I wanted to ask for your assistance regarding a private matter."

"How can I help you, Señor Sanchez?" Luis asked, recognizing this was the man Lorena had pointed out during her performance.

"Would it be possible for me to thank Señorita Santoya in person for her kind gesture?"

"Señorita Santoya is changing right now, but I would be glad to inquire if she would meet with you in a few minutes."

Luis immediately returned to Lorena's dressing room and knocked on the door. Lorena reluctantly invited Luis inside. She had already changed into a new dress and was sitting in front of the mirror brushing her tangled hair.

"I'm so sorry to bother you, but I've had an unusual request from a special fan," Luis said teasingly.

"Luis, you know I never receive fans in my dressing room," she curtly told Luis.

"Well, you might want to change your mind. It is Señor Sanchez, who has requested to thank you personally for your gracious gesture."

Lorena was momentarily flustered, and Luis could see it by her blush reflected in the mirror.

"Shall I tell him you're too busy?"

Lorena waited a few seconds and then responded. "No, give me ten minutes and I'll be ready to receive Señor Sanchez." She paused and turned to peer at Luis saying, "Remember what we talked about earlier regarding this issue. Absolutely no press!"

"Yes, I understand....but he *is* rather dashing, don't you think?"

Lorena ignored Luis and continued brushing her hair.

Luis returned to where Diego was standing and told him that Señorita Santoya would be honored to meet with him in her dressing room in ten minutes. Diego thanked Luis and sat down to wait. He nervously checked his watch every minute or so, making sure that he wasn't losing track of time. In exactly ten minutes, he started toward the stage door.

Lorena sat facing the mirror, fidgeting with her makeup kit. She was more anxious about meeting Diego in person than she was dancing in front of the huge audiences. She realized Diego was fifteen years her senior, but she was struggling to ignore her attraction to him. Luis was right about one thing—

Diego Sanchez was as handsome as reputed. *Was it possible that he was also attracted to her? How should she react if he approached her for an engagement this evening? Why was she so worried about it?* After all, she was free from any attachments since Chase had so carelessly deserted her.

As the time for Diego's appearance approached, Lorena could feel a slow gnawing pang in her stomach. She couldn't decide whether to act as if she were still in the process of nonchalantly grooming herself or to face the door as though she was expecting him. She decided to continue facing the mirror, not wanting to act too excited that one of Mexico's national heroes was coming to her private dressing room. She heard a knock on her door and her heart started racing.

Lorena calmly answered, "Please come in."

The door swung open, and when she looked at the image in the mirror, she almost fell out of her chair. It was Chase Chandler, and he was holding a large bouquet of long stem white roses. She blinked several times, thinking she was having a hallucination, but when she was finally able turn around, she could clearly see it was no mirage. It was Chase!

"Lorena, I'm so sorry," Chase declared apologetically.

Lorena was still too taken aback to answer.

He continued. "I left you a message at the restaurant in Ciudad Hidalgo explaining why I had to leave so abruptly but I learned after I got back to town that you never received it. I've been looking all over Mexico for you."

Every negative thought she had about him over the past few weeks vaporized. Lorena stood up and took the roses from him and set them on her dressing table. She hurtled herself into his arms. They kissed passionately, refusing to relinquish each other's embrace.

When Diego reached the door of Lorena's dressing room he saw the door slightly ajar. He innocently peered through the crack. Instantly he stepped back, not wanting to interrupt what was a very intimate scene between Lorena and a stranger. He froze, not knowing what to do next. He was so close to them he could easily overhear their conversation.

"Chase, I thought you had abandoned me. I didn't know what to think."

"I'm so sorry. I hope you'll never doubt me again. I went crazy trying to find you."

Chase paused as he looked into Lorena's watered eyes. "Let's get out of here, so we can talk in private. I have so much I want to say."

"I can't. I'm supposed to meet with the press in a few minutes," Lorena said, forgetting totally about the fact that Diego Sanchez was on his way to see her.

Diego felt guilty listening to their conversation, but he was uncomfortable about being discovered, so he slowly backed away. He could feel the sweat beading up on his forehead.

Chase beseeched Lorena to leave with him immediately. "Forget the press. Just come with me."

Just as Chase concluded his plea, Lorena heard a loud thumping noise outside of her dressing room and remembered her meeting with Diego Sanchez.

She stepped around Chase, opened the door, and looked down the empty hallway. She was sure she had heard something.

Diego's back was pressed up against the side wall near her dressing room. He was hiding behind a thick canvas curtain. He had knocked over a wooden crate trying to escape from being noticed. He held his breath so she couldn't hear him anxiously panting.

Lorena looked down the hallway one more time, but saw nothing.

"What is it, Lorena?"

"Oh, nothing."

Lorena knew that it would be too uncomfortable for herself and Chase if she tried to explain her arranged meeting with Diego. Now that Chase was back, she didn't want to do anything that could jeopardize their reunion.

Chase reached over, took her hand, and pulled her close to him. "What do I have to say to convince you to come with me right now?"

She had already made up her mind to go with him, but she had to make up some kind of excuse to give Luis for shirking her responsibility with the press.

"Give me one minute and I'll go with you," she pleaded as she broke away from his embrace. "I have to let my manager know why I'm leaving so suddenly. Wait here for me, and I'll be right back."

"I must be crazy to let you out of my sight after just finding you again."

She reached up and kissed him lightly on the cheek and said, "I promise, I'll be right back." Lorena exited her dressing room and headed in the direction of the stage door.

Diego could hear her approaching footsteps as she neared his hiding place. He froze in place, his body as stiff as a soldier at attention during dress inspection. As Lorena disappeared onto the stage, he crept into the hallway knowing this was his only chance to escape without being noticed. He crossed to the other side of the stage, opened the door to the rear exit of the theater, and stepped out into the cool night air. It was only then that he felt the true disappointment of realizing Lorena was involved with another man. The only thing he felt fortunate about was escaping the voracious jaws of the press without a major incident. He was sure they had already prepared numerous questions regarding his and Lorena's interaction during her performance. He could only hope Lorena's people would appropriately explain her gesture to the press and nothing would come of it. Not likely, he thought mockingly, as he headed in the direction of his hotel.

Lorena asked a janitor cleaning up the stage to get Luis, who was busy in the lobby impressing the press corps. Luis returned in a few minutes and found Lorena standing by the edge of the stage.

As he approached, he said somewhat impatiently, "Lorena, they are all waiting for you. Are you ready?"

"Luis, I've a big favor to ask you. I want you to meet with the press on my behalf."

He barely waited for her to finish. "Are you crazy? You can't leave them hanging after such an incredible performance." He scolded her. "What about what you said...."

Lorena interrupted him. "Luis, please." Her voice peaked and then softened. "Just make an excuse for me. You're good at that. Tell them that something has come up which requires my immediate attention."

"It's Diego Sanchez isn't it? You're ditching me to run off with him, aren't you?"

"No, it is not like that. He never even came to my dressing room."

Luis's mood shifted to one of concern. "This must be really important to you?"

Just then Chase stepped out from behind the stage door. He had become impatient waiting for her to return. It was not hard for Luis to notice the tall, handsome American. Both Luis and Lorena turned and looked in Chase's direction. Lorena had a guilty look on her face as she turned to face her manager.

"I think I understand now. Is he the reason for your odd behavior the last couple of weeks?" Luis said in slightly sarcastic tone.

"Luis, I can't explain everything right now. I'm just asking you to do me a favor this one time. Is that too much to ask?" Lorena pleaded, appealing to Luis's softer side.

"All right, but you owe me."

"Thank you, Luis," Lorena said, as she kissed him on the cheek.

"Get out of here before those reporters start sniffing around. Don't worry.... you can count on old Luis to wade through this without you."

Lorena turned and walked in the direction of Chase, who was waiting to see if she had been successful in convincing her manager to help with the escape plan. Luis could see the genuine excitement in her hurried pace as she moved toward the man standing at the stage door. It was only after a second look that Luis remembered Chase from Ciudad Hidalgo. This was the gringo Lorena had drinks with after her performance at the Tauromaquia. Luis thought at the time it was strange she had decided to socialize with a customer. Lorena almost always refused the numerous offers she received after every performance, but for some reason she had made an exception in this American's case. At the time, Luis really didn't think much about it, but now that Chase had shown up unexpectedly, he was worried that Lorena's affection for this stranger was more than a passing encounter. Luis watched them disappear behind the stage door and thought he would have to keep a close eye on her. He was not about to lose his prize possession to some gringo who was probably only interested in a brief affair.

Lorena and Chase returned to her dressing room, picked up a few of her personal items, and left through the same rear exit Diego had used only a few minutes earlier.

As they exited, Lorena looked both ways, making sure that there were no snooping reporters lingering in the shadows.

Chase put his arm around her and said, "I promise you won't regret this."

"I'm going to hold you to it," Lorena said, as she smiled seductively at him.

They walked down the back alley of the grand theater until they reached the main boulevard. Chase flagged down a cab and gave the driver the name of his hotel.

After returning from the Wallace mission and having found out Lorena's whereabouts in Mexico City, he had made reservations at the Posada Vista Hermosa, a converted convent from the mid-1800s. Chase knew he still had a lot to explain about his strange behavior after leaving her stranded after the first night together at the hot springs. Chase hadn't decided on what story he was going to tell her about the last few weeks, but he knew the truth was not an option—too much, too soon, he thought. He could only hope, whatever story he told her, that she would believe him and they could start all over.

When they reached the hotel, Chase escorted Lorena into the luxurious lobby. He went to the front desk and retrieved the room key. When he had made the reservation, he made sure it was the best room in the Posada, ensuring that he had the perfect setting for what he had to tell her.

They walked across a large, inner courtyard until they reached a small bungalow that was separate from the main structure. As Chase put the key in the door, she whispered to him in a soft, scolding tone, "You seem to have assumed an awful lot about tonight."

Chase was momentarily set back by her comment.

He replied apologetically, "I'm sorry. If you would rather go somewhere else to talk...."

She interrupted. "You're such a gentleman sometimes," she said, laughing aloud as she grabbed his hand firmly and whispered in his ear. "Well, are you going to stand out here all night gawking at me, or are you going to whisk me away to your room and make love to me with wild abandon?"

He swept her up into his arms and gently kicked at the door that was slightly ajar. They disappeared into the inner sanctum of the lushly decorated room and collapsed onto the large featherbed, tearing at clothes, breaking buttons, groping for each other's nakedness. There was a different intensity to Lorena's love making this time. At one point, the intensity of her frenetic movement almost scared him out of his sexual bliss. She was letting out all the frustration and anxiety she had felt during their brief separation pour out through her aching body. With the onset of her third climax, Lorena had to put her hands over her mouth afraid the hotel staff might hear her uncontrolled, high-pitched moaning.

Only after they had satiated each other's intense desires and collapsed from exhaustion, did they both finally drift off to sleep.

Lorena awoke to the sound of the door closing. She stretched her arms out high above her head and noticed Chase was not beside her. She bolted up and sat on the edge of the bed, imagining in her cloudy drowsiness that he had once again abandoned her. Her heart was racing even though she knew she was acting irrationally. She was just about to get up and start looking for him when Chase reappeared holding a tray of fresh orange juice, coffee, and croissants. He could see by the look on her face that she was surprised to see him.

He joked, "Did you think I had left you again?" Not knowing it was exactly what she had been thinking.

She lay back in bed and pulled the sheet up over her bare breasts. "No, of course not. I just missed waking up with you." Her eyes turned downward, not wanting Chase to know how vulnerable she still felt from having been abandoned by him.

"I'm sorry, but maybe what I have to say will make up it up to you."

Chase set the tray down on a small round table next to the French doors and opened the heavy curtains that looked out onto a private courtyard. He walked into the bathroom, retrieved a white terry cloth robe similar to the one he was wearing, and handed it to Lorena. Chase watched as she stood up, unabashedly naked, and put on the robe. He still could hardly believe he was fortunate enough to have found her again, and he was even more thankful that she had forgiven him for suddenly disappearing after their first night together. Lorena joined him at the table as he was pouring hot coffee into their cups. She sat down and glanced out at the beautifully landscaped garden surrounding the outer courtyard, trying to shake the cobwebs from her mind.

Chase sat across from her, anxiously fidgeting with the sugar spoon, and

Lorena sensed he wanted to say something of import. She thought about what he had just said about "making up for not being by her side when she awoke," and wondered what he meant by his comment. He finally broke the edgy silence.

The cadence of his speech was slow and deliberate. "Over the past couple of weeks, I've spent a lot of time by myself, mostly worrying about finding you. But I've also been trying to sort out what I wanted to do with the rest of my life." He paused, trying to fortify his courage. "I've never been close to anyone who could inspire me to ask those difficult questions. Then you came along, and I found myself trying to find the answers to something I had conveniently avoided my whole life."

Chase wanted to continue, while he had the momentum, but Lorena interrupted him. "Those are never easy questions to answer." She didn't know where Chase was going with the conversation, but she could tell he was struggling to communicate his feelings. She reached across the table and put her hand on top of his in a comforting gesture.

As he absorbed her consoling words, it was as if an emotional floodgate swung wide open. He peered into her eyes, hoping for any sign she might intuitively know what he was about to say.

"Lorena, I want you to come back to Texas with me."

At first, Lorena was too stunned to react to his request. She rocked back in her chair as if she had been given an electrical shock.

Her reaction was unsettling to Chase, and he was hoping he hadn't made a terrible mistake by moving so fast in their relationship.

She quickly tried to sort through the meaning of his request. Was it a marriage proposal? Or was Chase just asking for her to take a trip with him so they could spend some more time together?

"My God," she thought, "I don't know if I'm ready for this."

Her face flushed bright red at the realization of what he might be asking. They had actually only spent a total of two nights together. How could a man who appeared to be rational and somewhat cautious, ask her such an earth-shattering question? There were so many implications. What about her career? She had trained and lived her whole life for the sole purpose of becoming a career flamenco dancer. How could he ask her to give it all up?

After a belabored pause, she answered.

"I don't understand. Do you want me to go on a trip to Texas with you, right in the middle of my tour?" she asked, choosing the lowest common denominator of possible answers.

"I'm not talking about a vacation. I'm talking permanently. I'm sorry if I didn't say it directly the first time, but I want to marry you."

Lorena was staggered by what Chase had just asked of her. His words felt like a heavy stone resting on her chest. She almost dropped her hot cup of coffee into her lap. She knew by Chase's impassioned expression that he was serious. Obviously he had thought about what he was committing to for the rest of his life and was comfortable with it.

Chase continued, sensing her hesitation in answering his monumental question.

"Look, I know how important your dancing career is to you and I'm not asking that you give it up. I could never be that selfish..... but I'm sure if we both put our heads together, we can work it out. All I'm asking is for you to give it some consideration."

"Chase, I don't know how to respond. I need some time to think this over."

"Do you feel the same way as I do? Can you at least tell me that?"

"It's not that, Chase. You know a lot of people are depending on me."

"You didn't answer my question," he pleaded, begging for an answer.

"Yes, Chase, I love you. I haven't been able to think about anyone else since we met. It's just that...."

He interrupted her. "I don't need to know any more right now. I understand you have a lot to think about. I never thought I would ever get to this decision myself, but I have, and I don't regret it."

Chase stood up, walked to where she was sitting, and knelt down. He reached out, took her trembling hand and held it in his. "I think you know I'm the kind of man who would not make this decision lightly. You probably can't imagine what I went through before asking you to go away with me......to leave your home and family." Chase paused and squeezed her hand even more tightly. "Lorena, I wish there were a more original way to say how I feel, but there isn't.

I love you and want to wake up every morning with you for the rest of my life."

She leaned her head over and kissed him. She was scared to death of what she might say next. She had never felt such a powerful compulsion to throw caution and her entire career to the wind.

She turned her head and laid her cheek gently on top of his head, her words softly rolled off of her lips. "Chase, I want so much to be with you. I just have to finish this tour, and then we can be together. I hope you understand."

Chase raised his eyes up toward her face and could see a tear falling down her cheek.

"Does that mean yes?" he asked, as his eyes implored her.

"Yes, Chase.....it does."

They made love again; this time, any remnants remaining of their veiled emotions were fully exposed. They were more patient in their lovemaking, each unselfishly trying to satisfy the other's needs.

They spent the rest of the day walking through the old district of Mexico City, pausing every now and then to embrace and kiss. They were already starting to behave like newlyweds. Neither one of them could get enough of the other's affection. They talked about her tour, and she told Chase it would be over in three weeks. She hadn't figured out what she was going to tell Luis about her decision, but she knew he would take it very hard. Luis was already planning another major tour for the busy summer months.

Lorena explained to Chase that as much as she would like to have him accompany her on the rest of her tour, it would be just too much of a distraction. Even though she knew she had committed to joining her life with Chase's, she needed more time to make sure she wasn't sacrificing her career for marriage. She was sure Chase was the real thing, but she was never one to rush into anything.

Chase reluctantly agreed with her request. He didn't want to come between Lorena and her dancing. If he ever forced her to make that decision, he knew it could cause irreparable damage. She would have to come to her own decision about how she managed her career and her family life. He could only hope over time that she would want the same things in life as he did. He still couldn't believe he was thinking so far ahead. His life was so complicated, considering his ongoing role with the FBI. He didn't know if he would, or ever could, reveal to Lorena his double life. It was enough for her to consider marrying him and leaving her homeland. He wasn't about to drop that bombshell on her right now. He had successfully hidden his secret from everyone, including his family, and until he could figure out a diplomatic way of resigning from his work with the Bureau, he would have to keep it a secret. If he never had to tell her the truth, what harm would there be in deceiving her now? Chase didn't like his answer to his own question, but he was willing to accept it, given the present circumstances.

Lorena wasn't the only reason he was considering giving up his covert activities. This last episode with Wallace and the loss of Antonio had left him bitter and disillusioned. He knew that at some point in the not-too-distant future he would have to relinquish his position with the Bureau. Lorena was as good a reason as any other.

The day before leaving Ciudad Hidalgo in his search to find Lorena, Chase had asked Emiliano to find out the legal requirements to immigrate a Mexican national to the United States. Emiliano knew immediately that Chase's question was pertaining to Lorena Santoya. His first reaction to Chase's request was one of incredulity. What was Chase thinking after having spent only a few days with this woman? Yes, she was a beautiful, captivating woman, but he thought to himself, "*Chase, get a grip on yourself!*"

"Chase, are you sure about what you're doing?" Emiliano asked in total disbelief.

"Yeah, I know it's crazy, but I know she's the one."

"This could be complicated. Are you planning on having the ceremony here in Mexico?"

"No. I want her to be a U.S. citizen, and as I understand it, once you marry an American, you're automatically granted citizenship."

"Hold on Chase. It's not that simple. You have to prove that this is a serious marriage. Knowing someone for only a couple of days does not constitute serious intent," Emiliano charged, still not believing his normally rational friend. "They are going to question the hell out of your motives, especially given the high profile Lorena has in this country."

"Emiliano, I need you to pull out all the stops with your contacts. I don't care how much *mordita* you have to pay."

"Hell, Chase, you don't even know if she is going to say yes."

"Have you ever seen me fail an assignment yet?" he joked.

As he stood there holding Lorena's hand, Chase smiled, thinking back to that conversation with Emiliano two weeks ago. Staring at the magnificent cathedral in front of them, he was confident that all the problems confronting him and Lorena would all work out.

As they walked down the front steps of the cathedral, Lorena turned to Chase and lamented, "I never imagined in my wildest dreams it would be like this. Chase, I'm scared to leave. I've never lived anywhere but Mexico."

"You're not leaving here forever. We'll always have our home in Ciudad Hidalgo."

She looked up into his comforting eyes. "I need to know you'll always support me if I get crazy; if I need to come back home to live."

"Texas or Mexico? Where we raise our family is secondary."

"Family? Aren't you getting a little ahead of yourself?" Lorena queried, shocked by where the conversation was heading.

What if she didn't want children; would he still want to marry her? Would Chase love her regardless of her ability to have children? Every woman, in her heart, wanted to believe the answer to this question was an emphatic "yes". But how many times had she seen her friends betrayed by their husbands because they were unable to have a child.

Chase stopped Lorena, turned her toward him, and cautiously inquired, "You do want a family, don't you?"

She paused just long enough to concern Chase. He couldn't believe he hadn't asked the woman he intended to marry if she wanted to have children. The idea of having a family had never come up on his radar screen prior to meeting Lorena, but once he had made up his mind to get married, he definitely wanted children as a part of their lives together.

Finally, having recognized Chase was in anguish over her silence, Lorena responded.

"I was thinking of at least eight children. You know us Mexicans, we have very large families," she answered with a deadpan expression.

He was pleased to hear she wanted children, but eight seemed a few more than he had in mind. Maybe two or three, but not eight!

Lorena could see his mind spinning out of control. "See, you didn't know what you were getting yourself into, did you?" she said, twisting the blade of her stiletto wit a little deeper. "Relax. I'm not about to sit around the next ten years dropping babies out like a mother rabbit. Can we save this discussion for after we settle into our new lives? I'm sure when the time is right and we are both ready to start a family, we'll make the right decision."

"You're right. Speaking of family, what are your traditional parents going to think of you marrying some gringo?"

"I'm sure my mother will approve, but my father isn't going to be too happy that I'm marrying a rich Texan businessman who was born with a silver spoon in his mouth," she said with a sly smile.

Chase so badly wanted to tell Lorena that he was not a spoiled, rich Texan and to share with Lorena his background as a secret agent during Vietnam. Chase knew he could turn her hair white with the horror stories of the dangers he had faced as an agent for the FBI and as a war hero. As badly as he wanted to reveal his challenging past, he would have to save his stories for a later date—if ever.

"Texans *are not* born with silver spoons in their mouths; they're born on a silver saddle," Chase joked. "I've had plenty of tough times but I won't bore you with them right now. I'm sure over the next fifty years you'll get to hear every one of them more than once."

"I can't wait, but for now.... I think it's important for you to continue your dance lessons."

"Dance lessons?" He had a quizzical look on his face. He didn't pick up her hint at first. Lorena was referring to the first time they made love in the hot springs and how well they *"danced"* together.

The wires in his brain finally reconnected, and he blushed.

"I guess I could use a little more practice."

They started immediately back toward their bungalow. Chase had reserved the room for three days, but Lorena had to leave in two for the next stop on her tour. Both of them were reluctant to think about their impending separation. As hard as he tried not to think about her leaving, his mind wandered to the more serious issues concerning their future together. He was scheduled to return to Ciudad Hidalgo tomorrow to complete the arrangements for acquiring Lorena's U.S. immigration papers. They agreed on a fall wedding, which was six months from now, and which didn't leave him much time to work out all the arrangements. Chase knew Lorena would also need time to acclimate to her new life in Texas, so he wanted to look into the possibility of getting a temporary visa for her to visit his family's ranch outside of Pecos as soon as her tour was over.

Lorena noticed Chase's expression, as if he was off in another world.

"You're doing it again. I can hear those little wheels turning in your head," Lorena said somewhat seriously. "Was my blatant offer of wild sex not enough to keep you from getting distracted?"

"Sorry, it's a bad habit....and no, I'm not that distracted."

Their pace suddenly quickened in anticipation of stripping off their clothes and falling into the satin sheets of their bungalow hideaway. Just before they reached the Posada, they passed a newsstand and Lorena noticed the bold headlines in the local newspaper. She had forgotten all about last night and Diego Sanchez, but as she stared at the headlines she was pleasantly surprised. Instead of seeing her picture plastered over the front page with some salacious headline implying she was having an affair with Diego, there was an article about his feud with Lolo. Lolo had made accusations in his post-fight interview that the judges had clearly given Diego preferential treatment and that they had rated his performance more on reputation than skill.

Now this was news. It was exceptionally rare in the sophisticated sport of fencing for a fellow competitor to insult another competitor in public. Lolo had clearly stepped beyond the acceptable boundaries of this inner circle. Lorena knew from personal experience about Lolo' arrogance and how easily he could lose his temper but attacking Mexico's favorite son was even a surprise to her.

It was no secret that Lolo already had a bad reputation among colleagues and promoters; so he could ill afford any more bad feelings.

Lorena felt sorry for Diego, whom she sensed from their brief interaction was a man of honor and someone who would avoid controversy at all cost. She thought back to the night that Chase showed up in her dressing room unexpectedly. How she left without leaving even a note to explain her sudden disappearance. She could only imagine what he thought of her.

Lorena purchased a copy of the newspaper and tucked it under her arm. She was curious about the details of Lolo's accusations and wanted to see if in fact they had written anything about her performance. She hoped Lolo's behavior had saved her from the embarrassment of having to explain to Chase about her supposed relationship with Diego Sanchez.

Lorena was unaware that Diego had been backstage when Chase showed up, and how he had slipped out the stage door exit to avoid being caught in a compromising situation. After seeing Lorena and Chase in the dressing room, it was obvious to Diego what he had to do. He was keenly aware that if any speculative news leaked out about a potential affair between Lorena and him would jeopardize her relationship with her American lover. Even though Diego was disappointed, he was not about to let the press go wild with false rumors. It was clear from what little he had heard of their conversation that she cared a great deal about this stranger. As soon as Diego returned to his hotel room, he immediately called the chief editor of the largest newspaper in Mexico City.

As he sat waiting on hold for the Chief Editor to pick up, he rehearsed what he was going to say.

A gruff voice finally answered, "This is Carbajal Vargas. How can I help you, Señor Sanchez?"

"I want to talk to you about a possible story you might be running for the morning edition. It regards Señorita Lorena Santoya and I," Diego said, prepared to bribe the editor if necessary. He was willing to offer exclusive rights to the newspaper to assign a reporter to accompany him on the rest of his final tour of

Mexico. He knew there were several newspapers already vying for these rights.

"Yes, we were getting ready to print a story about you and Señorita Santoya, but something even more interesting just grabbed our attention."

Diego breathed a sigh of relief knowing the story about him and Lorena was off the front page.

"It seems as though you have enemies among your ranks," Vargas said in a gloating tone.

"What do you mean enemies?"

"One of my sports reporters was contacted by Lolo Nieto after the tournament. In fact, I'm very glad you called, because I was getting ready to assign a reporter to try to track you down. We thought it was only fair to get your side of the story regarding Señor Nieto's accusations."

"What accusations?"

"It seems that your colleague accuses you of receiving favoritism when it comes to tournament rankings. Señor Nieto said that although you fought well today, you did not deserve to be ranked so high at a national level. He implied that the Fencing Federation of Mexico put on their blinders due to your longstanding international reputation."

"Are there any other competitors who have contacted your newspaper making similar complaints?"

"No, on the contrary, they had the opposite opinion and when we contacted them, they were insulted by such accusations. They were very complimentary regarding your recent performances."

"At least someone's on my side."

"We'd like to get your side of the story. Of course, every paper in town will want it as their lead story."

Diego knew this was his opportunity to eliminate any story about him and Lorena permanently.

"If you agree to make no mention of Señorita Santoya in the paper then I'll give you exclusive rights to an interview with me regarding Señor Nieto's comments." Diego paused long enough for this to soak in and then continued, "but for the record, I want you to know Señorita Santoya and I have never personally met. Is that clear?"

"Yes, Señor Sanchez. When can I send a reporter over?"

"As soon as possible. I would like to put this matter to rest before it gets out of hand."

"Thanks for your cooperation."

"I have one other favor to ask you. If anyone inquires regarding my request to keep Señorita Santoya out of the newspaper, I would like you to deny it. I particularly would not want Señorita Santoya to know about our agreement. This matter, as far as I'm concerned, is between us. Agreed?"

"I understand completely."

Diego said good-bye and began thinking about his response to the reporter's possible questions. Usually he took the high ground regarding such stories and wouldn't comment to the press, but in this case, Lolo had exhausted his patience. He would not idly stand by and let Lolo get away with slandering his reputation. If Lolo wanted a battle outside of the court of honor, then he would be more than glad to accommodate him.

CHAPTER 10

Chase and Lorena parted company two days later in front of the hotel where she was meeting Luis. The emotional fabric between them had been tightly woven over the long hours of languishing in their bungalow; every thread, every new stitch of their relationship was reinforced by their commitment to each other. The *I*, had been transformed into *We*, as their separate lives folded into one future. The last two days together had given them an opportunity to stretch the boundaries of their relationship, a chance to know the man, to know the woman.

From the moment they woke up that morning, their apprehension about leaving each other was obvious. Lorena, in fact, had considered telling Luis she wanted to cancel the rest of the tour and run off with Chase to Texas. She knew this kind of self-serving act would not only be unfair to Luis, but would also cause her to regret the decision later. Lorena needed to prove to herself she wasn't giving up her identity to stand in the shadow of the man she loved. She could already feel the slicing curve of his silhouette starting to dim her sense of independence.

As for Chase, he was not relishing the return to his empty hacienda, especially knowing that Lorena would be out on the road entertaining droves of gawking men. He knew she considered her dancing an art form, but he had seen with his own eyes how men reacted to her sensuous moves. Chase was already jealous of their unwanted attention.

Watching Lorena wave farewell from the top of the hotel staircase as he departed for the train station tested the very limits of Chase's resolve to keep his promise to Lorena about letting her finish her tour without him. He wanted to turn around and convince her that he wouldn't be a distraction. He would do any menial task she asked of him—carry her luggage, fetch her hot coffee, whatever she wanted—just to be with her. The emotional chord that had so strongly linked them together was being severed and he hated being the victim of their forced separation.

Chase arrived in Ciudad Hidalgo after a brief stop in Morelia to give his personal condolences to Antonio's family. Meeting Antonio's wife and children brought back all the memories of watching Antonio die in his arms. He clearly remembered the warm, thick blood pulsing from Antonio's wound onto his hand and how helpless he felt. If he only had the power to turn back time, to forget this whole Wallace fiasco then maybe he could stop the unyielding guilt he felt for Antonio's family.

Looking across at the tearful eyes of Antonio's widow, Chase realized how fortunate he had been over his years to avoid serious injury or death. Never in the past had he questioned the motives of his profession, but now that his life had collided with this tragedy he could feel his deeply entrenched attitude shifting. He remembered being told early in his career by a senior agent that the moment you start to develop a conscience about losing a colleague in the field, it's time to call it quits. As cold as it sounded, Chase knew this was true. This lingering truth resonated even more strongly as he sat encircled by the anguish of Antonio's family.

By the time Chase was back on the road to Ciudad Hidalgo, he had pretty much made up his mind to conclude his operations with the FBI. He had only nine months left on his contract, and he was praying that nothing would come up requiring his services. He was finished; it was time to move on.

When Chase arrived in Ciudad Hidalgo, Fernando informed Chase that his father had left him an urgent message to return to Pecos as soon as possible. Chase immediately called his father, knowing something serious had happened. As he suspected, it was bad news. His Uncle Chas, the man Chase he had been named after, and his favorite uncle, had suddenly passed away. The funeral was in two days.

Chase's father, Wes, was not a man who procrastinated; he had already arranged to have his private plane flown to Mexico City to pick up his son. Chase immediately made arrangements for a driver to take him to the airport the next morning. Making sure not to repeat his earlier problems about suddenly disappearing without letting Lorena know what was happening, he left detailed instructions with Fernando to contact him immediately if she called or left any messages. He told Fernando he should be back in a week from Tuesday, which was the day he and Lorena had agreed to rendezvous at her family home outside of Ciudad Hidalgo.

Chase called Emiliano and made an appointment to meet with him in a couple of hours. He wanted to see if there was any fallout from the Wallace case and what progress Emiliano had made on greasing the skids for Lorena's immigration to the U.S.

Emiliano arrived promptly at seven. He was secretly hoping Chase had been unsuccessful in convincing Lorena to marry him, but as soon as he saw the glowing expression on his friend's face, he knew everything was about to change. There would be no more late night rendezvous or clandestine missions to hunt down the bad guys. *It was over.*

Chase had hinted before he went off to find Lorena that he was questioning whether he was still cut out for this line of business. Emiliano could sympathize with Chase's mindset, he wasn't feeling so excited about going out on another mission after this last fiasco. Emiliano had seen the mournful look in the eyes of Antonio's wife when he paid his respects to the family last week. He tried to imagine how his own wife would react to being told her husband had been killed in action. Emiliano's wife thought he worked for Chase's railroad company as a security consultant. He was positive his unforgiving wife would haunt him for the rest of his life if anything serious ever happened to him. All this thinking about future missions might be a moot point once Chase heard about the fallout from the Wallace episode. They both might need to high-tail it out of Mexico to escape Lorca's obsession for revenge.

Chase sat down across from Emiliano. Right away he shared his marriage proposal to Lorena. He was glad to announce she had accepted.

"Well, you're finally joining the ranks of the poor married souls. I would have been willing to bet my first child I would never live to see this day. Congratulations, my friend." Emiliano reached over and affectionately shook Chase's hand.

"Thank you, but I'm still on pins and needles that she might wake up one morning and have second thoughts."

"You're too good a catch to let go. She's a lucky woman."

"Speaking of Lorena, what have you found out about her immigration status?"

Emiliano was making good progress with the authorities and had confidence that everything would work out. He explained about all the paperwork they needed to file with the Immigrations Office. It was expected to take a couple of months before final approval was received. Chase thanked Emiliano for all his hard work.

"What about a temporary visa? We are planning a trip north as soon as her tour is over."

"I've already spoken with Immigration and it should be no problem." Emiliano handed Chase a short stack of papers. "You will need to have her fill these out and return them to the Immigration Office. Make sure you ask for Ignacio Vega. He owes me a couple of favors, and he'll make sure everything goes smoothly."

"Thanks. What about Wallace? Any fallout?"

"I wish I had equally as good news to report." Emiliano's expression suddenly turned dark.

"That bad?"

"It seems the guard Antonio rapped on the head didn't make it. From what little I could find out, he went into a coma and died two days later."

Chase shrugged his shoulders, almost making light of Emiliano's solemn admission. "If you're looking for sympathy, you won't get any from me."

"If you remember, Antonio told us one of the guards was the brother of a major drug lord, Fermin Lorca. He has a reputation for being a very bad dude. He once cut out the tongue of a man who cursed his mother's name. Lorca is not likely to let his brother's death go down without wanting serious revenge."

"Are you saying our cover was blown?"

"No. I haven't heard any rumors to that affect, but word on the street is that he has offered a handsome reward for any information regarding the men who killed his brother. Keep in mind; it's not only his brother he is pissed off about. We embarrassed him by taking Wallace right out from underneath his nose. This guy is going to be merciless in trying to hunt us down."

"In other words, he has a reputation to uphold. Well, tough shit! He's not the only one who is looking for revenge."

Memories of Antonio's ashen, pained face surfaced from the back of Chase's brain. Emiliano cringed at Chase's reaction. He wasn't interested in getting into a blood war with someone like Fermin Lorca. He hadn't been completely truthful with Chase regarding their cover not being blown. The morning before their raid on the compound, one of Lorca's men had spied Chase outside the Café Pato and put two and two together. Until Emiliano could confirm this information, there was no reason to get an already incensed Chase even more worked up.

"I feel the same way as you about Antonio, but this would be good time to keep a low profile. You know how money can ferret out even the most secret operations. Remember, you're in Mexico, not the good old U.S. of A. It's probably fortunate you're going back to Texas. In fact, you might consider extending your trip for a couple of months."

Chase immediately responded to Emiliano's suggestion, his face flushing with anger. "You can forget that idea! I'm not about to run scared from Lorca. Lorena is finishing her tour in a couple of weeks, and I plan on being here when she returns." Chase realized his voice was a couple decibels higher than normal. He wanted to make sure Emiliano understood he wasn't backing down from Lorca's threat.

"It's your call, but I'm taking my family to the coast for a couple of weeks while the dust settles. I've had enough excitement for a little while. I'll let you know if anything comes up regarding Lorca."

Chase understood Emiliano was trying to protect him, but he'd be damned if a second-rate drug trafficker was going to have him chasing his own shadow all over Mexico. He almost preferred that Lorca make some kind of play, so he could put this part of his life behind him.

Chase could sense that Emiliano wanted to continue discussing the problem of Lorca, but he was tiring of the conversation. They exchanged handshakes', and Emiliano told Chase he would give him a call if anything dramatic changed regarding Fermin Lorca.

CHAPTER 11

It had been less than a week since their first confrontation in the tournament in Mexico City, and Lolo was still fuming about Diego Sanchez. He was sitting in the office with his manager, Manuel Carbajal, discussing his upcoming schedule. Lolo was arguing with Carbajal about not wanting to be on the same program as Diego.

"Lolo, you can't avoid him forever. We've already passed up a couple of major tournaments," Carbajal insisted.

"Why not? You never know, maybe he might get injured or something..... and I won't have to worry about him anymore," Lolo said bitterly.

"Look....I'm not going to sit here and listen to this. Sanchez isn't my favorite person in the world right now, but I wouldn't wish that on anyone."

Carbajal could tolerate a lot from his brilliant client, but not his jealous insults aimed at Diego Sanchez. Carbajal realized Diego was hurting Lolo's career, but having followed the sport his entire life, he had to respect Diego's talent and longevity in the sport. He knew there were other ways to cut the great master down to size.

"Sorry, I'm just frustrated. Everywhere I go, everyone is talking about *him*."

"Relax, he is only going to be around for another year, and then you will have all the glory to yourself."

"A year! I could be a forgotten man by then. I was so close to the top of the rankings." There was a genuine aching in Lolo's voice.

"That's why you have to confront him directly. If the newspapers or fans even start to suspect you're avoiding him, we're finished."

"All right, but can't we do something about influencing the Federation officials? A little cash in the right hands never hurts."

"What are you suggesting?" Carbajal wasn't about to be a part of any payoff scheme, but he was curious about how deep Lolo's resentment ran.

"Look, it wouldn't be the first time officials padded their wallets in favor of improving someone's ranking. Why not use our resources in a more productive way?" Lolo squirmed in his seat.

"Let's drop this whole subject. Whatever you think it is worth, you're wrong. Understood?" Carbajal could feel the hair rising on the back of his neck.

"OK, but I can't just idly sit back and watch everything I've worked for be wiped out."

"Calm down. I have a plan. Part of Señor Sanchez's attraction to the public is his unblemished record as a man of honor. What if we had something that could knock him off his high and mighty pedestal?"

"What are you talking about?" Lolo's eyes sparkled with anticipation.

"I was approached a few days ago by a certain party who has damaging information about Señor Sanchez."

"What did he do....take a payoff or something?"

"Not exactly, but almost as repulsive to the public."

"Are you going to keep me in suspense all day?" Lolo was losing his patience with his manager's cat and mouse game.

"Well.... it seems in his younger days, he had an affair with a young woman."

"That's not exactly a criminal offense. In fact, in some cases, it can enhance a man's reputation with fans." Lolo cracked a smile at his cruel joke. Lolo was all too familiar with this kind of treatment of women. He used them up like a flu-stricken man tossing Kleenex in a waste paper basket.

"Be patient, my young friend. She got pregnant, and he left her to raise the poor bastard child herself. As told to me, Diego's family paid off the girl's family and shipped him off to France to avoid any chance of compromising his career. Can you imagine if the press somehow got hold of the story?"

"I see your point." Lolo's eyes narrowed. He knew if there is one thing the public wouldn't tolerate was a man refusing to accept his responsibilities for his patriarchal offspring.

"The press will go nuts over this. Sanchez is admired for being a man of honor. What do you think would happen if this nasty affair was exposed to all his loving fans?"

"Can we trust the source of the information?"

"We'll see. Our source for the information is sitting right outside of my office. His name is Pepe Robles. He has been the night watchman at the Plaza Quitzal for the last thirty years. He says he has intimate knowledge of the events surrounding Diego's affair."

Pepe Robles sat in the outer office, nervously waiting to be called into Manuel Carbajal's office. The night watchman had heard rumors about Lolo and his disdain for Diego Sanchez over the past few months. He knew he had valuable information and just maybe Carbajal would be willing to pay for it. Pepe would never have thought of betraying Diego, but he desperately needed the money to pay off his ever-growing gambling debt. He had lost his entire savings over the past few years and he had to come up with some quick cash or he would have to face the wrath of his notoriously merciless bookie. At the age of sixty-five, he only had a few more years before retirement and this kind of money could go a long way in securing his future. Pepe had already been visited by a couple of his bookie's goons who made it clear that if he didn't pay up by the end of the month, their next meeting wouldn't be so pleasurable. He tried to borrow money from his friends, but they had heard his sad stories too many times in the past. In desperation, Pepe contacted Diego's father, Don Julio Sanchez, who had helped him get the job at the Plaza Quitzal. Pepe figured Don Julio owed him a twenty year-old favor from for informing him about Diego's affair with Celaya. Pepe had never asked for any compensation regarding the matter, so he was sure Don Julio would help him out of his current financial mess.

Unfortunately for Pepe, Don Julio had heard about his gambling problems, and when Pepe begged him for a short-term loan, Don Julio refused. Pepe was infuriated by Don Julio's unsympathetic reaction. His anger festered, and he started to panic about what would happen to him if he didn't come up with the money. A few days before while finishing up his rounds at the Plaza Quitzal he overheard a conversation between Manuel Carbajal and a promoter. Carbajal was sharing his concerns about Lolo's career and the negative impact Diego Sanchez was having on it. Pepe seized the opportunity and approached Lolo's manager about selling him the information about Diego's affair with Celaya.

At first, Carbajal seemed uninterested in the night watchman's offer, but this latest episode where Lolo publicly insulted Diego had seriously backfired and they needed to counter the effects of Diego's damaging rebuttal in the newspapers.

The door to Carbajal's office opened and Carbajal waved Pepe in. "Please come in, Pepe," Carbajal squeaked in a friendly tone. "Of course, you know Señor Nieto."

Lolo stood up to greet the unkempt night watchman. He hesitated to shake hands with Pepe, afraid he might contract some communicable disease.

Pepe removed his tattered straw hat. "No, we've never met in person, but I'm a great admirer," Pepe said, nervously attempting to crack a smile.

"Please have a seat. Can I offer you any refreshment?"

"No, thank you." Pepe poured himself into a chair directly in front of Carbajal's desk.

Lolo turned to Pepe, not hesitating to get to the point. "So you have some information regarding Diego Sanchez. How can we trust that your information is reliable?"

Pepe nervously adjusted himself in the chair and answered.

"I'm not the only one who can confirm my story. Señor Alvarez, Diego's former maestro, is also aware of the situation."

Lolo wanted desperately to know all the dirt on Diego's illicit affair but he was more interested in Alvarez's role. "Are we talking about the same Señor Alvarez, one of the most respected teachers in the history of our sport? Are you saying he was aware of Sanchez's affair?"

"Yes. Not only was he aware of the affair, but he was instrumental in getting Diego out of the country and over to France."

"What good is the testimony of a dead man? I heard...."

Carbajal interrupted Lolo. "I also assumed the great maestro had died a few years ago, but he's alive and living in a sanitarium outside of Mexico City. He's ninety-four years old and in very ill health. They say he is not long for this world."

"Let's presume for a moment we can confirm your story with Alvarez. What kind of compensation are you expecting for this information?" Lolo caustically queried.

"Five thousand pesos," Pepe demanded, avoiding direct eye contact with Lolo.

"That's ridiculous!" Lolo barked, glancing over at his manager in disbelief.

"Hold on, Lolo. If in fact we can confirm his story, it would be well worth the asking price. Unless you have a better idea, I say we accept Señor Robles's offer." Carbajal was asserting himself, being much more familiar with the serious problems Lolo had recently caused with the press. Besides, some of the major promoters were starting to back off from selecting Lolo for exhibitions.

"All right, but you'd better not try to pull a fast one." Lolo glared at Pepe, leaving no doubt of his distrust.

"I've already made arrangements to visit Señor Alvarez at the end of the week to confirm Pepe's story," Carbajal offered.

The three men discussed the final details of the deal. When they were all satisfied, Pepe excused himself, having had enough of sitting on the hot seat. He felt torn betraying Diego, but he convinced himself that he had no alternative. Besides, after Don Julio Sanchez had treated him so callously, what obligation did he have to protect Diego's reputation?

Manuel Carbajal arrived at the Nuevo Vivo sanitarium early Friday morning. The nursing staff had informed him that this was the time Señor Alvarez was the most likely to be coherent enough to have a conversation. Typically, by afternoon he was exhausted and spent the rest of the day in a semi-comatose state. The old maestro was dying of lung cancer, and they expected him to live for only a few more weeks.

Carbajal had been wracking his brain for the last couple of days trying to come up with a plan for obtaining the information he needed from the old maestro. He finally had decided to pose as none other than the renowned swordsman himself, Diego Sanchez. Carbajal knew he was about the same age and stature as Diego. Lolo's manager could only hope the dying maestro's eyesight was failing along with his health. If he was going to have any chance of getting Alvarez to share what he knew about Pepe's alleged story, his disguise had better work. He was also banking on the fact that Alvarez had not seen his protégé in over twenty years. It was a risky plan, but at this point he had nothing to lose.

A heavy-set nurse dressed in scrub whites escorted Carbajal to Alvarez's private room. He watched as the overweight nurse waddled down the perfectly waxed floors, knowing his moment of truth was only a few steps away.

"You realize Señor Alvarez has terrible bouts of delirium, and he is only conscious for short periods of time."

"Yes, I understand."

This news was like sweet music to his ears. He needed every advantage he could muster in pulling off his disguise.

As they entered the sunlit room, the nurse called out to the wasted human figure that used to be one of Mexico's proudest maestros. "Señor Alvarez, you have a guest. It is Señor Diego Sanchez, your former student."

At first, the frail figure lying in bed did not respond. His shrunken, pale face looked void of any awareness that they had entered the room. There was only a slight flicker of light emanating from his glazed-over eyes. A thin, gooey stream of phlegm dripped from the corner of his parched lips.

Carbajal wondered for a moment if he had arrived too late. Carbajal moved closer to the bed, leaned over and spoke directly in the old man's ear.

"Maestro, it's me, Diego Sanchez."

Alvarez struggled to crease his lips, attempting to form Diego's name.

Carbajal knew this was it. There was no turning back now.

"My son, you...you have...returned to me," The decrepit maestro whispered, struggling to peel the words from his dry cracked lips.

Carbajal pulled up a chair next to the bed and took hold of Alvarez's hand. It was cool to the touch, and his skin was translucent, revealing a network of broken, purple veins that poured out into pools of ugly bruises.

"I've come here to ask a favor, Maestro. It is very important to me."

"How...can...I help you?" His breathing was labored. He stared up at the empty ceiling as if something compelling was drawing his attention away from the matter at hand.

Carbajal asked his next question as deliberately as he could. "Do you know what happened to the young lady I was in love with before I left for France?"

"You mean...Celaya.........Flores?" Every word seemed to have a rounded edge to it, as they bubbled out of his cancer-ravaged voice box.

The name struck Carbajal like a lightning bolt. He couldn't believe what he was hearing. It couldn't be true..... Celaya Flores! Could it be just a bizarre circumstance that the maiden name of Lolo's mother's was Flores? What were the chances that Diego Sanchez was Lolo Nieto's *father*?

Carbajal was aware of Lolo's family history and that his mother had died shortly after giving birth to him. He also knew from what little Lolo had told him about his mother's tragic death that she had never revealed the name of her lover to anyone. Lolo had taken on the name of his maternal grandfather, Lolo Nieto, to avoid the stigma of being a bastard child. His real name was Amado Flores.

Carbajal's mind was reeling as he quickly tried to do the math. He knew Diego was about the right age to have been Lolo's father, and it jelled with everything Pepe Robles had relayed to him in his office.

"Yes, Celaya Flores. Do you know where she is now?" Carbajal asked, bursting at the seams and struggling to contain his excitement. He had to confirm whether it was the same Celaya Flores.

Alvarez closed his eyes as tears welled up. He lay there motionless, as though he had fallen into a mindless stupor. Several seconds passed, and then the old man spoke as if he had never left the conversation.

"She died...in childbirth...bearing your son," Alvarez whispered, almost choking on the sorrowful words. "I'm....so....sorry, Diego." He gripped Carbajal's hand as if begging for forgiveness.

Alvarez seemed to have been given a sudden burst of energy as he expelled his next words. "I've lived with this secret....for too many years." He paused, struggling to get his words out. "I'm not proud of what I did—but I did it....I did it for you, Diego. All....for you." He made a feeble attempt to reach up and touch Carbajal's face.

"I forgive you, Maestro. Does anyone else know about this?"

"Only Pepe Robles... and...your father." He closed his eyes again and faded into unconsciousness.

Carbajal released his hand from the Señor Alvarez's grip. He had what he came here for. Carbajal shook his head in disbelief. He was so dumbfounded by what he had just found out that he had no idea what he would do with this startling news. If he revealed his secret to Lolo, it could set him into a violent rage. Carbajal had heard Lolo on several occasions vent his disdain for the man who had abandoned his mother. He could ill afford losing all the investment he had put into Lolo because of the muddled ramblings of a senile old man on his deathbed. Until he could positively verify Alvarez's account, he would have to keep it his little secret. Carbajal was sure of only one thing: the deal with Pepe Robles was off the table.

He couldn't imagine what kind of flash fire it would cause if anyone discovered such a bizarre story. He was confident the information he had just acquired could ultimately damage Diego Sanchez's reputation, but it would be a hell of a lot more destructive to Lolo. He had visions of Lolo spinning out of control and doing something that could permanently damage or even end his career. No, this secret would have to remain locked up in the mind of Señor Alvarez as it had for the last twenty years.

Carbajal met with Lolo in his office a day after his visit with Señor Alvarez.

"So, the night watchman was lying," Lolo coldly stated, having heard Carbajal's recounting of his meeting with the dying man.

"Not completely. Diego did in fact have an affair, but it never led to anything as preposterous as Pepe's story. I guess he thought he could just make up the rest and we would buy it."

Carbajal paused long enough to make sure Lolo was convinced of his story. "You know how some people will try to take advantage of any situation."

"We can't use any part of Pepe's story?" Lolo's disappointment was clearly registered on his face.

"I'm afraid not. We can't take any chances after this last problem we had with the press."

"Where do we go from here?"

"I've already started to work on damage control with the newspapers. All you have to do is continue to perform brilliantly." Carbajal knew this was a decoy strategy to get Lolo back on track and off Diego's trail.

"I still can't believe that slimy little night watchman thought he could pull the wool over our eyes," Lolo said, as he stood up to leave.

"You let me deal with him. You just do your job and in time, everything will work out."

The two men shook hands and Lolo left the office.

Carbajal didn't tell Lolo that he had already made arrangements with Pepe Robles to keep his mouth shut. He paid Pepe his five thousand pesos and made him promise never to share their arrangement with anyone, not even Lolo. Carbajal lied to Pepe and told him that Alvarez was totally incoherent and unable to corroborate his story.

Given his precarious financial circumstances, Pepe had no choice but to accept Carbajal's offer. Carbajal made it clear to Pepe that if he backed out on the deal at any time, he would make sure Pepe was fired from his job at the Plaza. Carbajal was confident he had covered all the bases. As he sat alone in his office, pondering how this bizarre scenario would play itself out, he momentarily felt a sense of guilt about not telling Lolo the truth. Carbajal was even more curious what Diego would do if he found out that his biggest antagonist in the sport was actually his own son.

Strange bedfellows indeed, Carbajal thought, as he picked up the phone to call his bank and make the payoff arrangements for Pepe Robles.

CHAPTER 12

Chase stood on the runway in Mexico City waiting for Dutch Evans to finish his preflight checklist. Dutch had worked for the family since the end of World War II. As Dutch lumbered around his Twin Engine Cessna UC-78, banging on the engine compartment, checking the torque of the propeller, and testing the ailerons for the appropriate tension, he whistled the "Yellow Rose of Texas" over and over. The four-seat aircraft was the same model as the TV show hero *Sky King* had flown into fame. The plane's fabric-covered wings and fuselage made it look flimsy to an already skittish Chase.

Dutch had picked up the plane in a war surplus sale. Its reliability was well known, and it was a gem to fly for experienced pilots like Dutch. It had one special feature even Chase would appreciate. The small Cessna had retractable wheels that never completely retracted. Just in case there was malfunction and belly landing was required, the plane could set down on the landing strip and leave thirty inches between the passengers and the ground. Dutch, knowing Chase's dread of flying, decided not to share this tidbit with his uneasy passenger.

Chase was anxious to get going but was not about to disturb Dutch during his pre-flight check. He trusted Dutch, who was the same pilot who had safely ditched the plane in a rancher's field when Chase was sure they were goners. They were on their way to San Antonio when they had a mechanical failure, causing the plane to lose total power. To this day, Chase still couldn't believe how Dutch was able to glide the plane in for a safe landing among the scattered cattle and dead oak trees.

Dutch knew Chase had a strong aversion to flying, so he always put on the appearance of being serious when he went through his pre-flight checklist. When Dutch was in rare form, he would shake his head and feign disgust, as if something was seriously wrong with the plane, all the time watching Chase rock back and forth in an attempt to control his anxiety.

When Dutch was satisfied that he had put on a good show, he motioned for Chase to climb into the cockpit and get ready for take-off. Once Chase was strapped into the co-pilot's seat, Dutch turned and calmly asked, "Are we feeling lucky today?"

Chase craned his head in Dutch's direction. "What do you mean by that?"

"Well, today is Friday the thirteenth. I don't know about you, but I'm a little superstitious," Dutch offered, in his slow, deliberate southern drawl.

"Could we just get the hell out of here?" Chase didn't want to hear anymore about Dutch's superstitious ideas.

"No problem, but if something does go haywire, you've got a parachute right behind your seat."

Dutch looked over at a perspiring Chase. He could hardly stop from breaking out in laughter as he watched Chase sneak a reach behind his seat to make sure his chute was readily accessible.

After they reached cruising altitude, Chase was finally able to relax enough to broach the subject of Lorena and his future plans. Chase wasn't planning on revealing his engagement to Lorena his parents, given the somber nature of this trip home, but he knew Dutch would have a good feel for how they would react when he did tell them. Chase wasn't worried about his mother's reaction. He knew she would be ecstatic that he was finally settling down. He could already hear her trying to influence him and Lorena on when they should start a family. She had been waiting years for a chance to become a proud grandmother.

It was his father who was making Chase nervous as hell about going home. Wes Chandler never got too excited about anything, and the fact that his only son was getting married probably wouldn't get much of a rise out of him, until he found out that Lorena was Mexican. Then, all hell might break lose. The senior Chandler had a traditional Texan attitude concerning his southern neighbors, and it wasn't always positive. His father was still fond of blurting out the fight slogan from the Battle of the Alamo. He saw Mexicans simply as a valuable resource for picking cotton or doing other menial jobs no one else wanted. The only exception to his opinion was the high regard he held for the *caballeros* that he sometimes hired for his annual cattle roundups.

Chase could recall on several occasions hearing his father refer to Mexicans as hard working people, but when it really came down to it, they were just ignorant wetbacks. Chase knew differently, having seen their work ethic in action. He had argued with his father about his bigoted opinion more than once over the years. How was Chase going to explain to his father that his future grandchildren were all going to be half wetback? It was a looming confrontation he was not looking forward to. He could only hope once his father had a chance to get to know Lorena, he would appreciate her as a woman of grace and sharp intelligence.

Chase glanced over at Dutch, still not sure about revealing his secret. The man sitting next to him knew his father better than anyone, so who better to confide in? Chase decided it was safer to start with some small talk.

"Dutch, how long have you been flying this old crate?"

Dutch knew right away Chase was up to something. "You know damn well how long I've been flying it. What's on your mind, son?"

"I need a blood oath that you won't share anything I'm going to tell you with my parents."

"Jesus, this must be serious."

"Do I have your word?" Chase asked tentatively.

"Yeah, kid. Fire away." Dutch couldn't wait to hear what his godson was so all-fired up about.

"Well, I met this young lady in Mexico."

Dutch looked over at Chase. He could not recall having ever seen Chase's cheeks so red. "Holy shit, you're in love," Dutch accused, as he smirked in muted laughter.

"I didn't say anything about being in love."

"You didn't have to. It's written all over your face."

"OK, so I'm in love. There is a little problem.....she's Mexican."

"Why is that a problem? You have something against Mexicans?" Dutch laughed out loud, shaking his head from side to side. He knew Chase went out of his way to stand up for Mexicans, particularly when it involved his father.

"You damn well know I don't have anything against Mexicans. It's my father I'm worried about. They aren't exactly high on his list of favorite people."

"Sure, your old man is likely to raise some hell at first, but your father is more talk than walk. Do you remember a couple of years ago when that Mexican migrant farmer's truck broke down not far from the ranch?"

"Vaguely, what about it?"

"Well, your father paid to have the damn thing fixed. He had to replace the entire engine. On top of that, your old man made sure they had plenty of pocket money. Of course, he didn't say a word to anybody about what he did. He isn't as hard-assed as you think he is about our friends south of the border."

Suddenly, Chase felt a tremendous weight lift off of his shoulders. Hearing Dutch's story opened the door for the possibility that his father might welcome Lorena into their family. He certainly hoped so because he had not yet told her about his father's attitude about bringing a Mexican into their traditional Texan family.

"I hope you're right, because we plan to marry in the fall, and I would like to have the reception at the ranch."

"Just curious, how did you meet this new love of your life?"

"I was at one of her performances."

"Oh, please don't tell me she's a stripper or something."

"Of course not!" Chase shot back. "Lorena is one of Mexico's most respected flamenco dancers. She is currently on a national tour. Not only is she well-educated and drop-dead beautiful, but she also has spunk. She has a great deal of pride in her heritage and family. I can promise you she won't back down from any confrontation—even if it is from a tough old wrangler like my father."

"Sounds like you found yourself a jewel. Congratulations."

"Thanks, and I guess I'll just have to trust your opinion about my father."

"Just give him some time to get used to the idea. I'm sure he'll come around." Dutch was trying to reassure Chase, but he knew Wes was probably going to throw a shit-fit when he heard the news. Wes and he had talked for hours about all the hopes he had for Chase. Dutch was positive they didn't include some fancy Mexican tap dancer.

The rest of their flight was uneventful and they arrived in the late afternoon at the ranch. Chase again reminded Dutch of his promise before departing the aircraft.

Wes greeted them at the flight hanger, "Smooth flight, I hope."

"Just fine," Dutch responded, as he winked, hinting they would have to get together later to share a laugh or two. "I'm going to put this old jalopy to bed. You two need to catch up with each other anyway."

Chase turned to Dutch and thanked him for the ride.

"See you on Sunday, Dutch," Wes said, referring to his older brother's upcoming funeral service.

Wes turned to his son and said, "Sorry you had to rush home under these circumstances son, but I know how close you were to your Uncle Chas." Wes reached out and gave his son a warm embrace.

His father's affection surprised Chase. Wes was from the old school; men very seldom displayed any kind of affection toward other men—even a son.

"How are you holding up?" Chase asked.

"I'm doing fine, but your mother has been bawling her eyes out for two days."

"Not surprising. She always felt sorry for Uncle Chas for having to live his entire life as a lonely bachelor."

"Lonely, hell! He had more women in and out of his place than the revolving door of a department store during a women's shoe sale."

"I guess you're right, but I'm sure he regretted not having someone there during the last days of his illness. Did he go peacefully?"

Wes picked up his son's bag as they started walking toward an old army jeep. "The last thing he said to me was, 'Could you get me a cigarette and a shot of Jack Daniels?' Chas was never one to go quietly," his father recalled, as he shook his head with a sad smile.

"Sounds just like Uncle Chas."

"Well, I wasn't about to deny a dying man his last wish, so I headed to the kitchen and was on my way back when I heard a deep wheeze coming from the bedroom; and before I got back, he was gone."

Chase could see his father's eyes beginning to well up with tears.

"Sorry, I couldn't be here."

Wes continued as if he hadn't heard Chase's last remark. "There I stood, with a lit cigarette in one hand and his shot of Jack in the other. I downed the Jack, figuring your uncle wouldn't want it to go to waste." A crooked grin slipped onto his craggy-tan face.

"Is there anything I can help with?"

Wes threw Chase's bag into the Jeep and jumped into the driver's side seat. "Yeah, there is. You know I'm no good at speeches, so I would really appreciate it if you would give the eulogy. You were his favorite....so it only seems appropriate."

"Of course. What time is the service?"

"High noon. He made me promise not to make a big fuss, but once word got out it was hard to turn away all his friends."

"Well....he had plenty of them, didn't he?"

Uncle Chas had a reputation for being unselfish with his money. He had made a couple of million from oil wells discovered on his ranch. Chas figured he couldn't take it all with him, so he squandered it showing his friends a good time. Unfortunately, he lived too long on the edge, and it cost him his life. He smoked three packs of Lucky Strikes a day and ended up with lung cancer. The doctors and the family tried to talk him into a treatment program, but he wouldn't hear of it. He told Chase six months ago, if that's what God intended for him on this earth, then he was damn well going to accept his destiny.

Chase did everything he could to try to change his mind, but Uncle Chas persisted. It was the only time in Chase's life that he could recall crying in front of another man.

"I just hope all his ex-lovers behave themselves," Wes said, with a hint of skepticism.

"I'm sure they'll mind their P's and Q's. After all, it's his funeral."

They both laughed, knowing that the kind of woman Chas hung out with didn't always follow the rule of proper decorum.

As they approached the main road to the ranch house, Chase was able to spot the outline of the large, two-story home built in the 1890's by his great-grandfather, Harlow Chandler. The somewhat garish house reflected his great-grandfather's brash, Lone Star attitude. Harlow was not about to let anyone in the county have a fancier home than the Chandler family. After all, they had the Chandler tradition to hold up.

Chase's mother, Rebecca, referred to the house as the "Gray Ghost," due to the fact the white paint had faded to a dingy gray after years of fighting off the brutal winds of west Texas. Rebecca wanted to build a smaller, less ostentatious house when they got married, but her husband would not hear of it. Wes was born in this house, and he damn well planned on dying there.

Rebecca Chandler stood anxiously awaiting her son's arrival, while the Jeep made its way up the driveway. She was waving a white handkerchief as if surrendering to the approaching Union army.

Chase prepared himself for a tearful reunion, even though he had been gone for less than two months. He jumped out of the Jeep and slapped the ever-invasive dust off his clothes, then started up the brick walkway. He could already see his mother's arms spread open, waiting for a bear hug.

Rebecca was decked out in her best white cotton dress, and it was obvious she had been to her hairdresser earlier that day. Her appearance seemed more appropriate for attending a church rather than simply greeting her son.

"That's my mother, in all her splendor," Chase mused.

"Chase, my darling boy," she called out to him, with a slight hint of a cozy Georgia accent. The tears were already glistening in her eyes.

Chase stepped into her open arms and lifted her diminutive body off the ground. "Hello, Mother. You look as ravishing as ever," Chase offered as he unlocked himself from his mother's embrace.

"Chase, you're such a tease. I'm so glad to see you." She was dabbing her watery eyes with a white silk hankie.

"It's good to be home. Sorry about Uncle Chas. I know you were very close to him."

"It's a sad day, son, a sad day," she whimpered, as she wiped her eyes again. Rebecca locked her arm around his and escorted Chase onto the wraparound front porch.

They sat down next to each other in high-back caned rocking chairs. His mother poured a glass of ice-cold fresh lemonade and handed it to Chase.

"I thought you said you would only be gone a couple of weeks, not of a couple of months."

Chase made up some business-related reasons for his longer than expected absence, knowing full well he couldn't reveal the real reason for his extended stay—meeting the woman he intended to marry. Wes joined them, and they spent the next couple of hours reminiscing about Uncle Chas. They had a good laugh, sharing stories about Uncle Chas's sordid adventures chasing the opposite sex.

Mother, which is how Rebecca Chandler preferred to be called by both her husband, son and just about everyone else in the family, chuckled as she recalled the time Uncle Chas decided to run off with a neighbor's wife. He literally got caught with his pants down by the angry husband, who was wielding a shotgun and taking dead aim at Uncle Chas. He barely escaped before the first round ripped a gaping hole in the screen door.

"So there was Uncle Chas, running down the streets of Pecos with only his skivvies on and the enraged husband in hot pursuit. Thank the good Lord he was a terrible shot or we might have buried your uncle years ago." Mother shook her head in disbelief, wondering how her womanizing brother-in-law had survived as long as he had.

"How'd he finally get away?" Chase inquired.

"Your uncle wasn't any dummy. He ran straight to the police station and made a beeline into the office of the Chief of Police, Hank Stone, who was an old high school buddy."

Wes piped in, "But Hank was tired of your uncle's antics and called a newspaper reporter to come down to his office right away. Ole' Hank made sure Chas was photographed in all his half-naked glory. The next day his picture appeared on the front page with a caption that read, 'Town Streaker Interrogated by Chief of Police.'"

"You would have thought he would clean up his act after such an embarrassing episode, but no, he continued on with his foolish ways till his dying day." Rebecca said, smiling as if Uncle Chas was sitting right across from her.

Just before they were summoned to the dinner table, Wes informed his son that there was going be a reading of his brother's will on Sunday evening after the memorial service, and Chase should plan on attending.

His uncle's estate included fifteen thousand acres of rich grazing land just west of Pecos. Uncle Chas seldom spent much time there. He preferred the rowdy streets of Pecos to the quiet solitude of his ranch.

Chase told his parents he was planning to stay only through the weekend since he needed to conclude some important business in Mexico. He hated lying to his parents, knowing that the real reason for leaving so soon was to get back to Lorena, but he wanted to avoid a major confrontation.

The service for Uncle Chas came off without a hitch. Chase's eulogy was heartfelt and honest. He didn't try to disguise his uncle's shortcomings, which were common knowledge to everyone in the territory. Instead, he chose to share a couple of endearing stories interlaced with plenty of humor, which garnered quite a few laughs from the melancholic crowd. He was confident his uncle would have preferred the boisterous laughter to tears.

Following the memorial service, family and friends gathered at the Chandler ranch for a Texas-style barbecue with racks of ribs, plenty of Lone Star beer, and a fair share of hyperbole regarding his uncle's exploits. Chase was sure his uncle was laughing from his grave from all the ridiculous attention he was receiving. As much as Uncle Chas would have hated it, he was becoming a legend before the last shovel of dirt was drying on his grave.

After everyone had their fill of Chandler hospitality, Chase and a small group of relatives adjourned to the living room to hear the reading of his uncle's will. Chase sat down next to one of his cousins from Oklahoma, who was hoping Uncle Chas had left him something that could help him settle some serious debt, the result of four marriages to women who had taken him to the cleaners.

Blake Norman, the family lawyer, had reviewed the will in preparation for the evening's event but no one in the family had any idea about the details. In fact, they were all shocked that Uncle Chas had taken the time or expense to make out a will. Chase neither cared nor had any expectations regarding his uncle's financial holdings. If he received one of his uncle's personal mementos, that would be enough.

When Blake Norman was sure everyone was comfortable, he sat down behind Wes Chandler's desk and addressed the family.

"I'm sure you're all surprised that Chas went to the trouble of a last will and testament."

A shudder of stilted laughter resonated through the small gathering.

"Well, I won't take a whole lot of your time. As you would expect, Chas's will is short and to the point." Blake put on a pair of reading glasses and began.

This, being the last Will and Testament of Chas R. Chandler, I hereby instruct the Executor of my will, Blake Norman, Esquire, to dispense my holdings as follows:

To my brother, Wesley Chandler, I bequeath our Grandfather's railroad pocket watch. It needs some work, so I am also bequeathing you an additional fifty-dollars for the repair bill.

Wes snickered at his brother's reference to the fifty dollars, but he was obviously genuinely touched. Chase thought to himself, "So much for getting the watch." He was disappointed for himself but happy for his father.

Blake continued,

To my brother, Frank Chandler, I bequeath my favorite shotgun. It's in good working condition but will need a good cleaning every now and then.

Uncle Frank didn't even flinch when his meager inheritance was mentioned, but his wife, Lulu, could hardly hold herself back from jumping up and screeching out her disappointment. Her husband rested his hand on her thigh, signaling for her to remember her place. Lulu was not a favorite of the Chandler family, given that she lived a luxurious lifestyle but never seemed to be satisfied.

To my nephew, Chase Walker Chandler, I bequeath the remainder of my estate, which includes the following holdings:

1. *All my land holdings of approximately fifteen thousand acres.*
2. *All my cash holdings of approximately $2.5 million.*
3. *My ranch house and all its contents, including my favorite rocking chair*
   Signed by: Chas R. Chandler
   Witnessed by: Blake Norman, Esquire
   On the Seventh day of May, Nineteen Hundred and Sixty

Blake stopped reading and looked up to the awestruck faces in the crowd.

Utter disbelief raced across the faces of Chas's stunned relatives, whose faces were frozen into blank expressions that would not crease fine French wallpaper. It wasn't that they were all expecting to get rich from Chas Chandler's holdings, but they thought it would at least be distributed equitably. They all turned in Chase's direction, just in time to see a puzzled look of shock on his face. Before Chase could react, Blake peered directly at him making sure he had good eye contact.

"Chase, there is also a letter from your uncle stamped "Personal" and addressed to you. I believe, among other things, it has specific instructions regarding the management of his estate." Blake stood up and handed the sealed envelope to Chase, whose hand trembled slightly as he accepted the envelope.

Aside from the fact that Chas had made Chase the sole heir of his estate, Blake could sense a great deal of surprise regarding the amount of cash in his client's estate.

"For those who were wondering how the hell Chas could have acquired so much money, let me just tell you he was much shrewder than you gave him credit for. He invested in the steel industry right after the Great War, suspecting a lot of countries would need rebuilding, and he was right on the mark." Having answered the burning question of the day, Blake started gathering up his papers and said, "Unless anyone has any other questions, I believe that concludes my business. I'm sure you would like to spend some private time as a family."

Blake Norman was positive there were family members who had questions, but they were not about to embarrass themselves by asking them in front of the rest of the family. If Texans prided themselves on anything, it's discretion when it comes to private family affairs, especially concerning money matters.

When everyone was sure Blake Norman was out of earshot, Chase's father burst out in hysterical laughter. "Well, that old scoundrel brother of mine. He did have the last laugh on us." Wes had tears in his eyes from laughing so hard.

No one else in the family but Chase and his Uncle Frank appreciated his father's humorous outburst. They were still reeling from the bombshell that just landed in their laps.

Wes slapped his son on the back. "Well, son, you were never too enthusiastic about being a big- time rancher, but now I guess....you don't have any choice."

"Very funny," Chase said, wondering if his newfound wealth was going to be more trouble than it was worth.

"Hey, it's your problem now. My brother's old place is pretty run down. It's going to need a lot of work to make it into a respectable cattle ranch."

"*As if I don't have enough to contend with already in life!*" Chase thought, as he tried to accept his newly found wealth.

"It's been a long day, so I'm going to get some shuteye. I'll see you in the morning, son. What time are you planning on leaving tomorrow?"

"Sometime in the early afternoon," Chase answered, still not believing what had just happened to him.

"It's a lot to think about. Anything I can help with, all you have to do is ask."

"Thanks. You may regret the offer."

Wes patted his son on the shoulder and told him to get a good night's rest. He had no idea how much his son had on his mind. Hoping the fresh, night air might help clear his head, Chase went outside, poured himself into a rocking chair and, under the dim bulb of the porch light, he started reading the letter his uncle had written to him.

Dear Chase,

I would love to have seen the shock on your face when Blake read my will. I didn't do it just to get a rise out of you. I know I can trust you when it comes to doing the right thing with my land. I am sorry I left the ranch in such bad condition, but I never was really cut out for the ranching life.

You may try and deny it, but ranching is in your blood. Someday, you're going to want to raise a family and my only hope is you will choose to do it on my ranch. I promise not to haunt the old place.

By the way, if you get any fancy ideas about giving it away or sharing my land or money with any other relatives, I have instructed Blake, as executor, to cancel all your rights to my estate and give it to the local dog pound. Sorry kid, you're stuck with it. Well, I can hear Gene Autry in the background singing "Happy Trails," so I guess it's time to say good-bye. I wish the best for you. Try, once in awhile, when you're sitting in my old rocking chair, to think of your old Uncle Chas.

The letter was signed in his uncle's barely legible handwriting. Chase continued to stare at the words, hoping somehow his uncle's raspy voice might lift off the page and speak to him. He thought about all the summer nights, when he used to lean up against the rail of his uncle's front porch and listen to his daring stories of the old west. He could remember many a night falling asleep to the rickety cadence of his uncle's rocking chair.

Chase closed his eyes and tried to imagine the soft creaking of his uncle's chair as it swayed back and forth. He was just about to drift off when he heard the phone ring in the background. He rushed over to the phone and picked up the receiver. It was Emiliano.

CHAPTER 13

Chase held the phone to his ear, refusing to believe what Emiliano had just told him. His thoughts were clustered into a tight fist of anger.

"Chase, are you still there?"

"Yes, ...I'm here. When did you find out?" Chase's voice almost broke in two.

"I received a call from her manager Luis Goya three hours ago. It took him almost a day to locate me."

"When did they take her?"

"Saturday evening after her last performance. Lorena was coming out of the theater when three thugs pulled up, put a gun to her head, and threw her into the car. Luis was just coming out of the theater behind her and saw the whole episode take place."

"Do we know who took her?"

"You're not going to like my answer. It's Fermin Lorca, the drug lord I warned you about before you left Mexico. I don't know how he found out about you and Lorena, but he must have spread a lot of cash around to come up with your name so quickly."

"That son of a bitch!" Chase yelled over the phone loud enough for his mother to hear from the upstairs bedroom.

The sound of his angry voice splintered the quiet of the house. His mother called out from upstairs, "Chase is everything all right?" Her voice registered concern over her son's language.

"Yes, mother. Sorry, but one of my deals in Mexico has gone south on me. I didn't mean to upset you. You can go back to bed now."

The last thing Chase needed was for his mother to get involved.

But everything wasn't all right. Chase's mind was raging with anger and fear, swimming with a glut of questions. Chase returned his focus to Emiliano.

"What details do we have so far?"

"They called Luis two hours after they snatched her to inform him that

Lorena was safe for now, but if he didn't follow their exact instructions, he would find his lovely dancer in pieces at the local dump."

"How much do they want?"

"It's not how much they want, it's *who* they want. Lorca's demanding that you meet him face to face." Emiliano paused for a moment to let the gravity of what he had said sink in.

"How do we know she is still alive?" Chase was almost afraid to ask the question.

"When they contacted Luis, they put her on the phone. I guess she was in pretty bad shape. He could hardly understand anything she was saying between her captors screaming instructions and her incoherent ramblings. Luis suspected she was drugged."

The thought of Lorena being drugged and beaten at the hands of Lorca made every muscle in Chase's body tense. He was struggling to get enough oxygen into his lungs. His heart felt as if it was going to burst from the thunderous pounding in his chest. Chase took a deep breath, trying to regain his composure.

"Was Luis able to understand anything she said?"

"He couldn't catch it all, but he said she rambled on about warning you not to try and save her, almost as if she was trying to protect you."

Chase paced back and forth like a caged animal, gripping the phone as if trying to squeeze the pain out of Emiliano's words.

Emiliano continued, "They told Luis to pass this message on to you. If you want her released unharmed, you need to meet Lorca at his hacienda outside of Morelia. There is only one problem—you have only forty-eight hours from now to make the meeting. They also told Luis that if there was even the slightest hint of involvement with Mexican authorities, the deal is off, and you'd need to look for a new girlfriend."

"How many people besides you and Luis know about this?" Chase was still concerned his cover might have been permanently compromised. It would only complicate things if the Mexican government found out that he was involved in covert activities on behalf of the FBI.

"Only Luis knows. He thinks it's strictly a kidnapping involving a ransom. He has no idea about our recent activities with the Wallace case. I told him to keep everything he heard to himself or he might cost Lorena her life."

"Are you positive Luis didn't contact the newspapers in hope of garnering a little publicity to help the cause of getting her release?"

"No. He's scared shitless his meal ticket might end up in a body bag. I told him to keep his mouth shut and lay low until we tell him differently."

"All right. You get back to Lorca's people, and tell them I've accepted his invitation," Chase exclaimed, leaving no room for discussion.

"Chase, don't do this! You know Lorena won't be worth anything once you agree to his terms. If this guy is really serious about getting revenge, then you've got to play this one differently."

"Look, Emiliano, this son of a bitch has me boxed in. I'm not about to jeopardize an innocent victim to save my own ass, especially the woman I love."

"Will you listen to me for just one minute?" Emiliano was adamant.

"OK, but we're wasting valuable time. Make it quick," Chase demanded impatiently.

"If he wants to play this game, then let's turn it up a notch, and see how he likes the heat."

"Get to the point."

"He has a twelve-year-old daughter going to a private school here in Mexico City. I suggest we pay her a little visit. Tomorrow is a regular school day, so we shouldn't have any problems."

"Are you suggesting what I think?"

"Look, Lorca is playing hardball. If we don't get in the game and let him know we're just as serious as he is about winning, then forget about any chance of getting Lorena back in one piece."

"I hope Lorca is in the trading mood. I'll leave tonight and meet you at the airport in Mexico City. I'll call you before we take off to let you know my arrival time."

Chase heard a noise at the top of the staircase. He turned around to see his father starting to descend the stairs.

"I need to get going if we are going to pull this off. Thanks, I owe you one," Chase said, trying desperately to calm his rattled nerves. He hated feeling out of control.

"I'll see you at the airport," Emiliano told him confidently, as if trying to assure Chase everything would be all right.

Chase hung up the phone and waited for the inevitable question from his father.

"Chase, what the hell is going on?" The furrows on his father's forehead curled up into tight rows.

"I can't explain right now. You just need to trust me on this one."

"It sounds like you're in over your head," his father exclaimed with a grave look of concern.

"No. I'm OK, but I've got to get back to Mexico tonight. Could you do me a favor and shake Dutch out of the rack? Have him meet me at the landing strip in half an hour."

"This must really be bad if you're willing to fly at night."

"Sorry Dad, I don't have time to discuss my fear of flying right now. I've got to pack a few essentials and get the hell out of here."

The essentials he was talking about were his firearms. He would be packing his favorite .357 Magnum and a .30 caliber Beretta as a backup. If Lorca wanted a fight, then, by God, he was going to get one.

His father could see the seriousness of his son's mood. "All right, I'll call him, but you better have a damn good excuse for all this commotion when you get back here."

The night sky was teeming with blue diamond pinholes as Chase rushed across arid desert to the small hanger at his father's private airstrip. He had never flown at night in a small plane, but his normal anxiety was replaced by his concern for Lorena and the terror she had to be experiencing at the hands of Lorca. He met a groggy Dutch at the airstrip.

"Do you mind explaining to me why you're so hell bent to get back to Mexico in the middle of the night?" Dutch grumbled.

"Dutch, it's personal, and I don't have the time or the inclination to explain it right now. Can we just get this bird airborne?"

Dutch knew something had gone seriously awry. Chase didn't even ask if the plane had been safety checked before takeoff. He threw his bag into the cargo section, jumped into the plane, and strapped himself into the co-pilot's seat. His mind was racing with the possibilities of what could go wrong with Emiliano's plan. He had always been meticulous in his planning of operations, but this time he would have to trust his natural instincts and hope for the best results. With the stakes so high, he knew there was no margin for error. The probability of getting Lorena back unharmed was low, especially when dealing with an unpredictable heavyweight like Fermin Lorca.

Chase arrived in Mexico City at four in the morning; Emiliano was waiting with a car at the airport. The flight had taken an excruciating five hours. Counting the thirty hours from when Lorca's people had originally contacted Luis, it left them only twelve hours. They had to kidnap Lorca's daughter, race across rutted highways of the high desert, meet Fermin Lorca at his hacienda, and hope he was in the bargaining mood. If everything fell perfectly into place, it was going to be a close call at best.

Neither man loitered as they greeted each other. The friendly bantering that was normally part of their conversation was absent, and pressure-cooker stress was etched into both of their faces.

Emiliano spoke first. "The school opens at seven. Children start arriving at around seven-thirty."

"Do we know if she is accompanied by bodyguards?" Chase asked flatly.

"Not from the little information I've been able to gather. Her nanny normally drops her off and picks her up."

"Do we have a picture yet?"

Emiliano anticipated Chase's question. He handed him a manila envelope. Chase pulled out a small clipping from a newspaper containing a photo of Lorca's daughter taken six months ago at the birthday party of a prominent politician. He looked at the picture closely and felt the slow rumbling of regret welling up in his stomach. Lorca's daughter was sitting at a birthday banquet table, beaming a bright, effusive smile. Her eyes sparkled with innocence. Chase wondered how it could come down to this and cringed at the thought of kidnapping this defenseless child. He started having second thoughts about following through with Emiliano's plan. But the thought of Lorena brought him careening back to the reality of the situation. Desperate circumstances required desperate measures.

Emiliano could sense Chase's hesitation. "Chase, if you're not a hundred percent committed, let's call it off."

There was a lingering moment of silence before Chase responded, "I'm in. Let's go."

Emiliano sped off through the rain-slicked streets knowing time was their number one enemy.

They stopped off to pick up a few items from a friend of Emiliano's and to exchange cars. They needed a bigger trunk to comfortably accommodate their victim. Neither Chase nor Emiliano wanted to injure the young girl or frighten her any more than required. Both men knew the experience was going to be traumatic enough for her. They could only hope she would quietly cooperate once she realized they didn't intend to harm her.

They pulled up in front of the school at six-thirty, positioning themselves in the ideal spot for observing each child entering the school. The plan was to wait until Lorca's daughter was sitting quietly in her classroom then Emiliano would impersonate a police detective, informing the school that she was in imminent danger. He would explain to school officials that she needed to be put under protective custody as soon as possible. He expected school officials would buy the story, knowing Lorca's suspected criminal background. In preparation for the morning's ruse, Emiliano had one of his underworld contacts forge appropriate police credentials. Given his former police background he was very comfortable pulling off the ruse. All they had to do now was wait and hope that everything fell into place.

As Chase peered through the fogged car window, he kept counting the minutes ticking off before his forty-eight hours were up. Ten and a half hours to go before Lorca snuffed out his dreams for a life with Lorena. If Chase believed anything about Lorca, it was that he would follow through with his threat to end Lorena's life. If they were one minute late, Lorena would be a casualty of their tardiness.

Seven-thirty came and went with no sign of Lorca's daughter or her nanny. Chase turned to Emiliano out of frustration. "Where the hell is she?"

"Let's give them a few minutes. Maybe she got delayed in traffic."

Eight o'clock rolled around, and the last of the children dribbled into the front entrance of the school. Their plan was blowing up right in front of their faces. Chase could barely stand being in his own skin.

"Could we have missed her?" he asked, already knowing the answer to his question.

"No. "I'm going inside to see if can find out anything."

Just then a black Buick pulled up in front of the school and a conservatively attired, middle-aged woman exited. The car license plate matched the car they had been waiting for all morning.

Chase and Emiliano watched as the woman entered the school. A few minutes later, she exited the school and started down the long stairway toward her car.

Emiliano opened the car door and said to Chase, "Wait here!"

Emiliano met the woman halfway up the stairs. He turned to her and said in a friendly voice. "Aren't you Adriana Lorca's nanny?"

The woman was tentative and hesitated to answer at first, but finally nodded. She was naturally wary of strangers, being the governess of Lorca's daughter.

"I thought so. My daughter is Maria. She goes to school with Adriana." Emiliano had chosen a common name, hoping the nanny wouldn't doubt his story. At hearing the name, the nanny relaxed her suspicious composure.

"I'm Franco Munez. I've seen you a lot of mornings and meant to introduce myself on several occasions," Emiliano said modestly.

The nanny smiled and introduced herself as Griselda Ortiz. To his surprise, the woman volunteered the information they were desperately hoping for. "Adriana is ill with the flu and won't be coming to school today. I'm just here to pick up her homework."

"My daughter has the same flu. It must be going around."

"Well, I better get going. I've got to get back to Adriana. Nice to meet you, Señor Munez."

Emiliano wished her well and continued in the direction of the school entrance. Chase could only watch the drama unfold in front of him.

The nanny returned to her car, and as soon as Emiliano was sure she was a safe distance down the street, he returned to an anxious Chase. Emiliano jumped in the car and started the engine.

"Bad news. She's got the flu and won't be coming to school today. Her nanny was only here to pick up her homework assignment."

"All right, that's it. We can't delay any longer. I'll just have to take my chances with Lorca.

"I've got another idea," Emiliano said, pleading with Chase to listen.

"Look, we only have a little over eight hours before Lorca slams the door on us. It's a six-hour drive if we don't run into any problems. That leaves us only two hours to spare."

Emiliano hit the accelerator and sped off in the direction of the main highway. "Bear with me, I'll explain along the way."

CHAPTER 14

Chase peered through the wrought iron gate of Fermin Lorca's hacienda in Quiroga. Two hulking guards stood on each side of him. Chase had arrived with only twenty minutes to spare. He was perspiring from the brisk walk up the dirt road from where Emiliano had dropped him off. The two guards at the gate were brandishing shotguns loosely slung over their shoulders. They stared straight ahead, avoiding any eye contact with Chase. They kept their focus aimed at the front of the hacienda, waiting for instructions from the main house.

The guards had already frisked Chase when he boldly strolled up to the gate. Chase had handed his weapons over to Emiliano before heading to Lorca's hacienda. He knew there was no chance he would make it into such a heavily guarded compound with any kind of weapon. The only thing he was carrying was a frayed leather case strapped to his waist belt containing a pair of small binoculars. One of the guards had removed the binoculars from its case and was attempting to focus them when a signal came from the house. The guards reacted immediately and escorted Chase through the gate.

The three men ambled toward the large adobe hacienda. With every few steps, one of the guards would shove Chase in the back with the barrel of his shotgun to make sure he was keeping the right pace. Chase did a quick survey of the compound to determine what escape options he would have if presented with the opportunity. The ten-foot-high walls surrounding the entire perimeter of the complex were topped off with triple strands of coiled barbed wire. The only exit out of this fortress was the gate he had just entered.

He tried to assess the firepower and number of guards stationed inside the compound. In addition to the two thugs escorting him, there were two guards stationed at the front corners of the house. Chase could see the faint outline of at least three other guards milling around inside the house.

It was clear from the manpower surrounding the compound that Lorca wasn't taking any chances of something backfiring. Chase tucked the cursory data into his already jam-packed brain on the chance he might need it later. He knew his first obligation was to get Lorena safely out of the compound. Then he would see what Lorca had in store for him. All he could really hope for at this point was that the plan he and Emiliano had hastily designed only a few hours earlier was successful. Otherwise, Lorena would be a bride left standing at the altar, waiting for a groom destined never to show.

As they approached the long covered portico, Chase could make out a figure sitting in an oversized wooden chair. The bulky man rose to his feet as the three men quickly closed the short distance between him. Fermin Lorca was large-framed man and had a bigger than normal head for his body size. His clean-shaven face revealed a long broad scar that traveled from his left sideburn to the mid-point of his jaw. Aside from this conspicuous distraction, he was a ruggedly handsome man. Lorca's dark rutted skin added to the menacing scowl draped on his face. He reminded Chase of old black and white photos of Pancho Villa astride his white stallion, glaring fiercely at the camera. His upper lip was adorned with a large, black bushy mustache not unlike that of the notorious Mexican revolutionary.

Lorca appeared at first glance to be in his fifties, but as Chase came closer, he realized his nemesis was probably only in his mid-forties. He was dressed in matching tan khaki slacks and a short sleeve shirt. If Chase hadn't known Lorca's background, he would have thought Lorca was just another wealthy Mexican businessman. Lorca puffed on a thick Cuban cigar he had obviously only lit a few moments earlier. He left no doubt who was in charge.

Just before they reached the edge of the portico, the two guards abruptly stopped Chase in his tracks. Lorca boldly paraded forward. He walked directly over to Chase and backhanded him with all the force he could muster. Chase was caught off guard by Lorca's violent welcoming gesture. His head spun half way around, but he was somehow able to stay on his feet. Chase was hoping that the sick shattering sound he heard ringing in his head wasn't his jaw breaking, but there was no mistaking the searing pain throbbing in his left cheekbone. In spite of it, Chase had enough adrenaline and hatred toward the man standing directly in front of him to ignore the pain.

"So you're the infamous Fermin Lorca," Chase shot back.

"We'll see if you're so insolent when I finish with you," Lorca sneered.

"Where is Lorena?" Chase demanded in a biting tone.

"You will see her when I damn well say so—if at all. First of all, you're going to answer a few questions; then maybe I'll grant you an audience with your famous dancer."

Chase thought this was no time to back down. Lorca was definitely testing his mettle. "I'm not answering anything until I see that she's unharmed."

"Unharmed? I don't know about that.....but alive, yes."

Chase rushed forward in an attempt to throttle Lorca, but he was struck from behind by a guard. The butt of the shotgun caught him between the shoulder blades, and the vicious blow knocked him to the ground. A flash of silver light exploded in his brain. He struggled with both hands to find the ground, then quickly rose to his feet and angrily spat.

"You son of a bitch! If you've hurt her..." Before he could complete his threat, Lorca ordered the two guards to escort him into the house.

The two guards each grabbed one of Chase's arms and started dragging him through the living room. When they reached the end of a long hallway, the two guards slammed him face first into the wall. As they pinned him to the rough plaster wall, Chase tried to regain his senses. His vision was still distorted from the blinding pain raging in the back of his head. He blinked several times trying to refocus his eyes.

When his vision finally cleared, he saw that he was standing next to a door guarded by a paunchy man who had been half asleep before all the commotion disturbed his siesta. Lorca walked up and viciously kicked the chair out from under the dazed guard and ordered him to open the door. The two guards holding Chase simultaneously shoved him forward, and for the first time he saw that Lorena was alive.

At first, he was so relieved to see she was still breathing that he didn't notice the ugly purple bruise on the side of her right cheek and the trickle of blood on her upper lip.

From behind, Lorca placed one of his alligator skin boots into the small of

Chase's spine, shoving him toward the reclining Lorena. Chase tried to catch himself, but he landed with his full body weight on top of her. She let out a deep, agonized moan as if all the air had been knocked out of her. Chase rolled to the side as quickly as he could.

"It's a touching sight to see lovers so warmly embracing," Lorca spouted. He let out an evil, demented laugh. His subordinates readily joined their boss, snickering at his cruel antics.

As Chase peered down at the woman he had proposed to only a few days earlier, he could see she had been beaten badly. He rose up and knelt beside her. It was only then that a disoriented Lorena recognized him. Her drooping eyes suggested to Chase she was still under the influence of a heavy drug dose. Aside from the bruise below her right eye, she had superficial contusions on her forehead and chin. Her normally well-groomed hair was a matted, unraveled rat's nest. Her torn cotton dress was soiled with dirt and blood. She looked as though she had been dragged by wild horses and left to die.

Lorena's swollen lips trembled as she tried to mumble his name. Tears started to glass over her eyes. Chase could see the absolute terror in her bloodshot eyes and the trauma she must have gone through over the last couple of days. A rising wave of guilt welled up in him until he almost choked on it. As his hand stroked her knotted hair, he felt sick inside. Never had he felt such empathy and fierce anger at the same time.

"Don't worry; I didn't let my men have their way with her yet. She is still your little virgin. I must admit though, she's got guts. She never did reveal your whereabouts."

Chase started toward Lorca but stopped himself when the two guards raised the butts of their rifles menacingly at his head. He knew it wouldn't do either him or Lorena any good if he were unable to carry out the rescue plan.

He turned to Lorca and threatened, "You're going to regret the day you ever started this goddamn war."

"How ironic, Señor Chandler, when you're the one who murdered my brother. On top of that, you stepped on my reputation and, as you know, for a man in my line of business, my reputation means everything." He dispassionately chuckled as a puff of smoke curled from his lips.

"I would like to offer my condolences on your brother's death, but I guess I'm just not in a sympathetic mood."

"If you're not in the mood now, I can promise you by the time I finish with you and your lady friend, you'll have much better manners," Lorca scoffed at Chase's insult. "I have to say I'm a little surprised that a man of your experience and skill would walk into his own death sentence, armed only with only this." Lorca held out the binoculars Chase had strapped to his belt.

"Who says that's all I walked in here with?" Chase proclaimed defiantly, as he coolly smirked at Lorca.

Lorca suddenly stepped back, suspecting Chase might have armed himself with hidden explosives. It would not be the first time someone in his position had been assassinated by such surprise tactics.

"Did you frisk this guy completely?" he charged, as he shot an angry look at one of the guards. The guard nodded his head with a panicked expression. Lorca eased his stance and resumed the debate with Chase. "And what exactly do you have to bargain with?"

"Step outside into your courtyard and look due east at the knoll about a quarter click from here."

"I warned you if you involved the authorities, you and your girlfriend would be going out in the same body bag."

"Let me ask you something, when was the last time you saw your daughter? How do you expect her to keep her grades up when she keeps missing school like this?" Chase coldly stared into Lorca's black eyes. "That's a pretty fancy private school she goes to, isn't it? It must cost you an arm and a leg. We thought about bringing her nanny along to keep her company, but she was just not the cooperative type." Chase stood up boldly, setting his face only inches away from Lorca's.

Lorca grabbed a pistol out of a guard's holster and placed the octagon-shaped barrel firmly on Chase's forehead.

Chase heard the distinctive click of the trigger hammer being pulled back. He expected at any moment to feel the searing sensation of cold lead passing through his brain. Chase didn't hesitate. He had nothing to lose.

"Go for it, asshole, but it will be the last time you see your precious little girl." The barrel tip shivered against Chase's indented skin. Lorca un-cocked the gun then gradually dropped it to his side. He shrieked at the two guards to drag Chase out to the open courtyard. Lorca rushed to the middle of the compound and turned due east, as instructed by Chase. He fumbled with the binoculars for a moment and then froze his attention on the objects standing on the knoll. He could barely make out the two forms that were slightly obscured due to the long distance.

Through the hazy binoculars, he could tell there was a large, robust man holding onto a young girl the same age and stature of his daughter. Her hair color and style was an exact match for his little Adriana. She was innocently waving with both hands in Lorca's direction as if she was saying good-bye to her father for the last time. Emiliano was staring back at Lorca through his set of binoculars and pointing with his other hand as if it were a gun aimed at the back of the little girl's head.

Chase calmly commented to Lorca, "I believe in your country you call this a Mexican standoff. You have five minutes by my watch to free us, or your daughter will disappear from your life forever."

Lorca ordered one of the guards to go inside and call his home in Mexico City to verify if his daughter was safely at home. He had just spoken to her last evening and knew she was sick. Lorca desperately thought she just had to be home and all this was a desperate bluff.

Chase seized the opportunity to shove the knife in deeper. "You're wasting time Lorca; three minutes and counting." Chase glanced down at his watch.

"Shut the hell up. You better not be bluffing, or I'll turn your little dancer over to my men for some more fun and games." Lorca snarled, as he impatiently waited for the guard to return.

After two excruciating minutes, the guard rushed out of the house and ran over to where Lorca was standing. His expression was embossed with quizzical apprehension. He cautiously leaned over and whispered to his attentive boss. Lorca stood stock-still, still not facing Chase. His shoulders slowly slumped, registering the crushing blow of the truth. Lorca's whole physical demeanor had changed from one of unquestionable arrogance to total defeat. It was the confirmation Chase had been fretfully awaiting. Without turning toward Chase, Lorca heatedly ordered a guard to go retrieve Lorena.

The guard returned a few minutes later and threw a disoriented Lorena into Chase's arms. She was still recovering from the effects of the drugs so Chase had to hold her up. He wrapped his arm around her waist to reassure her she was safe. He could feel her relax her body against his as if to say, "Don't leave me here."

"Nice doing business with you, Lorca," Chase retorted. "I can assure you, we were better hosts to your daughter than you were to Lorena. When we are safely out of sight, we'll drop your daughter off a mile down the road. Until then, if we see anybody leave this compound, the deal is off. Are we clear?" His stone-cold tone left no doubt about the gravity of his question.

Lorca didn't respond to Chase; he just slowly shook his head in confirmation.

Chase leaned his face toward Lorena and said, "You're going to be all right now. I promise."

She muttered through her swollen and bruised lips, "I love you, Chase."

Lorca had a chilling parting shot for Chase. "I look forward to seeing you again, Mr. Chandler," Lorca barked, sneering at Chase. He let the cigar dangling from his fingers fall to the ground, crushing it with the heel of his boot.

Chase continued walking, ignoring Lorca's threat. He had what he came for, and all he wanted to do now was to get Lorena safely home. When they reached the open gate, Chase glanced back to make sure all of Lorca's goons were still accounted for. Just as they stepped through the gate, the car Emiliano was driving skidded to an abrupt stop. Dust billowed around Chase and Lorena as they poured themselves into the back seat.

Emiliano slammed the car in gear and sped off down the dirt road toward the main highway back to Mexico City. After they had traveled a couple of miles, Lorena vaguely remembered Chase telling Lorca they would release his daughter a mile down the road. She looked in the front seat and could still see the outline of the young girl.

Lorena turned to Chase and whispered, "I thought you said you were letting her go?"

"It was a bluff. This is Emiliano's niece, Eva. We borrowed her for the day from her parents. It was pretty chancy, but we had to take the risk."

The young girl turned and smiled innocently at Lorena. Lorena smiled back, thanking her for being so brave and helping to save her life.

Emiliano's plan had worked flawlessly. After leaving Adriana Lorca's school empty-handed, they drove to Emiliano's brother's house. They pleaded with her parents to let them borrow Eva to assist them in their elaborate hoax. Reluctantly, Emiliano's family agreed, once they were assured she would never be out of Emiliano's sight.

Having set the first stage of the plan, Emiliano called one of his old buddies on the police force to seal the deal. The police showed up at Lorca's home, where his daughter was recovering from the flu, and told the nanny that Lorca was in a terrible accident, and that they should leave for the hospital immediately. Emiliano knew Lorca would want to confirm their story. Fortunately for Chase and Lorena, the plan went off without a hitch. Chase was positive that right about now Lorca was boiling over with hysterical rage, realizing the very culprit he wanted dead had hoodwinked him.

Chase understood for the first time the value of all the late nights Emiliano had spent hanging out in bars, making friends, and building a network of contacts needed for moments just like this afternoon. As he looked over at Lorena, he wasn't sure how he was going to return Emiliano's favor, but he knew he would never forget his friend's unselfishness.

When they reached the main road, they met up with another one of Emiliano's contacts, exchanged cars, and headed for one of the alternate routes to Mexico City. They were taking every precaution to make sure Lorca couldn't track them.

Lorena slept most of the seven hours back to Mexico City. They arrived at eleven at Emiliano's brother's house. Chase effusively thanked Eva and her parents for everything they had done and made it clear that, without their daughter's help, their rescue plan would have failed.

Emiliano drove Chase and Lorena directly to the airport. Dutch was waiting for them at a private hanger. Before they exited the car, Chase reached over and said to Emiliano, "I don't know how to thank you. I'm sorry I was so hard on you earlier."

"You're welcome, my friend, but once you're married and bored stiff with each other....I don't want you blaming me for saving your ass."

Chase and Lorena both smiled. It was the first time anyone dared to hint at a joke since this whole episode started.

"I'm actually hoping life will get a little more boring. I'll call you when we've safely landed at the ranch," Chase said.

It was only then that Lorena realized where they were going. Even in her exhausted state, she could feel the apprehension and fear of leaving her homeland. She wanted to protest, but she cared more about being protected and given a sanctuary from the horrors of the last three days than anything else. Lorena couldn't force herself to relinquish the grip she had on Chase's arm. She was willing to trust him with every aspect of her life. Somehow, she sensed she would always be able to trust that Chase would be there for her.

As the car approached the plane, Dutch could see by the silhouettes in the car that there was a woman snuggled up next to Chase. Chase helped Lorena from the car and directed her toward the plane. Dutch greeted them both with a nervous smile. Still weak, Lorena needed assistance getting into the passenger's seat. Dutch gingerly helped her in her seat. Chase draped a wool blanket over her and told her that before she knew it, they'd be home.

The word "home," in relationship to Texas sounded completely foreign to her. The only home she had ever known was Mexico.

As Dutch prepared for takeoff, he whispered to Chase, "So this is why you got me up in the middle of the night."

"Yes, and I can guarantee she's worth every bit of the effort." Chase looked tenderly at Lorena.

Despite her bruised face and the appearance that she had just been dropped from a tornado, it was clear to Dutch that she was a beautiful woman. Besides, he thought, anyone who could cure Chase of his fear of flying had to be pretty damn special.

As the Cessna taxied down the runway, Lorena peered out the small side window, wondering when or if she would ever return to Mexico. She had never seen the expansive lights of Mexico City glitter so beautifully. As she watched them slowly vanish into darkness, she felt a debilitating remorse for her homeland and knew that no matter where her new life led her that her heart would always belong to Mexico.

Once they were airborne, Chase came back and sat next to her. He pulled Lorena towards him, as she nudged her head into the crook of his shoulder, and reluctantly closed her eyes. It was the first time since being kidnapped that she felt safe enough to fall asleep without being afraid for her life.

The plane safely landed at his family's ranch the next morning. Chase knew he would have to explain to Lorena why she was the target of Lorca's vengeance, but for now they were both badly in need of some peace and quiet.

Wes Chandler stood on the dirt runway anxiously waiting for Chase's return. He curious about how his son was going to explain his sudden departure and unusually frazzled behavior when he left two days ago.

Dutch had called his friend on his short wave radio a few minutes before they landed. He didn't say anything to Wes about the extra "package" he was carrying. He was leaving the responsibility of explaining Lorena's presence in Chase's competent hands.

Chase stepped off the plane first, as his father approached from behind waving the rising dust away from his face. "Welcome back, son. You have an awful lot of explaining to do. What the hell was exactly..."

Wes Chandler stopped dead in his tracks when he saw Chase assisting a young lady from the passenger side of the plane. He could see she had a large bruise on the right side of her face. Her lips were still slightly swollen and her hair was a mess. Her dress looked as though she had just returned from working all day in a sharecropper's field.

As Lorena's feet hit Texas soil for the first time, she could feel the intense glare of the senior Chandler's piercing eyes. She was embarrassed by her condition but knew she could not change the circumstances of her first meeting with her future father-in-law.

Chase and Lorena stepped towards Wes, as Dutch watched curiously from a safe vantage point. Dutch wanted to make sure he was a fair distance from where he suspected all hell was about to break lose.

"Dad, I would like to introduce you to Lorena Santoya. She'll be our guest for a few days." He was not about to dump a bombshell on his father by introducing Lorena as his fiancée.

Lorena held out her hand and offered it to Chase's father. Wes was so shocked by her presence that he completely ignored her offering. It wasn't until Chase gave him a glare of disappointment that Wes finally accepted Lorena's petite hand into his parched hand.

"It's my pleasure, Miss Santoya." His voice was filled with reluctant sincerity.

She could sense his uneasiness. Lorena was hoping it was because of her bedraggled state of dress rather than a genuine dislike for her. "The pleasure is mine, Mr. Chandler."

Chase broke into the strained introduction, knowing his father would have a hard time stopping himself from asking Lorena all the intrusive questions raging in his mind.

"Lorena has had a couple of difficult days. I'm sure she would like to clean up and get some rest. There will be plenty of time to get more acquainted later."

It was obvious to Wes that his son was being extremely protective. What was Chase thinking, bringing a stranger unannounced to their home? Had he totally lost control of his senses?

Chase could tell that his father was uncomfortable with his evasiveness regarding this mysterious woman and why had he brought her home? Chase knew he had an obligation to answer his father's question, but for right now he just wanted to make Lorena feel as comfortable as possible. He could only imagine what she was going through at this very moment, having just narrowly escaped with her life, been uprooted from Mexico and then confronted with strangers in an unfamiliar country.

To avoid any further interrogation, Chase took Lorena's arm and escorted her to Wes's jeep. Wes looked over at Dutch for some reassurance, but Dutch just shrugged his shoulders as if to say, "Don't look at me for an answer."

Lorena and Chase climbed into the back seat of the old jeep, and Wes chauffeured them across the wide-open expanses of his ranch. Occasionally, Chase's father would sneak a peek in the rear view mirror, trying to catch a hint that would reveal Chase's relationship with their new houseguest. What little he saw told him everything he needed to know. Chase had his arm around Lorena, and her head was resting peacefully on his chest. Their embrace was innocent enough, but it was the uncharacteristic look of serenity in his son's eyes that revealed the depth of his feelings for Lorena. Wes Chandler might be an old, insensitive fool, but he knew love when he saw it.

They arrived at the ranch house that was dusted in the glow of early morning sunlight. Even though it was only eight o'clock in the morning, Rebecca was dressed up in all her glory. She wore a long, pleated, yellow cotton dress and polished white high heel shoes. Her silver-blue hair was styled and combed as though she had just stepped away from one of her afternoon bridge parties. With the constant threat of summer heat, she always carried her faithful hand fan. She waved it delicately through the air, ensuring that even the slightest hint of perspiration would be quickly whisked away. She was truly a vision of dignity and traditional southern poise, bringing a needed grace to this stark, barren landscape.

Rebecca could hardly hold herself back as Chase and Lorena approached the freshly painted white porch. Her famous intuition had warned that her son was involved with a woman when he hurried back to Mexico following Uncle Chas's funeral. She never believed Chase's weak "business" excuse for extending his stay in Mexico.

As soon as they were close enough for her to make out Lorena's facial bruises, Rebecca's heart sank. She gasped in revulsion, wondering what kind of trouble this girl had been in.

Chase proudly introduced Lorena. "Mother, I would like to introduce Miss Lorena Santoya."

"Oh, Chase, enough with the formalities," Rebecca scolded, gently locking her arm with Lorena's. "My dear, you must be exhausted from your long journey. Let's get you inside and into a hot bath."

"Thank you. You're very kind, Mrs. Chandler," Lorena said, walking alongside

Rebecca arm in arm.

"Please call me Rebecca. We may seem a little tight-stitched and proper at first, but I can assure you we're just common folk. That is, of course, with the exception of my husband, who occasionally gets on his high-horse, but don't worry.....he's more bark than bite."

Lorena gave Chase an inquisitive look.

Rebecca scolded her son again. "Just don't stand there; go get her bags."

What Chase's mother didn't realize were the dire circumstances under which Lorena had left Mexico. All she had to her name were the tattered, soiled clothes and her pride.

Wes stood back, curiously watching the whole scene with his wife and Lorena. *Rebecca to the rescue as usual, he thought.* His wife was noted in the community for being the redeemer of the less fortunate. She had started several charitable organizations in Pecos and never let an opportunity pass to make her bleeding heart liberal point of view clearly known.

Wes crept up behind Chase and whispered in his ear. "Yes, Chase, why don't you get the young lady's bags?" Wes had already checked the luggage compartment on the plane and had seen there were no bags to load into the jeep.

"Very funny, Dad. This is difficult enough, and you're not helping the situation with your cheap cracks," Chase shot back.

"Losing our sense of humor, are we? It might be helpful if you explained what the hell is going on!" His father's voice constricted with each faltering word.

"I know I owe you an explanation, but can it wait at least until we get settled in?"

Neither man spoke another word as they headed for the front entrance of the house. By the time Chase and Wes reached the bottom of the long curving stairway, Rebecca and Lorena had disappeared into the upstairs guestroom.

Upstairs Rebecca started drawing the bath water and laying out toiletries for her guest. As uncomfortable as Lorena was with her new surroundings, the warmth emanating from Rebecca's genuine concern for her was just what she needed.

When Rebecca reentered the room, Lorena started to try and explain her disheveled appearance.

"I suppose you're wondering why your son has shown up with a strange woman who looks like she's been in a cat fight."

"My dear, you needn't explain anything to me or my husband. That is not to say I'm not as curious as the next person, but I make it a rule not to pry into other people's personal lives; including my son's." Her voice was as sincere as her soothing words.

"Thank you, but I want to explain why...."

Rebecca stood up insisting, "All in due time, my dear. Your bath water is ready. We'll have plenty of time to talk later."

Lorena stood up and warmly embraced the older woman. Rebecca was touched by Lorena's affection, and knew that there was something special about this woman whom her son was being so protective over.

"I have some cream that will help reduce the discoloration of those bruises. When you're finished with your bath, just ring the bell, and I'll bring it up." Rebecca pointed to a braided gold rope used for ringing the bell in the servant's quarters. Then she exited the room, closing the door behind her, and went downstairs to join her husband and son.

As she approached the double doors separating the sumptuously decorated salon, she could hear the raised voices of two men arguing. Rebecca heard the deep, hardened voice of her husband first.

"What the hell were you thinking of bringing her here unannounced?"

"Sorry, but it's not like I had a whole lot of choice. We were a hair's breadth away from ending up in tomorrow's obituaries."

Rebecca momentarily paused before entering the room. She was shocked and concerned at what she was hearing, but not wanting to interrupt, she waited patiently outside the door.

"You can't be serious about this woman? You said she is some kind of gypsy dancer?" Wes bitterly asked.

Chase's voice rose in agitation as he answered. "Lorena is a highly respected flamenco dancer. Her family has carried on the tradition for over three generations. Look, I'm not here to defend her or what she does. She is going to be my wife, and you will just have to accept it," Chase said, emptying his determination into his father's eyes.

"You're making a big mistake, Chase. I thought you would be more sensible in your choice of a wife. A woman like this...."

Chase rudely interrupted his father. "A woman like this? You mean a Mexican woman!"

"Let's not get into that." Wes glared angrily at his son.

Rebecca stepped into the room, abruptly interrupting their conversation.

"Yes, Wesley, for once you're right. Let's not get into that." Her eyes snared her husband's and they were not about to let go. "Wesley, I would like to suggest you have somehow misplaced your manners and hospitality. Miss Santoya is a guest in our house and we'll *all* act appropriately." Chase's mother only referred to her husband as *Wesley* only when she was really angry with him.

It was only on rare occasions that Chase could recall his mother speaking so pointedly to his father, but when she did, there was no doubt that she meant business. Rebecca turned to her son. "I thought I asked you to get Lorena's bags."

"Without having to explain the entire story right now, the only clothes she brought are the ones on her back." Chase put his hands in his front pockets, rocking side to side, fearing that he might be the next in line to face his mother's wrath.

Without hesitation, Rebecca offered, "Very well, then. I think I have some dresses from your Cousin Caroline's visit last year. You know how finicky she is about her clothes. I've been waiting to give them to someone in need, and they should fit Lorena perfectly. Since you can't be of any more assistance, I suggest you get yourself cleaned up." Rebecca eyed her son as if he had some communicable disease.

Rebecca turned to her husband. "Wesley, I would like to speak with you in the other room." She turned and headed for the small parlor adjoining the living room, not giving her speechless husband a chance to argue with her. Chase had always admired his mother's composure in the midst of anger.

As Chase started walking up to his room, he could hear his mother's voice scolding his father for his rude behavior. He couldn't pick out all the details, but he could tell she was laying down the law regarding her husband's opinion of Lorena and his reaction to Chase's choice for a wife.

Chase continued up the marble staircase, confident that at least he had his mother's support. How he was going to bring his stubborn father around was still another matter.

Lorena felt rejuvenated after her bath, having lingered longer than usual. As she sat, facing the dresser mirror brushing her hair, she felt the overwhelming impact of the last twenty-four hours hit her with astounding force. *What would happen to her dancing career? What about her parents?* She hadn't been able to give them a warning about leaving Mexico or the fact that she was about to marry a man they had never met. The questions were rolling like thunder through her brain, and she didn't have any answers to calm her anxiety. She felt as though she was spinning out of control with no way to pull back on the throttle. A flood of emotions, unfamiliar to her, brought her almost to the state of total panic. She was more frightened now than she had been at any time during her kidnapping. She started to cry uncontrollably and put her hands over her mouth to mute the heaving sighs of sadness.

Rebecca passed by her room and heard the distressing sounds. Normally she would have not intruded, but her concern for her almost-daughter-in-law got the better of her.

Rebecca lightly knocked on the door and called out Lorena's name. Lorena tried to quickly brush away her tears with the back of her hand. Rebecca called out again. "Are you all right, my dear?" She almost always used this term of endearment when referring to someone younger than she.

"Yes.....I'm fine," Lorena answered trying to quell her irrepressible sobbing.

"May I come in?"

"Yes," Lorena whimpered, not wanting to embarrass herself anymore than she already had.

"I brought some cream to help with those bruises," Rebecca said, gracefully pretending to ignore Lorena's distressed state.

"Thank you," Lorena mumbled, still having a hard time holding back the tears.

"My poor girl. You have had such a hard time. You go ahead; let it all out." Rebecca sat down next to Lorena on the bed, and Lorena's head collapsed into Rebecca's lap.

Lorena sobbed openly, trying to exorcise the flood of fear and pain she had experienced over the past few days. Rebecca lightly brushed her damp hair with her hand. Lorena instantly recognized this soothing touch as one that can only come from a mother who has consoled a child. Lorena knew from this moment on, Rebecca would always be there for her.

"I'm sorry... I've been...so much trouble," The words fell from her lips like slow, tumbling dominos.

"We'll not have that kind of talk. We all have our bad days."

Lorena sat up, wiping the tears from her bloodshot eyes. Rebecca took her every-ready handkerchief out of her dress pocket and handed it to Lorena.

"You'll feel much better once we fix you up." Rebecca opened a small white jar of cream and started gently applying it to Lorena's cheek.

Rebecca could see that the young woman sitting in front of her was strikingly beautiful. Her skin was soft to her touch, and it was clearly apparent why her son was so enamored with Lorena. Taking a closer look, she saw that Lorena was a few years younger than Chase, but it was clear she had sensitivity and maturity that was beyond her years. Rebecca trusted her instincts when it came to recognizing important traits in a person, and she suspected Lorena was a woman of remarkable character. Besides, she knew her son had extremely high standards when it came to women, and if Lorena was good enough for him, she was good enough to be a Chandler.

"Does that feel a little better?" Rebecca asked as she closed the jar of cream.

"I don't think I've ever felt so confused," Lorena blurted out, unafraid of confiding in her new surrogate mother.

Rebecca suspected part of Lorena's uncertainty was aimed at her relationship with her son. "Do you love him?"

Lorena was initially set back by her host's straightforward question. "Yes....I love him very much."

"Then, welcome to the family. We won't have any more discussion about whether or not you belong here. Do we understand each other?" Her closing words were more an affirmation of fact than a scolding question.

"What about Mr. Chandler?"

"You leave him to me. I've been dancing around that old codger for over thirty years now. Don't worry; I know just how to keep him in his place. In fact, I'll be glad to give you free lessons if Chase ever starts to get out of hand."

They both had a good laugh and joked about the sometimes quirky, sometimes, harsh behavior of men.

Rebecca helped Lorena finish getting her makeup on, and they headed downstairs to join her husband and son for a late breakfast.

Chase was just coming out of his room when they started down the stairway. He saw his mother and Lorena smiling, busily talking, and acting as though they had been lifetime friends. Seeing his mother and Lorena so relaxed together helped him to release some of the tension he felt from his heated argument with his father. He felt sorry that he had accused his father of bigotry, but his only choice was to stand up for Lorena. As angry as he was, he intended to apologize to his father when they could again speak in private. Regardless of different philosophies, he respected his father.

Chase quickened his step to catch up with his mother and Lorena, who were halfway down the stairs.

"What have you two been up to? No good, I'm sure," Chase teased.

"Oh, I'm just filling Lorena in on a few of your curious habits," his mother shot back.

"What curious habits?"

"You know, like your obsession with the bedroom window having to be open when there is a full moon." His mother was delighted at the thought of revealing one of her son's childhood secrets.

"Really? You never told me about this, Chase," Lorena said, as Chase tried to ignore their taunting.

"OK, you two. I can see I'm not going to get out of this one. When I was five years old, my Uncle Chas told me a story about a wild stallion hypnotized by the path of a full moon on the prairie. The stallion was so enamored by the light that he foolishly followed the moonbeam all the way to the stars. My Uncle Chas told me if I left my window open during a full moon, and if I were *real* lucky, I might hear the stallion's hoofs galloping from star to star. So, when the moon was full, I would lie awake listening for the sounds of that wayward stallion. Sooner or later, it just became a habit."

"Such a romantic," Lorena jested.

"I can have my moments."

The three continued down the stairs and joined Wes in the living room. Chase's father was still sulking over the argument with his son and the subsequent scolding from his wife. He knew he was wrong about Lorena, but his pride would not let him acknowledge it in front of his family. As they entered the room, Rebecca, who had been arm in arm with Lorena, handed Lorena's arm over to Chase and then boldly made an announcement.

"Wes, I would like you to meet your future daughter-in-law, Lorena Santoya. I would suggest we need to get started on planning their engagement party."

Before Wes could react, Chase, who was totally surprised by his mother's announcement, jumped into the fray. "Mother, what are you trying to do, give him another heart attack?"

"As usual around here, when you guys decide to team up on me, I don't have any say in such matters." Wes stepped forward, and asked his son's permission to kiss his new fiancée. "You're not going to refuse an old cowpoke the pleasure of welcoming her into the family, are you?"

Chase looked at his father, apologizing with his eyes for his previous condemnation. "No, of course not, but just don't make it a habit."

Wes lightly kissed Lorena on the cheek and held both of her hands, gripping them tightly as if to say he was sorry for his earlier rude behavior.

Chase felt that for the first time since they had arrived, he could finally relax and enjoy his parents' company. If Lorena and he were going to start off on the right foot, having the blessings of his parents was very important, particularly his father's. Maybe Dutch was right; his father was more bark than bite.

Chase and Lorena were married two months from the day a bedraggled Lorena arrived at the Chandler ranch. They would have preferred a small, intimate wedding, but it was impossible to stop Chase's parents from putting on a big-time traditional Texas wedding. Everyone from Chase's family, including a few relatives he had never met, was invited. Lorena's parents even made the trip from Mexico. Chase had enlisted Emiliano's help in acquiring a temporary visa for them. It meant everything to Lorena that Chase had gone to such an effort. He had also made arrangements to have the ceremony in the oldest mission church in Pecos, fulfilling Lorena's childhood dream of being married in a grand Mexican style church.

Rebecca had the wedding gown she had worn over 30 years ago altered for Lorena and presented the pearl studded cream dress to her future daughter-in-law at the engagement party. Rebecca's unselfish gift solidified Lorena's confidence that she had truly been accepted by Chase's family.

The Chandlers spared no expense in planning the wedding festivities. Dignitaries from the political and business community were invited to assure that no one important was insulted. Anyone who was someone wasn't about to miss one of the biggest shindigs the territory had ever seen.

Wes surprised the newlyweds by hiring the best mariachi band in west Texas, and of course, he requested the first dance with his new daughter-in-law. Everyone got a kick out of watching Wes escort his new daughter-in-law around the dance floor. The old cowboy with two left feet was trying to lead one of the best dancers in all of Mexico through a Texas two-step.

Even though the band did not traditionally play flamenco music, they had taken the time to learn one of the better-known songs to entice Lorena to perform. Only after being pestered relentlessly by Chase and the wedding party, did she reluctantly agree to dance. Lorena hadn't performed since she had been kidnapped. No one would have noticed that she was rusty, watching the first few graceful moves she made across the dance floor. The wedding party watched in awe as she danced around the stage, snapping her heels on the oak floor. Lorena seemed possessed as she elegantly flipped the hem of her wedding dress. It was as if she was trying to paint the pale blue Texas sky with wide sweeping brush strokes of her white gown.

Chase watched from the sidelines and could see that familiar far-off look in her eyes. He knew she was in a uniquely private place, a place he couldn't share with her. His eyes were beaming with pride, but he felt a strange sense of jealousy watching her dance. He knew he had promised to help her resume her performance career, but seeing Lorena so happy scared the hell out of him. *What would the future hold for them if she actually resumed her career? What would their life be like if she was always traipsing across country on a tour?*

Chase hoped that once they were married, this whole issue would simply play itself out in his favor, and over time she would want to settle into the quiet life of being a wife and mother. As he intently watched her dance, he felt his dream of a normal family life disappearing with each dramatic step she took across the floor.

For Lorena, dancing on her wedding day brought back the memory of why she loved her art so much. As she concluded her performance, she firmly tapped her heels down in one final motion, lifted her eyes to the open sky and whispered a prayer of gratitude. At least, for this one immaculate moment in time, she had her dancing, Chase's undying devotion; but more importantly her world was back in balance again.

CHAPTER 15

It had been five months since Diego stood outside Lorena's dressing room his heart pounding in his chest in anticipation of meeting her. Even though he never had a chance to get to know her, there had been a rebirth in him that night backstage. Not since Celaya had he felt so enamored with a woman, so alive. Memories of his love for Celaya inspired him to start a search he should have begun long ago.

Since his arrival in Mexico over nine months ago, Diego had been using his busy schedule as an excuse not to resume his search for what happened to Celaya. Now that the season was over, he could no longer avoid the inevitable question. He needed to know why she had abandoned him after having sworn her undying love for him that night at the Plaza Quitzal. Diego was determined to do whatever it took to find her. He knew he could be confronted with his worst nightmare. Celaya could have simply fallen out of love with him. She could have lost her will to wait for his return from France. Had another man come along and swept her off her feet? Whatever the reason, he had to find out the truth.

He had no idea where to begin his search, but he decided to start looking at the place where it all had begun over twenty years ago—Don Roberto Castillo's home. He knew Don Roberto had passed away a few years ago, and his wife was living in the U.S. with one of her daughters. With the help of a mutual friend, Diego found out that Rafael Castillo was still living in his parent's house.

Rafael was out of town on business and Diego made an appointment with his secretary to meet his childhood friend on this weekend.

As Diego's cab pulled up in front of Rafael's home, he wondered if he was fully prepared to hear the truth about Celaya. Stepping out and looking up at the grand façade of the Castillo home, his mind was flooded with the memory of seeing Celaya for the first time. It was almost the exact scene as when he arrived with his best friend Ignacio twenty years ago. He remembered walking up the steps to the house and seeing Rafael waiting to greet him. Looking up at an older Rafael standing at the same doorway sent an eerie sensation coursing through his body. He almost tripped on the first step of the stairway. As he reached the top of the steps, he hardly recognized his old friend, who had put on a considerable amount of weight and looked slightly haggard. Rafael's hair was sprinkled with gray, and he had dark bags under his eyes. The only thing recognizable was his familiar broad smile. Diego had heard through the rumor mill that his friend had been married four times and was working on his fifth wife. No wonder he looked a little weather worn, Diego thought.

Rafael warmly greeted Diego. "Well if it isn't the famous fencing champion, Diego Sanchez. So good to see you, my friend; how many years has it been?"

The two men shook hands, and Diego thanked Rafael for seeing him on such short notice. Rafael motioned him into the foyer. As Diego looked around, he could see the place had changed very little since the last time he had visited.

"I've been reading about your success in the tournaments. Congratulations."

"Thanks...from what I've heard you've been pretty successful with your businesses."

"Yeah, I've done alright, but if I could have only been half as successful with all my wives, I would be a rich man." Rafael belly laughed. "What about you? Did you ever find the love of your life?"

Diego hesitated and tried to gather himself before responding. He knew once he started down this path, there was no turning back.

Diego tried to make light of Rafael's stinging question. "Not yet, but I'm still holding out hope."

"Why don't we go into the garden? We have a lot of catching up to do."

They passed through the same French doors through which he and Celaya had exited after their exhilarating tango display the night of the anniversary party. As Diego sat down at the table, he could see the edge of the Jacaranda tree he and Celaya had sat under. The tree was in full dress with its bright purple blooms, and he could smell the sweet faint fragrance as it wafted through the garden.

"I'm very curious. You mentioned to my secretary that it was really important that we talk."

Diego could hardly bring himself to begin the conversation, not knowing where it might lead.

"Rafael, do you remember your parent's thirtieth anniversary party?"

"Of course; it was quite the affair, and, if I remember correctly, you made quite an impression with my cousin Celaya on the dance floor."

It was the first time Diego had heard her name spoken in over twenty years. He felt that all too familiar twinge of pain whenever he thought of her name.

"I vaguely remember dancing with her but that's about it. Did she ever finish her degree at the University?" Diego asked nonchalantly.

Rafael's engaging smile instantly disappeared, and his face faded into a sullen expression.

"It was a great tragedy. Shortly after my parent's anniversary, she had an affair with a young man, and a few months later she found out she was pregnant." Rafael shook his head in disgust.

Diego felt a flush of pain drain through his body. *How could it be she betrayed him so easily?*

"So....she is married and has children?" Diego reluctantly asked, digging his fingernails into the palm of his hand.

"No, unfortunately the young man in question never stepped forward to take responsibility for his actions. As you might have noticed in your brief encounter with my cousin, she was a very proud and stubborn woman. We all suspected it was someone she went to school with, but we'll never know."

Diego chuckled inside at his friends' remark, remembering how impressed he was with Celaya's straightforwardness when they were initially introduced, how she cut him down to size with a few slicing quips.

Rafael continued. "It was very hard on her family. You know how cruel people can be. The fact that Celaya refused to reveal the identity of her lover's name didn't help. She took full responsibility for her condition."

Diego understood why Rafael referred to it as a great tragedy. In Mexican high society, having a child out of wedlock was the kiss of death. It must have been a terrible experience for Celaya and her family.

"I'm so sorry she had to go through such humiliation. I assume everything is fine with her now?" He felt the exuberance of hope surge through his veins.

"I wish that were true. Unfortunately, she died a few days after childbirth."

Diego could barely contain the unmitigated pain he felt at hearing Rafael's harsh words. His body shuddered as he tried to regain his composure. Of all the possibilities, he never suspected the truth would be so cruel.

There was a long, sustained silence before he could muster the ability to offer his condolences.

"I apologize. I didn't mean to bring up what must have been a very painful experience for your family." His voice trailed off as he struggled to hide his anguish.

As much as Diego tried to hide his feeling, it was obvious to Rafael that the news of Celaya's death had sincerely affected him. "I didn't know you were so fond of her, having met her so briefly."

"Even though I barely knew her, it's always a tragedy to hear about someone dying so young. It is just that I found something during my last move," Diego lied, as he pulled out the scarf Celaya had given him at the train station before he left for France. The scarf looked as new as when Celaya had draped it around his neck and kissed him good-bye. It was everything Diego could do to continue with the conversation.

"Part of the reason I came here today was to return this to her." Diego said, as he handed the scarf to Rafael. "She said it would bring me good luck. I think at the time she was only half-serious." Diego knew he was lying, but it was the only excuse he could come up with to keep Rafael from suspecting he might be the scoundrel who deserted a pregnant Celaya.

Diego hesitated before asking the next question. "If it would not be too much to ask, I would like to give this back to her family. If I remember correctly, they live near Guadalajara."

"Yes, her parents live on a ranch outside of Guadalajara. I'm sure they would appreciate getting her scarf back. Her family practically went into seclusion after her death. I have their address upstairs in my office. If you don't mind waiting, I'll go get it." Rafael stood up and handed Celaya's scarf back to Diego.

"Thanks," Diego answered, finding it hard to believe that after all the years of wondering what had happened to Celaya, he might finally have his answer.

Once Rafael was out of sight, Diego stood up and walked down the gravel pathway to the Jacaranda tree. He sat on the bench where they had sat over twenty years ago. He gently stroked the cream scarf hoping somehow its magic powers might erase the truth of her tragic death. He remembered how boldly she made the first move, kissing him underneath the fragrant umbrella of the Jacaranda. How cleverly they planned their getaway from the party. Diego could still smell the musty bouquet of the old fencing uniforms where they made love. Everything about that night was fresh and unblemished in his mind. Suddenly, the overwhelming reality of his role in her short life slammed down on him like a carnival sledgehammer. *Was I the young man in question who started this whole tragic chain of events? Had she tried to secretly contact him to tell him she was about to bear his child?* The only message he had ever received from her was via his old maestro, Señor Alvarez. Señor Alvarez made it very clear that Celaya wanted nothing to do with Diego, and that he wasn't part of her future plans. *Had his trusted maestro lied to him about Celaya when he inquired about her?*

If he wasn't determined before today to find out the truth about Celaya, hearing the news about her death reaffirmed his commitment to get to the bottom of this tragic story. He made a vow to himself to find the answers, no matter how much time or money it cost him. He had to have the truth.

Rafael returned a few minutes later and handed him a piece of paper with the address of Celaya's parents'. "Sorry it took so long. By the way, did you ever see Celaya after my parents' anniversary?"

Diego nervously put the slip of paper in his coat pocket and coughed up an answer, "No, unfortunately, I never had the occasion to meet her again."

He thanked Rafael for his hospitality and offered his condolences once again for Celaya's passing. As he left Rafael's house, he turned back and saw Rafael peering out of the window through the curtains. He wondered if his old friend was already growing suspicious, he couldn't worry about that now; he had to make arrangements to go to Guadalajara to meet Celaya's parents.

Diego arrived in Guadalajara three days later. Over the phone he had convinced Celaya's parents that he was an old college friend and had a personal item of Celaya's he wanted to return to them. They reluctantly agreed to meet with Diego the next morning.

Diego was parked just outside the entrance to Celaya's family ranch. It was just as Celaya had described it to him at the train station. Diego was apprehensive about meeting Celaya's parents. What little Diego had found out about her family in his limited research was that Celaya's father, Bernardo Flores, was a well-respected rancher and a no nonsense business man. Celaya's mother on the other hand was an icon in the community for her work with the under-privileged. This matched everything Celaya had shared with him about her parents. There were rumors that Señor Flores had started to drink heavily after his daughter's death, and that his business had suffered considerably. Señora Glorietta Flores, although initially distraught over the tragedy, recovered quickly and focused all her energy on raising her illegitimate grandchild. Beyond this sketchy information, Diego was left in the dark regarding Celaya's pregnancy and the child who would now be in its early twenties.

Diego sat in his car for almost a half an hour trying to work up the nerve to face the only two people he knew could answer all his questions about Celaya and her abruptly ended life. He took a deep breath, started the engine and drove through the stone archway, making his way around the circular driveway to the front of the Flores's expansive hacienda.

He had decided to pose as an old college friend just in case Celaya had revealed to her parents on her deathbed that her lover was an aspiring swordsman. The one thing Diego did not want to do was raise any suspicion that he was the father of their bastard grandchild. He knew he was taking a huge chance, but he needed to know if Celaya had abandoned him for someone else. Disguising himself would also protect Celaya's parents from what could be a painful truth. There was no reason, at this late date, to stir up the still waters of their terrible loss.

Diego knocked on the front door and was greeted by an older man whom he mistakenly assumed was Señor Flores. The distinguished looking gentleman immediately informed Diego that Señor Flores asked him to wait in the library. He escorted Diego to a well-lit room and informed him that the master of the house would join him momentarily.

Diego seated himself in an overstuffed chair across from a large oak desk scattered with papers and stacks of books. He glanced at the titles, trying to get a sense of the reader's interest and saw the subject matter of almost every book was related to the history of breeding prize bulls. It was something Diego knew a little about, having grown up on a ranch, and if necessary he could use it as an icebreaker with Celaya's father.

As he sat waiting for his host to arrive, his only concern was whether they might recognize him from all the press he had received since returning to Mexico. To avoid such a situation, Diego wore a short brimmed brown felt hat and a pair of round spectacles resting halfway down his nose. He was dressed conservatively in a slightly rumbled-brown pin striped suit. To accentuate his new appearance, he brushed some gray dye into his hair, thereby making himself appear slightly older. Diego looked more like a disheveled college professor than a fencing champion. He could only hope his feeble attempt at creating his disguise was enough to protect his true identity.

After what seemed like hours, Señor Flores finally entered the room. He was dressed impeccably in a black suit, white shirt, and silk tie. The older man appeared to be in good physical shape, aside from the excessive wrinkles beyond his years. His hair was totally gray, matching his thin, closely cropped mustache. His disposition was stern and serious.

As with all strangers who were guests in his home, Señor Flores greeted Diego with a firm handshake. "I understand from our brief conversation on the phone that you knew our daughter, Celaya, during her college years?"

"Yes, we were friends at the University. Please let me offer my sincere condolences on your tragic loss. Unfortunately, I only recently heard of her passing from an old friend. Celaya was a bright star in a dark sky."

Señor Flores ignored his compliment and moved on to the business at hand. "So you studied with Celaya."

"Yes, we were interested in the same field of psychology. Of course, she was a much more serious student than I."

"If I may ask, what is your profession?"

"Actually, I continued with my studies and have a private practice in Mexico City." Diego looked downward, not wanting his eyes to reveal his blatant twisting of the truth.

"I understand you have something that belonged to our daughter."

Just as Diego was reaching into the briefcase to retrieve the scarf, Señora Flores entered the room. She was a woman of medium stature and build, but carried herself in a way that suggested she was a woman of formidable inner strength. Her long black silk dress was obviously finely tailored to conform to her willowy form. Even though she had the complexion of a woman in her sixties, her face revealed the genuine beauty of a much younger woman. It was apparent to Diego where Celaya had gotten her grace and stunning looks.

Señora Flores walked confidently over to where Diego and her husband were sitting and politely scolded, "Bernardo, where are your manners? Why have you not offered our guest some refreshments?"

Before her husband could respond, she walked over to the double doors of the library and told the housekeeper to prepare some refreshments and bring them to the library. Satisfied she had taken care of her guest, Señora Flores returned to join Diego and her husband. Both men stood when she presented herself.

"Please excuse the interruption. It is a pleasure to meet you in person, Dr. Zavala."

It sounded strange, hearing his counterfeit name roll so respectfully off her lips. Diego took Señora Flores' hand in his, raised it to his lips, and gently kissed it. "It is my pleasure. Thank you so much for your hospitality."

"Please, don't let me interrupt. Where were you?"

"We were just discussing Dr. Zavala's profession and his relationship with Celaya. Dr. Zavala is a practicing psychologist," Señor Flores somberly declared.

"You knew my daughter well, Dr. Zavala?" Señora Flores inquired.

"Yes, we attended the same classes together but I don't think it would be fair to say we were close friends," Diego said cautiously. "I lost contact with her after she left school. Unfortunately, I just recently heard about her untimely passing. Please let me assure you, my intention for coming here today was not to intrude on your painful past."

"I trust that your motives are sincere, Dr. Zavala. Yes, it was a very difficult time for us, but one has to move on in life. Our daughter died giving the greatest gift that anyone can give. We have a wonderful grandchild."

"Glorietta, I'm sure Dr. Zavala did not come here to discuss our family history," Señor Flores said abruptly.

Señora Flores ignored her husband's impatient comment and continued. "You must have all wondered what happened to Celaya after she disappeared so unexpectedly."

"Well, in fact, I did, Señora Flores. I was very concerned about her when she so suddenly left the University. We all tried to inquire about her whereabouts without intruding into her personal life. If I recall, it was a couple months after spring break when she dropped out of school. I was surprised and disappointed about her decision. Of course, at that time, I did not know the reason behind her leaving."

Diego was taking a chance, guessing this was close to the time Celaya left college. He knew she was on spring break when they met, and it would have taken a few months for her to discover her condition.

"Yes, unfortunately, she had an affair with a young man who, we suspect, was an acquaintance she met during her stay at my brother's home in Mexico City. Were you acquainted with my brother, Don Castillo?"

Diego paused for a moment before answering her. He didn't expect to be asked this question about his relationship with Rafael's family.

"No, I never had the pleasure. I heard Celaya speak of her relatives in Mexico City but, no, I never met them. During that particular spring break, I was visiting my family in Hermosillo." Diego was making sure there was no suspicion raised about his relationship with Celaya.

"Perhaps you might have known the young man and not realized Celaya's secret affection for him. Even though it has been all these years, we are still curious as to who fathered our grandson, Amado."

The name sliced into Diego like a dull knife. It was as if his heart had stop beating for a brief moment, and he wondered if he would ever feel the familiar thumping against his chest again.

Señora Flores continued, not recognizing her guest was temporarily paralyzed. "The only clues Celaya revealed to us about the young man's identity was that he might have been involved in the world of sports. We also think she was calling out his name while giving birth to our grandson. She kept mumbling *mi amado* over and over, as if hoping for him to appear by her bedside. When we asked her about it the next day, she refused to acknowledge that she had called out his name. She was determined to take her secret to the grave. Unfortunately, she had complications during childbirth and she left this world two days after she bore our grandson. Before she died, she scribbled a brief note asking that we christen the child *Amado*."

Señora Flores' body language noticeably changed after describing her daughter's death. Her shoulders slumped and her eyes glassed over with tears.

Diego was still reeling from Señora Flores' words. He sat motionless, unable to respond. Everything in the room seemed out of focus. All he could see were visions of Celaya lying there on her deathbed imploring him to embrace her; to hold her *amado* one last time. He could barely imagine the infinite loneliness she felt before her last breath.

When he finally gathered himself, there was no doubt about the truth. Amado Flores was the product of their one night of passion. *Why hadn't she told me? Was she trying to protect his reputation and career?* She must have known he would have done anything for her. His mind was reeling with the possibilities of why Celaya kept the truth from him.

"Dr. Zavala? Are you all right?" Señora Flores questioned. Diego at first didn't recognize his counterfeit name. He was still numb, barely able to claw his way out of the dark abyss of guilt he had fallen into.

"Yes....yes, I'm fine. I apologize. I never imagined this tragic end to Celaya's life."

"Did Celaya have any friends nicknamed Amado that you were aware of?" Señora Flores inquired, hoping this stranger might be the source of the answer to her lingering quest for truth.

"No, I'm afraid not." Diego paused, wanting to scream out, *"I am her Amado! I am the one you have been looking for all these years!"*

Diego battled to regain his composure. He was finally able to eke out a few words of concern. "I wish I could be more help."

Diego could see the pained look on Señor Flores' face.

"Could we please get to the point as to why you came here today, Dr. Zavala?" Señor Flores was clearly at the end of his rope.

Diego wanted to inquire about the whereabouts of *his son*, but he could see that any further inquiries would only cause his hosts more pain, and possibly raise their suspicion about him being the culprit they had been looking for all these years.

Diego opened a tattered leather briefcase and retrieved the scarf Celaya had given to him. He had worn the scarf at every tournament and exhibition for the last twenty years, just as he had promised Celaya. He was reluctant to give it back to her parents. It was the only tangible remnant he had of their brief time together. He told himself it was worth the sacrifice, having now learned the truth about Celaya's life. He was still fighting off the fact that Amado Flores was his child as he turned his attention back to his hosts.

Señora Flores was the first to recognize the scarf he was holding. Her stare was stock-still as she looked down at it.

"Celaya was so kind to have loaned her scarf to me one night after I forgot my coat. It was not unlike her to be so generous. I thought you would like to have it back." Diego let the long scarf slide through his hand for the last time into Señora Flores' small, wrinkled hands.

As he watched Señora Flores nestle the scarf next to her cheek, he felt the sense of true loss. "Thank you. It was so kind of you to have gone to so much effort. Her grandmother swaddled her in it when she was born. She always said it would bring her good luck." It was obvious Señora Flores was genuinely touched by Diego's gesture.

Señor Flores, on the other hand, was not so moved and seemed disappointed by the simple article of clothing. Diego, sensing that he had over extended his welcome, stood up, and thanked them for taking the time see him. Even though he was disappointed at having to leave without knowing the details of his son's childhood or his current whereabouts, Diego finally knew the complete story of the young woman he had fallen in love with on that warm spring night in the Plaza Quitzal. All those years of thinking Celaya had coldly abandoned him were just not true. He knew, for the first time in over twenty years of unrelenting sorrow, that Celaya had loved him to the very end.

As Diego parted, Señora Flores asked his discretion in not sharing their conversation about Celaya and her tragic death. Diego assured them that he would never speak a word of this private family matter to another person. It was only then that he felt the full weight of guilt for having disguised his identity. At a future date, he knew he had an obligation to tell them the truth about his relationship with their daughter, but now was not the time.

As Diego climbed into the driver's seat and circled back to the main road, he knew his search was not ending here, he had a son somewhere out there to find.

CHAPTER 16

Chase and Lorena honeymooned in southern Spain. Chase had originally told Lorena that they were going to the coast of California but surprised her when they arrived at the Dallas airport with tickets to Granada, Spain. He knew that she had always dreamed of going to the birthplace of flamenco.

For the two weeks they were there, Lorena was in heaven. Almost every night they wandered through the carved out caverns of Granada. In small, smoky taverns filled with fanatical patrons, she watched the best of the fiery gypsy dancers and for the first time felt a true connection to her artistic heritage. The experience re-ignited her passion for dancing, and she swore to herself that as soon as they returned home, she was going to rededicate herself to her career.

During the ensuing months after their return to Texas, Chase officially informed the FBI that he was no longer interested in working on their behalf. The Assistant Director tried every trick in the book to convince Chase to hold off on his final decision. The Bureau knew they were losing one of their top operatives. Chase was firm in his conviction; besides, he had promised Lorena never to go out on another operation.

A few days before they moved into Uncle Chas's ranch house, Chase finally revealed the real reason why Lorca had taken her as a hostage. The truth shocked Lorena to the very core. At first, she couldn't believe Chase had kept such a monumental secret from her. She assured him it would not have made a difference in her decision to marry him, but to have hidden it from her all this time was inexcusable. Chase explained that he had never told anyone about his clandestine life—not even his own family. He told her that when they first met, he was too afraid the truth might scare her off. Chase said he was going tell her after her national tour was over, but the whole kidnapping episode spoiled all his plans. He pleaded with her to forgive him. Chase showed Lorena his resignation letter to the Bureau and swore he was finished with that part of his life.

Even with Chase's apologies, Lorena felt deeply betrayed. She fumed over how she was willing to temporarily give up her career for him, yet he couldn't tell her the truth about his secret life. It took her over a week to finally forgive Chase. It was the first major test in their young marriage. As difficult as it was for her to let go of her anger, Lorena felt fortunate to have survived the temptation to just walk away. Even after assessing all of her misgivings about Chase, she was positive she had fallen in love with the right man.

Lorena settled into her new world, having endured this potential disaster. She had a lot to learn about the American way of life, and more importantly, the Texas way of life. Rebecca was very supportive, guiding her through the do's and don'ts of being a good wife. Lorena had to learn how to run a household and also to constantly deal with the cultural differences. She couldn't understand why a young woman with her education and experience couldn't join the men during their political discussions. All she had ever heard about America prior to arriving on its doorstep was how it was the land of the free! What Lorena soon found out, through a couple of uncomfortable confrontations, was that this important constitutional principal only applied when the men granted women permission to speak their mind. Yearning for some kind of intellectual outlet, Lorena forced herself to join the local Ladies Auxiliary; but even among the high society of Pecos' most prominent women, speaking her mind on controversial issues was frowned upon. Sex, politics, and a husband's business matters were totally off-limits topics.

Lorena soon found herself desperately longing for the one thing she could rely on—her dancing. Unfortunately, it was almost impossible to find someone who would act as her agent in acquiring performance dates. As well known as she was in Mexico, in the U.S. she was just another aspiring dancer. Chase pretended to make some contacts on her behalf, but his heart wasn't really in it. Lorena finally had to accept the fact she would have to wait until she returned to Mexico to resume her career. The problem with returning home was that she had left the country illegally. Chase said he was working on trying to resolve the problem, but it was going slow. With each day that passed, Lorena grew more impatient. She wasn't about to forget Chase's promise to support her career and her plans to return to Mexico. She had spoken several times with her manager, and Luis assured her that he was already working on plans for another national tour in Mexico for the upcoming summer. Luis was also impatient with Chase's progress. During their last conversation, Luis told Lorena that he was going to hire his own lawyer to investigate why it was taking so long. He suspected some corruption involving Immigrations, but couldn't fathom who would be behind such a plan to keep her out of Mexico.

For his part, Chase tried to quell Lorena's impatience by remodeling the old barn into a fully equipped dance studio. While the practice studio soothed some of Lorena's angst, it could never replace the joy she felt from performing in front of a live audience. She missed the nervous tension shuddering through her body just before stepping into the bright lights of the stage, the satisfaction of knowing all her hard work was appreciated. She wasn't sure that Chase fully understood that dancing was a spiritual tether to her identity; there was no replacing it.

Chase tried to ignore his new wife's uneasiness by keeping busy with his railcar leasing business. Lone Star was expanding its operations into the Far East. He turned over all his operations in Mexico to Eduardo Munez. He was pretty sure Lorca was still intent on getting revenge for his brother's death, so there was little chance Chase could return to Mexico in the immediate future. Emiliano had been keeping tabs on Lorca to make sure he wasn't making any plans to cross the border and finish off what he had started. Chase knew he could never be assured Lorca wouldn't go to such an extreme, but he could only hope Lorca was smart enough to know there would be major repercussions from the U.S. government if he ever tried anything so desperate. He was positive of one thing, as long as Lorca was still in Mexico, Lorena could never safely return to her homeland. When she had asked him about the possibility of going back, he lied and told her she would have to wait until they were able to straighten out the mess with Immigrations. Chase had no idea how anxious Lorena was to return to Mexico or how she would have gladly taken her chances with Lorca to resume her career.

Lorena never suspected that Chase, in his eagerness to protect their life together, had asked Emiliano to pay off certain officials to assure she was not allowed to return to Mexico. Lorca wasn't the only thing Chase was afraid of facing. He was positive that if she started performing again, he would lose any chance of having a normal family life. As hard as he tried, he just couldn't envision how they could have a life together if Lorena was on the road all the time and he was back in Texas. After all, he had just given up an important part of his life for her; wasn't it only fair that she make a similar sacrifice? He wasn't sure how long he could continue the deception, but he was hoping Lorena's passion for dancing would dissipate over time and she would get more comfortable with her new life in Texas. He knew deceiving her again was a dangerous strategy, but he felt like he had no alternative.

As the harsh winter of 1984 settled in with a vengeance, Lorena struggled to stay focused on her dancing. As she stared out her studio window at the rolling hills smothered in snow, she cursed at her powdery nemesis. She couldn't believe the weather could be so dreary and cold in February. Back in Mexico, she would have already been bathing under crystal blue skies in the warm rays of the midday sun. Even though Chase had kept his promise and had the ranch house renovated, the frigid winds somehow seemed to find their way into every corner of the house.

It had been nine months since their wedding day, and so much had transpired. In so many ways she felt disconnected, living in some artificial reality, a pretender in another person's body. On mornings like this, it was a struggle to remember how she ended up here on this windswept, barely habitable desert. Her brief life with Chase had been a combination of getting used to each other's eccentricities, sharing passionate nights of lovemaking, and fighting off her temptation to run away and go back home no matter what the consequences. She never questioned her decision to marry Chase, but she knew she was never going to feel truly content having to live in Texas. She was unwavering in her commitment to resume her career in Mexico. At times, it was the only thing that kept her from feeling totally trapped. As determined she was to dance again, hearing week after week the bad news from Chase's lawyer in

Mexico about her legal problems caused from her leaving the country illegally, began to slowly take its toll on her. It didn't help that Chase was starting to put pressure on her about wanting to start a family. From the very beginning, she was adamantly opposed to the idea, still holding onto the hope of returning to Mexico. The final blow came when Chase's lawyer informed them that it would be a minimum of at least a year before her legal situation would improve. Her hopes dashed and Christmas tugging at her emotions, Lorena finally consented to Chase's wishes to try and have a baby.

Chase did everything he could to convince Lorena that she could have a career and be a mother at the same time. He gave example after example of women who had successful professional careers and raised a family at the same time. It wasn't that Lorena didn't want a family, but she was afraid motherhood would consume all her energy. She had visions of dirty diapers, crying babies and sleepless nights devouring every spare minute she had to herself. She had seen it happen too many times to other dancers, including her own mother. In fact, if it were not for her grandmother helping out, her mother would have had to give up her dancing career when she gave birth to her.

They decided two months ago to stop using any form of birth control. They waited month after month, hoping to get positive news, but each time they were disappointed. She knew Chase was feeling the pressure of starting a family much more than she was. At twenty-four, she told herself she still had several good childbearing years ahead of her, but now that they had been trying for over two months, she was getting worried that something might be wrong with her.

Chase agreed to go through his own battery of tests, to make sure it wasn't something physically wrong with him. It was a sign of how badly he really wanted to have a child. In such a male-oriented culture, it was rare for a macho Texan to potentially put to question his manhood.

Lorena knew her inability to get pregnant was in no way related to their sex life. They had not lost any of their fervor or passion for each other. In fact, their lovemaking had become more robust and experimental. It wasn't uncommon for Chase to escape from work and come home to make love in the middle of the day. No, sex wasn't a problem, but Lorena sensed that something was wrong.

Lorena was particularly uneasy this morning as she watched one of the ranch hands scrape a path through the snow that led to the front of the house. She had a doctor's appointment with the Chandler's family doctor in the hopes of solving the mystery of why she unable to get pregnant.

Dr. Kittles did a complete workup and told her that he would have the results back in three weeks. He reassured her from the preliminary tests that there no reason she shouldn't be able to have children. Three weeks later, just as Dr. Kittles had promised, Lorena received her test results. There were no indications from her fertility tests that there were any problems. The doctor told her they should just be patient. He said very often with newlyweds, "nerves" can play a role in preventing pregnancy. Lorena had never heard of nerves causing such a problem. She was pretty sure it was just an old wives' tale used by doctors to ease the concern of struggling couples.

When she informed Chase of the news, he was ecstatic. To her surprise, and disappointment, Chase told her he had yet to make his doctor's appointment for his tests. He promised as soon as he got back from an upcoming business trip to China that he would take care of it. Their first major argument occurred two weeks after Chase returned from his trip to the Far East. Lorena found out that Chase had not made an appointment with the doctor as he had promised, and she wanted to know why. Chase knew in his heart why. Once having heard Lorena had received a clean bill of health, he was afraid that he might be the one with the problem. His masculinity was directly threatened and Chase didn't know if he was truly prepared to hear bad news regarding his potency. How would Lorena react if she found out he wasn't capable of fathering an offspring? He knew how important having children was in the Mexican culture. Would she still want to be married to a man who couldn't fulfill his part of the bargain? What about his parents who were expecting their only son to carry on the Chandler name?

Chase was really feeling the pressure. He was hoping that by ignoring the problem, it would go away, and Lorena would surprise him one day with the happy news she was bearing their child.

Lorena could sense his edginess ever since he had returned from China, but her patience was wearing thin. Chase hadn't been interested in making love even before he left on his business trip. This in itself was enough to alarm her that something was wrong with him. She wondered if Chase had changed his mind about wanting to have a baby.

One afternoon, shortly after he came home from work, she decided to confront him. "Chase, have you made your doctor's appointment yet?"

"Not exactly," he hedged, browsing through his briefcase.

"Are you avoiding taking these tests?" she demanded impatiently.

"Look, I said I would take care of it, and I will!"

"We can't wait forever. As soon as my immigration papers get approved, I plan on spending some time in Mexico. It has been almost ten months since I've seen my family. What about my career?" She folded her arms across her chest. "I'm not going to put my whole life on hold because you won't take responsibility and make a simple doctor's appointment."

"Is that a threat?" Chase snarled, snapping his head in her direction.

Lorena tried to regain her composure and lowered her voice. "No, Chase, it's not. Do you really want to have this child?"

"Of course I do! It's just that I have been very busy lately. Can we not talk about this anymore?"

Their conversation quickly escalated.

"No, Chase, we need to talk about this now! You've been avoiding me ever since you returned."

"You may not be finished with this conversation, but I am!" With that, he slammed his briefcase shut, and stomped out of the room.

They avoided each other for the rest of the evening until it was time to go to bed. Lorena was already in bed, and the lights in the bedroom were off when he entered. He could hear the quiet whimper of Lorena crying into her pillow. Chase knew he was the one in the wrong, and whether he liked it or not, he was going to have to consent to the tests and apologize to Lorena.

He crawled into bed and cuddled up next to Lorena's stiff body. "Please forgive me. I don't have any excuses." He draped his arm around her and turned Lorena's face toward him. Her eyes were swollen from crying.

"I know my reasons for not going through the tests are foolish, but I'm afraid that if they are negative, you'll be on the first train out of town. I am scared."

She raised her hand to his dejected face and softly stroked it. "My darling, Chase, I'll love you no matter how the tests turn out. I didn't marry you just to have your children."

"Lorena, I'm so sorry. I'm such a stubborn fool sometimes."

She kissed him and slid her hand down inside of his pajama bottoms. He was already starting to get hard. He ripped away the skimpy cloth of her silk negligee as Lorena climbed on top of him. She put him inside of her, bent down, and lovingly laid her head on his chest. The intensity of their lovemaking was so fervent that they both were left with superficial scratches. The next morning, having seen the result of their sexual acrobatics, they joked at the breakfast table about how they should argue more often, particularly if making up was going to be so much fun.

Lorena wasn't naïve enough to believe that everything between them would always be a smooth journey but she was reassured looking across the table at Chase's smile, which indicated to her that they had the basic tools to survive any crisis.

Chase left for his office later that morning, promising that he would call Lorena as soon as he knew his appointment time with Dr. Kittles. Lorena spent the rest of morning lavishing in the comforting sensation left over from their intense lovemaking. She found herself getting excited about the potential of being a mother. In fact, she thought, it could have happened last night. Could Dr. Kittles have been right about their problem being merely a case of newlywed "nerves?"

Lorena's face broadened into an effusive smile, as she chuckled out loud. There sure weren't any signs of "nerves" last night, she thought.

CHAPTER 17

Chase sat in his office in downtown Pecos. He was feeling relieved that the tension of the past two weeks was over. It was too bad Lorena and he had their first major fight last night, but it had all turned out for the best. Hearing Lorena affirm her love for him, no matter what the results of his fertility test, went a long way toward making him feel more comfortable about seeing Dr. Kittles.

Chase was just getting ready to pick up the phone to arrange for his doctor's appointment when it rang. It was Carl Eddings from the FBI.

"Chase how have you been?" Eddings said, in a saccharine tone.

Chase knew something major was up. Eddings wasn't calling to catch up on old times.

"Fine, but I'm a little busy right now."

"Chase, an urgent matter has come up, and we need your help."

"Carl, you know I'm not in the business anymore."

"Well, you may want to hear what I have to say. We have a situation in Mexico. We need some local knowledge and thought you would be the best source. One of the major drug kingpins down there is willing to turn state's evidence against his fellow drug lords. We've been working on this for six months. If we can get him back to the States and offer him immunity, then we'll be able to break one of the biggest drug rings in Mexico."

"There are a lot of guys at the Bureau who have operated out of Mexico. Why me?"

"I believe you know this guy. Does Fermin Lorca ring any bells?"

There was dead silence on the Chase's end of the line for a good ten seconds. Chase had tried to forget about his brief episode with Lorca, but hearing his name again brought back all the anger. Chase tried to disguise his feelings as he answered Eddings.

"So what does that have to do with me?"

"Look, Chase, we know the background on you and Lorca. We know you and your wife barely escaped with your lives from this asshole. That aside, we need to get him safely out of the country or the deal is off. You know how much drug traffic comes into our cities and into the hands of our children because of these slime balls?"

Eddings knew Chase was aware of the answers; playing the guilt card was his best chance of getting Chase on board.

For Chase's part, he knew that breaking into this almost impenetrable drug ring would be a major coup for the Bureau. If Lorca was ready to roll over and assist the Bureau in breaking down this drug powerhouse, he couldn't blame them for showing up on his doorstep. After all, he knew more about operating in Mexico than just about anybody at the Bureau.

"Why don't you just go down there and get the guy out?"

"We would, but part of the deal is that he wants you to be his escort. He's currently living like a prisoner in his own compound. One of his business colleagues, Remo Navarrete, suspects that he is about to jump over to our side, and he's making sure Lorca stays put. Navarrete has the backing of his fellow drug lords. There is really only one road in and out of town, and Navarrete has the place guarded like Fort Knox." Eddings stopped to catch his breath. "Lorca and his former compadres are in a standoff right now; but we don't know how long he can hold out. Both sides are heavily armed, and it won't be long before all hell breaks loose. We could lose Lorca in the crossfire and then we've lost six months of hard work. Lorca is unwilling to take the risk of trying to escape unless you're in charge of the operation. He knows all about your track record, and you're the only one he is willing to trust with his life."

Chase couldn't believe what he was hearing. Why the hell did Lorca want him to be his personal escort? There was no way he was going to involve himself in anything having to do with Lorca.

"I'd like to help you out, but I made a promise to myself, and more importantly, to Lorena, that I'll never take another assignment."

"Chase, we know you want Lorca out of Mexico as much as we do. Your wife can't return while Lorca is still in the country. We also know about your deal with certain Immigration officials and how you paid them off to keep your wife out of Mexico. I think she would find this interesting news, don't you?"

"You son of a bitch! You think you can blackmail me?"

"Cut the crap, Chase. I'm not bluffing."

"I don't give a damn what you tell Lorena. I'll call her right now and tell her the truth."

Eddings had worked with Chase long enough to know he would fight back if he was cornered. But Eddings had one more card in his hand to play, and Chase wasn't going to like it.

"I don't doubt you would come clean with your lovely bride, but if you don't accept our offer, I'm afraid U.S. Immigrations will have to arrest your wife for illegally entering the country. You know how the courts work, Chase." Eddings paused to let the gravity of what he was saying sink in. "They'll immediately deport her to Mexico, and now that we've cleared the way with Immigration for her to return to Mexico, she could be back in her homeland in less than a week. Of course, we can't predict what Lorca might have in mind for her upon her return. As I understand, he was about to have his way with her just before you showed up to save her ass. I suggest you reconsider our offer."

Chase knew Eddings had him boxed in. He had no alternative but to accept the assignment. Chase couldn't believe he was potentially jeopardizing his relationship with his wife to act as Lorca's personal babysitter. More importantly, what did Lorca have up his sleeve, requesting him as his guardian? It could all simply be a ploy so that Lorca could finish off what he had started when Chase left him with his balls in his hand. Chase could only imagine the rage festering in Lorca when he found out he had been bamboozled into thinking Emiliano's niece was his endangered daughter.

"All right, I'll do this one job, but if you guys ever try to come back and threaten me or my wife again, I'll be sitting at the desk of the chief editor of The New York Times spilling my guts out. Do we understand each other?"

"Nice to have you back, Chase. By the way, if you get any ideas about telling your wife about this mission, the deal is off. Understood?"

"Yes. Let's move on. What's the plan?"

Eddings told Chase he would be flying to Texas the next day to fill him in on the details of the operation, and Chase should be ready to leave the following day for Mexico City. He would work with his old friend, Emiliano, who was getting briefed as they spoke.

"You were pretty sure of yourself, weren't you?" Chase vented sarcastically.

"Meet me at our regional office at 10 a.m. tomorrow." Edding's earlier congeniality was replaced with a hard-edged, business-like tone.

They hung up without saying good-bye. Chase slumped back into his chair. What excuse was he going to give Lorena for suddenly leaving on such short notice? Once again he was faced with the prospect of lying to the woman he loved. The last time he attempted to deceive her on such a major scale, it almost cost him his marriage.

Chase left his office early to give himself time to pack and, hopefully, console Lorena about his sudden departure. He told his staff that he was going to Sao Paulo on urgent business, and he would return in a week. He didn't know how long his assignment in Mexico was going to take, but he wanted to make sure no one started asking questions. As extra insurance against raising suspicion, he told his secretary that he would be visiting sites in remote areas. There was a good chance he would be out of phone contact for most of his trip, so there was no need to try to call him. It was the same story he was planning to tell Lorena.

Lorena was excited to see him when he arrived home and the first thing she asked was about his doctor's appointment. Chase had totally forgotten about making the appointment after Edding's call. Reluctantly he lied. "It's a week from tomorrow," he said, as his voice trailed off.

"I'm sure there is nothing wrong, so don't worry," she said, as she leaned over and tenderly kissed him.

"I've got some bad news. I have to fly down to Sao Paulo tomorrow on some urgent business. It seems that some of the sites we chose for rail stations have turned into major problems with the local Indian tribes." Chase could see the disappointment on Lorena's face.

Lorena knew the trip must be important if he was willing to get back on a plane so soon after returning from the Far East. He still had an aversion to flying, but the recent expansion plans for Lone Star left him no choice.

Nevertheless, she attempted to make a plea for him to stay. "Why can't someone else go in your place? What about Hendricks? He's been down there before."

"They asked for me specifically. Besides, Hendricks almost died from dengue fever the last time he went out in the rain forest. I promised I wouldn't send him again."

"Oh, and that is supposed to make me feel better about you going."

"Not exactly. Unfortunately, I'll also be out of phone contact for most of my trip. If you need to get a message to me, call my office. I'm not making any promises that they'll be able to get hold of me, but it's worth a try."

"How long?"

"Not more than a week." His eyes twitched as he made a feeble attempt to console her.

Lorena resigned herself to Chase's leaving and offered to help pack. They spent the evening quietly enjoying each other's company and made love before going to bed early.

Chase lay awake for several hours, trying to sort out the insanity of this mission. He was glad Lorena bought his lie, but if anything went haywire with the operation, he knew he was in deep shit with her. He would not only be in major trouble with the Bureau, but his marriage probably couldn't sustain another major hit. He silently cautioned himself, "*Be careful Chase. Everything you care about is riding on this one last mission.*"

The next morning, Eddings feigned an apology for having put the pressure on but said he had no alternative. Chase ignored his apology and asked if they could stick to the task at hand. He was anxious to get started and get back home to Lorena. The longer the mission, the greater chance for a fuck-up, Chase thought.

The basic plan was pretty simple as Eddings explained it. Chase was to meet Emiliano in Mexico City and go to Ciudad Hidalgo under the cover of conducting business on behalf of Lone Star. From there they would sneak their way into Quiroga, snatch Lorca from under the nose of Navarrete's people, and whisk him off to the awaiting FBI agents at the border.

Before Eddings could finish, Chase interrupted him. "You're joking, right?

This is your brilliant master plan? I need some goddamn details."

"Relax," Eddings joked, having had his fun teasing Chase. Eddings knew Chase was a stickler for details. Eddings started rattling off every detail of the plan the Bureau had worked out. He told Chase that the only time Lorca was allowed to leave his compound was to go to confession and pray every Saturday evening at the local church. Lorca may have been a murderous, kidnapping drug dealer, but he still was a devout Catholic. He was chaperoned by several, armed gunmen working for Remo Navarrete to ensure he didn't try anything funny. As long as he played by the rules, they weren't going to deny Lorca his right to be with his God one day a week.

Chase asked for a profile on Navarrete. He wanted to know every detail about the man he would have to out-fox to get Lorca out of Mexico. Eddings was prepared for this question and handed him a thick folder containing all the background. Chase quickly glanced through the file.

"This guy sounds like a real sick puppy. Did he actually have his uncle killed because the old man tried to rip him off for two grand?"

"That's affirmative. But wait until you get to the part about chopping off one of his son's fingers for the same kind of reckless behavior. We don't know a lot about Navarrete, but we are pretty sure he takes his business seriously."

Chase was ready to move on. He would have plenty of time to review Navarrete's file later. He still had a lot of questions he needed answered before leaving. "What's the general layout of the church?"

"The church is about a half-mile from Lorca's hacienda. There are only two entrances to the church. A front and rear door. The road leading up to the church is a dead end. One way in, one way out."

"That doesn't seem to leave a lot of options." He would figure out his escape route later. "How does Lorca get there?"

"He rides in his own car, but like I said, he is escorted by Navarrete's men in a surveillance vehicle. We considered trying to snatch him while he was on the move, but it's just too risky."

"How long does he stay in the chapel?" Chase was firing questions off at the rate of a semi-automatic weapon.

"Lorca and a few local patrons are generally the only ones in the church. He goes to confession first, says a few prayers, and he's out of there. It takes no more than an hour. It's the only time he is left alone by Navarrete's men. We realize it's a small window of time, but we think it's your best shot. Once he's back in his compound, Lorca's essentially in lockdown."

"Once we have him, what then, transport him to the airport?"

"No planes!" Eddings emphasized. The airport was too dangerous. Navarrete would be looking for them to use the airport as the primary escape route. Any public transportation just wasn't a viable option.

Chase was clearly irritated by Eddings' answer. "You mean I have to baby sit this son of a bitch all the way across Mexico in a car?"

"I'm afraid so. You'll have better control, and we won't have to worry about any outside influences."

Chase was already putting a skeleton plan together in his head. He and Emiliano would have to make a surveillance mission to the church in Quiroga first thing out of the chute. He needed to know every nook and cranny in the old church. Then there was the task of making sure they had all the escape routes covered. If Chase had heard Eddings correctly, there weren't a lot of alternatives if they got trapped in at the church. Designing an escape route Navarrete and his men couldn't trace would be the key to their success. The job was dangerous enough without having a group of thugs chasing them all the way to the border. If Navarrete suspected for even a moment that foreign agents were escorting Lorca out of the country, they could all end up being shipped home in body bags.

Chase would use his house in Ciudad Hidalgo as a staging area for equipment and supplies. When everything was set, they would sneak back into Quiroga, extract Lorca and hightail it for the border. If everything went as planned, Chase would be back at his ranch in six days, longer than he wanted. It was a risky plan at best, and the thought of having to put their lives on the line for Lorca turned his guts inside out.

After Chase heard all Eddings had to say, he stood up and charged, "Your guys better damn well be there when they're supposed to, or I'm leaving the son of a bitch at the border to fend for himself."

Eddings handed Chase an envelope, which contained cash, information about his chartered flight to Mexico City, and a false passport for Lorca. It was a precaution in case they were stopped *en route*. Eddings held out his hand to shake Chase's, but Chase ignored it. He picked up his bags and exited the office without another word.

Eddings ran to the door and yelled down the hallway, "How will I know you have him?"

Chase continued walking straight ahead and barked, "Just be there on time."

Chase called Lorena from the Pecos Airport before his chartered plane took off and told her not to worry. He still felt guilty about having to lie to her about his mission, but he was positive of one thing; Lorena would never let him go if she knew it had anything to do with Fermin Lorca.

Chase arrived in Mexico City later that same afternoon and Emiliano was waiting for him with a car at the airport.

"Sorry you had to return under such unpleasant circumstances. How is Lorena handling this?" Emiliano looked exhausted.

Chase threw his bags in the open trunk and answered his friend. "She doesn't know I'm here or anything about the mission."

Emiliano had assumed that Chase wouldn't have told Lorena about returning to Mexico as Chase had told him how angry she was when she learned of his work for the Bureau. If Chase thought telling Lorena about this mission was uncomfortable, he should have been in Emiliano's shoes when the Bureau contacted him. Emiliano was furious that they had threatened both him and his family. He almost backed out until they said that Chase would be running the show.

They drove the five hours to Ciudad Hidalgo, hardly speaking a word to each other. Neither man was in the mood for idle conversation.

When they arrived, Chase's house was empty. They immediately began making more specific plans to get in and out of Quiroga without any collateral damage. Neither of them wanted to make the same mistakes of their last mission. They discussed all the possible options, and after several hours of wrestling with alternatives, they settled on a strategy. It wasn't a failsafe plan, but it was the best they could come up with given the limited time.

The plan required them to split up. If they were going to pull off this caper, they needed all the time they could muster between the two of them. Chase would have to make the surveillance run to Quiroga on his own while Emiliano worked on getting supplies together. Emiliano also needed to make special arrangements in Quiroga that were critical to ensuring their success. Chase asked if he thought it was possible to pull it all together. He told Chase that it would be a tough go, but that he would try and make it happen. Normally, Chase would not have accepted such a lack of confidence, but he knew what kind of pressure they were both under, so he let it go.

When they finished around eleven-thirty neither man had eaten since breakfast. There was no food in the house, so they decided to go to a small, discreet cafe. Chase had always kept pretty much to himself during his short visits to Ciudad Hidalgo, so there was little chance of running into someone he knew. But why take the chance?

They ate in a business-like fashion. Both men were exhausted from the long hours. Chase paid the bill, and they exited. It was twelve-thirty and the streets were empty. Chase turned the corner to where the car was parked and saw a man across the narrow street who looked familiar. He did a double take, but the man disappeared before he could get a second look. He tried to remember where he had seen the stranger but couldn't immediately come up with an answer.

Luis Goya, Lorena's manager, ducked inside a dark alley, making sure Chase Chandler did not see him. He waited until Chase and Emiliano drove off before stepping out of the shadows. Luis had been in Ciudad Hidalgo for the past week trying to find out why Lorena's papers were still held up at Immigration. He had finally talked to enough people and paid enough *mordita* to discover that Chase was involved and that his partner in crime, Emiliano, had paid off several officials to prevent Lorena from returning home. Seeing Chase walking down the streets of Ciudad Hidalgo raised Luis's suspicion that something major was up.

Luis rushed to his hotel and immediately dialed Lorena's number.

Lorena was dead asleep when she heard the faint sound of the phone ringing. She realized it could be Chase calling from Sao Paulo, so she fumbled for the receiver and answered. "Hello, Chase?" Even though she was groggy, Lorena was anxious to hear the sound of her husband's voice.

"No, it's me, Luis."

"Luis, what are you doing calling me at this hour?" Her voice registered a hint of anger.

"I have something very important to tell you." Luis panted, still out of breath from running to his hotel room.

"Can't it wait until tomorrow? What could be so important that you have to call at this time of night?" Her impatience was growing.

"Bear with me. You won't believe who I just saw walking down the streets of Ciudad Hidalgo."

"Enough with the suspense, Luis."

"Your beloved....Chase Chandler."

Luis was still angry with Chase for having stolen his meal ticket. He was hoping he could convince Lorena to come back to Mexico and forget about her rich, gringo husband.

"You're mistaken, Luis. Chase is on a business trip to Sao Paulo. He left this morning, and I don't appreciate your insinuation."

"It's no mistake. I just saw him and Emiliano coming out of a restaurant. I may be tired, but I'm not blind."

Questions started careening through her mind. *How could it be true? Why would Chase lie to her about where he was going? What was he doing with Emiliano?* She raced through the labyrinth of possibilities, trying to sort out what Luis was telling her.

"That's not all, Lorena. I did a little investigating into why your immigration papers were being held up and found out that your devoted husband has been paying off officials to keep you out of the country."

"That's a vicious lie!"

"I'm sorry, Lorena....but it's true. You could have returned months ago."

Lorena's end of the phone went eerily silent. She couldn't fathom why Chase would do such a thing. Chase insisted that he was doing everything in his power to help her return home. He knew how badly she wanted to see her parents. What about all the times they had sat across from the dinner table and discussed her career and performing again in Mexico? Was this just another one of his lies? Lorena thought back to how he had hidden the truth from her about being an FBI operative, and even more recently, how he had lied about not making his doctor's appointment. Did his deception go that deeply? Couldn't he even tell the truth about such a simple matter as a doctor's appointment? Was her whole life with Chase one big lie? The questions kept hitting her like a driving hailstorm. She pinched her cheek to make sure she wasn't having a horrible nightmare.

"Lorena, what do you want me to do?"

"Nothing, Luis. I need some time to think this through."

Luis could hear that her voice was resigned to the truth. She reluctantly thanked Luis for calling and took down his number at the hotel. She was glad he had called, but in some small way, she would have rather just blissfully carried on with her quiet life. She went into Chase's library, pulled out a bottle of aged-rye whiskey from his private stock and poured herself a stiff drink. It was one o'clock in the morning, and there was no way she could sleep with Chase's lies on a collision course with her need for the truth. She tried to think of every possible reason why Chase felt he had to lie to her about where he was going and—more importantly—what he was doing. She couldn't force herself to believe that the man she had fallen in love with had been deceiving her all this time.

She knew he must have taken another assignment with the Bureau. It was the only legitimate reason she could come up with. Maybe he never resigned, and his trips to the Far East and South America were really trips on behalf of the FBI. She couldn't decide which was worse, breaking his promise about resigning from the Bureau or trying to keep her out of Mexico. Every thought she had about Chase's motives for lying to her became twisted. Maybe his business trips were a ploy so he could be with other women. It wouldn't be the first time a man had betrayed his wife's trust for a roll in the hay with another woman.

She wracked her brain for answers but finally concluded the only way to know the real truth was to find out for herself. The decisions about the rest of her life depended on verifying Chase's current whereabouts and his reason for being in Mexico.

Lorena started packing some clothes; she was prepared to overlook the risk she was taking by going back to Mexico illegally. Chase had given her the combination to his hidden safe, so money wasn't an issue. She would need plenty to buy her way back into Mexico. She called Luis back at his hotel and told him she was on her way. Once she was sure of her arrival time, she would call him. She asked him if he knew anyone in Mexico City who could help eliminate any sticky problems with her re-entry to Mexico. Luis had a close contact in the Vice President's office, and told her that he would see what he could do. She rifled through the Pecos phone book and scribbled down telephone numbers for private charter plane services. As soon as she was convinced she had covered all the bases, she got into their old pick-up truck and drove toward her in-law's house.

She turned off her lights as she approached their mailbox and slipped in a note to explain that Chase's Sao Paulo ploy was just another one of his planned, romantic getaways. She wrote that she was meeting him in Dallas, and they expected to return in a week. His parents had seen Chase and Lorena run off in the past on secret holidays, so she knew they wouldn't doubt her story. She just hoped a week would give her enough time to find her husband.

Lorena drove down the dirt road, the dust billowing behind her, determined to find out if her entire life with Chase Chandler had been a charade.

CHAPTER 18

Chase left early Friday morning for Quiroga to scout out the village and the small church that Lorca attended. He had gotten very little sleep the night before. He still couldn't believe he was on a mission to rescue a man he despised. On top of that he was highly suspicious of the Bureau's intelligence regarding Lorca. He suspected that Lorca's real motives were not purely based on wanting to get out of the country to turn evidence on his fellow drug lords. He wouldn't put it pass Lorca to have set up this whole scam in retaliation for the killing of his brother. He promised himself that if Lorca even blinked the wrong way, he would waste him and face the consequences later.

Chase arrived in Morelia at midday and decided that it would be better to lay over in the bustle of the city rather than raise suspicion by wandering in Quiroga. He would set out for the small village a couple hours before dark, leaving him ample time to collect the information he needed.

Chase started testing his photographic memory, trying to recall every detail from his last visit to Quiroga but the last time he was there, his only concern was getting Lorena safely away from Lorca. After struggling to jog his memory, Chase realized he would have to rely on the sketchy plans of the village Eddings had provided for him.

As soon as the sun dripped down below the midday cloud cover, Chase was on the move. He drove to the center of Quiroga and went into a small restaurant announcing he was a professional photographer doing a story on the regional culture. After having sufficiently pumped the locals for information, he meandered through the streets under the pretense of taking photographs. The entire time he was memorizing every detail of the village. Quiroga barely qualified to be called a "town." The narrow cobblestone streets were lined with eroded adobe-walled homes built in the eighteenth century. The dim lamps lining the streets were turned off by nine o'clock. With the exception of a few stragglers, most of the villagers would be tucked away in their homes, recuperating from the daily grind of surviving in this rugged environment. All this was good news from Chase's perspective; the fewer people around the better.

As Chase surveyed the only road in and out of town, he knew there was no room for error. The south and west ends of town backed-up against Lake Pátzcuaro. A swim would be a daunting task at best, given that the lake was over twenty miles long and seriously polluted from all the sewage pouring in from the surrounding villages. Chase made a few more mental notes and then started walking the half-mile toward the church to get a feel for the landscape and see what he and Emiliano would have to deal with during their escape route. The sun was diving into the distant rosy haze as he reached the steep road up to the church. He paused for a moment, looked west to the lakeshore and calculated how long it would take a man to cover the distance from the church to the lake. He thought it was no longer than fifteen minutes at a good clip.

Eventually, Chase reached the small church of St. Ignacio. The church was perched on the hill overlooking the lush farmland of corn crops and avocados. Eddings had been right about the road dead-ending at the church steps. The structure itself was larger than he expected for a village the size of Quiroga, but this wasn't unusual in Mexico. Chase had often wondered how these little villages could afford the opulence they spent on their beloved churches; St. Ignacio was no exception. The façade was covered with carved statues of both indigenous Indians and Spanish religious figures. The matching steeples were adorned with two sets of stained brass bells.

As he entered through the termite-pitted doors, he made note of the large crossbar standing in the corner, used to secure the door from the inside. Chase stepped into the arched marble portico as the last rays of sunlight poured through the stained glass image of St. Ignacio just above the cracked, pink agate altar. Chase was not looking forward to disturbing the solitude of such a holy place to carry out his mission. Aside from the two elderly, pious women in the front row devoutly lost in prayer, the church was empty.

He walked down the center aisle, admiring the dedication of the church's patrons. The walls were adorned with huge Romanesque paintings depicting scenes from the Twelve Stations of the Cross. The paint was barely visible from years of billowing candle smoke and black soot. When he reached the point opposite to the mesquite confessional, he turned right and gingerly made his way over to the confessional. He opened the ornately carved door and sat in the same seat where Lorca confessed his sins. Chase wondered whether his adversary was truthful in his confession, and if so, how the priest must have sat in horror, knowing he had to find forgiveness for Lorca's horrific acts. Chase slid open the small window between the sinner and the priest, noting the size and dimensions of the sitting areas. Once he was satisfied that he had put to memory every aspect of the confessional, he turned to survey the rest of the church's interior.

While Chase was completing his end of the plan, Emiliano was busy making calls and collecting equipment. He had turned Chase's living room floor into a mini-warehouse. Emiliano was sitting in one of the over-stuffed chairs, sorting and packing each item, when someone knocked on the door. The harsh rapping surprised him since he was positive nobody knew he and Chase were staying at the house. He cautiously approached the door and opened a small security window.

Emiliano quickly slammed it shut, reacting as if he had seen a ghost. The shock of seeing Lorena on the other side of the door caused him to begin sweating profusely. Reluctantly, he opened the door and greeted her. "Hello, Lorena. What a pleasant surprise," he said, almost choking on his words. It was one of the rare times in his life when he was at a loss for words.

"You damn well know why I'm here. Where's Chase?" Lorena was in no mood for playing games with Emiliano.

"He's out of town on business. I thought it was illegal for you to come back to Mexico?"

"Thanks to you, I understand! Are you going to invite me in, or do I have to stand outside of my own home?"

"Sorry. Please come in," Emiliano politely offered, hoping to ease the tension.

Emiliano was so distressed by Lorena's presence that he completely forgot about the equipment scattered around the living room floor. Lorena walked directly into the cluttered space.

"Starting a new business are we, Emiliano?" Lorena mocked as she set her purse down on a nearby end table.

"Not exactly. It's some old stuff Chase had sitting around the house that he asked me to get rid of," he stated, hoping he might just get away with this lame excuse.

"Let's cut through all the lies. I know why Chase is here." Her intense stare could have weakened even the strongest fortitude.

"You do?" Emiliano said, feigning shock. He was still not ready to give up the charade.

"You and Chase are down here working on a case, and don't try to deny it." She paused long enough for her words to register with Emiliano. "I also know both of you have been involved in paying off officials to keep me out of the country."

"Look, it was for your own protection."

"Since when did I ask for your help?" she growled, peering at him with unfettered anger.

"Chase was afraid you might try to come back while Lorca was still settling his account with him. Lorca's not the kind of guy to give up after just one try."

"I don't care what Chase thought he was doing. He should have told me. Instead, he lied about keeping me out of Mexico and about working for the Bureau. He swore to me he would never take another assignment. I wouldn't have married him if I had known he was a scheming liar." She turned and surveyed the array of gun belts, knives, and other supplies scattered around the living room floor.

"Don't say that, Lorena. You know he cares deeply for you."

"If this is how he defines love, then I've been sadly mistaken my whole life about what the word really means." She shot back a glance of total disdain. "Enough about our personal life. When do you expect Chase back?"

"Tomorrow sometime, late afternoon." Emiliano looked beaten down from Lorena's barrage.

"*Oh, great; all we need now is a pissed off wife getting in our way.*" Emiliano reflected. This mission was almost impossible anyway, without having to contend with Chase's marital problems. He hoped Chase could calm Lorena down once she heard the circumstances behind this particular assignment.

"I'm staying at the Hotel San Cristobal. I suggest you let Chase know as soon as he gets back into town."

"Yeah, sure. Just curious, how did you know we were here?"

"Don't worry your little brain; I can assure you that I haven't caused a major security breach for your operation. Let's just say, I've got my own spies." Lorena let Emiliano's mind spin in place for a good ten seconds, then she let him off the hook. "Luis saw you coming out of the restaurant the other night and called me. At least someone is looking out for my interests."

"I'm sorry about this, Lorena. I know if Chase could have avoided this, none of us would be here right now."

"I don't care what his reasons were. All I want from Chase is to hear the truth from his own lips. Just tell me one thing, Emiliano." Her voice softened for just a moment. "Is it another woman?"

"No, Lorena. If he isn't anything else, he's faithful. He would do anything for you." Emiliano's eyes pleaded for her to believe him.

"I don't want *anything*; I just want the truth!" At that, Lorena stomped out of the room and headed for the front door, slamming it behind her.

Emiliano plopped down in an over-stuffed chair and tried to imagine how he was going to explain to Chase that his wife was here and she was waiting for him with both barrels loaded. He started to wonder which of the two problems was going to be more dangerous for Chase, extracting Lorca or facing the fury of his young bride. Emiliano was sure Chase had seen his fair share of angry women before, but knew that there was nothing like a hot-blooded Latin woman to rattle the constitution of even the most brave-hearted man.

Emiliano returned to sorting out the supplies, Chase would not be in the mood for any excuses when he returned in the morning from his surveillance mission.

Chase arrived at ten o'clock and was greeted by an anxious Emiliano. Chase immediately suspected something was awry. Emiliano was uncharacteristically fumbling over his words as he tried to give Chase an inventory of the last twenty-four hours.

Finally, Chase couldn't stand it any longer. "Emiliano, what the hell is going on?"

"I don't know exactly how to tell you this, so I'll just give it to you straight. Lorena is here in Ciudad Hidalgo."

"What!" Chase's voice raised two octaves as he turned to face Emiliano in disbelief.

"She came to the house last night and practically gave me a heart attack."

"How the hell did she get here?"

"I don't know, but I suspect Luis helped her grease the skids with Immigration."

"Luis Goya, her manager?" Before Chase finished uttering his question, a vision exploded in front of him like flashing camera bulbs. Luis Goya was the stranger he saw the other night coming out of the restaurant. How could he not have remembered?

"Where is she now?"

"At the Posada de Cristobal."

"Well, she can't stay here in Mexico. It's too dangerous. She has to go back to Texas immediately," Chase stated in a matter of fact way.

"Chase, I'd be a little cautious if I were you. She is not exactly in the mood for being ordered around."

"Emiliano, don't tell me how to manage my personal affairs!" Chase rebuked, as his head snapped around to face a somewhat stunned Emiliano.

"All right, but she knows you were involved in the plan to keep her out of the country."

Chase stopped in his tracks. "How the hell did she find that out?"

"I'm not sure, but you can bet her sneaky little manager was in on it. Somehow, she figured out you're down here working on an assignment for the Bureau. It would be an understatement to say she's furious."

"I don't care what she knows or how pissed off she is at me. We can't afford to have her butting into our business and jeopardizing the mission."

"I don't think she cares anything about the mission. She's feeling betrayed right now, and she needs to hear a reason other than it's none of her business."

"Betrayed or not, she can't stay here." Chase was even more adamant than before. "Does she know any details about our mission, or that it involves Lorca?"

"Fortunately, no, but I wouldn't put it beyond her to try to find out. She's desperate for any answers right now."

"I'm going over to the hotel to straighten this out. When I get back, I'll fill you in on what I found out in Quiroga. Any problems on your end?"

"No, I think we are all set."

"See you in about an hour."

Chase turned and marched off, determined to confront Lorena and demand that she leave for Texas as soon as possible.

Emiliano laughed to himself at the thought of the inexperienced newlywed Chase thinking he was going to take the "bull by the horns" and solve his problems with Lorena so effortlessly. Having been married for thirteen years, he knew Chase had little or no chance of cleaning up this mess in an hour. Chase would be lucky if he had it straightened out by the time they had to leave the next morning.

Chase walked into the lobby of Lorena's hotel and headed to the front desk. "I would like the room number for Señora Chandler, please."

The front desk clerk checked the guest list and told Chase there was no Chandler registered at the hotel.

Chase persisted, "Please, check again. I'm positive she is staying here." He nervously looked around the lobby maybe hoping to see Lorena.

The clerk carefully glanced through the registration list again and informed the impatient Chase, "Sorry sir, there is no one registered by that name."

Chase didn't want to believe what he was thinking. "Could you check under the name of Santoya?"

This time, the clerk confirmed that she was registered. "Unfortunately, sir, she is not in right now."

"Did she leave any messages?"

"No sir, but she said she would return later this afternoon."

Chase could barely contain his fury. If she was out trying to stick her nose into his business, then all hell was going to break loose when he found her.

"Sir, would you like to leave a message for her?" the clerk asked politely, sensing Chase's irritation.

"Yes, please tell her that her husband was here, and he'll call her later."

"I'll make sure she gets the message, Señor Santoya," said the clerk.

Chase rudely stomped out of the hotel ignoring the clerk's remark. He returned to the house and immediately set to the task of filling Emiliano in on the details from his trip to Quiroga.

They made a few key changes to their plan and went through the checklist to make sure they hadn't overlooked any details. Around six o'clock, they finally finished packing and loading everything into the car.

Twice, Chase called the front desk at the hotel to see if Lorena had returned, but he was disappointed she hadn't returned. His anger was turning to concern with each unanswered call. He waited another thirty minutes and called again, but still no Lorena. Emiliano offered to take him to dinner, but Chase refused. Emiliano's appetite finally got the best of him, and he decided get a bite to eat on his own. Returning from the restaurant, Emiliano checked in on Chase one more time before heading to bed.

"Any word from Lorena?" Emiliano nervously inquired. He could see the answer to his question from Chase's rumpled posture.

"Not yet."

"I'm sure she'll show up. I'm going to catch some shuteye, and I would suggest you do the same."

Chase didn't respond to Emiliano's suggestion.

"See you in the morning. Seven o'clock, right?"

There was a long pause before he answered. "Right. Seven o'clock." He continued staring straight ahead into the dwindling flames in the fireplace.

Chase had no idea that while he was pacing nervously around his living room, Lorena had been spending the day with Lolo Nieto, whom she had run into at breakfast. Even though she was still aggravated with him for his behavior last year at Tauromaquia, it was nice to see a familiar face. After trying to ignore his glaring stare from across the restaurant, she finally relented and invited Lolo to join her.

As Lolo approached her table, Lorena wondered if she had made a mistake. Was she so in need of company that she would lower herself to spending time with an ex-lover whom she could barely tolerate?

Lolo reached her table and he bent over to kiss her on the cheek, but she turned her head to avoid his welcoming gesture.

"Don't think for a moment, just because I've invited you to join me, I've forgiven you for the way you treated me the last time we met."

"I know this is asking a lot, but can we please bury the hatchet? I had had too much to drink, and seeing you that night at Tauromaquia brought back all the pain of losing you. I'm sorry," Lolo eyed Lorena, hoping she could see the sincerity of his words.

"I'll accept your apology this time, but if I see even one sign of your treating me that way again, I can promise you there won't be another second chance. And on the subject of being deserted, you deserved everything you got and more. If you recall, you were the one who couldn't restrain from extra-curricular activities with the young ladies."

"All right, you win. I was an inconsiderate asshole. Look, we've known each other for a long time, and I wouldn't want one foolish act on my part to destroy years of friendship. Agreed?" His puppy dog expression begged for forgiveness.

Lorena couldn't believe what she was hearing. Was he admitting that he actually was wrong? Could it be that he was starting to show some signs of sensitivity? Lorena stared at the man taking a seat across from her; still not sure she could trust his motives.

"Is this a new Lolo I haven't met before? Are you turning over a new leaf?"

Lolo chuckled. "Sarcasm will get you nowhere. If anyone should know, it's me."

"Sorry, that was uncalled for. Can we start over?" Lorena was willing to give him the benefit of the doubt for now.

"Why not?" He smiled cautiously. "What are you doing here anyway? I heard rumors you married a rich American gringo and were living the good life in the U.S.A."

She hesitated before answering his question. "Yes, I got married about ten months ago. I believe you met him, Chase Chandler."

"He wouldn't happen to be the gentleman in shining white armor who was ready to rearrange my face last year at the Tauromaquia?"

"Yes, that's him."

Lolo denoted a touch of cynicism in her tone of voice. "Well, how is married life? Is it everything they say it is?" Lolo chuckled, not knowing the level of pain she was feeling at this very moment.

With his innocent question, Lorena could feel the sadness and betrayal starting to well up in her again. She struggled to find an appropriate answer. Her eyes dampened with tears. She started to reach for a napkin to dab her eyes when Lolo handed his handkerchief to her.

"Sorry, I can see I put my foot succinctly in my mouth again."

"It's just...you think you know someone; then all of a sudden, you feel like you're living with a complete stranger."

Lorena couldn't believe she was sharing her feelings about Chase with him. Of all people, why had she chosen him? Maybe, it was because at one time they *were* good friends. Maybe because she felt safe with him, knowing there was no way she could ever feel anything other than a cautious friendship with Lolo.

"You sound like you could use a little distraction right now. I'm going out to look at some property at one of the nearby ranchos. Would you like to come along?"

"I don't know." She was hesitant to go anywhere with Lolo; but she also didn't want to mope around waiting all day for Chase to show up. Every time she thought of him and how he had lied, her heart felt like it was going to implode and disappear into the emptiness of her sorrow.

Lolo asked her again. "Come on. It'll be good for you. Besides, my reputation and ego could use a little help right now."

"All right, but I have to be back by no later than five o'clock."

They drove through the lush hill country outside of Ciudad Hidalgo; their conversation was still somewhat stilted. As much as he was tempted, Lolo made sure to avoid any further inquiry about her personal life. He could tell from her somber mood that she was suffering from a recent incident with her husband. He recognized the familiar symptoms from his brief relationship with Lorena and knew this was not a time to pressure her for answers. Lolo decided to keep the conversation focused on his troubles, hoping it might distract Lorena from her own. He told her about his recent problems with Diego Sanchez and how his dreams had been dashed when Diego showed up on the scene.

Lorena hadn't thought about Diego Sanchez since Chase surprised her after her performance in Guadalajara. Her life had been in such chaos since Chase swept her away and proposed. After her kidnapping, Chase's rescue, and her recent marriage, it was a wonder she could recall any of the circumstances of that eventful evening. Lorena remembered feeling guilty about stranding Diego when she so mysteriously disappeared without a word of explanation. Although they had only interacted from a distance, Lorena still felt an unexplainable attraction to Diego Sanchez. She could tell from her conversation with Lolo that he did not share the same feelings for Diego. Lolo was openly bitter toward his rival, and couldn't wait until the great master retired at the end of the next season. She was thankful that Lolo was so self-absorbed in his own problems. It provided her with a needed respite from facing her own emotional dilemma.

On their way back into town, having looked at several properties, they stopped at a small village and ate a late lunch. Lorena ordered several margaritas during the meal, hoping the tequila would take the edge off of the unrelenting tension she felt. The two old friends reminisced about some of the foolish situations they had gotten themselves into in their late teens as they explored the nightlife of Mexico City.

Before Lorena realized it, they had spent the entire day talking about old times. When Lorena looked out the window of the restaurant, she saw that the sun was already starting to set. A vision of Chase frantically searching and not finding her waiting at the hotel came hurtling into her mind. The sudden reality of what was awaiting hit her like a cold shower. She abruptly ended the conversation midstream, and told Lolo that she really needed to return to town. She apologized for the urgency but hoped that he understood. Lolo paid the bill and they drove back toward Ciudad Hidalgo.

The joviality of their earlier conversation vanished. Lorena hardly spoke another word the rest of the short drive back to town. Lolo tried on more than one occasion to reengage Lorena, but she was not in the mood for any more small talk.

Lorena was trying to prepare herself for a potentially volatile situation when she confronted Chase with all his lies. She knew the events of the last few days could easily spell the end of their brief marriage. Even though she was overwhelmed by the prospect of losing her comfortable life with Chase, she preferred to face this minefield of emotions than live a life of deception. As Lorena watched the last glimpses of daylight disappear, she hoped Chase had a rational explanation for his behavior. She was willing to listen to any legitimate reason that could stop the impending train wreck from tearing their lives apart.

Chase called the hotel one last time before trying to get some badly needed sleep. The front desk clerk was just about to inform Chase that his wife was still out, when Lorena and Lolo walked into the hotel lobby. "Sir, your wife is just coming into the hotel. Would you like me to hold the line until she gets to her room?"

The clerk was reticent to hand the phone directly to Lorena, not knowing what the situation was with the handsome young man escorting her. He had seen lovers use the hotel for a secret rendezvous in the past.

"No, that's all right. I'll be right over," Chase said, and he hung up the phone before the clerk could warn him about the possible compromising situation confronting him once he arrived at the hotel.

Lolo escorted Lorena to her room on the second floor. They stood outside her door sharing small talk about when she might be back in Mexico City. Lorena told Lolo she was unsure about her future at this point, but if and when everything was straightened out, she would be glad to be his guest at one of his tournaments. They both were feeling good about having reconciled their strained relationship.

Chase was almost to the top of the stairs, when he heard Lorena's voice echoing down the hallway. He stopped on the last stair, posing cautiously at the corner of the staircase. He was about to round the corner when he heard the distinct lower tone of a man's voice. He froze in his tracks.

Lorena opened the door to her room and stepped halfway inside. Feeling much more comfortable with Lolo, she felt compelled to let him know how much she appreciated his kindness. She leaned over and innocently kissed him on the lips. Her gesture even shocked Lolo. He knew it was nothing more than a platonic kiss, but it clearly sent a sign that he had redeemed himself.

Just as Lorena's lips lightly touched Lolo's, Chase peeked around the corner, instantly recognizing the man kissing his wife as Lolo Nieto. It appeared that his devoted wife was inviting Lolo into her room. Revolted, Chase jerked back from the scene and, in a cat-like motion, made his way down the stairs, and then rushed through the lobby and out into the street. All he could think about was what Lorena had told him about her previous relationship with Lolo. His blood boiled with jealous rage at the thought that Lorena had rekindled her relationship with the arrogant Lolo.

Chase turned into a nearby alley and waited to see if Lolo would exit the hotel. He waited for over a half-hour with no sign of Lolo. His mind was flooded with visions of Lolo's sleek hard body writhing on top of his wife. Chase felt his fingernails digging into the soft adobe wall of the building he rested against. His body shuddered with each excruciating thought of them together. How could it have come to this?

A good part of his incentive for taking this mission was to get Fermin Lorca out of the country so Lorena wouldn't be arrested by U.S. authorities and deported. He was risking his life to save Lorena's! How could she betray him so easily? Chase lost track of the fact he was the one who had originally deceived her with his lies.

While Chase was imagining the worst case scenario, Lolo was saying goodnight to Lorena and wishing her the best. Heading out of the hotel, Lolo ran into an old friend in the lobby and joined him for a drink in the bar.

After forty minutes of sheer misery, Chase saw Lolo exit the hotel. Lolo turned in his direction and Chase edged farther back into the dark alley, contemplating what action he might take next against his unsuspecting victim. He thought about snatching Lolo as he passed by and interrogating him about whether he enjoyed screwing his wife. He even thought about ending Lolo's life then and there. He knew it wouldn't be hard to make it look like a simple robbery gone awry.

Before Chase could react, Lolo's image flashed in his mind. Chase reached into the depths of his self-control and decided to wait for another time. First, he would deal with his adulterous wife.

Chase waited until he was sure Lolo was safely out of sight before slithering from the shadows of the alleyway. He stood under the amber glow of the streetlight, still trying to decide whether he had the guts to confront Lorena. He was torn between wanting to know the truth and begging for her forgiveness. All the anger he felt toward her for having come back to Ciudad Hidalgo and jeopardized the mission was evaporating. The anguish of seeing her with Lolo was replaced with the thought of losing her forever. Through all these conflicting images and emotions, Chase came to the realization that he only wanted to know one thing, was she still in love with him?

He stood in front of Lorena's hotel room door, hesitating before knocking. He knocked twice, heaved a deep sigh, and waited to find out the destiny of his relationship with the woman he loved.

Lorena, hearing the rapping sound on her door, thought it was Lolo returning. She was unprepared when she peered through the peephole and saw her husband fretfully rocking back and forth on his heels. For some reason, she was expecting him to call first. Lorena closed her eyes tight, unlatched the safety lock and opened the door.

They stood facing each other without speaking a word, neither one of them wanting to take the first step toward reconciliation. Chase's eyes nervously swayed as Lorena stared straightforward. She could feel the rapid thumping of her heart on the inside wall of her chest. Standing face to face with Chase brought back all the angst she had felt for the last twenty-four hours. She wanted answers, and she wanted them now! They clumsily interrupted each other as both tried to speak at the same time.

Finally, Chase prevailed. "Can I come in?" he asked cautiously.

Chase was determined to try and restrain his rampant emotions. All his training as an agent during the war should have prepared him for this kind of predicament, but he could feel years of discipline slipping away.

A simple, solemn "Yes" was all Lorena could muster as she stepped aside to let Chase enter the room.

He walked to the balcony overlooking the street below then turned to face her. "I know I owe you an explanation, but I want you to know I would never have done anything to purposely hurt you."

"Chase, I trusted you. My God, I was willing to give up my life, postpone my career for you, and this is how you repay me."

"I know you must be feeling terribly hurt right now, but I need to ask you to go back to Texas. I'll explain everything when I get back home. This is just not the time or place."

His innocent request re-ignited the firestorm in Lorena that had slowly started to subside throughout the day. Just before Chase arrived, she had promised herself to try to stay composed and give him an opportunity to explain, but his bullying remark put her over the edge.

"This is going to have to be the time and place!" She started to pace around the small space she occupied. "I am not going to be the good little Texas wife patiently waiting for her man to return. You owe me an explanation for your behavior and I'm not leaving until I get one," she angrily demanded.

"Lorena, I'm down here trying not to get killed in the next couple of days, and you're making it difficult as hell."

"*I'm* making it difficult? You're the one who had the audacity to look me straight in the eye and swear you would do anything to help me get back to Mexico? Try explaining that for starters. How much did you have to spend to keep me out of Mexico? Was everything you promised just a long list of lies?" Lorena sat down on the edge of the bed trying to calm her nerves.

"Lorena, you know in your heart I'm not that kind of person." Chase could feel his temper beginning to swell inside his chest.

Their anger was becoming contagious, spreading at a fever pitch.

"I'm not so sure who you are anymore. If you remember, you swore to me that you would never go out on another mission. If that's what you're really doing down here..."

"What are you implying?" His voice rose in volume and pitch.

"For all I know you have been having affairs with other women right under my nose. What kind of business trips have you really been taking?" Lorena knew she wasn't being rational, but she needed to eliminate the possibility of her husband's infidelity. She stood up and walked across the room until she was standing next to Chase.

Chase turned in her direction. They were standing face to face, only inches away from each other. Both their faces were flushed red. Neither one of their rigid bodies had the posture of someone who was about to back down.

"I wouldn't call the kettle black, if I were you. I just saw you with Lolo Nieto in the hallway. And by the way, where were you all day, with your ex-lover?" His words were accusatory and biting, he stepped toward the door as to leave. Chase wheeled around and confronted her with a stare so ruthless that it startled even the stoic Lorena.

Lorena held her ground and lashed out at his threatening look. "I see your spying doesn't end with your professional life! I won't stand here and have you insult me when you're the one who has filled our lives with vicious lies. I want you to leave right now." She turned and faced the balcony window.

"You're going back to Texas where you belong," Chase ordered. "We can finish this conversation later. Don't force me to call the local authorities and have you deported."

Chase reeled around and started out of the room. Lorena rushed toward him and grabbed his forearm. As she clutched at him, he flung her hand off, accidentally losing control. In one violent motion, his clenched fist struck her squarely on the right cheek, just below the lower ridge of her eye, grazing the bridge of her delicate nose.

The force of the blow sent her stumbling to the floor. Lorena scrambled away from him, her back landing hard against the foot of the bed. She cowered in pain from the violence of Chase's blow.

When Chase realized what he had done, a sick empty feeling ascended from the pit of his stomach. He had never struck a woman before or even considered that he was capable of such a despicable act. He felt as though he were sliding down a dark chute into a ghastly hell solely created for wife-beaters. As much as he tried to convince himself it was an accident, he knew there was still no excuse for his behavior.

Lorena lay crumbled on the floor against the edge of the bed, holding her hand to her throbbing cheek. The force of the blow had caused her nose to bleed. The physical pain was bad enough, but the fear and disgust she felt sickened her almost to the point of vomiting. Tears started streaming down her already swollen cheek. She put her hands up to her face, glaring at Chase through the spaces between of her fingers.

Her anguished expression left Chase paralyzed. He was trying desperately to rewind the last few minutes as if it had never happened. Chase rushed over trying to console her and sputtering about how it was an accident, but Lorena already was on her feet and running for the door.

"Lorena, please wait! I'm so sorry. It was an accident. Can't you believe me?" The words couldn't roll off his lips fast enough. Never had he felt so helpless. He started after her but he was too afraid to rush toward her again and repeat the same horrifying mistake.

Ignoring his plea, Lorena frantically rushed to the door. She clawed at the doorknob with her tear-drenched hands. All she wanted to do was get out of the room and away from him. She finally managed to fling open the door and escape. Chase was fast on her heels as she raced down the hallway.

"Lorena, please don't go. I can explain everything." His petition of honesty and concern fell on deaf ears.

Lorena couldn't hear anything but the sound of disgust ringing in her head. She was halfway down the hotel stairs before Chase realized that pursuing her would probably only make the situation worse. He stopped, slumped against the hallway wall and put his hands over his temples, trying desperately to squeeze the grief from his guilt-ridden mind. *This couldn't be happening! They had it all!*

Lorena ran out into the street, looking in both directions, confused about which way to go. Her cheek was still pounding with the sting of Chase's blow. She could already feel the swelling under her hand as she tried to hide her embarrassment. She turned right and ran down the sidewalk, careening off unsuspecting bystanders. Everything seemed distorted, as if she were lost in a hall of mirrors at a carnival show. A stranger on the street pleaded with her to stop so he could help her. She ignored his plea and continued to run down the street. When she reached the corner, she turned and disappeared into the seclusion of the unoccupied alley.

Chase spent the next few hours roaming the streets, hoping to find Lorena. Coming up empty handed, he returned to her hotel, hoping she might have returned. After waiting for over an hour, he left. It was eleven-thirty, and Chase had only a few hours remaining before leaving for Quiroga.

Reluctantly, he returned to his home and found Emiliano anxiously pacing back and forth, anxious and worried about the outcome of Chase and Lorena's meeting.

"I was just getting ready to send out a search party. What the hell happened?" Emiliano could see Chase was upset.

"Let's just say things didn't go as planned."

"Sorry to hear that, my friend. Are we still on for tomorrow?"

Chase didn't answer Emiliano initially; then he slowly nodded his head affirmatively.

Chase was torn between fulfilling his mission or continuing his search for Lorena. He knew Eddings was serious about having Lorena arrested for illegally entering the U.S. The only chance of reconciling with Lorena and having a normal life again depended on completion of the mission. He could only hope that once Lorena knew the whole story, she would forgive him. Chase realized that he would still have to convince her that everything that had happened in her hotel room was irrational and an accident in the heat of argument, and that it would never happen again. She *had* to know he wasn't the kind of man who would purposefully harm her. Chase closed his eyes and recited a silent prayer, hoping somehow his message would be channeled to Lorena. Chase hoped that his prayer wouldn't fall on deaf ears and she would go home to their ranch and wait for him to return.

"Chase, is there anything I can do?" Emiliano sympathetically asked.

"Do you have the power to turn back time?" he sighed pitifully.

"I'm afraid not." Emiliano felt defenseless to comfort his friend.

Chase shifted back to the task at hand. "I'm going to get some shut eye. We'll leave at six in the morning."

He turned away from Emiliano and headed toward the library. His body language said it all. Once inside his private sanctuary, Chase opened the liquor cabinet and poured himself a stiff drink of Johnny Walker Red. He sat down in his favorite overstuffed chair and leaned his head against the headrest. He raised the glass, took a sip, and placed the outside of the glass on his forehead. He couldn't get Lorena out of his mind. He finally fell asleep but not before shivering with the thought of Lorena wondering alone through the empty streets of Ciudad Hidalgo.

CHAPTER 19

Diego had a successful winter season and was looking forward to the last legs of his final tournament schedule, which culminated in Mexico City on the Dia de la Revelucion, on November 20, 1985. It had been a long season and his last few tournaments had been physically and emotionally taxing. He was so distracted by his efforts to locate Amado Flores that there were times when he barely avoided losing several major bouts. Every time he stepped onto the fighting strip, Diego wondered if his son just might be a spectator in the crowd, watching, unaware that it was his own father was standing before him, fighting to uphold his reputation in the fencing world.

Diego still had Lolo Nieto biting at his heels, taunting and challenging him on every occasion. In fact, promoters had picked up on the heated rivalry and were pressing for more and more exhibitions involving the young upstart and the older master. Whenever they were on the same card, the stadium was sold out. Although Lolo was getting his fair share of acclaim in the press, he was still bitterly angry with Diego for constantly upstaging him. The fans were also getting caught up in the conflict, started to divide their allegiance equally between the brash, flamboyant Lolo and the calm, collected Diego. Both men were fighting brilliantly, even though Diego always ended up on top it was clear Lolo was gaining ground on the old master. They were in each other's face constantly and it was subtly taking its toll on both of them. In fact, it seemed Diego couldn't even avoid Lolo when he was on vacation. A few months ago while Diego was in Ciudad Hidalgo having lunch with a friend, he spotted Lolo in the restaurant. The two men acknowledged each other from across the room, but bolts of hostility arched over innocent diners like streaks of lightning.

It wasn't just a coincidence that Lolo and Diego were in the same town. Lolo spent a great deal of his off-time visiting friends and hanging around the local bar scenes of Ciudad Hidalgo. He had done some of his novice training in nearby Querétaro, and was considering the purchase of property on the outskirts of town. Diego was home enjoying the peace and quiet of his ranch outside of Ciudad Hidalgo. He was on a rare break from his other promotional commitments that seemed to consume his life outside of tournaments. *Ten months and counting*, he thought with a sense of relief.

February was normally the month when everyone caught up on badly-needed rest. It was also the chance to take care of personal business, such as visiting family or, in Diego's case, working on his obsession with finding his son, Amado Flores. It had been almost six months since he had visited Celaya's parents and every spare moment had been dedicated to finding out as much as he could about his newly discovered son. At one point, he was so desperate to discover Amado's whereabouts that he even considered going back to Celaya's parents' ranch and revealing the truth about his true identity. Try as he might he had made little progress in his search for the truth about his son. Time constraints between his busy schedule which included helping his ailing father, had consumed most of his free time over the past six months. In fact, Diego had cancelled two tournaments to take care of his father, who recently had had a couple of minor heart attacks. Frustrated, and realizing he was fighting an uphill battle in the search for Amado, Diego hired a private detective two months ago.

The detective discovered that Amado Flores had changed his identity to avoid the stigma of being a bastard child. Celaya's family was very protective of their grandson's privacy, making a pact to never reveal his new identity. The detective confirmed what Diego had found out from other relatives; Amado had been a very rebellious child. When he turned twelve, his grandparents sent him to a private school, hoping it would straighten him out. The prestigious school was known for educating some of the most prominent families in Mexico and school officials prided themselves in protecting their students' personal information. It was in this sheltered environment that Amado adopted his new name and where the trail disappeared to Amado's new identity.

In reviewing the transcripts of the interviews the detective had conducted with teachers and former classmates, Diego was only able to glean tidbits about Amado's early life. What was clear from the interviews was that Amado was a loner and had made very few friends at school. Complicating the mystery even more was the fact that Amado unexpectedly left the school when he was fifteen and virtually disappeared from sight.

The one pertinent piece of information that intrigued Diego about the detective's report was the fact that Amado was noted for his total disregard for danger. A fellow student recalled in one of the interviews an incident when a local rancher near the school was transporting fighting bulls to Mexico City and had accidentally run off the road and into a ditch. The students having heard the commotion immediately rushed to the adjoining fence line to watch the rancher and his hired hands as they tried to corral three disoriented, angry bulls. The rancher was successful in recapturing two of the confused animals, but the last one was not about to cooperate without a fight. The large, black beast with wide jutting horns had already severely injured one of the ranch hands. Having seen the result of the bull's fury, the hired hands were doing their best to keep a safe distance from the bull. It was then, out of nowhere, that Amado appeared with a swath of red cloth he had taken from the school cafeteria table. He jumped into the fray, taunting the bull with his pseudo cape. Onlookers watched in horror as he positioned himself in front of the gate where the ranch hands were attempting to herd the infuriated bull. Amado assumed the classic position of a matador and crept slowly toward the bull. His fellow students and instructors called out to Amado demanding that he get the hell out of there before he got himself killed. Ignoring their desperate pleas, Amado continued to goad the snorting beast. All at once, the bull put his head down, shook his horns violently from side to side, and charged full speed in Amado's direction. Instead of running as any normal person would, Amado stood his ground, arched his back in complete defiance of the ensuing danger, and held his red tablecloth steady. The bull struck the cloth with a furious hooking motion as Amado slowly lifted the cape over the animal's back. Before the beast realized it, the bull was on the other side of fence and the ranch hands were slamming the gate closed.

The students who recounted the story told the detective, "Amado simply ignored our calls of praise, nonchalantly walked off the field and returned quietly to his studies in the library."

Diego laughed out loud as he finished reading the interview and could only hope his son had learned to be a little more caution as he matured.

Diego was just finishing off the last part of the interviews, when his housekeeper came rushing into the room.

"Señor Sanchez, you have an urgent call from the hospital." Diego hurried to pick up the phone. It was his father's physician, Dr. Franco Gutierrez.

"Diego, your father has had a major heart attack," said Dr. Gutierrez in a somber tone.

"Is he still alive?"

"Yes, but I'm afraid he won't last long. I suggest you come to the hospital immediately."

"Is he still conscious?" His voice strained to complete his question.

"He's fading in and out. I can't guarantee what state he'll be in by the time you get here."

Diego was a little over two hours from the hospital in Guanajuato. He could only hope that his father had the strength and will to live long enough for him to get there.

Diego raced through the narrow, underground tunnels of Guanajuato. He reached the hospital, and rushed to the intensive care ward, hoping he would still find his father alive. Dr. Gutierrez was standing at the nurses' station when Diego crashed through the heavy double doors. Dr. Gutierrez turned toward Diego, who couldn't tell from the expression on the doctor's face whether his father was alive or dead.

"Relax, Diego, your father is resting peacefully. His condition has not improved, but he is stabilized for now."

"Is he alert? Can I see him?" Diego pleaded.

"Your father has been in and out of a semi-conscious state for the last few hours. He keeps calling out your name, Diego. You have to understand, he more than likely won't make it through the night."

"Thank you for everything you've done. I would like to see him now, if that's all right." Diego started down the hallway in the direction of his father's room. When he reached the door, he stopped to prepare himself for the worst. He slowly pushed the door open, making sure not to disturb his father and stepped over to the side of the bed. His father was staring at the ceiling, mumbling incoherently.

Diego quietly called out, "Father, it's me."

At first, the shell of the man he once knew to be so robust didn't recognize his son's voice, but then he slowly turned his head to face Diego. His father's eyes welled up with tears. Diego's heart filled with pain as a tear trickled down his father's weathered face. He reached over the bed rail and kissed his father's forehead. "I'm here, father."

The senior Sanchez motioned for Diego to come closer. He had only enough energy left in his failing body to whisper to his son. Diego leaned over until his ear was almost touching his father's ashen lips. Don Julio took a moment to try and gather his strength, and then whispered in his son's ear. "I'm so sorry. Please forgive me."

"You have nothing to be sorry for. You've been a wonderful father."

His father shook his head from side to side, denying his son's acknowledgement. "I've kept a dark secret from you for too many years. I'm not....a man of honor." His father paused to catch his breath. He reached up and grabbed Diego's collar, staring straight into his son's blue eyes. "You have a son."

His father's words rang through Diego as though he was standing next to one of the huge church bells at high noon. "What are you saying, father?" Diego's face was pained by his father's confession.

Don Julio released his grip, and Diego stood back far enough to see the truth reflected in his father's eyes. He was too stunned to react to the shocking news that his father had been involved in the conspiracy against him and Celaya. Diego didn't know whether to be angry or thank his father for finally being honest about his role in the conspiracy.

Diego remembered how adamant his father had been about sending him off to France and how reluctant he was to contact Celaya's family on his behalf. He looked down at the pitiful figure lying in bed and although he was sadly disappointed in his father's role in the deception, he could only feel compassion for the man who had raised and supported him for so long.

"I forgive you, father," Diego offered, not wanting to believe his father was the sole conspirator in keeping truth about Celaya away from him.

His father's eyes flickered as his breathing slowed measurably.

Diego called out to his father, "Father, please don't go. I still need your help."

Don Julio didn't respond. Diego called out loudly to the doctor. He leaned as close as he could to his father's ear and whispered, "Where is my son?" He repeated his desperate request again. "Where is my son?"

Don Julio did not respond to Diego's plea. His chest was still. Then he took one last heaving breath, and all the tension slowly slipped from his face. Dr. Gutierrez rushed over and placed his stethoscope over his father's heart. After a minute he lifted his hand from Don Julio's chest and sternly looked at Diego, "I'm sorry, Diego; he's gone."

Diego sat by his father's side for over an hour, not wanting to let go of the only remaining sliver of his family's long heritage. He thought about all the times he had spent away from his family selfishly chasing his career. Diego knew he should have come back years ago, but he was so haunted by the memories of Celaya he couldn't force himself to come home. He had used his career to build a wall around himself and kept everyone important out, including his family. Diego had hoped his adoring fans would be a substitute for his family, but staring down at the lifeless body of his father now, he could clearly see they were a poor substitute for his real family.

Before he left the hospital Diego took care of the arrangements for moving his father to the mortuary. As he drove from the parking lot of the hospital, he glanced in the rear view mirror and thought to himself, "*What a horrible place to die.*" Having lived much of his life on the edge, Diego couldn't imagine the banality of lying in a sterile hospital, gasping for his last breath.

On the long drive back to Ciudad Hidalgo, his thoughts returned to the conspiracy against him and Celaya. He knew someone other than his father was involved. The most likely candidate was his old maestro, Señor Alvarez. He was the sole person who had communicated all the messages regarding his inquiries about Celaya and her whereabouts. Alvarez had to be the one holding the answers to his son's identity. Unfortunately, he had just found out just a few days before that his former maestro had recently passed away. Diego regretted not making the time to visit his mentor at the sanitarium before his death. He was sure that had he made the effort, his search for the truth might be over. Diego decided that once his father's memorial service was over, he would contact Señor Alvarez's family in the hopes that he might find some scrap of evidence that could finally put all the pieces together for this tragic puzzle.

CHAPTER 20

It was almost midnight when Diego arrived in Ciudad Hidalgo from his father's memorial service in Guanajuato. It had been a little over a week since his father had passed away. He couldn't sleep, so he decided to take a walk. As he passed by the dimly lit Parroquia, he felt drawn into the church. The Cathedral was unoccupied as he crossed the threshold of deeply worn limestone pavers and made his way to the front row of the wooden pews. He genuflected, forming the sign of the cross and kissing his pinched index finger and thumb to conclude his holy reverence to the crucified Jesus overhanging a large marble altar.

He knelt down on the bench, stared up at the blood-drenched figure and recited several Hail Mary's and Our Fathers. He prayed that his father would be reunited with his beloved wife, Doña Maria. Their lifetime devotion to each other deserved to be consummated in heaven.

After Diego finished whispering his last prayer, he stood up and made his way to the marble rail in front of the altar. As he was lighting a candle for his mother and father, he heard the soft, whimpering sound of someone crying to his left. He looked over to one of the adjoining chapels and saw the outline of a slumped-over woman. The echo of her sobbing pierced the dry silence of the towering ceilings.

Normally, Diego would not have interfered with a stranger's private moment, but her sobbing was so pained that he felt compelled to ask her if she was all right.

He approached her from behind, not wanting to startle the woman and asked in a faint whisper, "Are you all right, Señora?"

A stilted response came from the sobbing woman, "I'm not really sure."

He took another step forward. "Can I help you?"

She slowly curved her head toward Diego, wiping the tears from her bloodshot eyes. Diego recognized her immediately; it was Lorena Santoya.

Lorena couldn't tell through the tears fogging her vision that the man standing in front of her was Diego Sanchez. The same man whom she had invited to her dressing room after reuniting with Chase in Mexico City.

"Can you heal a broken heart?" she asked, finally realizing that she had met this man before. She tried without success to place a name with the face.

"Señorita Santoya, if I had the power to help you, I can promise you I would." The grace of his words suddenly repaired her poor memory. "Señor Sanchez?" she whispered as her forehead crinkled in disbelief.

He knelt down beside her. "We finally meet in person; although I would have preferred it was under more cheerful circumstances....and please call me Diego."

"I must look like a mess," she said apologetically.

"Quite the contrary...you're as stunning as ever," he lied, flinching at the sight of a deep purple swelling on her right cheek.

"You're very kind. I'm surprised you're even speaking to me after my rude behavior in Mexico City."

"It's not the first time I've been stood up by a beautiful woman, and I'm sure it won't be my last."

Lorena smiled at his words. Diego assisted her to a wooden bench inside the small chapel. "Why don't we sit for awhile, and clean you up a little."

They sat under the statue of the Virgin Mary, whose mournful eyes were a close resemblance to Lorena's. Diego retrieved his white handkerchief from his coat pocket and dipped it into a marble holy water font. He lifted Lorena's chin up and began wiping the tears from her cheek.

Lorena looked up into his eyes and could see the genuine concern Diego had for her condition. As his hand neared the large crimson bruise, his touch became even more delicate. His eyes darted away from Lorena, as if trying not to acknowledge the embarrassing circumstances under which he had found her. Diego dabbed the wet cloth near her upper lip, wiping away a small trickle of dried blood from her nosebleed.

Lorena felt compelled say something about her condition. "I would explain, but it's a long story."

"Please....don't feel obligated to justify anything. This is obviously a personal matter, and you hardly know me," Diego offered, as he finished cleaning up her face.

"Thank you. Are you always such a gentleman, coming to the rescue of ladies in distress?" Lorena said, as she attempted to straighten out the front of her blood-stained blouse. Her normally perfectly groomed hair was frayed into a tangled mess. What little makeup she had on was smeared and gave her eyes the appearance of a raccoon. She felt as if she was in a freefall, plummeting into a hellish firestorm, every excruciating detail of her confrontation with Chase passing before her eyes; leaving nothing but the rubble of her marriage in its wake.

Diego could almost measure the pain she was feeling from the deep creases of her blackened eye. "Would you like me to drive you home?" Diego cautiously inquired. "It's late, and I would hate to see anything else happen to you."

The scene of her and Chase in her hotel room seized her thoughts again. The searing pain of his knuckles smashing into her face was as fresh as the shock of falling through an icy pond. She could feel her emotions starting to spin out of control again. The prospect of returning to her hotel and finding Chase waiting for her was too much to bear. She wondered if she would ever be able to return to a man who treated her so callously. Even if his jolting slap was an accident, how could she ever forgive him for his complicity in keeping her out of Mexico and lying to her about working for the FBI?

Diego could sense that Lorena was still hesitant to accept his offer. "I hope you don't think I'm being too presumptuous but my rancho is only a few miles outside of town. You're welcome to stay there tonight."

"Thank you for your offer, but I don't want to be a burden," she said, hoping Diego would persist with his offer.

"It's not a burden. You're welcome to stay as long as you need."

"You may come to regret your offer. I'm not sure I'll be very good company right now."

"Any company right now would be welcome." Diego said, feeling a tinge of excitement.

"How can I refuse the great Diego Sanchez?" Lorena teased, knowing from what she had read about him in the press that he hated any reference to his greatness.

"Haven't lost your sense of humor, I see. Can we go now before I change my mind?"

Both their faces broke into a cautious smile. They exited the side entrance of the church and walked to Diego's car that was parked down the street. The night air had a slight chill. Diego removed his black blazer and draped it over Lorena's shoulder. As her hand reached up to straighten the collar of the coat, she touched the back of his hand. Lorena held it just for a brief moment as if to thank him for all of his help. Her soft touch sent a shock wave through him. All the past feelings he had tried to ignore after first seeing her performance in Mexico City came rushing back. He felt guilty for having such strong feelings toward a woman who was obviously suffered a recent catastrophe in her personal life. Add to that the fact that she *was* a married woman, and Diego could barely stand to face the immorality of his own thoughts.

Diego had read in the newspapers that she had married an American businessman and the accounts of how she had suddenly disappeared and deserted her career. The tabloids made up a ridiculous story about how she had run off with a rich gringo to help pay off a large family debt. Finally, after two months, a persistent reporter tracked her down in Texas. The article didn't give any background on her marriage, but Diego was pretty confident she had married the man who had been in her dressing room the night he had first seen her dance.

After a short drive through countryside, Diego and Lorena arrived at his rancho. Diego pulled up in front of the large-adobe ranch house. The front courtyard was landscaped with an array of lush tropical plants, and three, forty-foot date palms that towered above the red, oven clay tile roof. It looked slightly out of place juxtaposed against the high desert fauna surrounding the rancho.

As they exited the car, a small hunched-over man with salt and pepper hair greeted them. His left foot dragged on the gravel driveway as he made his way toward them. The old man's face was pasted with a broad, cheerful smile.

"Felix, this is Señora Lorena Santoya. She'll be staying with us for a few days."

Felix had been with Diego's family for over forty years. When his father's health condition worsened, Diego brought Felix to administer the staff at his rancho. Felix wasn't able to perform all the tasks, as he had in the past, due to a stroke he had suffered two years ago, but he was faithful to the family, and Diego totally trusted him.

When they were out of earshot, Diego apologized for introducing her by her maiden name. "I'm sorry....but I forgot to ask what your new married name is?"

"Let's just leave it as Santoya for now." It was Lorena's way of distancing herself from Chase.

Diego could tell from her body language that Lorena was exhausted. He escorted her directly to the spare bedroom in the left wing of the house. The room was spacious and beautifully decorated with European antiques, including a matrimonial bed with a birds-eye maple headboard that was ornately carved with a scene of a unicorn carrying off a maiden in distress. Looking at the exquisitely carved figures, Lorena thought how ironic that her host had rescued her from the arms of overwhelming sadness only a short hour ago.

"I can't thank you enough for your generosity," Lorena said as she looked around the room.

"You just get some rest, and I'll see you tomorrow. Buenas noches." Diego turned and walked back down the long hallway toward the main part of the house.

Diego was wide-awake from the experience of discovering Lorena in the church. He went into his study, dimmed the lights, turned on his 8mm projector, and studied old films of fencing champions. He needed something to distract him from thinking about Lorena, who was sound asleep, only a few steps down the hall. He didn't hold out any hope that their relationship could be anything other than platonic, but for some reason, having her around filled the house up with an uncertain expectation. As the flickering light from the projector filled the room, Diego tried to convince himself that his motives for helping Lorena were untainted. He caught himself wishing Lorena was free, and that somehow, he could fill the void in her life.

After watching film for well over an hour and still struggling to clear his mind of Lorena, he headed for his bedroom. As he walked by her room, he could hear the faint sound of Lorena crying. He wanted so much to open the door, take her in his arms and console her, but he knew he would be crossing a boundary that would compromise both of their lives. Whatever desires he had for Lorena needed to be buried the same way he had hidden his dark, lonely feelings about losing Celaya. Over the years, he had not only become a master of controlling his emotions, but of denying his true feelings. This time would be no different.

CHAPTER 21

Chase awoke to the metallic clank of his alarm clock. He reached over, slamming down the palm of his hand in an attempt to stop the annoying sound. In his drowsiness, he forgot where he was and reached over, searching for the familiar outline of Lorena. As his hand groped around the empty sheets, he realized he wasn't safely within the confines of their ranch house in Texas. He had been so restless with thoughts of Lorena that he got up several times in the middle of the night to call her hotel, only to find out that she had not returned.

As the fog started to clear in his head, the vivid scene of Lorena crumpled on the floor of her hotel room shoved him back into the harsh reality of the previous night. The same sick feeling he had experienced after striking Lorena gripped his chest with a paralytic spasm and he wanted to crawl under the sheets and suffocate in the shame. His guilt was immediately replaced with genuine concern. Why hadn't she returned to her hotel? Would she ever come back to him?

Chase was trying to reassure himself that his wife was safe when Emiliano knocked on the door and poked his head into the room.

"Chase, it's five o'clock. I just wanted to make sure that you were up."

"Yeah, I'll meet you downstairs in half an hour." He rolled over and covered his head with a pillow hoping it would drown out the cruel voices pounding in his head.

Emiliano could tell from Chase's tone of voice that he was having a hard time shaking off the effects from last night. Emiliano had no idea what had happened between Chase and Lorena, but it was apparent that his normally focused companion wasn't firing on all cylinders. For the first time, Emiliano was unsure about going out on a mission. He was going to keep a close eye on Chase; any missteps and he would sit this one out.

Chase took a quick shower and tried to focus on the mission. His concentration was sabotaged with the image of Lorena fleeing like a wounded creature. He wondered how was he going to stay focused and not compromise the operation. It was going to be a crapshoot at best. Chase considered asking Emiliano to head back home and dealing with Lorca on his own. In all fairness, he didn't feel that he had the right to risk Emiliano's life because of his personal life was in shambles. On the other hand, Chase knew, without Emiliano's help, he had little or no chance of pulling off the mission.

Chase met Emiliano downstairs. He could sense that Emiliano was uneasy. Emiliano had seen firsthand how personal problems could affect the outcome of such a dangerous undertaking. One of his best friends had been killed six years ago because he worried about his wife giving birth to their first child in his absence.

As Emiliano studied Chase, he could see all the familiar signs of a man who was thinking more about troubles with his marriage than about the task at hand. Chase was putting on a good show, but he wasn't fooling anyone.

Emiliano checked with his friend one more time to make sure it was still a go. "Are you still up for this, Chase?"

"Do I have a choice?"

"Wrong answer," Emiliano said, in a reprimanding tone.

"Sorry. Forget what I said. I'll be all right as soon as we get on the road."

"OK, but if you have any second thoughts, all I ask is that you let me know before we get our heads caught in nooses."

Chase shook his head, grabbed one of the duffel bags and headed for the car.

While Chase was closing the trunk door, Emiliano patted him firmly on the back and offered sympathetically, "It'll all work out, Chase. She knows you love her."

"I wish I could believe you." The sound of defeat echoed through Chase's voice.

They headed off in the direction of Morelia, Chase hoping to finally close the book on Lorca. When they reached the outskirts of the city, Chase glanced one more time out the rear window knowing Lorena was alone somewhere out there, trying to mend her shipwrecked life.

The soft, amber light of morning streamed through the large window of Lorena's room. She rolled her face away from the intrusive rays and felt a faint throbbing from her bruised right cheek as it touched the pillow. She reached up and gently touched the swollen knot on her face. It felt as though someone had implanted a large cotton ball under her skin. The physical pain from the night had subsided, but the agonizing, emotional memories remained intact.

Lorena forced her aching body out of bed, anxious to see her face. She hesitated momentarily as she stood facing the bathroom mirror. As she slowly raised her head and peered into the mirror, she could see an oblong purple pattern radiating from the lower corner of her right eye. In its entirety the bruise was about an inch and a half long and two inches wide. It wasn't a full-blown shiner, but it was enough to remind her of what had transpired between her and Chase. She expected much worse damage from the initial pain of the blow. Hopefully, with a little creative use of make-up, she could make herself presentable. She reached up and wiggled her nose, pleased to find that nothing was broken.

Felix, always the alert guardian, heard Lorena's light footsteps on the bedroom floor. He had seen her bruise and was already preparing a remedy his mother had taught him. With the first light of sunrise, Felix had been out gathering medicinal herbs from his garden. He always made sure he had an assortment of plant remedies available for Diego when he returned with bruises and aches after hard-fought contests.

Felix cautiously knocked on Lorena's door while balancing the beautifully decorated breakfast tray accented with two yellow roses. Lorena had just finished taking a shower and was feeling almost alive again when she heard the tapping on her door. She tiptoed up to the door, placed her lips next to it and purred, "Señor Sanchez?" She used his proper name in case it was the housekeeper.

"No, Señora. Señor Sanchez left early this morning to run some errands in town. I made some breakfast for you."

Lorena breathed a sigh of relief. Although she was still reticent to appear in such a condition, even in front of Felix, she opened the door.

"Good morning, Señora," Felix said, avoiding direct eye contact with her.

"Good morning." She stepped back, as he shuffled past her with his staggered gait. He placed the tray on a small antique table in front of the window.

Lorena followed him over to the table and scanned the fare he had prepared.

The only thing she didn't recognize on the tray was the dark brown paste in a small bowl with a homemade wooden applicator.

Felix did not wait for her to ask about the strange-looking potion he had concocted.

"Apply this to your face first thing in the morning and just before you retire for the night. You should see significant improvement immediately. Is there anything else you need, Señora?"

"No, thank you very much, Felix. You've been very helpful. When do you expect Señor Sanchez to return?"

"He should be back later in the afternoon. He had several arrangements to make regarding his father's estate."

"Let me offer my condolences. I understand from Señor Sanchez that you were very close to his father."

"Thank you. You're very kind, Señora. Diego's father was a good man. If that is all, I'll return to my duties." As efficiently as he had come, Felix disappeared from her room.

Lorena sat down, poked at the brown paste and said out loud, "What kind of strange potion has this old man cooked up for me?"

She devoured breakfast and decided it was time to test the magic of Felix's potion. She took the wooden applicator and scooped out a fair amount of the thick paste, gently applying it to the bruised area on her cheek. She immediately felt a cool tingling sensation. After covering the entire area under her eye, she stretched out on the bed and followed Felix's instructions, to keep the gooey substance on her bruised cheek for at least an hour.

As she stared up at the white gauze canopy above the bed, she started to try to sort out what really happened last night with Chase. She re-created every action that led up to his violent outburst, from her bitter accusations of betrayal, to Chase's jealous remarks, to the brutal blow that left her sprawled on the floor in disbelief. After replaying the scene over in her mind, she tried to convince herself that Chase would have never purposely hurt her. Even as she tried to reconcile herself to the possibility that it was an accident, she was still no closer to forgiving him for lying and paying officials off to keep her out of her homeland. His unwillingness to apologize and make amends until they were safely in Texas was completely unacceptable. And what was he thinking, trying to order her back to Texas like some wayward child? Lorena seriously thought for the first time that maybe she had made the biggest mistake of her life marrying a man she barely knew.

Tired of confronting her troubles and having exceeded the time Felix had suggested for his magic potion to work, she got up and finished dressing. When she looked in the mirror, to her amazement she saw that the swelling and most of the bruising were appreciably reduced. After she skillfully applied some make-up and was satisfied that she was somewhat presentable, Lorena made her way downstairs. She strolled through the large living room decorated with oversized mesquite chairs and tables. Everything in the room felt powerful and masculine. In front of the fireplace lay a large sheepskin rug with its thick fur perfectly combed. Over the stone hearth, splayed out in all its grandeur hung a bright crimson matador's cape.

"It was a gift from a special fan in Spain." Felix surprised her from behind.

"Was he loved by his fans as much as everyone says?"

"Even more; he gave so much of himself to the people, and they paid him back in kind."

"I don't mean to pry into his personal life, but why has he never married? There must have been plenty of women standing in line."

"Senor Sanchez was married to his craft. He never found a woman who could replace his love for fencing."

"I don't want to intrude but I would like to know more about this mysterious knight who rescues ladies in the middle of the night." It felt good to make an attempt at humor, given the events of the last twenty-four hours.

Felix escorted Lorena to Diego's private study. The well-lit room was cluttered with the evidence of Diego's accomplishments. Every shelf was filled with accolades and awards from politicians, royalty, aficionados and, most importantly, from charitable organizations Diego had supported throughout his long and successful career in France. Photographs of him standing next to prominent people were scattered throughout the room.

Lorena perused her surroundings and realized she was in the home of a man who was not only highly respected by aficionados of his sport but also sincerely loved by the people of France.

"He saved all of this from his years in France?" She was somewhat surprised such a modest man as Diego would have kept so many mementoes.

"No, Señora. This represents only about a third of his awards. If it weren't for his mother and father, this room would be empty. His father kept everything. When Señor Sanchez returned to Mexico, his father had it all moved to this room as a homecoming surprise. Señor Sanchez would have preferred to have all these items removed, but he was very careful not to hurt his father's feelings."

Felix directed Lorena over to a large, oval table stacked with old scrapbooks. He politely pulled out a chair for her. Lorena sat down, reached over and took one of the tattered scrapbooks. She opened the scrapbook containing newspaper clippings from 1963 through 1964. The first page contained an article on Diego's international tournament debut in Paris and she read the vivid description with total amazement. In his first tournament, and at the age of twenty, he finished in second place among contestants far more experienced. As she continued to read the early history of Diego, every story of his exploits in tournaments seemed to repeat itself. Then something curious happened; there was an unexplained gap in time. During the period from March to June 1964, Diego mysteriously disappeared from competitive tournaments. There were no newspaper articles regaling his brilliant swordsmanship. Had his parents simply stopped saving the articles for a short period of time? Lorena knew from reading the other clippings that Diego's disappearance was during the height of the international tournament season. Had he been injured? If so, why weren't there any articles indicating that he had been injured? What could have stopped someone who had skyrocketed in world rankings? It was as though he simply vanished.

Lorena turned the page; as suddenly as the articles had disappeared, they reappeared—four months to the day.

Lorena's curiosity tugged at her as she quietly uttered, "What dark secret would have taken a man like Diego away from fulfilling his dream so early on in his career?"

Lorena spent the rest of the morning reading through the scrapbooks and scanning the photographs of a young Diego. It was no wonder he captured every woman's eye. As she read further, Lorena became even more curious about his personal life. Why had a man of his prestige and stature never married? Lorena found herself fantasizing about meeting Diego when he was young and dashing. If Diego was only half the man now that he was in his younger years, he would still be a major catch for any woman.

In the midst of her curious search for answers, Felix interrupted her, announcing that he had prepared a light lunch for her out on the veranda overlooking the garden. After eating every delicious morsel, Lorena decided to take a short siesta. She still wasn't feeling a hundred percent after the trauma of the previous night. She knew she would need all of her strength to deal with sorting out her future. She was still confused about whether to go back to Texas and wait for Chase, or move on and chalk up her brief marriage to a misguided decision. She felt as though she were on a teeter-totter; one moment her heart said yes to Chase and then in one, rising and falling motion, an emphatic no!

Felix told Lorena he would probably be gone when she awoke. He spent Saturday afternoons and Sundays with his sister in Guanajuato. He expected that Señor Sanchez would return from his errands around four o'clock, and she should make herself at home.

Lorena thanked Felix for all his help. She asked him if he wouldn't mind leaving a copy of his healing potion on the kitchen counter. Felix seemed pleased by her request, and he could already see the positive results of his mother's medicinal recipe.

"I hope to see you in the very near future, Señora," Felix said, with an encouraging tone. It was clear there was a deeper message in his parting words.

"It would be my pleasure."

As she climbed up the stairs to her room, Lorena prayed that the nightmares from last night would not invade her midday nap. She badly needed to be lost in the comfort of more pleasant dreams.

CHAPTER 22

Chase and Emiliano arrived in Morelia in the early afternoon. Not unlike Chase's earlier surveillance of Quiroga, they decided to use Morelia as their final staging area to avoid raising suspicion in the village. They spent the rest of the day going over their provisions and reviewing every detail of the plan. Emiliano could still sense Chase's distraction, but he seemed to be coming out of his dazed state. He hoped Chase would be firing on all cylinders by the evening. Chase checked in with Eddings just before they left Ciudad Hidalgo, and Eddings confirmed that Lorca would be at St. Ignacio as planned, an hour after dusk. As far as Eddings knew, nothing had changed as to the logistics or the number of guards watching over Lorca's movements. Remo Navarrete, Lorca's self-appointed warden, had not given up on his promise to make sure Lorca stayed put. There would be three armed guards from Navarrete's entourage accompanying Lorca to the small church overlooking the village. Lorca would leave his compound promptly at seven-fifteen, and the slow procession of Lorca's car trailed by Navarrete's people would make its way to the church. While Lorca was pretending to salvage his soul, one of Navarrete's hired guns would stand watch at the front entrance while another protected the rear entrance. The third guard always sat in the escort car. One of Lorca's bodyguards would accompany him to church, but it was only for show. Lorca's man was totally out-numbered by Navarrete's manpower, but it at least assured him some privacy during the short time he was in St. Ignacio.

Two hours before sunset, Chase and Emiliano headed down the deeply pitted dirt road to Quiroga. They were driving a 1962 pickup truck so as not to attract any attention.

Both men were dressed shabbily in old Levis and worn-out plaid shirts. They arrived in Quiroga an hour before sunset and parked the truck on a side street at the edge of town. They had stashed two small bags of provisions, including weapons, in some thick brush a few hundred yards from the church.

They traversed the empty back streets and alleyways of Quiroga. With the exception of an occasional old man and his burro heading into town, the streets were empty. They made their way to the outskirts of the village unnoticed.

After a twenty-minute hike through sagebrush and cactus, they relocated their stashed bags, which were undisturbed, aside from a scorpion that had decided to use the underside of Chase's bag as a sun block. All they had to do was wait until darkness fell and they could get on with the mission they both wanted over as quickly as possible.

Lorca and Navarrete's entourage arrived at the church on schedule and Navarrete's people positioned themselves as usual. The leader of the small brigade stayed with the car while the other two guards positioned themselves at the front and rear entrances of the church. Lorca's bodyguard stationed himself just inside the large double wooden doors, making sure his boss could pray in peace, while Lorca entered the unoccupied church and slowly made his way toward the second row of benches that faced the front of the gilded altar.

He felt uneasy as he knelt to pray, turning his head from side to side, as if looking for some sign that he was not alone. After feigning a few prayers, Lorca stood up and made his way over to the confessional booth. He looked both ways before entering the parishioner's side. Lorca gingerly opened the door, knelt down, and closed the ornately carved door behind him. He sat for well over a minute in uncomfortable silence.

Slowly, the small-screened window on his left side slid open. A strange, eerie voice spoke out in fluent Spanish, "You have come to confess your sins, my son?"

Lorca was surprised by the priest's pointed question. Having no choice, Lorca answered the voice on the other side of the blurred partition, "Yes, my father."

"Are you ready to repent for having kidnapped and beaten an innocent victim?" the voice snarled from the other side of the veiled partition.

"Who the hell are you?" Lorca protested, visibly shaken by the priest's question.

"Quiet, you son of a bitch! Don't you realize you're in the house of God?" Chase fired back sharply.

"Señor Chandler, how nice to hear your voice again," Lorca's sneered at Chase as he tried to make out the face framed on the other side of the gauzy screen.

Chase cringed at the thought of sitting in such close proximity to a man he so much detested. He wanted to leap from the confessional booth, race to the front entrance of St. Ignacio's and inform Navarrete's thugs their prisoner was trying to escape. Chase envisioned the guards mowing Lorca down with their sawed-off shotguns and then standing over Lorca's buckshot-riddled body, watching him struggle for his last desperate breath.

Just as Chase was about to stand up and make his fantasy reality, a vision of Lorena burst into his mind and he sat back down on the small, caned seat. He knew if he had any chance of a future with Lorena, it all rested on getting Lorca out of Mexico alive.

"Enough of the bullshit. Here's how it's going to work," Chase growled.

Chase proceeded to give Lorca instructions on how the escape plan was laid out. If everything went as designed, they should be out of any danger and on the road to the border within the hour. Lorca quietly listened to the details of Chase's plan. When Chase was satisfied that everything was clear in Lorca's mind, he stood up and barked one last cutting remark.

"I don't know what your real motives were for having me come here, but if you even blink sideways, you're a dead man. Understood?" Chase barked, repeating the threat he had made to Eddings in his office.

"So nice to see you haven't lost your manners, Señor Chase. I understand you married the lovely young lady who was my houseguest, and that you two lovebirds are living the good life on your ranch outside Pecos. I would be careful who you threaten. You never know who might pay you and your young bride a visit someday." Lorca's snicker was a haunting reminder of his demented mind.

Chase wanted to reach through the screen and silence him forever, but Lorca interrupted, sensing the depth of Chase's fury.

"As you said earlier, Señor Chase, let's not forget we're in the house of God." Lorca stood up, opened the door, and stepped outside into the cool, musty cavity of the church.

A moment later an unrecognizable figure appeared from where the priest sat in the confessional. Chase was dressed in a thick brown friar's robe, the hood draped over his forehead to hide his pale gringo appearance. His hunched posture made him appear much older. Chase shuffled over next to Lorca, quickly frisked him for any weapons, and then led Lorca in the direction of the altar.

They both made the sign of the cross as they passed in front of an impaled Jesus, and walked through a granite-arched doorway leading to a tight passageway behind the marble altar. Chase stopped when they reached an alcove just inside the rear entrance threshold.

While Chase and Lorca were making their way to the back entrance of St. Ignacio, Emiliano, also dressed as a friar, was positioning himself next to a thick, frayed strand of rope dangling from the steeple of the church. It was from here the friars rang the two large bronze bells every hour and half-hour of the day.

The lone guard, stationed in the rear of the church, made a quick glance over in Emiliano's direction, but let the slightly pudgy friar go about his daily responsibilities.

Emiliano firmly grabbed hold of the thick rope and pulled down, using his body weight to tilt the heavy wooden yoke from which the bells were dangling. When the bells reached horizontal, he released the rope, and the bells swayed back to their vertical position and up to the opposite side of the steeple. The huge carillons sent out hollow, ricocheting echoes across the barren landscape. Emiliano repeated the same process seven more times, signifying the hour of eight.

Chase waited for the last reverberations of the bells to disappear, and then motioned for Lorca to follow him to the back door of the church. He looked at his watch and turned his head as if listening for another signal before cautiously cracking the door open.

Chase heard the sound first and then he saw a bright white flash pierce through the stained glass windows of the church. Seconds later, he heard another cannon blast and a flash of light, followed by another, then another. The fireworks show Emiliano had arranged was right on schedule. Emiliano was now making his way to the rear of the church, having successfully signaled his counterparts in the village to begin the fireworks show. The front entrance guard and the guard in the escort car were already distracted from their duties by the pyrotechnics. As Emiliano approached the back corner of St. Ignacio's, the guard watching the rear entrance was attempting to sneak a peek at the fireworks while continuing to glance over in the direction of the rear entrance.

Emiliano bowed his head as he neared the guard and said, "A beautiful night for fireworks, wouldn't you say?"

"Yes, Father," replied the spellbound guard, whose eyes sparkled with the glow of blue and green streamers falling from the sky.

Emiliano could see the guard was struggling to get a clear view of the bursting lights. "Why don't you go out front, where you can really get a good look?"

"I would like to, but I can't leave my post."

"I'll stand watch for you if you want to take a quick look."

The guard edged his way a little more toward the front of the church, which was still obstructing a clear view of the fireworks, now in full bloom.

Emiliano egged the guard on, "Go, my son; I'll make sure no one leaves the church."

"Thank you, Father," the guard said tentatively as he moved along the stone edifice of the church, creeping closer to his fellow companions.

As soon as Emiliano was sure the guard was far enough away, he turned and quickly headed to the rear entrance. He tapped out a pre-arranged signal on the back door.

The door slowly creaked open, and Chase whispered, "All clear?"

"Yes. Let's get the hell out of here. I don't know how long this charade is going to last."

Chase pushed the door open, and he and Lorca emerged. Emiliano ran over to the corner of the church to make sure the rear guard wasn't on his way back to his station. When he reached the corner, he signaled that everything was still a go. Emiliano rushed back to where Chase and Lorca were standing. Chase and Emiliano stripped off the heavy robes and directed their reluctant guest toward Lake Pátzcuaro.

Under the amber glow of the fireworks, the three men made their way out through the scrub brush and tamarack trees. Emiliano was leading the way, with Lorca between him and Chase. The lakeshore was about a half-mile scramble through rolling gullies. At a good jogging pace, the distance could be easily covered in ten minutes. It was obvious to Chase that the slightly overweight and out of shape Lorca would need more time than they had allotted. Lorca was already gasping for breath in the first hundred yards.

"How much further?" Lorca pleaded.

Chase was curt in his response, "Just keep moving or none of us will make it out of here alive." He was pretty confident that right about now the guards were figuring out something was wrong with the timing for this pyrotechnic display. As usual Chase's intuition was right.

The rear entrance guard warily approached his two companions, who were still hypnotized by the fiery display. The guard in charge, stationed at the car, noticed and screamed out, "What the hell are you doing here? Who told you to leave your post?"

"The priest told me he would watch the door."

"The priest? You idiot! When was the last time you heard of a fat priest volunteering for guard duty?"

The three men frantically rushed toward the church. As they approached the threshold, Lorca's bodyguard attempted to stop their progress. The lead guard, who was brandishing a .45 pistol, didn't hesitate to shoot the unsuspecting man right through the base of his neck. Lorca's bodyguard dropped to the floor, gurgled for a breath through the thick red blood then stopped breathing.

The three guards unsympathetically stepped over the fallen man and rushed into the church. They immediately saw that Lorca was nowhere in sight. They made their way toward the rear entrance of St. Ignacio's, checking out every possible hiding place, constantly bellowing out Lorca's name in fitful desperation. When they reached the door of the church, they noticed that the door was slightly ajar. The lead guard kicked the door open, prepared for a firefight with the escaping Lorca. As the three guards stepped into the warm night air, they spotted the priests' robes crumpled on the ground and the tracks of three men leading out into deserted landscape. They looked at each other simultaneously with excruciating dread. They had all witnessed the wrath of Navarrete firsthand. They knew if Lorca escaped under their watch, they might as well put a gun to their heads and save their boss the trouble.

The leader bent down and studied the footprints. He could see by the impressions in the soft desert sand that their prey was heading for the lakeshore. He frantically signaled to his partners, and they all started running at full speed through the darkness, their weapons drawn.

Meanwhile, Lorca was still having trouble keeping up with Chase and Emiliano. Chase had to practically shove Lorca along to keep him going.

At one point, a frustrated Lorca roared at Chase, "Keep your filthy hands off me."

An unsympathetic Chase countered, "Pick it up, or I'll leave you here to die."

"I don't think so, Señor Chase. I'm your meal ticket out of here."

"Maybe you'll save me the trouble. Doesn't sound like you're up to this."

Lorca was still struggling to catch his breath when Chase heard the faint sound of other voices in the distance. Chase needed something to put a fire under Lorca's ass, so he called out to Lorca, "Quiet. Do you hear that? I think we have company."

It was even obvious to an exhausted Lorca that the sounds of the angry voices were getting closer. Lorca straightened up, turned in the direction of the lake and starting running at a faster clip.

Chase estimated they were only about five minutes away from the shoreline, but he could tell their pursuers were quickly gaining ground. Lorca kept looking back, making sure he was not about to take a bullet in the back.

Chase yelled at Lorca again, "You're wasting time! Just keep moving."

Chase saw the look of fear on Lorca's pained face, who knew if he was captured that Navarrete would take great pleasure in watching him die a slow, torturous death.

Emiliano reached the shoreline first and doubled over trying to catch his breath while he nervously waited for Chase and Lorca to arrive. He could hear the muffled voices of the guards approaching through the darkness. It was excruciating for him to stand there and peer into the darkness, knowing their pursuers were rushing at full speed in their direction, ready to deliver a death sentence at any moment. He was starting to regret having offered to help Chase on this assignment. Emiliano was positioned next to their only hope for salvation, but if Chase and Lorca didn't pick up the pace, it would all be for naught. Emiliano had arranged to have a seventeen-foot fishing *ponga*, equipped with a twenty horsepower engine, waiting for them at the lakeshore. He desperately wanted to jump in the boat and rip at the pull cord to start the engine, but until he could see the whites of Chase's eyes, he would have to wait. Emiliano was smart enough to know that all he would accomplish by starting the noisy engine was to alert the guards to their means of escape.

After what seemed like an unreasonable amount of time, Emiliano finally saw Lorca approaching. Chase was only a few steps behind, but for some unexplainable reason he stopped twenty yards from the shoreline. Emiliano was helping an exhausted Lorca into the boat and yelling at Chase to hurry.

Chase, his eyes peeled in the direction of the oncoming voices, called out loudly to Emiliano.

"Start the damned engine, and get the hell out of here. I'll cover for you."

Emiliano's head snapped up, with a look of utter disbelief. "No way! You get your ass in this boat now!" he demanded.

At that very moment, two shots rang out from the darkness. Chase immediately hit the ground in a prone position, ready to fire back at the guards.

Chase bellowed at Emiliano, who had managed to get the engine started. "Go! That's an order, god dammit."

Chase fired off four quick rounds from his 9mm Beretta. He was barely able to make out the rushing onslaught of guards in the darkness. He took aim again, spraying the approaching figures with another sweeping barrage. He had little hope of hitting his intended targets. He was just hoping to give Emiliano some breathing room. Chase could hear the thump of Navarrete's men scrambling for cover. Then he heard one of them screech out in pain.

Chase had wounded one of the guards, and it was obvious from his anguished cry for help that he was seriously hurt. The other two guards fired shots in Chase's direction. He could hear the thud of lead hitting the sand only a few feet away.

Emiliano shoved the heavy wooden fishing craft from the shore while pleading with Chase to join them in the boat. Lorca was sitting mid-aft, yelling at Emiliano to forget about Chase. Emiliano jumped into the rocking vessel and was heading back to man the engine when Lorca pulled out a six-inch switchblade and, in one violent sweeping motion, plunged it into Emiliano's chest. The bright glimmering blade pierced him just below the right lung, fortunately missing all of his vital organs.

Emiliano cried out from the grating pain, as Lorca used the hilt of the knife to shove the paralyzed man overboard. The ponga was thirty feet from the shoreline when Emiliano's heavy body landed in the frigid waters of Lake Pátzcuaro. The blood from his wound had already turned the murky waters a dingy maroon as the disoriented Emiliano flailed to keep his head above the waterline.

Chase's head pivoted violently when he heard the desperate cry of his friend. What Chase saw when his eyes came into focus left him cringing in disbelief. Emiliano's body looked as if it was being catapulted out of the ponga by a canon. He could see Lorca holding the bloody stiletto.

Lorca glanced in Chase's direction, and then ducked low in the boat, using the high arched bow for cover. Chase tried to get a shot off at Lorca but couldn't get a clear line of sight. Just as he was about to pull the trigger for a second try, a volley of gunfire came from his opposition in the field behind him. Chase reloaded his pistol with another clip and fired several shots to keep his pursuers at bay. He turned back in the direction of Emiliano and could see his friend was alive but helplessly floundering with his one good arm in an attempt to make it to shore. It was apparent to Chase that his partner had little or no chance of making it to safe ground without his help.

Lorca's plan had worked perfectly so far, even the idea of struggling to keep up with Chase during their frenzied run from the church to the lake. He knew the guards would eventually discover him missing, and with just the right amount of delay, he could cause trouble for his rescuers. Lorca could not have hoped for a better result, as he watched Chase, who was pinned down by Navarrete's thugs, and Emiliano, who was struggling for his life in the polluted waters of Lake Pátzcuaro. Lorca felt confident as he sneered down at Emiliano. There was nothing to prevent him from making his escape. The most ironic part of the whole farce was that two days ago Chase's own man, Eddings, had filled him in on every detail of the escape plan, thus allowing Lorca ample time to plan an alternative escape and exact his revenge on Chase.

Lorca had made arrangements to be picked up by his own people on the other side of the lake; where they would safely escort him to the U.S. border. Lorca had even fabricated a story about what happened to Chase and Emiliano to tell Eddings. He would sympathetically explain how they lost their lives in a bloody skirmish while trying to save him. From the beginning, when he first contacted the Bureau, Lorca had planned on using Chase and Emiliano as pawns. Asking for Chase as an escort was a perfect ploy for the anxious Eddings, who had always wanted to upstage Chase. The FBI had fallen right into his trap. Lorca reveled in the fact that Chase's own colleagues had inadvertently helped him exact the revenge he had so patiently planned since Chase had deceived him last year.

As Lorca looked over at Chase's vulnerable position on the beach, he knew the gringo had little chance of escaping from Navarrete's men. Emiliano wasn't finished off yet, but he was in too bad of shape to be any help to Chase. Eventually, Lorca knew Navarrete's thugs would overtake Chase, and that would be the end of the story for his two gallant, but foolish rescuers.

Chase's mind was bouncing off the walls, racing with alternatives. His first priority was to help Emiliano, who was quickly losing his battle with the water. Emiliano's heavy clothes and the severity of his wound were making it impossible for him to make progress toward shore. Chase could hear the gurgling sound of his drowning friend echoing through the still, night air. He decided he had to make his move now. He wasn't about to have to face Emiliano's family and tell them of his tragic death, as he had done with Antonio's family.

Chase let off several rounds from his Beretta in the direction of the guards, then stood up and ran in a zigzagging path toward Emiliano. The guards were still face down from his volley when Chase took off for the shoreline. They didn't look up to see the scrambling figure until Chase reached the water's edge.

Chase's pursuers fired off four quick rounds, barely missing a diving Chase only by inches. Chase hit the water at full speed and started stroking frantically toward the floundering Emiliano. He reached Emiliano just before his friend was about to go down for the last time. Chase wrapped his arm around Emiliano in a swimmer's rescue hold and kicked parallel along the shoreline until he reached a small outcropping of heavy brush they could use for cover. Even though it was a short distance to dry land, lugging the dead weight of Emiliano's limp body left Chase gasping to fill his lungs.

Meantime, Lorca struggled to gain his balance in the unstable, shifting boat. He finally made his way back to the engine and twisted the handle of the throttle. Unfamiliar with boat engines, Lorca turned the throttle in the wrong direction, shutting off the engine. He cursed out loud; "Fuck!" then tried to restart the engine.

Chase finally dragged Emiliano's hulking body up onto the shore. He glanced down at the thick trail of his friend's blood staining the sand. Chase rolled Emiliano over and saw the entrance hole in his shirt where Lorca's knife had cut into his chest.

"How bad off are you?" Chase's whispers were smothered in concern for his friend's life.

"I don't think he hit anything major, but it hurts like hell," Emiliano whispered, holding his hand tightly over the entrance wound.

"We're in a tough spot here," Chase said, as he wiped the dripping sweat from his brow. He could still hear the rustling as their pursuers repositioned themselves just over the rise to his left.

Emiliano looked Chase straight in the eyes and angrily proclaimed, "Don't you let that son of a bitch get away.... I'll live. Our only chance is for you to get to the boat. I've got enough rounds in my gun to give you cover. Take off, now!"

"Are you sure?"

"Go!"

Chase knew Emiliano was right. Emiliano rolled over, positioned himself in the direction of the guards and nodded at Chase to make his move. Chase stood up, took a good run at the lake and dove toward the surface. Simultaneously, Emiliano fired off a flurry of rounds in an attempt to keep the guards at bay. Chase landed hard on the lake surface and started stroking hard toward the boat.

Lorca heard the thud of Chase's body hit the water and could see that his adversary was making good progress in his direction. He frantically he pulled on the starter cord to the engine but there was no response. Lorca's eyes widened with fear as he stared out at the quickly approaching Chase. He turned and ripped hard on the starter cord. The engine sputtered, backfired twice, and then started.

Just as the engine started to rev, Chase reached up out of the water, and gripped the port side gunwale with his left hand. He was about to grab hold with his other hand, when he felt the sharp pain of Lorca's switchblade pin his hand to the gunwale. He let out a throaty grunt, trying to contain the blinding pain. Somewhere on the outskirts of his mind he remembered his pistol was stuck in his waist belt. He reached down with his free hand, grabbed hold of the handle and pointed the gun at Lorca, who was standing directly above him.

Lorca, shocked by Chase's resiliency, tried to move slightly backward, but had nowhere to go in the small craft. He cowered at the sight of the narrow barrel of the 9mm Beretta as Chase pinched the trigger with his index finger. Simultaneously, both men heard the sharp clicking and metallic sound of the firing pin striking the casing of the shell; nothing happened. Chase pulled back on the trigger again and again, but all he heard was the clicking of the firing pin striking the spent shells. In all the confusion and concern for Emiliano's life, he had forgotten to reload.

Lorca roared out a sinister laugh as he peered down at a helpless Chase, whose bloody hand was still impaled on the gunwale. "You see, Señor Chase, I always make sure I repay my debts."

"You can rot in hell, Lorca."

Lorca lowered his face until it was only inches from Chase's. "Maybe later, my friend. Right now, I have an appointment to keep with a few of your old friends north of the border. I'll make sure Eddings knows you died heroically trying to save my life." He stood up and with a scolding waggle of his index finger sneered down at Chase.

Suddenly, Lorca's head rocked violently back on his shoulders and recoiled. As his face momentarily returned to its original position, Chase could see the perfectly round hole of a .45 caliber bullet in Lorca's forehead. The projectile from one of the guards' guns had struck Lorca dead center, blowing the back half of his head off. Lorca's lifeless body tumbled backward, slapped the surface of the lake and began slowly floating away like a half submerged log.

Chase reached up with his free hand and removed the switchblade from his skewered hand. He dropped the knife and pulled himself into the boat. He took a moment to gather himself and realized their situation was only marginally improved by Lorca's death. Emiliano was still bleeding to death on the shore, while he was stuck in the boat without any ammunition.

He yelled over to Emiliano to check on his condition. "Emiliano, are you still with me?"

A faint voice answered back. "Yes, but I can't hold out much longer."

Unexpectedly, out of the shadows came a stranger's voice. At first, Chase thought he was hearing things. Then he realized it was coming from one of Navarrete's people, who was still perfectly positioned to heap their vengeance onto Chase and Emiliano.

In broken English, the man called out to Chase, "Señor, it seems we are in a standoff. You have one down and so do we. Lorca is dead, and that's all our boss cares about. Why don't we call it a draw?"

Chase couldn't believe what he was hearing. They obviously didn't know he was unarmed and Emiliano was barely struggling to stay conscious from all the blood he had lost.

"How do I know I can trust you?"

"Our battle is not with you, Señor. We can wait this out and watch our friends die, or call it a night. Your choice."

"All right, but don't forget, we still have plenty of firepower, and if this doesn't go down like you say, all hell is going to break lose." Chase tried to make sure his voice was firm enough to pull off his bluff.

"Agreed. Hasta luego, my amigo."

Chase could hear the whimpering sound of the wounded man as the other guards lifted him up. He could see the faint outline of two figures dragging a third man draped between their shoulders.

He waited until he was sure that they were out of sight before manning the engine. He tore off a piece of a rag in the boat and wrapped it around the gaping wound in his hand. Chase turned the throttle of the engine, pointed the bow in the direction of Emiliano. Chase slammed into the shoreline, beaching the boat only a few feet from his wounded friend. He leapt out of the *ponga* and ran to where Emiliano lay.

"How are you holding up, my friend?"

"I always knew there was a reason not to play poker with a Texan. That was a hell of a bluff."

Once he heard Emiliano had not lost his sense of humor, Chase knew his partner was going to pull through.

"Let's get you out of here," Chase said with a sense of relief in his voice.

Chase tore off his shirt, unfastened his leather belt and removed it. He placed his folded shirt over Emiliano's wound and tightly cinched a belt around his torso to act as a temporary bandage. The bleeding had slowed down significantly, and he felt for the first time it was safe to move him.

As Chase was assisting him into the *ponga*, Emiliano huffed, "By the way Chase, this was my last assignment. I think we're both starting to slip a little."

"That's a nice way of putting it, but I'm with you. I'm finished with this cloak and dagger crap for good."

Chase helped Emiliano into the boat, pushed off from shore, climbed in, and headed for their rendezvous point. He looked out over the glassy black waters of Lake Pátzcuaro, and felt a quiet calm come over him. It was the first time since leaving Texas over a week ago that he felt could let down his guard. He knew he still had a lot of work ahead to regain Lorena's trust; it was going to be a difficult reconciliation at best. Knowing that this part of his life was behind him, Chase hoped that he would finally be able to concentrate all of his energy on healing the wounds of their fragile relationship. Maybe, just maybe, he could get her back.

CHAPTER 23

Lorena awoke to the soft glow of the fading day. She couldn't believe she had slept three hours in the middle of the day. Feeling guilty, she quickly dressed and headed downstairs in the hope of finding her host, but the house was empty. Felix had already left for his sister's in Guanajuato.

Lorena stepped through the door leading to the courtyard and was immediately enveloped in the pungent fragrance of the wisteria vines climbing up the granite pillars that supported the tiled veranda. She casually made her way out to the garden overlooking Diego's rancho. From this elevated position, she could see the mosaic of rock walls forming the different buildings.

As the sun edged toward the horizon, Lorena walked down to a small rectangular building. From her vantage point she could see through a large arched window the faint outline of a figure standing in the middle of the room. Hidden from the view, Lorena watched the lone image slowly pivot and lunge forward with his foil in hand. Diego's graceful movements were more calculated and slower than they would have been in an actual contest. Lorena moved closer to get a better view, hiding behind the finely trimmed hedges that lined the gravel pathway. As she watched Diego go through his moves, she was fascinated by his meticulous footwork. Every movement had to be done with exactness, while at the same time appearing to be instinctive. It is the illusion of this unconscious perfection that always captivates the observer, that special quality that separates greatness from mediocrity. It was all done with the same artfulness of her own dance steps.

Lorena followed the lush pathways meandering down to the open double-door entrance to the practice hall, all the while trying to not make her presence known.

Diego seemed totally lost in his practice session. From her close proximity, she could see the intensity and focus radiating from one the world's greatest swordsmen. Diego's back was still facing Lorena as he imagined an opponent charging toward him, and raising his foil in one fluid motion while pivoting in a willowy pirouette that left him prepared for his next parry.

In that instant, she recognized part of her undeniable attraction to Diego Sanchez. They shared the same rare experience, in which body and soul are united into one moment of physical and spiritual fulfillment. Lorena knew, as she watched Diego masterfully perform his graceful waltz, that he was one of the few people on earth who could truly understand why dancing was such an integral part of her life. Unconsciously, Lorena suddenly started to applaud, as if she was part of an audience. The singleness of her clapping startled her, and she realized she was the lone voice in the imaginary crowd.

Diego turned and bowed in the direction of Lorena.

She stumbled over an apology. "I'm so sorry; I didn't mean to disturb you."

"Would you like to try your hand at it?" he asked encouragingly.

"I don't think so. It looks very complicated."

"Don't be shy. From what I've seen of your performances, I think you're a natural."

Diego escorted her to the center of the fighting strip and handed her the foil.

"It's much lighter than I expected," she observed, eyeing Diego as she took hold of the foil.

"Just try to imagine it's the same as holding the hem of one of your dresses when you're dancing. Firm, but light at the same time."

Diego helped arrange the position of her feet and knees in the classic *en garde* position. He turned, faced off in front of her with the foil in hand and motioned for her to engage him in battle.

Lorena made a valiant attempt to strike Diego in the torso, but stumbled forward, almost falling face-first onto the cloth mat of the *piste*.

"I thought you said I would be a natural."

He laughed and added cautiously, "OK, you might need a little instruction." He knew it was difficult for a woman of Lorena's grace to look clumsy.

Diego stepped behind her, tentatively reached over with his right hand, and took hold of her hand holding the foil. He wrapped his other hand around her waist and placed his palm on her abdomen to help guide her body through the intricate moves. Lorena didn't resist the closeness of his body. Even though he was almost twenty years her senior she could feel the fitness of his body as he slowly moved her into the appropriate position. She felt his taut thigh muscles pressing against her body. It was impossible not to notice the strength of his forearms and biceps as he wrapped one around her waist and took control of her hand with the other. She had danced with a lot of male dancers during her career, and Diego's firm body reminded her of their physical strength. Her face flushed slightly as she encouraged his gentle touch.

As for Diego, just being so close to a woman of Lorena's beauty was enough to give him an adrenaline rush. Her natural fragrance was the first thing Diego noticed. Her hair blossomed with the bouquet of fresh lavender. He could smell the light scent of perfume on the nape of her neck. Her body relaxed into his light embrace. Lorena had been working out almost every day in her dance studio in Texas, so her muscles were lean and hard.

Diego's left arm unintentionally brushed against the side of her breast. There was no mistaking the soft curve of her roundness. He could feel the goose bumps budding on the skin of her arm as he lifted it to raise the foil in the air.

Lorena turned her face to her left, providing a perfect profile of her delicate features. His face was only inches from hers.

Because of their close proximity, Lorena only had to whisper her question for Diego to hear. "How is my form?"

"Very good. Now let's try a lunge. Let the tip of the foil lead your feet," Diego coached, thankful for her question.

Diego started by slowly guiding her right hand in a quick, fluid motion, while using his left hand to move her hips forward.

Lorena's footwork was flawless, as he would have expected from a highly trained dancer.

They moved as one single fluid unit. Lorena could feel the full length of his body pressed against her. The soft touch of his hipbones in the small of her back unexpectedly heightened her senses. It was as though he were a skilled puppeteer and she were a marionette, willing to entrust all her physical abilities to his nurturing hands. Diego continued to lead her through several moves as their bodies melted into one. It felt to Diego as if Lorena had been doing this her entire life.

In one graceful final move, Diego stepped away from Lorena and grabbed his foil and faced her. Lorena quickly lunged forward. Diego moved in closer and performed an effortless parry. Their faces were within inches of each other. Their eyes were locked onto each other. Lorena leaned forward and lightly touched Diego's lips with hers. Diego instinctively pulled back.

Lorena lowered her eyes away from him and gratefully purred, "You're a very good teacher."

"It's much easier when you're inspired by your student."

Neither of them wanted to acknowledge what had just happened between them. Even though they were standing only a few feet from each other, they could still feel the afterglow of the sexual energy springing from their bodies.

Lorena felt confused, knowing she was still a married woman and having unsettled feelings regarding Chase.

Diego, on the other hand, could not in all good conscience let himself take advantage of a woman still struggling to sort out her personal life. Still, it was almost impossible for him to ignore his attraction to Lorena.

Finally, Diego took charge of the tense situation and offered, "I think we've had enough lessons for the day. It's getting dark."

"I guess we have," Lorena reluctantly agreed, as if thanking him for saving them from a moment of indiscretion.

Diego took the foil from her, and they walked toward the door.

Lorena remained pleasantly haunted by the feeling of his body pressed tightly against hers. It was so much more soothing to linger in this moment with Diego than to have to confront the sadness of her troubled relationship with Chase.

Once again Diego broke her trance. "Are you hungry? Believe it or not, I'm not a bad cook."

"Is there anything you don't do well? Defender of ladies in distress, noted champion, gifted teacher and now a great cook!"

"I promise if you watch close enough, you will see I have more than my fair share of flaws."

"I'll have to keep my eyes open." She teased him and smiled.

When they reached the house, Diego excused himself, went out to his car and retrieved a package wrapped in a plain brown paper bag.

When he returned, he went over to Lorena and handed her the package.

"What's this?"

"I noticed you were a little light in the clothing department, so I picked a dress up for you in town."

"You're very kind," she told him. "If you don't mind, I would like to get cleaned up before I try it on," she said, thanking him again for the gift.

"Take your time. I'm going to the kitchen to throw something together for dinner." He suddenly remembered she had yet to formally accept his offer for dinner. "You *are* staying for dinner, aren't you?"

It was the first time Lorena had confronted the notion of staying another night or returning to her hotel. She hesitated, while her mind wrestled for an answer.

"Yes....I'll stay. After all, I have to see if you're truly as good a cook as you say you are."

"Now the pressure is really on."

Lorena turned and headed up the stairs to her room.

Diego watched her climb every step, transfixed by the natural swaying of her hips. He felt guilty for having flirted with a married woman, but he couldn't resist the attraction he was feeling for her.

Lorena took a long bubble bath, the entire time trying to gather her thoughts about what was happening. Her recent experience in the practice hall with Diego was causing more confusion than clarity. She was aware in her current vulnerable state that spending time around another man to whom she was attracted could be dangerous, but nothing else seemed to make her feel better right now.

After lingering for more than half an hour in the bath, she toweled off and readied for dinner. She hesitated before looking in the mirror, and was shocked to see her bruise had nearly disappeared. Felix's concoction had worked its magic and she was confident that with a little make-up, she could easily cover what remained of the bruise.

Lorena had yet to open Diego's gift, and she was curious to know what kind of taste he had in clothing. She walked over to the bed, sat down, and began carefully un-wrapping the package. She could tell immediately that the dress was of a high quality. The cloth was bright crimson in color with fine silk embroidery across the V-shaped neckline. Lorena unfurled the dress and saw it was a classic flamenco dancer's dress. It was tightly fitted for the upper torso and accented with long, flowing pleated cloth that stopped just below the knee.

She held it up to her body, pressed the edges of the waistline close and saw immediately it was going to be a perfect fit. Not only did Diego have great taste, but also he had somehow guessed her measurements perfectly.

While Lorena was paying particular attention to how she looked in her new dress and trying to do justice to her host's gift, Diego was busy preparing dinner. Diego picked out a fine, aged wine from his cellar and set the table with candles and silver. As he completed these final touches, Diego realized that this was the first time he had entertained a woman in his house since he purchased the ranch over two years ago. He had left himself just enough time to take a quick shower and throw on a pair of cream linen pants and a long-sleeved black shirt. It was simple, but with his good looks, he didn't need much to make an impressive appearance. He was just coming out of his room when Lorena stepped from hers.

At first glance, Diego only saw her from behind, but he could tell that he had chosen her size correctly. The dress fit her trim body flawlessly. When she turned to face him, he was totally taken aback. Her auburn hair was slightly tousled, giving her an untamed look. Her face glowed with a bright sheen, highlighting her piercing dark eyes. The V-neck of her dress dipped down to expose just the right amount of cleavage, and her firm breasts filled out the upper portion of the dress fully. The dress curved around her flat abdomen and flowed out from her thin waist just below her knees. Her bare feet peeked out from the hemline. There was something raw and completely natural about her appearance.

Lorena spoke first. "I have to compliment you on your taste. It's a wonderful gift. I hope I won't have to be like Cinderella and return it at the stroke of midnight."

"Of course not. Until now, I never fully understood the old cliché, 'Clothes are simply a means to accent the true beauty of a woman.' Never has such a statement been so true."

"Thank you." Lorena blushed, knowing she had surpassed her own expectations in doing justice to Diego's gift.

He held out his left arm forming a perfect cradle to wrap her arm around. Diego led her down the long flight of stairs and into the room adjoining the comfortably decorated living room. The house had flagstone fireplaces in both dining and living rooms and Diego had lit fires in them just heading upstairs to dress.

The glow from the fireplace, with several candles placed along the length of the mesquite dining room table, provided the perfect lighting. The shadows cast by the flames played on the high wooden beamed ceiling, dancing like nymphs above their heads.

Lorena lingered for a moment, taking in the entire scene, amazed that Diego had accomplished so much in so little time. From the lovely decorated table, to the fresh cut flowers, to the wonderful aroma wafting from the kitchen, everything was perfect.

Diego escorted Lorena to the far end of the table where he had placed two table settings. He pulled back the red velvet chair that almost matched the color of her dress, and Lorena sat down. He poured her a glass of his finest *vino tinto* and sat down at the head of the table.

There was a strained silence between them as they avoided direct eye contact.

Lorena broke the ice first. "What are your plans after you retire?"

Diego, relieved that she had taken the lead, answered. "To live the quiet life here on my rancho and raise prize bulls."

"No plans for a family?"

"I'd say it is a little late for that, wouldn't you?" said Diego, taking a sip of wine.

"I think any woman would be crazy not to want to be with you."

Diego was uneasy with the direction of the conversation. He had already accepted his destiny, that he would never have a wife or a family.

"Speaking of that, I need to go and check on the dinner." He stood up and headed for the kitchen. He returned a few minutes later with a tray containing two oval platters. He had prepared one of his favorite dishes, Tampiquena—

braised marinated flank steak—roasted, red potatoes, and julienne carrots with pine nuts. Diego placed one of the plates in front of Lorena and refilled her wine glass. Before sitting down, he stirred the fire and added another log. Lorena politely waited for him to sit before taking her first bite.

"How is it?" Diego nervously inquired.

"Wonderful. How did you find time with your busy career to learn to cook so well?"

"I spent a lot of time at my home outside of Paris learning from my housekeeper. She was a wonderful woman, with abounding exuberance for teaching me her cooking skills. She told me if I was intent on not ever getting married, then I had to learn to cook for myself."

"Well, obviously, she taught you well. This is delicious. You never answered my question about wanting a family."

"It's not a subject I think about very much." Diego nervously peered over the rim of his wine glass.

"Why is that? I can't believe you haven't had someone in your life that really mattered."

"I did once, but it was a long time ago."

Lorena saw Diego's expression suddenly darken. "I'm sorry. I didn't mean to pry."

Diego wasn't ready to talk about Celaya Flores, so he changed the direction of the conversation.

"What about you?" Diego asked.

Lorena looked downward, not wanting to revisit the painful memory of her argument with Chase.

"I guess we both have parts of our lives we're better off not re-living." Diego offered.

"I guess I do owe you an explanation."

"No, you don't. That's my point. We all have secrets."

"You're right. Sorry, I didn't mean to spoil this wonderful dinner."

They spent the rest of the meal talking about their childhood and laughing at each other's traditional upbringing. They talked about their parents being perfectionists and wanting their children to follow in their footsteps. Even though they were from different generations, the more they talked, the more they realized how much they had in common. They both admitted to being totally obsessed with their individual art forms. They laughed about how easy it was to detach from the real world and only focus on their individual obsessions.

Having consumed their fair share of wine, they were starting to feel the mellow warmth of intoxication. After finishing desert, they retired to the overstuffed couch in front of the living room fire to enjoy a glass of Diego's best port.

Lorena was still curious about the large cape hanging above the fireplace that Felix mentioned earlier that morning. "Is there some significance to the cape over the fireplace?"

"It was a gift from a friend of mine who was a famous matador in Spain."

"Do you miss being in Europe?" Her eyes focused tightly on his reaction.

"Sometimes, but Mexico has always been my real home."

"I have to apologize for snooping around your office today, but Felix said it would be all right."

"I hope it didn't bore you too much."

"On the contrary, I found it fascinating. I didn't know I was in the presence of such an important figure in the world. The President of France even vied to be in your presence? That's a pretty big deal."

"Please, I came back home to get away from all that insanity." His eyes glanced downward.

Lorena leaned closer to him. "I am curious. There was a gap in the newspaper clippings in your scrapbook. If you don't mind my asking, why at the beginning of your career, did you suddenly disappear for over four months, or is this another one of your dark secrets?"

"Actually, it's connected to your earlier question."

Lorena felt terrible for having once again raised what obviously was a painful experience for her host. "I'm so sorry, I didn't mean...."

Before she could finish, Diego interrupted her, "I'm sure you meant no harm."

"Was she beautiful?" Lorena cautiously asked.

"Yes. She was a woman who lit up a room when she walked through the door. I'm sure you can understand what I mean," Diego said, waiting to see if his compliment registered on Lorena's face.

She coyly smiled back at him.

Diego continued, "But it was her inner beauty, her strength of character, that set her apart from most women. She put me in my place the first time we met," Diego laughed at the thought of Celaya's straightforwardness on their first meeting.

"Why aren't you with her now, if you were so much in love?"

Diego breathed in a deep sigh, refilled their glasses and answered, "She died during childbirth. I never knew until recently that she bore my son."

"You have a son?" There was genuine shock on Lorena's face.

"Yes, but he changed his identity to avoid the humiliation of being born out of wedlock. On top of losing the only woman I loved, I have a son who doesn't even know I exist....and probably doesn't care," he reluctantly offered, his face bearing the naked grief.

"I'm sorry for your loss."

Lorena could feel the full weight of the burden Diego had been carrying all his life.

Diego thanked her for her concern and then surprised himself by sharing the entire story of his brief affair with Celaya. He told of how they first kissed under the shadow of a jacaranda tree and about the promises they made to each other after making love in the Plaza Quitzal. He painstakingly told Lorena of their sad parting at the train station and how he had lied to her about leaving for France. He shared the desperation he felt when he thought Celaya had abandoned him and the darkness he experienced when Señor Alvarez passed on the message telling him that Celaya was not interested in continuing with their relationship.

"Was that when you stopped competing for four months?" Lorena sympathetically asked referring to the articles she had read earlier in the day.

"Yes. I was in no shape to compete in tournaments."

As Diego continued, Lorena listened attentively, captivated by the dark events of his experience with Celaya. He described how he pleaded for his family's help in trying to find her. He vividly recounted how his mother told him that life must go on when all he really wanted to do was give up.

When Diego finished, Lorena could feel a trickle of a tear trailing down her cheek. Having just experienced her own angst over Chase's betrayal, Lorena knew of the despair that comes with losing someone you thought was going to be your life partner. Her tears were as much for herself as they were for Diego's unfortunate story.

Diego reached over and caught one of her tears with the curve of his finger. She reciprocated by taking hold of his hand and tenderly kissing his palm. Diego felt his eyes welling with tears and realized that it was the first time he had shared Celaya's story with another human being.

Lorena knelt down next to Diego and took his face in her hands and kissed him tenderly. She didn't know if it was out of empathy, or the emptiness in her own heart but she could feel herself being drawn to him. Although she sympathized with the void Celaya Flores left in Diego's life, there was something else attracting her to Diego. Maybe she needed to be unconditionally loved by a man again, to feel as she had with Chase the first time they made love. Whatever the reason, she couldn't stop her uncontrolled emotions.

Diego was swept away by her passionate kisses. He tried to pull himself back from her embrace, but all his steadfast resistance was being worn away with every stroke of her hand on his face. Ever since the sparks flew between them earlier that afternoon in the practice hall, he felt powerless to deny his attraction to Lorena.

They fell into the soft confines of the overstuffed sofa, Lorena tearing at the buttons of his shirt. His hands were exploring, plunging into every angle of her body. He pulled up the hem of her dress and was surprised that she wasn't wearing any panties.

Lorena could no longer stand the restrictions of her dress; she wanted to feel his hands all over her body. In the glow of the fireplace as Diego watched, she slowly peeled the silk dress off over her head. In one slithering motion, she was naked. The rays of the fire were a perfect backlight for her statuesque figure. He could see the flames of the amber fire flickering through the crease between her legs. She turned, and facing the fireplace, reached up above the stone hearth. Gingerly, she pulled down the matador's cape down and wrapped it around her waist, leaving her upper torso bare. She stepped onto the sheepskin rug directly in front of him, lifted the hem of the cape and slowly began to dance.

Diego watched as her bare feet pounded into the thick nap of the rug, her head slowly revolving on her shoulders, her long hair dangling freely toward her waist. Her upper body writhed in an undulating motion from her navel to her breasts. Within seconds, her entire body seemed to become enraptured in a fever pitch. It almost seemed as if she were on the edge of becoming out of control, but amazingly, Lorena was conscious of every subtle move—and Diego knew it.

He gazed at her, mesmerized by every sensual motion of her body. Watching her brought back the intense sexual sensations he felt at seeing Celaya lying naked in the discarded fencing garb at the Plaza Quitzal.

Lorena, lost in that mysteriously joyful world she hadn't felt since her last performance in Guadalajara, danced effortlessly. Her eyes closed tightly; enraptured by every note of the music she was composing in her head. She was in that special place where time, space, and the physical world meld into one seamless dimension. In one last graceful swooping move, she collapsed onto the sheepskin rug, splayed out, her entangled arms above her head and her hair hiding part of her face.

Diego, spellbound by the vision that lay before him, hadn't noticed Lorena's hand reaching up to pull him down toward her. She un-wrapped the cape from around her waist and stretched out, naked on the sheepskin rug. A slick coat of sweat glistened over her entire body, as he watched her breathing slow to a metrical cadence. Diego at first resisted her invitation, wanting only to savor the temptation. Then he stood up and stepped out of his slacks. He lay down beside her and began to gently kiss her, first on her lips, then her neck, all the while gently caressing her. She could feel the maturity of his lovemaking; every move was done with patience and the same care she had seen him demonstrate while practicing his fencing moves.

They made love for hours, watching the fire ebb and flow with their unbridled pleasure. When they thought they had both satisfied their hunger for each other, one of them would feel the flush of eagerness again and awaken the other for another round of love making.

In the aftermath of the final and unconditional release of energy, Lorena whispered what she had reserved only for Chase, "I love you." She was unaware she had even spoken them, but her words had not escaped Diego. Having heard them, Diego clung to her tightly, not wanting to really know how much truth there was in her spontaneous outburst.

It wasn't until the morning light eased through the cracks in the courtyard doors that they both fell into a deep slumber. Diego woke first and sat up on the couch where their night of uninhibited lovemaking had begun. The mid-morning sunlight was cascading its bright silver-blue light onto Lorena's cocoa skin. He peered down at her and froze the scene in his mind, knowing it would probably be the last time he would see her like this. For some unexplained reason, he knew he couldn't hold onto someone so special. There was also the matter of her estranged husband. As much as he wanted Lorena to be part of his life, he was unwilling to steal another man's wife. If he didn't have anything else after this night of betrayal, he still had his conscience. Diego knew Lorena had yet to come to terms with her relationship with Chase, and until she settled the ensuing crisis in her life, their night together could never be anything more than a frivolous affair between two wounded souls.

He stood up, put on his trousers and headed for the kitchen to make coffee. He needed some time to prepare for telling Lorena she needed to go home to her husband. It wasn't guilt that drove him to this decision, but his own selfish needs. If he were ever to have Lorena's love, it was going to be when she was free of her relationship with Chase.

When Lorena finally awakened, a floodgate of fear and remorse saturated her thoughts. She woke up in a cold sweat, having had a horrible nightmare. She had dreamed Chase was drowning in a stormy sea, while she, in a lifeboat fended him off with an oar in an attempt to keep him from getting in the boat with her. Each time Chase tried to approach the lifeboat, she would furiously slap at him. Finally, after what seemed like an eternity, the exhausted Chase stopped struggling, gave her a look of absolute forgiveness, and disappeared below the dark blue surface. Lorena watched her husband drown before her eyes. It was only after he was gone that she realized how much she cared for him. She dove into the churning waters in an attempt to save him, but as she flailed around, screaming out his name, all she could hear was the stark silence of emptiness. Her tether to the lifeboat mysteriously disappeared, and she was adrift alone in the chilling waters. The horrendous fear of living the rest of her life thrashing around in an ocean of total isolation shook her violently from her sleep.

Sitting on the floor of Diego's hacienda, half naked and soaked in her own sweat Lorena was unaware how her dream had almost come true only a few hours earlier for Chase at Lake Pátzcuaro.

While Lorena had been in the throes of making love to Diego, Chase was risking his life trying to make sure they would have some kind of future together. She didn't know Eddings had forced Chase into the assignment, threatening him with her expulsion from the U.S. Whether Lorena's dream was a premonition of their future together or not, she knew she had betrayed their vows of marriage.

Diego reentered the living room to find Lorena draped in his cape, slumped over with a look of anguish, her face drenched in sweat and tears.

"Are you all right?" Diego asked, as he rushed over to comfort her.

"Not exactly. I had a terrible nightmare," she whispered through her weeping.

"It was about Chase, wasn't it?" Diego was hoping it wasn't, but he already knew the answer.

She slowly nodded her head. Diego could see the guilt plainly written on her face.

"You want to talk about it?"

"I don't want to involve you in my mess."

"I haven't often had the chance in my life to be there when someone really needed me."

Diego sat down next to her and she leaned over and rested her head on his chest. It was heart-wrenching for Lorena to hear Diego be so compassionate, so supportive. She felt a sudden rush of disdain for her behavior of last night. Not only had she cheated on her husband, but she had also involved a man whose only motive was to help her through a tough time.

For the next hour and a half, Lorena poured her heart out to Diego, detailing every phase of her life with Chase. She spoke of her traumatic kidnapping and her whirlwind marriage. She hoped that in hearing her own recounting that she might find some answers to confusing questions that were hounding her about the future of her and Chase's relationship. Chase would be furious if he knew she had revealed his FBI operations to a complete stranger. She wasn't sure it would matter anyway after he found out about her night with Diego. The only thing Lorena left out of her life with Chase was their recent struggle over trying to have a child.

Somewhere during her desperate confession, the reality of the past few days started to form the clear edge of truth and the role she had played in the disaster. In that moment of clarity, Lorena realized she had no choice but to tell Chase about Diego if they had any chance at starting over.

Diego attentively listened to her story, trying to sort out why her husband had treated her so callously. He had the perfect opportunity to belittle Chase after hearing how he had struck Lorena in the hotel room, but he would not lower himself to such pettiness.

When Lorena concluded her story, Diego pulled her close to him and tried to reassure her. "I wouldn't give up all hope. I don't know your husband, but I don't believe he would treat you like this without a good reason. It sounds like he would do anything to make you happy. I know I would." Diego couldn't believe what he just heard himself say.

"I'm sorry, Diego. I need to give Chase another chance."

"I understand," Diego reluctantly agreed.

She reached up and kissed him tenderly on the cheek. Once again, he felt the angst of love slowly slipping away from him, and not unlike with Celaya, he felt defenseless to change the path of his destiny.

"I think we should take you back to your hotel," Diego offered.

She nodded her head, stood up and headed to her room upstairs.

When she came downstairs, Lorena was dressed in the clothes in which she had arrived. In her arms, neatly folded, was the dress Diego had given her last night. She handed him the dress.

"I think it would be best if you kept this," she said softly, almost apologetically.

Diego nodded in agreement and set the dress on the table at the front entrance.

They drove into Ciudad Hidalgo without talking. There were no words that could erase the memories of last night or soothe the pain of their ensuing separation. When they arrived in front of Lorena's hotel, Diego started to get out of the car to open the door for her but she clutched his forearm and pulled him toward her. "He might be waiting for me."

"Of course," Diego said, understanding her caution.

They sat for a moment staring into each other's eyes. Lorena leaned over and kissed him. Diego did not want to let go of her, but they both knew they were past the point of no return.

"Diego, if things were different...."

Diego put his fingertips to her lips. "I know, but promise me, if you ever need an old, worn-out swordsman to come to your rescue again, don't hesitate to call."

"I'll always know I can count on you, Diego. Good-bye." Lorena lightly brushed his cheek with the back of her hand, turned, and exited the car, never looking back.

Just as she was stepping out of the car, Lolo was exiting the hotel, having just finished breakfast with his close friend. He glanced over at Lorena, surprised to see that she was still in town. Lolo immediately saw that she was upset.

Diego remained at the curb and saw Lolo approach Lorena near the hotel entrance. He watched to make sure everything was all right, knowing something about the bad blood between them.

"Lorena, I was wondering what happened to you. I checked at the front desk, and they said you had not checked out, but they hadn't seen you since Friday night," Lolo said, as he glanced in the direction of Diego's car.

Diego, who had been staring in their direction, quickly turned his head but Lolo immediately spotted him. Lorena seeing Lolo's attention drawn to Diego, tried to distract him, but it was too late.

"Lolo, I would like to talk to you, but I'm really tired. So, if you don't mind, I'm going to go up to my room and get some rest," Lorena said in a defeated tone.

"No problem. I guess you've had a *long* night," Lolo remarked sarcastically, as he again looked in the direction of Diego's car, which was slowly pulling away from the curb.

Lorena ignored his stinging words but noted to herself, "*The same old jealous Lolo.*" His comment had been aimed at her obvious indiscretion with Diego, and any hope she had of Lolo turning over a "new leaf," evaporated before her hand struck the brass handle of the hotel door.

Lorena walked briskly to the front desk to inquire if she had any messages. The front desk clerk reached over, retrieved a thick envelope from the counter behind him, and handed it to Lorena. She looked at the handwriting on the outside of the envelope, which simply read, *My Dearest Lorena.* It was in Chase's handwriting.

CHAPTER 24

Emiliano was resting quietly in a private room and recovering from his wound. Fortunately, Lorca's switchblade had only struck muscle and fat, just missing the lower lobe of his left lung. The doctor's prognosis was positive; Emiliano should be back on his feet in a couple of weeks. Chase was relieved he wouldn't have to make the same tragic visit to Emiliano's family as he had with Antonio's. He stood by the bedside of his friend, searching to find the appropriate words to thank Emiliano for almost having made the ultimate sacrifice.

"Why are words such a sorry excuse for how we really feel?" Chase's heartfelt sentiments shocked Emiliano.

"Save it for another time, my friend. I've never doubted your devotion. Just promise you won't be calling me in the future except to catch up on our boring personal lives."

"I'm not sure I have a *personal* life anymore." Chase's expression turned somber.

"You won't....if you don't get the hell out of here. I don't know what happened between you and Lorena, but standing here moping around about it won't solve your problems. You've never been one to give up easily, so why start now?"

"Are you going to be all right?" Chase asked, feeling somewhat guilty about leaving so soon.

"Yes, as long as I don't starve to death from this poor excuse they call hospital food."

The two long-time associates fondly said good-bye to each other and affirmed once again that they were finished with their covert operations. They were both looking forward to cruising into the quieter side of life, as mundane as everyday existence could sometimes be.

His narrow escape on the shores of Lake Pátzcuaro left Chase exhausted, but all he could think about afterwards was getting back to Lorena. He left the hospital and drove the five and a half hours to Ciudad Hidalgo without stopping. Chase arrived at his home early Sunday morning and rushed straight to Lorena's hotel to see if she was still registered.

The front desk clerk gave Chase the news he was hoping for: his wife was still a guest.

He decided it was too early to wake Lorena. Besides, he looked like hell and he wanted to get cleaned up first. Chase left an envelope with the front desk clerk to give to Lorena. It contained a letter he had written to Lorena while waiting in the hospital for the status report on Emiliano's condition. He could only hope Lorena would read it and give him another chance to explain. Unbeknownst to Chase, at that very moment Lorena lay in the arms of Mexico's most notable swordsman.

Chase was grateful that he still had a little more time to sort out exactly what he would say to Lorena. He would have liked to blame his behavior on the predicament associated with the Lorca, but he knew it wouldn't wash with her.

"*No more excuses!*" Chase swore under his breath. He was ready, for the first time since he had started down this dead-end road of lies and deception, to accept full responsibility for the all mistakes he had made. If he was going to have any chance of salvaging their relationship, he had to start with a clean slate.

He knew he had some legitimate concerns about letting Lorena return to Mexico while Lorca was still on the loose, but he should have been honest with her. He also knew, in all good conscience, that he probably could have worked something out with Immigration so that Lorena could remain in the U.S. He had lied to himself for selfish reasons; he wanted to finish Lorca off for what the bastard had done to Lorena. Chase knew he had taken the easy way out when Eddings blackmailed him. He was no better than Lorca when it came to being obsessed with revenge. How he was going to explain all this to Lorena seemed an almost insurmountable task.

Chase took a long hot shower and lay down in his room to try to catch up on sleep. He made sure the phone was right next to the bed. If and when Lorena decided to call, he didn't want to take any chances of missing her call. Chase's head hit the pillow; two minutes later, he was sound asleep.

Lorena sat in her hotel room, staring at Chase's letter sitting on her bureau. She hesitated opening it, fearful that it would be filled with more lies. Everything had gone totally haywire since they had last seen each other. She had foolishly let herself slip into an affair with Diego, but she wasn't absolutely convinced that her feelings for him weren't more deep-rooted than a passing infatuation. Whatever the reason, it seriously complicated things. She kept vacillating over her decision to tell Chase about her affair. She wanted to make sure her motives were pure, and not aimed at paying back Chase for the pain he had caused her. Every time she had convinced herself that the right strategy was to reveal the truth about last night, another legitimate reason would materialize for not telling him. She worried that even if she and Chase could work out their problems dropping such an emotional bomb would eliminate any chance of reconciliation. Lorena made a commitment to herself; if Chase was willing to acknowledge his mistakes, she would consider trying to work things out. Whatever the outcome, she now knew that she was strong enough to move on in her life. If her recent circumstances with Chase and her brief affair with Diego hadn't done anything else, they forced her to look at herself and what she really wanted out of life. Somehow, she had lost that sense of empowerment, her sense of self, when she had decided to marry Chase. Her inner strength had been rejuvenated over the past few days with Diego and she was never going to let it go again. If she went back to Chase, it wasn't because she felt sorry for him or was too weak. She would go back on her own terms or not at all.

Lorena finally relented and opened the four-page letter. It was clear from the beginning that he had not taken the task lightly:

My Darling Lorena,

I love you! That may sound strange coming from a man who lied to you, who held you back from your dancing and in a fit of anger, accidentally struck you. But I have no other way of conveying my true feelings for you than to tell you that I still love you deeply. I understand I've betrayed you, and I can understand if you decide to move on without me but please read what I have written.

Where should I start? I guess with the truth.

Lorena stopped momentarily. Reading his words was almost like hearing his voice. She knew it was irrational to be feeling remorseful for Chase's admission of guilt, but she suddenly felt the overwhelming shame for having slept with Diego. There was no question any longer; she would have to postpone her plans for telling Chase about her affair.

Lorena continued reading.

First, I want to say that this is not about asking for forgiveness. I am not asking you to try to erase all the pain I caused you. All my errors in judgment and dreadful behavior are inexcusable, but I am asking for your understanding. First, and foremost, I need you to understand I am just an ordinary man, with flaws and faults like any other human being. One of these is thinking I needed to provide for your every need, including protecting you from harm's way. Somehow, in my devotion and love for you, I lost sight of the fact that you needed your own independence, to make your own decisions about your life. I thought, by trying to protect you, I could have you to myself. I was wrong! In attempting to make a perfect life for us, I almost destroyed it.

Chase's words splashed off the paper like soothing waves of warm water. Lorena read his apologies for having participated in paying off officials in Mexico, and how frightened he was that she would return to Mexico to resume her career. He wrote about how he woke up many nights in Texas in a cold sweat, imagining her back in Lorca's treacherous grip. He wanted her to know that he was not using any of it as an excuse, but hoped she could understand his need to protect her. Chase spoke honestly about lying to himself concerning his motives for keeping her out of Mexico and his fears about Lorca. He admitted being afraid that she would return to her dancing career, and she might not want to start a family. Chase openly acknowledged his jealously of other men watching her performing and his fear of losing her over time to someone else. He wrote that he understood the frustration and anger he had caused by not letting her fulfill her dreams. Chase apologized for not keeping his promise to support her career and vowed that from this point on, he would to do everything in his power to help her accomplish her goals in life. What Lorena read next even surprised her. Chase detailed how he was forced into the mission. When

Eddings threatened to take away the only thing in life he cared about. Chase shared the frustration he felt when she showed up in Ciudad Hidalgo, and how, later on, he realized his anger once again revolved around his fear of losing her, or worse, seeing her murdered at the hands of Fermin Lorca. He wrote of his re-ignited anger for Lorca, and that he accepted the mission because he had a chance of permanently eliminating Lorca from their lives.

Chase's appeal for sympathy was desperate at this point in the letter. He begged her to try to understand that he would never intentionally hit her, under any circumstances. She had to believe what happened in the hotel *was* an accident. He described in excruciating detail about what happened at Lake Pátzcuaro, about how the whole time he was in danger of losing his life he could only think about getting back to her. When he was sure he was about to die at Lorca's hand, he only regretted not having had a chance to tell her how much he loved her.

Lorena turned to the last page of the letter and read his final words:

Lorena, I realize there is nothing I can do to change the past. All I can do is hope that your heart is not closed to me. If you choose to turn your back on our life together, then I'll understand and support you. But, if you can find it within yourself to take me back into your life, then I swear by all the powers of God above, I will never betray or lie to you again.

With everlasting love,
Chase

Lorena read and reread his last, earnest words and knew she had to give him another chance. She now understood why he had tried to keep her out of Mexico and was willing to acknowledge that he had a legitimate reason to go after Lorca. She also understood how the powers of love could corrupt even the strongest human beings. She had made her fair share of questionable decisions in her past and even more recently with Diego. She knew she wasn't going to give Chase a blanket pardon, but at least now, she felt for the first time in a long time that he was being honest with her.

Lorena picked up the phone, dialed the front desk and asked the clerk if the gentleman who delivered the letter had left any messages. The clerk told her he could be reached at his home in Ciudad Hidalgo. She hung up the phone, knowing the next move was hers.

Lorena knocked on Chase's door twice. At first, Chase, who was still in an unconscious stupor, didn't hear the knocking. Lorena knocked again and was starting to leave, when she heard the door open behind her. He stood at the door in a white terry cloth robe. His blond hair was disheveled; he only had the time to brush it with his hand in his rush to get to the door. He didn't care how he looked to Lorena; he was just relieved to see her standing at his door. *It must be a positive sign*, he thought.

Lorena turned around to face him. They stared at each other in complete silence. The tension was palpable, as thick as red Mississippi mud. Chase had tried to imagine what it would be like to see Lorena again. Would her eyes be filled with anger and disdain or with understanding and compassion? His mind was jumbled with possibilities. Maybe she wasn't even here to try and reconcile, but to say a good-bye? Should he say something first, or wait for her to speak?

Finally, he couldn't take the pressure. "I am so glad you came. Please come in." His words had the soft edge of reconciliation.

"Thank you."

Lorena walked past Chase, and wondered how long this uneasy feeling between them would last. She was barely three paces into the house, when Chase uncharacteristically blurted out an emotional plea, "Lorena, I want you back in my life so much." He stepped toward her, wanting to make sure that she saw the sincerity of his words on his face.

The intensity of his impassioned words almost struck her down. Lorena stood stock still for a moment, staring intently at him. Tears were starting to well up in Chase's eyes.

Lorena knew the next action she took would be a life-defining moment. Should she take him into her arms or turn around and walk out the door? Her mind rocked back and forth in an emotional tug-of-war.

Chase was paralyzed by her lack of response. He knew the wheels were turning inside her mind, but what choice would she ultimately make?

"Didn't you say once that everyone deserves a second chance?" There was a certain desperation to his words.

"I guess I did but I'm not so sure that applies here." Lorena let her tense expression relax, as she hinted at a smile.

Chase bent his head in defeat as Lorena moved closer to him. Chase raised his eyes as she lifted his chin. She cupped her hands around his face and slowly brought his lips to hers. They kissed tentatively at first, and then within seconds were passionately embraced. The intensity of their exchange was as if they were exorcising all the anger, betrayal, and frustration. Tears poured down their cheeks. Somewhere between their impassioned kisses, Lorena whispered, "I love you, Chase."

The sound of Lorena uttering those sacred words was like hearing shock waves radiating from distant shores, thundering together into one holy sound. Not since the horror of watching Lorena run away from him at the hotel had Chase thought he would ever have Lorena back in his life again. Now he knew it was possible.

Chase and Lorena spent the next few days reacquainting themselves. They shared their hopes and dreams for the future. Lorena became excited about the possibility of returning to her career. Chase's sole purpose now was to make Lorena happy, and if that meant chasing her all over the country on tour, then so be it. There would be plenty of time for having a family later. All he cared about was about being together, about being husband and wife again.

The first time they made love later that evening was slightly uncomfortable and tense, but by the following morning all their uneasiness had disappeared. Familiarity with each other's body seemed to act as a cleansing potion for their open wounds. Only once during their passionate lovemaking did Lorena think of her brief affair with Diego, but even then it was a fleeting thought of irrational, misplaced attention. She wanted to forget Diego ever happened.

Three days after reconciling, they made arrangements to leave for Texas on the next train. Anxious to get back to their ranch, they purchased two, first class tickets on the midnight express that would leave the next evening. On the way to the train station, they stopped off at the hotel to get her bags. In all the upheaval with her decision to patch up things with Chase, she had forgotten to check out and get her belongings. As they were leaving the hotel, Diego Sanchez entered the lobby. Lorena saw him instantly and her entire body tensed.

Diego had tried to erase their night together from his mind, but it was impossible. He had not heard from her since dropping her off, and he was trying to convince himself that he was at the hotel to see if she was all right. But he knew better. His real motive was based on selfish hope that maybe it hadn't worked out between Lorena and her estranged husband. Seeing her with Chase in the lobby now closed that chapter in his life. They passed within a few feet of each other. Diego conspicuously glanced at Lorena, no differently than he would have any other beautiful woman on the street. Lorena tried not to return his piercing stare, but she caught a glimpse of his eyes. His crestfallen expression told her everything she needed to know about Diego's state of mind. She looked straight ahead, not wanting to betray her feelings for Diego. As much as she wanted to turn and console Diego, she was helpless to help him.

Chase turned to Lorena and asked curiously, "Wasn't that Diego Sanchez, the fencing champion? I think I read in the local newspaper he bought a rancho outside of Ciudad Hidalgo."

Lorena hesitated before answering. "I'm not quite sure. It looks like him, but I wouldn't know, having never met the man personally."

"I thought flamenco dancers are famous for hanging out in the same crowd."

"Don't always believe the idle ramblings of the press." Lorena's palms began to sweat. "Have you ever known them to be accurate in their reporting? Can we go now? We have a lot to get done before we leave tonight."

While Chase and Lorena were slowly chugging across the high desert of central Mexico, Diego was back at his hacienda trying to put his life back in order. He sat in front of the same fireplace where he and Lorena had made love. He was holding the neatly folded dress Lorena had returned to him, staring at the blue-gold flames. He slowly leaned over and gently set the dress into the red-hot coals. He watched regretfully as the flames reached up and devoured the embroidered silk. As the ashes danced up the chimney, their fluid motion reminded him of the sensual moves of Lorena's body. He lay back into the comfort of the sofa, and when the dress was completely consumed by the flames, he closed his eyes, took a deep breath and tried to freeze just one frame of her poetic grace in the corner of his memory. She was gone from his life, not unlike when Celaya had disappeared from his life.

CHAPTER 25

Two months after Chase and Lorena returned to their ranch in Texas, Chase had his appointment with Dr. Livens, a local urologist. He hadn't forgotten about his commitment to Lorena to have a fertility test. He was positive the previous pregnancy problems were not due to infertility on his part. The subject of children hadn't come up since their return to Texas, but Chase wanted to demonstrate to Lorena that he had truly turned over a new leaf.

Dr. Livens did a full work-up on Chase and asked for a semen sample to send off to the lab for testing and told Chase the results should be back in a week. When Dr. Livens asked about any problems in the bedroom, Chase informed him that their sex life was very active. Ever since returning from Mexico, all the problems Chase previously had with his sexual libido had disappeared. The first couple of weeks while settling into life back on the ranch, they hadn't even thought about birth control. Chase didn't know whether this was a signal on Lorena's part that she was rethinking her attitude about having children or because their sexual encounters were so spontaneous. Whatever the outcome of their frivolous attitude toward birth control was fine with him.

Chase returned home early after his doctor's appointment. Lorena was in her dance studio busily practicing for an upcoming performance in Pecos. Chase had gone out of his way to contact a few friends in the entertainment industry. He convinced them that with the large Hispanic population in the southwest, Lorena's talent would be a perfect fit for promoting a concert. Chase had to put up part of the fees for the promotion and rental of a theater in San Antonio. It was all worth it when he saw Lorena's jubilant reaction toward his effort in helping her career along.

Chase crept into the studio unnoticed by his wife, sneaked up behind her, and lifted her into the air with a bear hug.

Lorena screeched with fright, "Chase, you almost gave me a heart attack!"

He lightly kissed her on the nape of her neck. "Guess where I was today?"

"I am almost afraid to ask, given your mood."

"I made a *contribution* at Dr. Livens' office."

"Who is Dr. Livens?"

"A urologist. I should have the results back in a week,"

Lorena released herself from his embrace. "Chase, I know we spoke about this before...." Lorena broke off, not wanting to bring up bad memories from their recent past.

"Lorena, it's all right."

"I'm not saying I don't want children right now, but I think we should give it a little time. Besides, I've been so busy getting ready for my performance next month that I really haven't even thought about it."

Chase had anticipated her answer about having children. "Hey, I'm not saying we need to get started right away, I just wanted you to know I kept my promise. No pressure, I swear." Chase held up his right hand as if being sworn into office. He was having a hard time hiding his disappointment, but he didn't want Lorena to feel threatened.

"Thank you. You know I want children, but all in due time."

"I should let you get back to work. I love you," he said as he exited the studio.

"I love you. See you in about an hour," she replied, hoping Chase was honest in his reaction about waiting to start a family.

A week later, while at one of her early morning practice sessions Lorena became tired and was on the brink of throwing up. She tried to ignore the nausea, deciding that it must have been something she ate the night before. But the next morning, she was still dragging, and there was no avoiding her upset stomach. She vomited twice before coming down to have breakfast with Chase.

Chase looked over at her and could see she was peaked. "Are you feeling ok?"

"Yes. I'm just a little slow this morning."

"Would you like some bacon and eggs?"

Even the thought of food almost sent her rushing back to the bathroom. "No thanks. I think I'll just have some toast and coffee."

Lorena had known for a while something was physically amiss. She had been struggling with her energy level during the last few practices. At first, she thought she was a little out of shape, but as time went on it really started to bother her. Her sleeping habits were totally off kilter. Several times over the past couple of weeks she had awakened in the middle of the night with strange, surrealistic dreams.

Her most recent concern was that she had not had a period in over a month. Lorena hadn't thought anything about her menstrual cycle, knowing she had occasionally missed her periods in the past. She knew she had been lax about taking precautions during sex in the first couple of weeks after returning from Mexico, but they were having such a great time she didn't want to spoil the spontaneity. Besides, she was convinced nothing had changed from before regarding their difficulty in getting pregnant. Why, all of a sudden, would it have miraculously changed? Lorena remembered joking with herself about the possibility of getting pregnant. She tried to reassure herself at the time that it was impossible. Once Chase had told her about her upcoming performance in San Antonio, she immediately started using protection to avoid the prospect of getting pregnant and spoiling her return to the stage.

All things considered, her stomach-turning experience this morning had her worried. She knew all the signs of a pregnant woman, and she was starting to show too many of them for her own comfort level. She decided she would make an appointment with Dr. Kittles to eliminate any possibility that she was carrying a child.

Three days later, Lorena was sitting in Dr. Kittles' office waiting to get the results from the pregnancy test she had taken earlier in the week. She was anxious, given that her symptoms continued to persist, but she tried to convince herself that the current maladies could be the result of any number of minor illnesses. As she waited for the nurse to call her name, she fretfully rubbed her hands together, praying for good news.

The nurse came from behind the closed doors of the examining rooms and called out her name. Lorena almost jumped out of her seat. She followed the nurse into the exam room, barely able to get her legs to work out of fear that her whole life could change within a matter of minutes.

"Dr. Kittles will be right with you," the nurse said, in a cooing tone.

Lorena knew Dr. Kittles was no different than any other doctor. He was always over-scheduled, and she would have to wait ten to twenty minutes to get her results. She sorted through several magazines, most of which had to do with prenatal care and child rearing. It was everything she could do not to run out of the room screaming with impatience for the doctor.

Fifteen minutes later, Dr. Kittles entered. He had his usual beaming smile. It was impossible to read from his expression the results of her tests.

"How are we doing today, young lady?"

She wanted to grab him by his white coat and shake the answer out of him. "Fine, thank you," she politely answered.

"Well, I got good news for you," he announced proudly.

How could he know what good news was to her? She was pleading inside her panicked mind for her "good" news and Lorena looked earnestly at Dr. Kittles, who was taking his time out the verdict. *Were the next two years of her life going to be filled with dirty diapers and sleepless nights? Could he please just give her the damn answer?*

Lorena finally couldn't stand the suspense any more. "Are the results negative?" she inquired directly.

"Hardly. The rabbit died....I'm pleased to announce, you're very pregnant, my dear. From the look of things, I'd say you're a little over two months."

His words resounded through her brain like jagged blue strobes arcing across two magnetic electrodes. She could hear everything he said, but it sounded as if his every word was played at a ridiculously slow speed on an old broken phonograph.

Lorena managed to mumble a question from her numb mind. "Are you sure?"

"Yes, quite sure," Dr. Kittles supplied, recognizing her state of shock. He had seen this blank expression of disbelief numerous times in his career. She would get over it, he thought.

"We'll need to set up a schedule of monthly appointments. I've already notified my nurses to start booking appointments. You're young and healthy, so I don't expect any problems. Just continue to eat right, try to exercise appropriately, and everything should be fine. Have you told your husband yet?"

"*Told my husband*!" she thought. "*What about me?*" She was three weeks away from her first major performance in America. Lorena was paralyzed. Her whole life had just turned upside down. She felt as if she was on a carnival ride, suspended upside down until all the blood rushed into her head. At any moment, she thought would pass out.

She finally mustered a response. "No, Chase doesn't know yet. I wanted to keep it a surprise."

"I'm sure Chase will be ecstatic. I know from his last visit here, when he talked a lot about wanting a family someday."

Lorena stood up. She had had enough of Dr. Kittles exuberance.

"Stop at the front desk on your way out, and they'll set you up for your next appointment. You take care now and congratulations."

Lorena was barely able to squeak out a thank you as she exited the examining room.

All the way home, she could think only about was how foolish she had been not to have taken precautions for those few weeks. She screamed, scolding herself in the privacy of her car. She wanted a little more time, a little more freedom before she had to commit to being a full-time mother. She was just turning twenty-four, hitting the prime of her dancing career. What kind of physical shape would she be in after lugging a baby around inside of her for nine months? She placed her hand on her hard abdomen and tried to imagine what it would look like after doubling or tripling in size. She had seen the dark purple stretch marks on other pregnant women and cringed at the thought. Would she ever be able to return to her life's work? Lorena pulled over to the side of the road and sobbed.

A policeman stopped his patrol car to ask if she needed assistance. She lied, thanked him, and made her way home.

It took Lorena two days to acclimate herself to the idea of motherhood. As the initial shock started to fade she began reading about the task of bringing a child into the world. The option of abortion never crossed her mind. First off, she would have to do it in complete secrecy in a town where there were no secrets. Besides, she wasn't about to deceive Chase again on such a major issue in their relationship. Then there were her parents, who would never forgive her for such a horrific act. No, she knew she had to accept the consequences of her actions.

The more she mulled it over in her mind, the more she forced herself to try and get comfortable with the idea of being a mother. While in town running errands, she had even caught herself staring in a window at baby clothes. As for her career, she convinced herself that somehow she would be able to do both. There was no reason why, with Chase's help, she couldn't continue dancing while also being a good mother. Yes, she would have to take a sabbatical, but as soon as she could get back in shape after the baby, she was determined to resume her career. Chase had promised to do anything to support her, and now she was going to hold him to it.

After keeping her secret for two days, the morning finally came when she decided it was time to tell Chase. Lorena followed every step Chase took as he came down the stairs for breakfast. She had been waiting for him since before sunrise, like a spider luring an unsuspecting bug into her web. Her excitement was growing as she edged toward the moment of truth.

She waited until Chase sat down at the breakfast table and poured himself a cup of coffee. When she was sure he was totally relaxed and starting to sink his teeth into the sports section of the newspaper; she decided the time had come.

"Sleep well?" she asked him innocently.

"Great. How are you feeling this morning?" Chase inquired from behind the rustling paper.

"Just fine.... aside from a little morning sickness."

Chase was so embroiled in checking out the box scores from the last night's ballgame that he didn't pick up her reference at first.

Lorena gave it one more shot. "Dr. Kittles will be calling your office to schedule some appointments with us."

"What for?" he asked, his head still buried in his newspaper.

"Well, generally the husband comes with his wife for her prenatal appointments."

Chase's hands clinched together, crumbling the edges of the newspaper. He peeked over the top of the paper and saw a beaming Lorena. Her expression told him everything.

"This is not a joke, is it?"

"I'm afraid not. You're going to be a father."

He jerked up out of his chair and rushed over to where Lorena was sitting. He got down on his knees so he could look straight into her eyes. He laid his head on her stomach, and then looked up at her with expectant eyes.

"When did you find out?" Chase asked, hardly able to contain his excitement.

"A few days ago. I would have told you then, but I wanted to wait till the right time." Lorena knew she was telling a little white lie, but Chase didn't need to know about her initial negative reaction.

"Are you ok with this?"

"Yes. It took me a while, but now I'm ok with it." She paused. "I'm going to need a lot of help, Chase. I want you to know I'm not going to stop dancing."

"Of course, you're not. We'll figure it out. I promise to do everything to support you." Chase was unsure what he was committing to, but he didn't care. He was going to be a father! They were going to have a family together. All the concerns about not being able to have a child evaporated with Lorena's joyful words. Chase couldn't believe that just a few short months before he was on the brink of losing the only woman he loved, and now she was about to bear his child.

For the next few days, Chase was walking on cloud nine. He could hardly wait to share the news with his parents. His mother cried at hearing the news that she would finally become a grandmother, which at times she was convinced might never happen. Rebecca was just as stunned as her son at the surprising but blessed news. She knew how important Lorena's career was to her and had been fairly sure that kids were not in their near future. Rebecca also suspected that something had been wrong between Chase and Lorena a few months before, but was never able to confirm it. She really had come to love and respect Lorena as her own daughter. Chase's father took the news in stride. The only thing he cared about was whether it was a boy. Carrying on the Chandler tradition was at the top of his list when it came to a first-born grandchild.

Lorena watched as an exuberant Chase told his friends and associates around town. His genuine elation was contagious. Lorena found herself getting more and more excited about becoming a mother. The motherly instincts she heard about from her grandmother so many times were really starting to kick in. She continued to practice for her upcoming performance, but her previous intense focus was now starting to take a back seat to her pregnancy. Lorena, for the first time since Dr. Kittles told her, could feel the new life springing within her body, and to her surprise, she was starting to feel a sense of peace within herself and her new role in life.

CHAPTER 26

Having laid his father to rest seven months ago, Diego was still trying to weather the emotional storm of losing his last family member while also trying to recover from watching Lorena walk out of his life. He knew it was foolish to ever think he could have had a chance with her, but the pain still lingered.

Fortunately for him, Diego was closing in on the end of his career, and he didn't have the time to wallow in personal tragedies. He had to focus all his energy on preparing for his last tournament, which were only a couple months away. There was one thing he was not about to let go of in his personal life, and that was locating his son. During the brief lull in his search to find Amado, Diego dismissed the detective he had hired, dissatisfied with the lack of results. He had a gut feeling that somehow he would find Amado on his own. With the death of his father, he realized he was the only surviving member of the Sanchez family. He knew somewhere out there though, amid the throngs of human chaos, was the last vestige of hope for carrying on the long heritage of his family's name, and he was determined to find him.

There was something even more powerful causing him to spend every waking moment on the search for Amado. Amado was the only remnant of fabric left between him and Celaya. Diego was not about to let go of this tether without a fight. He needed to look into his son's eyes and see the warm reflection of Celaya looking back at him, to let him know how much he truly loved his mother. More importantly, he had to correct Amado's perception that his father was a coward who had callously abandoned his mother. As long as these facts remained unspoken, Diego's universe would be unbalanced, tilted on its axis, wobbling with an unyielding guilt.

As Diego sat in his study resting after a successful Sunday afternoon in Monterrey, he reflected on his most recent tournament performances. The intensity of his artistry was becoming more pronounced with each outing. The flair of his sword work and the boldness of his moves exceeded even his own expectations. He felt as though he was in his early twenties again. Of course, this just further alienated some of his colleagues, particularly Lolo Nieto. Diego could see Lolo's frustration building with each contest. It had gotten to a point that whenever they were on the same card, Lolo would not even acknowledge Diego's presence. Lolo's disrespect for Diego was easily recognizable by both aficionados and the press and Lolo's rude behavior was starting to backfire with both the press and fans. The more he pressed in tournaments, the more his performances suffered. After the Monterey tournament, Lolo's manager suggested that his young protégé needed to use the time before his next contest to get his act together. The most prestigious tournament of the year was coming up, and he needed to be sharp. Carbajal reminded Lolo that he was still the heir apparent to Diego Sanchez, and he had to start acting like he was deserving of the honor. There were only a few more opportunities for him to show the proper respect before Diego retired and also Lolo had to take advantage of them before it was too late. Regardless of how he personally felt about Diego, Carbajal told Lolo, he had to mask his resentment and exhibit some class, or even his most faithful fans would abandon their allegiance to him.

Lolo knew that he had to take his manager's advice or he would end up despised by his fans for the rest of his career. As much as the press could influence the success of a sports hero, they really made or broke careers.

Lolo decided to take Carbajal's advice. He would visit his grandparents; whom hadn't seen in over nine months. Even though his grandparents had raised him, it was always traumatic for him to go back home. The painful memories of his early childhood, of knowing that his mother had died in their house was sometimes just too much to bear.

Lolo arrived early Friday morning at the Flores's sprawling rancho. After an onslaught of tearful kisses from his grandmother and a firm handshake from his stoic grandfather, Lolo was practically dragged into the large, formal dining room. Señora Flores had already prepared lunch, and the fare consisted of chilies en nogada, fresh tamales, chayote and luscious vanilla flan. Lolo could already see the rolls of fat building up around his thin waistline but it was her way of spoiling her grandson. Marta Flores always treated Lolo as if he was her own child and constantly worried about him. She had already had enough tragedy in her life without losing Lolo.

Their dinner conversation almost always revolved around Lolo's most recent tournament performances. Both of his grandparents paid close attention to his promising career in the newspapers. Not knowing of his hatred for Diego Sanchez, they asked him what it was like to fight in the same tournament as the great master. Lolo politely answered their question by complimenting Diego. He was practicing for his return to tournament play in Mexico City when he would have to face inevitable questions by the press regarding his feelings about Sanchez's upcoming retirement.

After eating, they retired to the living room. While Lolo and Señor Flores smoked cigars and sipped brandy, Señora Flores went to her bedroom to retrieve something she wanted to give to Lolo. She returned a few minutes later, carrying a colorfully wrapped gift. She handed it to her grandson.

"What is this for? It's not my birthday."

Señora Flores had been waiting with restrained excitement to present the gift to Lolo.

"Just open it." Her face beamed.

Lolo could see by the expression on his grandfather's face that he did not share the same excitement as his wife. Lolo carefully unwrapped the gift and immediately saw that it was some type of clothing. When he had completely exposed the creamy white strip of cloth, he turned to his grandmother and started to thank her but before he could speak, Señora Flores interrupted him.

"It was your mother's. We gave it to her over twenty years ago. Your great-grandmother made it for her as a going away gift when she went to the university in Mexico City."

Lolo was somewhat astonished by his grandmother's admission.

"Thank you very much." He respectfully stroked the cloth as if he were gently touching the cheek of his dead mother.

"It was given to her to protect her from harm's way," Señor Flores said with an air of skepticism.

Señora Flores frowned at her husband's insinuation, returning her attention to Lolo. "Your mother would have wanted you to have it."

"Where did it come from?" Lolo said, gazing at the scarf again.

"Strangely enough, one of her old acquaintances from the university returned it just recently. He said your mother had loaned it to him, and he felt compelled to return it when he heard that she had passed away."

"But she died over twenty years ago."

Lolo knew his grandparents had kept the situation concerning their daughter's delicate situation and untimely death a secret. It was no mystery why his mother's former associates were unaware of her passing and now only finding out now about her death.

"Yes, dear, but...."

Lolo interrupted his grandmother, whose eyes were starting to well up with tears. "I'll treasure it for the rest of my life." Lolo stroked the scarf again, and then placed it around his neck. "Thank you so much. If you don't mind my asking, what was the name of the gentleman who returned it?"

"Dr. Zavala. He is a prominent psychiatrist in Mexico City. He seemed to know your mother quite well during her time at the university."

Lolo banked the unfamiliar name in his mind. When he returned to Mexico City, he would make a point to look up this stranger and thank him for his kind gesture. Maybe this Dr. Zavala could tell him something about his mother's college days. As painful as it was for Lolo to recall his mother's brief life, the more he could learn about her earlier years, the better. He knew so little of the woman who had sacrificed her life to bring him into this world. The only reminders he had of his mother's youth were a few pictures his grandparents had given him. They had done their best to explain what kind of woman she was, but it was difficult for them to bring up painful memories. Even in his early childhood, Lolo recognized the angst his questions caused them, particularly his grandfather. What little he was able to garner from their recollections was that his mother was an independent woman noted for her intelligence and stunning beauty. To have lived his whole life without ever hearing a single tender word uttered from her lips or to know what really inspired her, left an uncompromising emptiness in him. The scar was so deep that it felt as though the insides of his heart had been spooned out and left hollow. Then there was still the question of this mystery man who had so coldly abandoned his mother, the coward who had made him a bastard child, who had created such suffering in so many lives. Just the thought of "his father" caused Lolo to want to strike out and kill the haunting spirit.

Lolo often thought that if he ever had the pleasure of confronting his so-called *father*, how he would relish striking him down unsympathetically. He thought he would not spare even one word of sorrow in gleefully watching the last breath wither from the chest of such a pitiful excuse for a human being.

Diego spent the last few days of his vacation cleaning up some of his father's affairs in Monterey. Needing a break, Diego decided to head to his family estate outside of town. He had been there only once since his father died. The rancho was being run by one of his cousins, but Diego had yet to sort through all of his father's personal belongings. He had been avoiding the task, but now was the perfect opportunity for him to conclude this difficult but important business.

He arrived at the rancho and took up residence in his old bedroom. Even though his cousin's family had moved into the large hacienda, they had respected Diego's wishes not to disturb his father's library. All of his father's personal items were right where he had left them over a year and a half ago.

Diego had a drink with his cousin, Franco, then politely excused himself and went to the library. He pushed open the two sliding doors, cautiously stepped inside, and closed the doors. The late afternoon sunlight streamed into the room. He walked through, brushing his hand along the way against the dusty bookshelves filled with his father's favorite books. It was almost as though he could feel the presence of his father as he glanced at the titles.

He made his way to a large mahogany desk and sat in his father's high back green leather chair. As he settled in, he could envision his father studiously rifling through his daily workload. He remembered that as a young child, how he would often slither into his father's office unnoticed, just to be near the man he so much loved and respected. He remembered sitting on the floor in the far corner, patiently waiting for his father to finish conducting his business.

Eventually, his father would beckon him over to the desk, sit Diego on his lap and begin regaling him with stories of spectacular confrontations between fencing champions.

Diego remembered his father telling him about a great swordsman, Jose Fernandez and how he broke his ankle during a bout but continued to battle to the bitter end, and ultimately winning the match. For hours, Diego would sit there listening to his father's colorful stories, all the while imagining himself in such a glorious role. As he sifted through the recollections of those comforting times with his father, it pained him to think his father had anything to do with the conspiracy against Celaya.

Diego started rummaging through some of the papers scattered on the desk. There were a few old bills and correspondence from his father's best friend, Roberto Soya. Diego avoided his natural curiosity, deciding it would be inappropriate to read his father's private letters. He reached over and opened the top drawer on the side panel of the desk, glancing through the neatly ordered files pertaining to the rancho's business. With the exception of an unpaid bill for recent roof repair, there wasn't anything of any consequence. He checked through the other drawers. There was nothing of any interest except in the bottom drawer, where his father stashed his private stock of premium tequila. Diego retrieved the bottle from the drawer, removed the cork and took a sniff. He recognized the brand as being one from a small distillery in Jalisco.

Diego took his father's shot glass out of the drawer and filled it to the rim. He raised the glass, said a toast of absolution to his deceased father, and took a healthy sip of the tawny liquid. He set the shot glass down and pushed the chair back so that he could open the middle desk drawer. As he pulled it open, he could see that with the exception of a few writing pens, it was almost empty. The drawer stuck about a third of the way out. Diego tried to gently coax it the rest of the way, but something was jamming it. He gave one good, solid tug, and the whole drawer landed in his lap. Diego immediately saw what caused the jam. Taped to the back panel on the inside of the drawer was an old skeleton key. He removed the tape holding the key and held it in the palm of his hand. He knew his father had a strongbox in his office, but for the life of him, he couldn't remember where it was. The last time he could remember seeing his father open the box was when he was about fourteen years old.

Diego took another sip of tequila, hoping it might jog his memory. He closed his eyes, trying to visualize where his father would have hidden the strongbox. He tried taking himself back to that day when he was fourteen as he watched his father opening the box. At first there was nothing, but the longer he kept his eyes closed, the clearer the picture came. Then, all of a sudden, his memory became crystal clear. The strongbox was behind his father's favorite set of books in the far corner of the room. Diego got up, walked over to the bookshelf, and removed several books by Carlos Fuentes and Octavio Paz. Just as he had remembered, there it was, carefully hidden behind a copy of *Los Muertos*. He removed the locked strongbox, placed the key in the hourglass shaped keyhole, turned it to the right, and watched the wooden lid snap open. Diego reached in and retrieved a large stack of yellowed papers and envelopes. He walked over to his father's desk and sat down again. The first few folded papers were copies of deeds for his father's land holdings. He set them aside, then looked curiously at a stack of envelopes tied together with a strand of old straw twine. They were weathered and equally old. Diego removed the twine and unfurled a separate piece of tattered paper wrapped around the letters. It was handwritten note from the son of his old maestro, Señor Alvarez. The note was dated over a year and a half ago. With strained curiosity Diego read the brief note addressed to his father.

Dear Señor Sanchez,

I am sure you have heard by now of my father's unfortunate passing. I know that you were dear friends. I found these letters among his personal effects and thought you should have them. I believe they are letters addressed to your son, Diego. I do not know the circumstances by which my father acquired them, but I am returning them to you with the hope you will forward them on to their rightful owner.

Sincerely,

Cesar Alvarez

Why would Señor Alvarez have personal letters belonging to him? Diego brushed away a thin layer of dust from the top letter and read the outside of the envelope. He was stunned. The letters were addressed to him in care of Señor Alvarez. The envelope trembled in his hand as he read the name and return address: Celaya Flores, P.O Box 264, Guadalajara, Mexico.

He flipped through the stack of letters. There must have been over thirty letters, all from Celaya and they were dated during the first nine months of his training in France. Every one of Celaya's letters had been opened. Diego felt as though he had been violated. It was apparent to him that Alvarez had invaded the privacy of his personal correspondence from Celaya. His rage was only temporarily postponed by his intense curiosity over what Celaya had written.

Diego opened the first letter, which was dated three weeks after he had left her at the train station in Mexico City. He carefully unfolded it and a dry rose bud fell into his lap. He retrieved the brittle flower, set it gently aside on the desk, and began reading the handwritten letter.

My Beloved Amado,

It has been over two weeks since I learned of your sudden departure to France. I understand, from speaking with Señor Alvarez, that you had no choice in the matter, so I forgive you, my love, for not saying good-bye.

From what Señor Alvarez tells me, this is a very important opportunity for your career. I am very proud you have been chosen to study in such a prestigious program. It doesn't mean I won't miss you terribly over the next few months, because I will. My heart is already heavy from the burden of missing your sweet touch.

Diego paused, dumbfounded by what he was reading. All these years, he had thought Celaya had abandoned him, when, in fact, she had been still deeply devoted to him. Why had Señor Alvarez kept this secret from him? What had he done to cause such deception by his maestro?

Every time he inquired about Celaya's whereabouts, his mentor's response was that she didn't want anything to do with him. Diego thought back to the circumstances of how he was swept off to France by his father and Señor Alvarez.

Was it just a coincidence that it happened to be at the same time that he met and fell in love with Celaya? Did Señor Alvarez somehow find out about their brief affair? Diego continued reading the rest of the letter, trying to restrain his growing anger.

I am back at the university, but I am finding it very hard to concentrate on my studies. I keep finding my mind wandering off to that wonderful night we spent in each other's arms in the Plaza Quitzal. Do you remember what we promised to each other that night? I hope the distance separating us won't diminish the intensity of your love. I promise I will never surrender to the temptation of another man. You're my soul mate, the inspiration for my life.

Diego, I miss you so much. Please write to me when you find time. I will wait with baited breath to read your words. Señor Alvarez has assured me that he will contact me as soon as he hears from you.

Goodnight, my precious love,

Celaya

Diego set the letter down and pinched his eyes together in anguish. The pain debilitating, so deep, that he felt as though he was paralyzed from the neck down. All the years of suffering and longing for Celaya raced back into his mind. Those early months, when all he could think about was trying to get a message to Celaya; how he had begged her to reconsider and not give up on their relationship. He realized it was all a vicious lie contrived by Alvarez to protect his precious property. His maestro had kept all of Celaya's letters from him to protect *his property.*

Diego was now positive that the letter he wrote on the passenger ship during his maiden voyage to France, the one apologizing to Celaya for not telling her about leaving, never reached her. He had entrusted the wrong man with his words of remorse in abandoning her. In fact, Diego suspected that none of his correspondence to Celaya had ever reached its intended destination. *How betrayed she must have felt!*

As Diego sat in the confines of his father's office, the magnitude of his father's apology on his deathbed came into full focus. His father had to have been in on the scheme to keep him away from Celaya. It saddened him deeply to think the man that he had so respected had caused so much pain in his life.

Diego tried to imagine what their life would have been like if it were not for the conniving efforts of his father and Alvarez. He knew he had a son somewhere out there in the world, but what other wonders might they've shared if he had only known the truth? He felt as though he had been deprived of every precious thing he had yearned for in his life.

As his mind raced from present to past, his thoughts shifted to the lonely plight of Celaya, how humiliated and ostracized she must have felt carrying his illegitimate son. Had she given up all hope, thinking she had been abandoned and tossed aside by a brash young swordsman? Would she have put up a tougher battle for her life after giving birth to their son if he had been by her side?

All these questions left him feeling helpless. He wanted to reach into the past and pull her from the depths of her anguish, to lift her up into the cleansing light of his love. He yearned to comfort her, to hold her and tell her it was all a terrible mistake. Her beloved Diego had not betrayed her devotion.

Diego slumped into the leather chair and opened the next letter. He read each one in chronological order, every letter containing one red rose. Each flower tore a new gaping wound into his already grief-stricken heart. When Diego got to the one that was dated three months after his departure to France, he could hardly bear the burden of her words.

My Beloved Amado,

Where are you, my love? My longing to hear from you is beyond words. I have not heard from you since you left over three months ago, but somehow I know you are out there and that you still love me. I have begged Señor Alvarez to contact you and let you know how desperate I am to know that you still care.

Of all my letters, I hope this one inspires you to write to me. I need you so much right now.

Diego, I am pregnant with your child. Knowing the child I am carrying is a part of you provides me great comfort, but I still need to know that you love me.

I had to leave the University and discontinue my studies, but as long as I know you will be there for me, it is worth the sacrifice. I am living with my parents in Guadalajara. I feel sorry for them having to defend my condition, but I refuse to let myself be humiliated by all these small-minded people.

I must leave you now, my love, but please be safe and write soon.

All my undying love,

Celaya

Reading her heartfelt words announcing that she was carrying his child almost took him over the edge. He slammed both hands down on the desk, cursing the soul of Alvarez.

Even though he knew his father had assisted his mentor, he still couldn't bring himself to hate his own father. Somehow, Diego knew his father believed what he was doing was the right thing for his son at the time.

Diego spent the next two hours reading the remainder of Celaya's letters, pausing just before reading the last one, which had no return address. What amazed him most, as he read and re-read her impassioned words, was her determination in the face of having heard nothing from him for over eight months. It demonstrated a love and devotion not even he thought possible.

When he finally opened the last letter, the soft glow from the window behind him left just enough light to read her final words. The slightly crumpled letter was on hospital stationary. He noticed right away that the handwriting was almost illegible. Diego could tell it was written by Celaya, but it was obvious that she was struggling to etch out her feelings. He envisioned her lying there in the hospital, pen in hand, desperately trying to scribble out her last words. Her normally fluid prose was replaced with short, staccato sentences.

My beloved Amado,

You have a son. I am very tired. He has your strong eyes. I prayed somehow you might have come to me in my hour of need. You must know, my love that I have not lost faith, but I so much need to feel your tender touch again.

I have christened our son Amado Nieto Flores. Amado is for you, my love,

Nieto for my dear grandmother. I only wish he could carry your family name.
Will we ever be together again, my love? I must rest now.
All my love,
Celaya

He read his son's name over and over. Amado *Nieto* Flores. It couldn't be true!

The name *Nieto* kept ringing in his head, like a fire engine siren rattling down an empty street. Lolo Nieto couldn't be his son—the same Lolo Nieto who was his nemesis, who had tried to undermine him on almost every occasion possible?

Diego now saw in Lolo the same fire that Celaya had shown when they first met. He tried to recall every facial feature of Lolo. As the young man's face came into focus in his tormented mind, Diego began to see the eerie resemblance to Celaya and himself. The crystal blue eyes, the dimpled chin, and high cheekbones became unmistakable signs of their genetic fabric. He was stunned that he had not recognized Lolo's distinctive physical characteristics as clear evidence of their relationship.

Diego studied the postage date of the letter, never wanting to forget the birth date of his son.

Even if it seemed like a plausible coincidence that Lolo Nieto was his son, Diego would need to validate the truth. He was not about to announce to Lolo that he was his long-lost father. As he looked at the date again, he tried to recall if he had ever heard or read about Lolo's age. He wracked his brain for an answer, and then suddenly it came to him. He had read a newspaper account about Lolo three months ago that mentioned he had just turned twenty-three. He quickly calculated the corresponding dates and knew instantly that Lolo was the right age to be his son.

What about his name? Why Lolo Nieto? It made all the sense in the world why Amado had changed his name when he was a teenager. He wanted to avoid the same humiliation his mother had experienced. He didn't want to carry the burden of being a bastard child his whole life, especially in such a prominent, public career as fencing.

As tragic as the letters from Celaya were, finding out that the product of their one night of passion potentially was Lolo Nieto lifted Diego out of the darkness of depression.

He held her last letter up and pressed it to his lips, thanking Celaya for unsuspectingly providing him with such a precious clue. All the anger he felt about Alvarez was temporarily set aside and replaced by a newfound exuberance. Having finally solved the mystery that had relentlessly obsessed him was like unleashing the floodwaters from an over burdened dam.

Diego gathered up the letters, retied them and put them into his satchel. He couldn't wait to embark on the next step of his journey to determine if Lolo Nieto was his long-lost son. If Lolo was his missing son how incredibly ironic that he had chosen the same profession, or was it?

Diego knew, once he confirmed his son's identity, there were no guarantees that Lolo would want anything to do with him. Lolo might despise him for having abandoned them but Diego was willing to take the risk. He was positive once Lolo knew the whole story and had a chance to read his mother's letters, everything would work out for the best. It was the least he could hope for after such a long, arduous search.

Diego closed his father's strongbox and exited the library. He told his cousin of urgent business that had come up in Mexico City; he would have to cut his visit short. All he could think about now was confirming the truth about Amado Nieto Flores.

CHAPTER 27

It was late fall in west Texas, and Lorena was grateful for the cooler weather. The last few weeks had been difficult for her. She felt like a beached whale. Her successful U.S. debut in San Antonio seven months ago was just a distant memory. Her once rock-hard body had turned a distorted shape she didn't recognize. The bulbous expansion of her waistline was stretching her skin so tight she was afraid she would burst at the seams at any moment. She was obsessive about oiling her stomach nightly to avoid stretch marks. To date, she only had one faint purple line on her left side. Her once beautiful, auburn hair was clogging up the bathroom drain trap on a regular basis. The prior week she had had a nightmare in which huge clumps of her silky mane fell in slow motion into the toilet bowl. In her dream, she sat staring in horror at her mangy scalp, looking like one of those half-starved feral dogs she had seen running loose in the streets of Mexico. When she woke from her nightmare, she rushed to the bathroom mirror, almost afraid of what she might find glaring back at her.

The relentless, Texas summer heat had made her slender feet swell up until she thought her toes were going to completely disappear into swollen feet. She continued to exercise in her studio, trying to stay in the best shape possible, but she realized in these last few weeks that she definitely was losing the battle of the bulge. Her body was betraying her, and there was nothing she could do about it. Every horror story she heard about having strange cravings in the middle of the night were true. She longed for lox and cream cheese at midnight. Before her pregnancy even the thought of eating half-raw fish was nauseating.

As with many first-time pregnancies, Lorena was a week overdue, and her patience was wearing thin. She was more short-tempered than she could ever recall. The night before last, Chase had been putting the final touches on the crib and didn't hear Lorena calling for help from the other room. When he finally appeared, he caught holy hell. A crazed Medusa could have not been more menacing.

Chase had been a saint through the entire pregnancy. Ever since she told him he was going to be a father, his whole disposition had changed. He even cut back on his office hours so he could help her out around the house. She often wondered what his colleagues at the Bureau would have thought to see their ex-macho agent slaving away as a handholding nurse. At times, his attention was almost too much for her. When Chase was home, he shadowed her every move, searching for opportunities to help her. And if the abundance of toys and baby furniture purchased by Chase were a manifestation of his proclivity for spoiling their unborn child, then Lorena couldn't imagine what it would be like when the baby actually arrived.

On top of all the gifts for the newborn, Chase had lavished her with so many presents Lorena felt guilty. From expensive diamond jewelry to a brand new Cadillac convertible, it was an endless barrage. When he presented her with the shiny baby blue Cadillac, he told her he wanted to make sure she had plenty of good old American steel between her and everyone else on the road.

When she scolded him for being so frivolous, Chase simply responded, "Who else should I waste my money on?"

The final straw had been his surprise of full-length mink coat. Lorena finally put her foot down insisting that Chase stop the insanity. What was she going to do with a mink coat in Pecos, Texas!

Chase's mother wasn't exactly helping the situation. Having learned that her first grandchild was on the way, she put together a busy social schedule for showing off her expectant daughter-in-law. Her friends, who had been teasing her for years about not having grandchildren, were about to get their comeuppance. The fact that Lorena was a stunningly beautiful woman and her son a ruggedly handsome man, gave Rebecca all the ammunition she needed to thwart her teasing friends. Everywhere Rebecca went, she would make a point of smugly noting, "Can you just imagine how beautiful this child is going to be?"

Lorena incessantly heard mother-in-law brag. It came to a point where Lorena began to wonder if an imperfect baby would result in the entire Chandler clan being forced to move out of the county due to the embarrassment.

Aside from these few little bumps in the road, Chase and Lorena had actually settled into a comfortable life together. Yes, the pregnancy was unexpected, but Lorena had worked hard over the last few months to acclimate herself to being a mother. Chase's railcar business was going gang busters. It seemed everything was falling into place for a new generation of Chandlers.

On this particular Sunday afternoon, she was relaxing on the front porch watching Chase wax her new Cadillac. His white T-shirt sleeves were rolled up around his bulging biceps, and his shirt was soaked with soap and water. Watching her well-built husband from the front porch, Lorena actually could feel herself becoming sexually aroused. They hadn't had intercourse in over two months. Chase was the one who suggested they restrain themselves from any activity that could harm the baby. Lorena asked Dr. Kittles about Chase's concern and he assured her that many men reacted this way toward the end of the pregnancy. The more she watched the sheen of Chase's flexed muscles flexing, the more the tightening of her abdomen increased, until she realized it wasn't that she was turned on; she was having contractions.

She waited for another ten minutes to make sure it wasn't a false alarm. When the sharp, stabbing pain returned, there was no mistaking it; their baby was on the way.

"Chase, could you stop waxing the car?" Lorena calmly called out to him.

Chase kept rubbing furiously on the hood of the convertible. "I only have a little bit more to do then I'll give you my undivided attention."

"Chase, I think it's time you stopped waxing the car." Her voice was a little more strained.

He looked up at Lorena and saw that she was in discomfort.

"Chase, would you mind getting my bags from upstairs?" Lorena said with a juicy, teasing smile. All of a sudden, the bells went off in his head, and Chase went racing up the stairs to retrieve Lorena's bag. She had already packed her things in anticipation of the momentous occasion. Before Lorena could count to twenty, Chase was back, standing by her side, panting with excitement.

"Just stay calm. Let me help you to the car," Chase nervously rambled, spilling out his words like marbles pouring out on a tiled floor.

"Relax, Chase. Don't worry, I promise not to have our baby in the backseat of the car." Lorena stood up and started toward the half-waxed Cadillac.

"Chase, I want you to go in and call your parents. Let them know we are headed to the hospital. Your mother would never forgive me if we didn't let her know that her precious grandchild is on the way."

He followed Lorena's orders, while she waddled to the car. Chase came bolting out of the house.

"They're leaving in a half hour. You know my mother; she wouldn't go to any event without being properly dressed."

Chase climbed in behind the wheel of the car and sped off down the road that led to Pecos. The dry dust swirled in horizontal tornadoes behind the extra-wide rear end of the Cadillac. They were on their way to start a new family.

Christina Rebecca Chandler was born fourteen hours later. She was healthy and as beautiful as her grandmother had predicted. Her hair was dark brown, and she had her mother's cocoa colored skin. Strangely enough, the baby's eyes were a light blue in color, which didn't match the color of either of her parents. Dr. Kittles told them it wasn't unusual for newborns to have lighter eyes at birth, and they would probably darken with maturity.

Lorena weathered the birth fairly well and was glad it was over. The first thing she did after leaving the delivery room was pull down the bed sheets to see the condition of her lower torso. She had only minimal stretch marks, but her stomach was sagging more than she had hoped. It had the texture of the rippled skin dangling from the neck of an old sea walrus. She took hold of the flabby mass, and let it drop back to where her once hard abdomen had been, and started crying. Dr. Kittles reassured her that within a couple of weeks she would see significant improvement if she exercised properly.

"*Thank God,*" Lorena offered to herself; maybe she could return to her old shape once she got back into her practice studio.

Chase was on cloud nine. Lorena never sensed from Chase his preference for a girl or a boy. She was sure her in-laws would have preferred a strapping boy to carry on the Chandler name, but watching her husband holding his new little girl, it was impossible to detect any dissatisfaction with the outcome.

It was strange to watch this man, whom she knew had lived his life on the edge for so many years, tenderly holding their baby girl. Lorena clearly understood for the first time why he had so desperately wanted to start a family. His eyes glowed with unbounded pride and affection. Lorena was genuinely touched watching Chase coo at his sleeping daughter.

Two days later, they left the hospital with their brand new baby. The first couple of days were a madhouse of activity. Every relative and family friend within a hundred miles had to see the new addition to the Chandler family. Chase played the role of the proud father with more exuberance than even Lorena expected. He hardly let Christina out of his embrace the entire time. Aside from breast-feeding her, Lorena almost had to fight Chase for her own daughter's attention. It was already apparent to Lorena; Christina Rebecca Chandler had no choice but to be her daddy's little girl.

The celebration would have gone on for weeks if Lorena had not told Chase that she was exhausted from all the company and in need of a break. What she really wanted was some time to bond as a family. As difficult as it was for him to understand his wife's unusual request, Chase ultimately capitulated.

Within a couple of days, they settled into the seesaw routine of being new parents. Sleep became a precious commodity, and personal time alone was practically nonexistent. They took turns waking up with the baby throughout the night. Chase was so supportive and anxious to help that sometimes he made Lorena feel guilty. One night, when he had volunteered to take Christina back to her crib after her nightly breast-feeding, he didn't return. After awhile, Lorena became concerned and went to check on them. When she entered the nursery, she found Chase sitting in the rocking chair fast asleep, with Christina peacefully asleep in his arms. It would not be the first time or the last time her devoted husband would go out of his way to be near his new obsession in life.

Chase was so engaged in the parenting process that he would cancel important meetings to attend Christina's weekly check-ups with their pediatrician. He wasn't about to miss any chance to demonstrate his dedication as a loving father.

This Friday was no different. It was time for her first monthly check-up, and Chase met Lorena at Dr. Kittles' office at ten o'clock.

The examination went just as expected. Christina was a healthy, happy little girl. Chase was standing out in the waiting room after the examination, waiting for Lorena, who had some questions to ask Dr. Kittles. He was proudly cuddling his precious, little girl.

From across the room, a doctor in a white frock waved at Chase and moved in his direction. At first, Chase didn't recognize him, but as soon as he spoke, he realized it was Dr. Livens, the urologist he had seen ten months ago for his fertility tests.

Chase had completely forgotten to follow up on his test results once Lorena told him the news that she was pregnant. Dr. Livens' office had called to set up a follow-up appointment, but Chase ignored the request, thinking it was a waste of time. Why did he need fertility test results? The proof of his manhood was alive in his wife's womb.

Dr. Livens walked up and peaked into the tiny bundle Chase was holding. "What do we have here?" he asked, smiling at Chase.

"Let me introduce you to Christina Rebecca Chandler. Isn't she a miracle?"

"I would say so, based on the results from your fertility tests."

All the color in Chase's face drained out. Every muscle in his body tensed.

"What do you mean?" Chase asked, almost afraid to hear Dr. Livens' answer.

"Well, your tests came back indicating that you were infertile, but like they say, miracles happen every day. Congratulations. I'd like to stay and chat, but I'm late for an appointment. Take care of that little package of joy."

How could the test results have been negative? Chase was holding his daughter in his arms. Chase looked down at Christina, trying to see his own features mirrored in her tiny face. He knew it was a foolish endeavor. Only old ladies and wishful grandparents saw those clear similarities between the parents and the child at this early stage of life. Dr. Livens had to be mistaken! He must have screwed up the test somehow.

Chase turned his focus to Lorena's role in such an improbable conspiracy. Could she have secretly had an affair without his knowing? His mind was reeling with possibilities, but none of them seemed plausible. His logic was failing him when he needed it most.

The test just had to be wrong! He tried to reassure himself but doubt had already made its cancerous inroads into his psyche. For a moment, he was so engrossed in the shock of Dr. Livens innocent statement that he forgot he was holding Christina. He felt his arms go slack but caught himself just before his unsuspecting daughter rolled out of them onto the green linoleum floor.

Chase tried to shake this insane nonsense out of his head. It couldn't be true! He said it over and over, hoping the truth would be erased if he said it enough times. Dr. Livens was just an old fool. He just had to be wrong!

A few minutes later, Lorena joined Chase in the waiting room and walked over to him. She could see something was bothering her husband.

"Are you all right?"

"Yes, fine," Chase coldly answered.

"You don't seem fine."

Chase realized he was exposing all his anxiety from his brief conversation with Dr. Livens. What was he thinking, treating Lorena like she was guilty of a crime? He shifted gears.

"I'm sorry. Just something at the office I was thinking about. Ready to go?"

He glanced over at Lorena as they walked out of the office, and tried to imagine her in the arms of another man, but all he could see was the mother of his child.

The day after Dr. Livens turned his life upside down, Chase made an appointment for the following Monday with another urologist. He needed a second opinion. Chase had to close the book on this whole question of his fatherhood, or it would drive him over the edge. For a man who had always been in control of his life, he was feeling like a whirling dervish. He tested his memory, again and again, trying to sort through all the potential possibilities resulting in Dr. Livens' innocent, but earth-shattering declaration.

Chase couldn't convince himself, no matter how hard he tried, that Lorena had cheated on him. They had practically been together every moment since they returned from Mexico. He was positive Dr. Livens had made a mistake in the testing process.

Chase was pretty sure he knew exactly when Lorena got pregnant. During the two weeks after they reconciled, Lorena never used contraceptives, preferring their wild and spontaneous lovemaking. Chase had reviewed his daily calendar from the last year and counted backwards from Christina's birth date. The timing was perfect. He just had to be the father of his beautiful baby daughter.

Chase arrived at his doctor's appointment the following Monday as scheduled. He was sitting in the waiting room of Dr. Jack Blaze, a highly respected urologist. He wanted to make sure he was seeing the best medicine had to offer.

Dr. Blaze put him through the same tests as before and asked him for another specimen. He reassured Chase that it was not uncommon for test results to be incorrect the first time. Hearing this news temporarily lifted the painful burden of apprehension that Chase had been feeling for the last couple of days.

Although he left Dr. Blaze's office feeling more positive, the next week was excruciating.

Chase was having a hard time controlling his anxiety, and it was apparent to Lorena. She noticed his edginess and started to worry that something was seriously wrong. Lorena asked him about it several times, but he blamed it on problems at work.

In fact, to avoid having to spend time with Lorena, Chase started working longer hours. Very often, he wouldn't get home until Lorena and the baby were fast asleep. His behavior over the two weeks while he was waiting for his test results to return was dramatically different than anything Lorena had ever experienced with him.

Before he couldn't get enough of Christina, and now he hardly paid attention to her.

Every time Lorena thought she was starting to understand the man she had married, he would throw her another curve. This endless, emotional roller coaster was starting to wear on her. She didn't know whether to wait this one out or jump in with both feet. She decided to give him a few more days, but if things didn't clear up she would have to confront him. She had learned her painful lesson about holding back her suspicions.

As hard as Chase tried, he couldn't stop thinking about the possibility that Lorena had betrayed him. He couldn't clear his head of those insidious thoughts of her writhing beneath the thrusts of another man. He knew he was jealous, but this was ridiculous! The only circumstance that came to mind was seeing Lorena kiss Lolo outside her hotel room. He never did get a straight answer from her when he accused her of having an affair with her old lover. It was just after his angry accusation regarding Lolo that everything went haywire, and she stormed from the room crying. Was she insulted by his allegation of indiscretion or had something really been going on between them?

Every time he came home from a long day at the office and looked into his wife's eyes, he was pushed back into his jealous rage.

Two weeks later, he received the call from Dr. Blaze's office. Chase tried to cajole the results out of the appointment nurse who had called him, but she insisted that Dr. Blaze wanted to see him in person.

Chase drove straight to Dr. Blaze's office that afternoon. He was not about to continue to wade in the quagmire of suspicion any longer than necessary.

As he sat in the examining room fidgeting with his car keys, he could hardly contain all his pent-up anxiety. Every time he heard the sound of footsteps marching past the closed door of the room, his chest would fill with an unbearable pressure.

When Dr. Blaze finally came into the examining room, Chase saw that from his expression something was wrong. His heart sank into the pit of his stomach.

Dr. Blaze got straight to the point. "Mr. Chandler, I unfortunately have bad news. Your test results came back confirming your earlier results. You're infertile."

The electrical current of his words struck Chase with a resounding jolt. Chase had not told Dr. Blaze the reasons why he needed testing. Dr. Blaze did not know Chase was a new father. Chase wanted to keep his appointment totally private, in case, for some unfathomable reason, his tests came back negative. How embarrassing it would be if anyone found out that he wasn't the father of Christina, and that his wife had betrayed the sacred bonds of marriage!

Chase was barely able to mumble out a response. "You're absolutely positive. It's not just a temporary condition?"

"Yes, we're positive about the results. Unfortunately, you have never been fertile. I checked your records with your family doctor, and it seems you had mumps when you were five. Mumps, in rare cases, can cause infertility in young children. I'm sorry, Mr. Chandler, but you will never be able to conceive children."

All his worst nightmares about the last couple of weeks were confirmed. Christina wasn't his daughter, and Lorena had deceived him. Chase felt as though a time bomb was ticking inside of him and if he didn't immediately leave the doctor's office, there would be serious causalities.

Chase abruptly got up and left. Every nerve in his body tingled with an intense burning, sensation. The entire time he took walking to his car, all he thought about was Lolo and Lorena in the hotel in Ciudad Hidalgo. The hallway scene was permanently and painfully etched in his mind: Lorena leaning over, kissing Lolo on the lips, then smiling as if having just concluded the shameful deed. The smirk on Lolo's face as he turned to leave, infuriated Chase at the time of the incident, but now it made him want to put a bullet smack in the middle of Lolo's brain. The rage was spreading like a wildfire out of control, burning away all the bliss of the past few months.

Chase drove to his office instead of going home to confront Lorena. He knew he couldn't trust himself in her presence right now. How could he face her, while she held their daughter and not want to scream at the top of his lungs, "*You fucking whore!*"

Chase was already formulating a plan to pay that little son of a bitch back. When he arrived at his office, he immediately picked up the phone and dialed his old friend Emiliano in Mexico City. Emiliano answered his phone and was surprised to hear Chase's voice on the other end of the line.

"Well, how is it being a brand new daddy?" Emiliano jovially inquired.

Emiliano's words felt like a punch from a heavyweight fighter, knocking the air out of his lungs.

"Fine," Chase curtly answered, not wanting to explain the real reason for his call over the phone.

"Emiliano, I need your help again."

"Look, Chase, as much as I would like to help you out, I told you after the last episode with Lorca, I was finished with all that business," Emiliano exclaimed, leaving no doubt about his conviction.

"It's not what you think. It's personal."

"The last job was personal, if you remember."

"No, I mean, it's very personal. Please, just trust me on this. It doesn't have anything to do with the Bureau."

"Chase, what are you up to?" Emiliano asked, challenging his friend to explain why he needed his help.

"I promise I'll give you all the details when I arrive tomorrow."

"All right, but if there is even a hint of shadiness involved, I'm going to have to beg off."

"I understand. Thanks, Emiliano."

Chase asked Emiliano if he could pick him up at the Mexico City airport tomorrow afternoon.

Emiliano told Chase he would have to make an excuse at work, but he would be there.

Chase thanked his friend one more time for his support and hung up the phone. He called his secretary into his office and asked her to make arrangements for a flight to Mexico City first thing tomorrow morning. Chase told her that some urgent business had come up which required his immediate attention.

After Chase was sure he had covered all his bases at work, he picked up the phone and dialed home.

Lorena had just finished putting Christina down for her afternoon nap, when she heard the phone ring.

"Hello?"

There was silence on the other end. Just hearing her voice made Chase want to reach across the phone line and choke the vicious lies out of her.

"Hello?" Lorena asked again and was just about to set the phone back on the receiver when Chase spoke.

"It's me, Lorena. Sorry, I was trying to do two things at once." His voice was tense.

"Is everything all right?" Given his most recent behavior, Lorena suspected everything wasn't.

"Yes, fine. Listen, something has come up in Mexico City, and I'm going to have to go down there to straighten it out."

Lorena's mind flashed back to the last time Chase told her he had urgent business outside of the United States. She didn't want to believe he was lying to her again but his strange behavior lately definitely raised some doubt.

She decided to confront him straight on. "Chase, what's going on?"

"Nothing, really. They are just having some problems closing off one of our contracts with the government, and they need my help."

Chase remembered how he had sworn never to deceive Lorena again, but that promise went out the window when he found out how she had betrayed him. It was as if she had blindfolded him, led him innocently to the edge of a cliff and nonchalantly shoved him over.

"All right, but when you get back, we need to talk."

"I promise I'll make time." Chase was scowling on the other end of the line.

"How long are you going to be gone?"

"Just a couple days." His guts felt like they were devouring themselves.

This was sounding all too familiar to Lorena. The tone of voice and the dry, edgy nature of his words scared the hell out of her.

"What time can we expect you to be home tonight?"

"Don't wait up for me. I have several things to close down here before I leave tomorrow. I'll pack in the morning."

They said a strained good-bye. Lorena, as hard as she tried, couldn't stop thinking about their conversation. Maybe it was her woman's intuition, but she knew he was lying to her again. All the bitter feelings of his previous deception came rushing back to her with a vengeance. Didn't he realize she was not about to give him a second chance?

Lorena went in to check on Christina. Looking down at her daughter safely cuddled in her blanket sound asleep, she tried to imagine what it would be like without Chase. Why was he so willing to risk everything, including his baby daughter, for the thrill of another mission?

She threatened Chase in her mind, "*I don't care what excuse you have. You go on another mission, and we are finished!*"

Her hands gripped the rail of the crib so tightly that her knuckles turned white. Her entire body was trembling with fury. She tried to settle herself, but to no avail; she was lost in a blinding storm of distrust and fear.

Chase awoke early the next morning. Lorena got up with him and made him breakfast. They hardly spoke a word during the meal. Chase pretended to be engrossed in the morning paper, but she could tell it was a sham.

Lorena stared across the table at him, trying to imagine what kind of addictive behavior caused a man to give up everything he seemed to value to risk his life on dangerous missions. Was the opiate of working for the Bureau stronger than the love he had for his wife and child? She so much wanted to confront him, but if he was going to fall into this trap, then she couldn't save him. She could only hope that somehow she was wrong, that her suspicions were unfounded.

After barely touching his breakfast, Chase grabbed his bags, kissed Lorena on the top of her head and told her he would see her in couple of days.

"Call me when you get there," she said, calling out to him as he walked out the door.

"Sure," he answered, not taking the time to look back at his wife.

There was no question in her mind now; Chase was lying.

CHAPTER 28

Diego Sanchez returned to his apartment in Mexico City hoping to confirm what he had discovered in his father's library about Amado Flores, alias Lolo Nieto. He had a hunch one person might be able to help him with some answers—the night watchman, Pepe Robles.

It was a long shot, but Pepe Robles knew Señor Alvarez better than just about anybody in Mexico City. If anybody knew about his former maestro's involvement in the conspiracy against him, it would be the night watchman of the Plaza Quitzal.

Diego had other reasons for wanting to enlist Pepe's favor. He was fairly sure Pepe could help him solve the puzzle of Amado Flores's true identity. The old scoundrel was noted for having all the dirt on the secret lives of every man who fought or trained in the Plaza. He knew every detail, every one of their wicked vices, from their clandestine late night affairs with starlets, to the bad habit of gambling their fortunes away. He even knew about their sexual preferences. Pepe kept track of every sordid incident regarding all the swordsmen who passed through these hallowed grounds, including whether a certain individual might have changed his name to protect his questionable heritage.

There had always been rumors that Pepe benefited financially from his scandalous knowledge. Word around the Plaza was that he had tried to blackmail a certain world-ranked swordsman to keep quiet about his indiscretion. Recently, he had heard, Pepe had tried to cut a deal regarding some very sensitive information on a prominent fencer, but somehow his scheme had fallen through. Regardless of his motives, Diego was hoping the old man might have some background on Lolo Nieto. Any information that could help him solve the mystery was worth a try.

Diego had given serious thought to directly confronting Lolo during an exhibition three weeks ago, but his better judgment told him it might just blow up in his face. He absolutely had to be certain that Lolo Nieto was really Amado

Flores before confronting him.

Over the last month, he had been asking a lot of questions around town about Lolo without trying to raise suspicion. Aside from learning that Lolo was quite the ladies' man and that he was despised by most of his fellow competitors, Diego learned nothing new. With only two weeks left before the Championship Tournament in Mexico City, Diego was prepared for the possibility that he might not resolve the elusive question before he retired.

The build-up in Mexico City for his last performance was out of control. His manager Roberto Nunez, wasn't helping to calm the situation. Every chance he had to talk to the press—which was often these days—Nunez raved about how Mexico was about to see one of its greatest fencing champions before he retired from the sport. In addition to drawing constant attention to Diego through newspaper stories, Nunez had put together a blistering schedule of press conferences and dinner engagements that required Diego's attendance. Everyone wanted a piece of him. All the insanity was starting to wear thin; he was ready for it to be over.

On a dreary October day, Diego sat in a cab headed for the Plaza Quitzal. He was hoping to meet with Pepe Robles. If he didn't get anything else done in the next few weeks, at least he was going to pump the night watchman for information. He knew Pepe was getting ready to retire after this season concluded, so he needed to seize the opportunity. Diego had known Pepe since he was a teenager. In fact, his father had been instrumental in helping Pepe get his job at the Plaza Quitzal, so he was hoping Pepe felt some allegiance toward him and would be willing to help him out.

Diego arrived at the Plaza Quitzal and went straight to see Pepe's boss, Jorge Reyes, who was in charge of operations at the Plaza. He inquired about Pepe's whereabouts and was told that Pepe was in one of the underground tunnels cleaning out a storeroom.

Señor Reyes asked if Diego needed any assistance in finding his way to Pepe. He thanked Señor Reyes, but assured him he could find his own way. Diego knew the Plaza Quitzal like the back of his hand.

Pepe was busy moving tables around and didn't see Diego approaching from behind. Besides being almost blind in his left eye, Pepe's was also losing his hearing. Diego walked up, tapped Pepe on the shoulder and sounded his name. The night watchman jumped back, startled to see Diego Sanchez in the musty confines of his world. He had seen Diego on numerous occasions when he was in tournaments at the Plaza, but Diego was always whisked away by his manager to meet the press before he could approach him to say hello. There were times when Pepe felt insulted by Diego's lack of interest. Pepe knew Diego was aware that he was still working at the Plaza, but the swordsman made no attempt to make contact and Pepe bore the insult in silence. He was thinking about it now as he surveyed the man standing in front of him.

In his gruff, gravelly voice Pepe cynically asked, "What are you doing here in the bowels of hell, Señor Sanchez?"

"Looking for you. Do you have a minute?"

"What for?" Pepe was getting suspicious of Diego's real motives for being here.

Had Diego heard about his deal with Lolo's manager, Manuel Carbajal? Was he aware Pepe had tried to use his knowledge about Lolo Nieto being Diego Sanchez's illegitimate son to raise cash for his gambling debt?

"I just have a few questions I would like to ask you about a certain individual."

"Who might that be?"

"Lolo Nieto. I assume you know him?"

Pepe stopped fiddling around with what he was doing when he heard the name. He shifted nervously from side to side. "What about Lolo?"

Pepe was not going to offer any more information than was needed to avoid Diego's suspicious question.

"Before I go on, I can assume that our conversation will be kept totally private?"

"Of course, Señor." He avoided direct eye contact with Diego.

"Do you know anything about his past?"

"I know a little about everyone's past," he slyly acknowledged. "I make it a point to keep my eyes and ears open around here. You never know when it might pay off. Why do you want this information anyway?" Pepe felt assured at this point that Diego was unaware of his deal with Lolo's manager.

"It's personal."

"Well, if it is none of my business, then I guess I'll get back to work." Pepe reached over and started rearranging the tables. He was starting to sense that he had the overconfident Diego right where he wanted him.

"All right. Let's just say I'm helping out a friend, and the information is very important to him."

"Very cute ploy, Diego, but I really know what you're looking for," Pepe scowled, becoming impatient with Diego's feeble attempt to hide the truth.

He stopped what he was doing and turned his full attention to Diego. Pepe was hoping there was still a chance to leverage the information about Lolo and Diego into some serious cash. He knew he had made a deal with Lolo's manager, but if Diego was willing to pay a higher finder's fee, then to hell with that deal. He needed all the cash he could amass to cover his most recent gambling losses. Pepe was still trying to fend off his bookie's threats of retribution.

Diego skipped right to the point. If Pepe knew the real identity of Lolo Nieto, he would see it in his eyes as soon as his question was answered.

"What about his family background? Do you know who his parents are?"

"Yes," Pepe flatly said.

"And......"

Pepe could hear the anticipation in Diego's voice.

"Well, that kind of information has a certain value, wouldn't you say?"

"What are you talking about?" Diego fired back, wanting to strangle the ungrateful old man.

"Eight thousand pesos sounds like a reasonable price to me."

"That's highway robbery. What makes you think my friend will want to pay that kind of money?"

"Let's cut the bullshit, Diego. You don't recognize this room, do you?" Pepe stepped aside, so Diego could see the entire room.

Diego peered into the dark confines of the cramped room, trying to recall why it would be important for him to remember this particular room.

Pepe interrupted his concentration. "Think back over twenty years ago when a certain young man brought a beautiful young lady into this room."

Suddenly, Diego's memory opened up.

"You son of a bitch! You were there!" Diego lurched toward Pepe, but stopped himself, realizing the decrepit man was too weak to strike.

Diego had forgotten Pepe was the night watchman the rainy evening he and Celaya made love in this very room. Diego glanced over at the silver light pouring in from the small window near the ceiling. It was the same light that lit up Celaya's naked body, as she lay in the mound of cluttered uniforms beckoning him to join her.

Pepe could see the lingering anger in Diego's eyes, but knew he had Diego right where he wanted him.

"Eight thousand pesos or the rest of your young lady's story dies with me."

Diego slumped down onto one of the broken chairs. He was boxed in by this simple night watchman and knew he didn't have any alternative but to meet his demands. Señor Alvarez and his father were the only two other people who could give him the answers he needed, and they were both dead.

"If I agree to your terms, then I want your word you will never reveal your secret to anyone else. Are we clear?"

Pepe was not about to tell him that Lolo's manager already knew his dark secret. He would deal with that later. Besides, it had been over a year since he told Carbajal, and he knew for a fact Carbajal was keeping the secret to himself. For what reason, he didn't know, but Pepe was banking on the fact, that neither Diego nor Carbajal would reveal where and how they obtained the information.

"You have my word on it." Pepe grinned like a carnival barker after taking a farm boy's last dollar.

"It's not your word I'm going to want, if you break your promise." Diego stopped himself from completing his threat. There was no question in his mind that Pepe's word was worthless, but he just hoped his forewarning was enough to keep Pepe's mouth shut.

Starting from the very beginning, Pepe shared how, while making his nightly rounds over twenty years ago, he had accidentally come upon a young couple embroiled in passionate lovemaking. When he realized it was his young friend, Diego Sanchez, he felt compelled to report the affair to Señor Alvarez.

Pepe wanted to make it clear his only involvement in the scheme was reporting Diego's youthful indiscretion to Alvarez. Diego's very own trusted maestro was the one who plotted with Diego's father to send him away.

Diego interrupted Pepe, "How did you know my father was involved?"

"About two weeks after I had told Señor Alvarez about your affair, I got a letter from your father containing five hundred pesos. He thanked me for my assistance in such a sensitive matter and for my loyalty in keeping his son's foolishness a secret."

Even though Diego knew his father must have been involved in the conspiracy against Celaya and him, he cringed at hearing how deep his father's involvement was in the scheme.

Pepe meticulously conveyed the rest of his story. He told Diego how he had seen Celaya come to the Plaza Quitzal one afternoon looking for Señor Alvarez. It was obvious that she was pregnant. Pepe recognized her immediately as the same woman who had been with Diego on that momentous evening. Pepe introduced himself to her, which is how he learned her identity. Pepe made a point of finding out a little more about Celaya so that he could use the information in the future if he needed it. He learned she had to leave the university and that she was living in seclusion with her family on their ranch outside of Guadalajara. As the story continued unfolding, the same emotions Diego had felt in his father's library returned. He vacillated between torrential anger toward Señor Alvarez to deep compassion for Celaya's condition.

Finally, after hearing all the excruciating details of Señor Alvarez's betrayal and Celaya's desperate effort to reach him in France, he interrupted Pepe. "When did you find out Lolo Nieto was my son?"

Pepe paused before answering him, questioning whether he should tell him the truth. "I was in Señor Alvarez's office one day after he fell ill, and ran across a stack of letters in his desk addressed to you. I was curious, so I read a couple of them. One of the letters had no return address and was on hospital stationery. It was the last letter Señorita Flores had written after the birth of her child. In the letter, she mentioned the name of her son, Amado Nieto Flores. At first I didn't think anything about it, until I overheard Lolo tell a close friend that his mother's first name was Celaya. I put two and two together and the whole puzzle fell into place."

Now Diego had no reason to doubt the night watchman's painful recounting of Celaya's short, but tragic life.

"Well, that's about it. When do I get my money?" Pepe callously inquired.

"You'll get your blood money, don't worry. Just curious....were you ever going to tell me?"

"I've got to get back to work. Meet me outside of the Plaza tomorrow at two o'clock or the deal is off. I am sure the press would love to get hold of this story. It might even spoil the plans for your celebrated sendoff." Pepe reached over and grabbed the handle of a broom and began sweeping the stone floor.

Diego had what he came for. But hearing the fact that this old night watchman, his mentor Señor Alvarez and his own father had invaded Celaya's privacy by reading her letters, left him feeling defiled. He didn't know where to direct his anger. As he walked down the dark passageways, Diego knew one part of his journey was over, but another was just about to begin. How was he going to explain to Lolo Nieto, who despised him, that he was his father? It would be one thing to drop such a mind-shattering bombshell on Lolo, but how was he going to legitimately explain that he hadn't abandoned Celaya? Would his estranged son understand that he was as much a victim as they were of Señor Alvarez's conspiracy against Celaya and him?

Diego realized in that moment that he wasn't finished with Pepe Robles. He would need Pepe as a witness to verify his innocence. If Lolo wouldn't believe his rendition of the story, he surely couldn't deny the truth after hearing Pepe confirm it. How ironic, Diego thought, that the one man who originally betrayed him twenty years ago was the same man he needed to get his son back.

CHAPTER 29

Chase and Emiliano were waiting outside of Pamplona, a favorite hangout of celebrities in Mexico City. It was one o'clock in the morning, and they had been sitting in Emiliano's '81 Buick for three and a half hours. Pamplona was still crowded with patrons, and there was no telling when Lolo would leave the bar. He was notorious for closing down places like this all over Mexico.

While they were waiting, Chase spilled his guts to Emiliano about what he had recently discovered about Lorena. For a man who was raised in the macho culture of Texas, it was difficult to reveal his own masculine frailties, yet he had no choice in the matter if he was going to enlist Emiliano in his plan. He needed to verify whether Lolo was the man who had had the affair with his wife. His old friend would have seen right through him anyway. They had been together too long to play games.

Emiliano felt a genuine sympathy for Chase's predicament and was touched by his honesty. He knew how much it must have hurt Chase when he found out the truth. It was hard for him to believe Lorena would have betrayed Chase for a low-life like Lolo Nieto. He would have wagered his first child that Lorena would have never gone back to Lolo, given the way he treated her when she was performing at Tauromaquia.

As Emiliano listened attentively to Chase's story, he could see the anguish, clearly exhibited by Chase's crestfallen demeanor. Emiliano recalled the elation Chase shared with him the day Christina was born. He couldn't imagine being a father of two daughters himself, how crushing it must have been for Chase to find out Christina wasn't his child, but Lolo's. Emiliano wasn't happy about going out on another mission with Chase, but he couldn't refuse a man who had stood by him all these years. Hell, he owed his life to Chase for dragging him off the shore at Lake Pátzcuaro; he couldn't just turn tail and abandon him when he was most needed.

At a quarter to one in the morning, the door to Pamplona sprang open; they both immediately recognized the man exiting the bar. Lolo Nieto was alone.

Lolo looked for a cab, but none was in sight. He started walking toward the main thoroughfare, Avenida Morelos. He had a loose swagger to his gait that indicated he had drunk his fair share of tequila. Lolo didn't notice the man exiting the parked car directly behind him on the same side of the street. He was walking at a leisurely pace, so it was easy for Chase to catch up.

About a pace away from Lolo, Chase pulled out his 9mm Beretta and tucked his hand into his lower coat pocket. Chase increased his pace and came directly behind Lolo. He raised his concealed pistol and pressed the narrow barrel firmly into the arch of Lolo's lower back.

"Stay calm and don't even think this gun in your back isn't loaded. Keep your eyes straight forward," Chase whispered menacingly. It was everything he could do not to pull back on the hair trigger of his Beretta and end it all right here.

"Look, whoever you are, my wallet is in my front coat pocket. Just take it," Lolo said, clearly shaken by the cold, threatening voice behind him. In that split second, he realized it wasn't a Mexican threatening him. He thought how strange that a gringo would be robbing him in the middle of his own country.

Chase could hear the fear in Lolo's voice. "This is not a robbery. I just have a few questions I want to ask you."

He signaled for Emiliano to bring the car up to where he was holding Lolo hostage. Emiliano pulled up, Chase opened the door to the back seat, forcefully shoving Lolo inside.

"Take it easy. Do you know who you're dealing with?" Lolo boldly declared.

"Unfortunately, yes," Chase barked, as he sat down next to Lolo in the rear seat.

"What's this all about?" Lolo had yet to recognize his captors.

"Before we start, let me make something clear; if you even think about making the wrong move, I won't hesitate to blow a hole in you. It would be a shame to bloody this nice car, but one way or another you're going to answer my questions!"

Lolo nodded that he understood. He realized he was in serious trouble and this was no time to play the tough guy.

"I doubt that you remember me. My name is Chase Chandler," he exclaimed as he turned to face Lolo.

Lolo peered across at the American who was sitting so close to him that he could feel Chase's hot breath warming the side of his neck. He struggled to recall where he might have met this stranger before. Then, all of a sudden, his mind became dead-sober clear. It was the guy Lorena had run off with and married. The last time Lolo had heard Chase's name mentioned was when Lorena was having breakfast with him at her hotel in Ciudad Hidalgo. He had taken her for a ride in the country to help distract her from what was obviously some kind of marital spat. That was over ten months ago. Lorena hadn't gone into a lot of details during their leisurely trip, but he could tell she was having a rough go of it with her marriage. Did this Chase Chandler think he had something to do with his marital problems?

"Yes, I remember you. You're Lorena's husband, correct?"

"I just want you to answer a couple of questions. I already know my wife was unfaithful and bore the child of another man. You're at the top of the suspect list, my friend. So let's get straight to the point. Did you have an affair with my wife?"

"Yes, but relax. It was over four years ago." Lolo felt reassured for the first time since being thrown into the car that he wasn't going to die.

"I saw her kissing you in the hotel outside her room last year!" Chase's tone was getting more aggressive with each question.

"Look, Mr. Chandler, as much as I would have liked to have gotten back together with Lorena, it was just an innocent kiss between friends. Nothing more, nothing less."

Chase looked into Lolo's eyes and could see he was telling the truth. He lowered his gun. "Look, I made a mistake, but someone had an affair with Lorena and I'm going to find the son of bitch." Chase realized he was back to square one.

Looking at Chase's defeated expression Lolo realized he was being presented with an opportunity to betray his archrival Diego Sanchez. He had seen Lorena get out of Diego's car in front of her hotel two days after he had said good-bye to her, and he was pretty sure Lorena and Diego weren't just casual friends. Even though Diego Sanchez was retiring from the sport in less than two weeks, he relished the opportunity to act as a spoiler for Sanchez's going away party. Creating a major controversy was just what Lolo was looking for. He could already see the bold headlines in the paper *"Diego Sanchez's Illegitimate Child"*. A crooked smile creased his face. Then, of course, there was the money. A rich, desperate gringo might be willing to pay a lot for the right kind of information. Lolo knew with some serious money he could encourage promoters to get him more prestigious exhibitions. Anything that could give him that extra boost would be worth it. Lolo decided to seize the moment.

"What if I could provide you with the information?"

"Let's not play games, Señor Nieto."

"I'm serious. I believe I know who you're looking for and I have the evidence to prove it."

"And what exactly are you asking for in exchange for this information?" Chase had dealt with slime balls like this before.

"It won't come cheap. I know you're a wealthy man, Señor Chandler." Lolo thought all gringos had money. In this particular case, he happened to make a lucky guess.

"How much?" Chase demanded.

As Emiliano listened to the conversation from the front seat, he couldn't believe Chase was desperate enough to deal with someone of Lolo's questionable character. He thought about jumping into the fray but knew it wouldn't do any good. It was obvious Chase was obsessed with finding the man who had caused him this personal holocaust.

"Look, I've been out all night drinking. I'd like to do this with a clear head." Lolo wanted some time to come up with a top dollar figure. He wanted to squeeze every penny he could out of Chase. There was no question; the roles had reversed in the last twenty minutes and he knew he was the one holding all the cards.

"This better not be some game you're playing. I'm not in the mood, nor do I have time to fuck around," Chase spat out, gritting his teeth.

"I can promise you, Señor Chandler, I have just as much incentive to make this deal as you do. Meet me at my hotel tomorrow morning at ten o'clock. I'm sure we can come to some arrangement."

Lolo gave Chase his address and asked to be dropped off at the next corner. When they reached Avenida Morelos, Lolo exited the car. Chase bent over in his direction to apologize. He needed Lolo on his side if he was going to close out this case. "No hard feelings, I hope?"

"Hey, we're partners now," Lolo boldly shot back. "See you tomorrow morning, and don't forget to bring your checkbook."

Diego arrived at the Plaza Quitzal at two o'clock the next afternoon, just as he and Pepe had agreed. He had Pepe's money with him and was anxious to close the deal. He had never been involved in anything so underhanded. The wad of bills in his pocket felt unholy.

Diego had already planned what he was going to demand of Pepe. He needed a witness to verify his innocence; Pepe either confessed the truth in front of Lolo or he could forget about the payoff. He was prepared to accept the consequences if Pepe decided to go to the press with his story. Lolo's knowledge of the real truth about him and his mother was more valuable to him than his reputation with the fans.

Pepe was over forty-five minutes late when Diego decided to inquire about missing their appointment. He walked over to the office of Pepe's boss and inquired about his whereabouts.

"I was supposed to meet Pepe Robles this afternoon. You wouldn't happen to know his where he is?

"You haven't heard? Pepe was found dead this morning in an alleyway not far from here."

"What? I don't understand." Diego was rocked by the shocking news.

"I'm afraid it's true. A garbage man found him during his rounds in one of the back alleys. Pepe's throat was slit from ear to ear. The police aren't sure who did it, but they suspect, with all his gambling problems, one of his bookies was a little too impatient in getting repaid."

Diego's stared blankly into the distance. No wonder Pepe was so anxious to cut a deal.

"I'm sorry it had to end this way." Diego tried to be sincere, but it was hard to feel any remorse for a man who had caused him so much pain over the years. He thanked Señor Reyes for the information and left his office.

As his feet hit the pavement outside the Plaza Quitzal, Diego knew that explaining the truth to Lolo had just become significantly more complicated, if not impossible. Pepe was his only viable witness. All he had left now were the letters from Celaya, and he wasn't sure they would convince Lolo of anything except his mother's undying devotion to him. He could only hope that once he explained the story, Lolo would recognize the truth. It was chancy, but what alternative did he have?

As Diego walked back to his apartment, he wracked his mind trying to think of something he might have missed, something that would help him verify his story with Lolo. He was just about to give up when he remembered the letters to Celaya he sent through Alvarez during his first six months in France. At least his letters would substantiate his commitment to Celaya. It was apparent from reading Celaya's desperate words that she never had received them. If Alvarez had kept her letters, then maybe his mentor had also kept the letters he had sent to her. It was a long shot, but he had to check it out. As soon as he got back to his apartment, he would contact Alvarez's son, Cesar, to set up an appointment for the next week.

Diego had a hard time locating Cesar Alvarez's home number, but eventually was able to locate his office number through a mutual friend. He called Cesar Alvarez, but the son was away on a business trip to Cuernavaca. The secretary told Diego that her boss would be returning in four days. Diego felt as if his patience was being tested at every turn. He was so damn close. If he could just put this last piece of the puzzle together, he could finally approach Lolo Nieto, and proudly proclaim that he was his father. It sounded so strange murmuring to himself—*his son, Lolo Nieto.*

Lolo and Chase met in the almost empty lobby of Hotel de Cortez. They sat down at a nearby table.

"So, have you settled on a number?" Chase prodded, wanting to get right to the point.

"Yes, for this kind of trouble I want twenty-five thousand dollars."

Lolo peered directly at Chase, hoping to get an initial reaction. Chase's poker face didn't flinch. Chase had been in so many negotiations over the years that dealing with someone like Lolo was child's play. He thought Lolo's offer was actually low. Lolo had no idea how wealthy his family really was if he was only asking for twenty-five grand. He had been prepared to pay more for Lolo's services, but he wasn't about to concede without some dickering.

"I like nice round figures, twenty thousand. Five up front and fifteen when I verify your story."

"And exactly how are you planning to substantiate it?"

"Leave that to me. You just provide the details, and I'll take care of the rest."

"That works for me." Lolo had been prepared to go down to ten grand. "Are you prepared to make the payment today?"

"I'll make arrangements to have the money transferred to your account later this afternoon. You can start talking anytime." Chase cringed at the thought of paying a lowlife like Lolo to find out who had been sleeping with his wife.

Lolo explained how he had observed Lorena exiting a stranger's car outside of her hotel in Ciudad Hidalgo. "Lorena was like a kid with her hands caught in the cookie jar. She tried to pretend like she didn't see me, but it was too late." He told Chase how angry Lorena seemed when he teased her about having spent the night with the man in the car.

"Enough with the details. Get to your point. Who was driving the car?" Chase leaned forward.

Lolo paused long enough to create the appropriate drama, and then blurted out, "None other than Mexico's most esteemed fencing champion, Diego Sanchez! You do remember Diego Sanchez, don't you?"

Chase had only seen him once during his performance in the exhibition in Ciudad Hidalgo. The only other time he could recall having seen Diego Sanchez was when he and Lorena were coming out of the same hotel after he had reconciled with Lorena. Chase remembered asking her if she recognized Diego, and how nervously she responded to his innocent question. He thought it was a little curious at the time, but didn't give it a second thought.

Lolo continued, "When I looked into the car through the rear windshield, Diego tried to conceal his identity, but I could never mistake that face."

Lolo explained how he had checked with the front desk the following day after their drive in the country to see how she was doing. The manager informed him that Señora Santoya had not checked out and also confirmed she had not returned to her hotel room the previous night. Lolo told Chase that he became suspicious, so he checked the following morning, and found out that she still had not returned. When he saw her getting out of Diego's car, he put two and two together.

"Are you absolutely positive it was Diego Sanchez?"

"When you battle with a man this close up....you can never forget his face. Unfortunately, I see him more often than I prefer." Lolo scowled. "When I tried to get a good, second look, Diego sped off like a race horse bolting from the starter's gate."

"Anything else?"

"Well, I did a little checking around the next day after I saw them in front of the hotel and found out that Diego Sanchez had been busy the previous day looking around town for a woman's dress. It's almost impossible for him to go anywhere these days unnoticed, particularly when it's a specialty item like a flamenco dress. From what little I could gather from the clerk at the dress shop, it was for a woman with a fine figure."

"Is that all?"

"Do you really need any more? If my wife mysteriously disappeared for two days, and then reappeared getting out of another man's car; that would be enough for me. By the way, Señor Sanchez just happens to be here in Mexico City as we speak. I've made the assumption you would like to have the address of his apartment." He handed a folded up piece of paper to Chase.

Chase abruptly stood up, not offering his hand in gratitude for all of Lolo's efforts. "I'll have the money transferred to your bank within two hours. As I said earlier, once I confirm your story, then the other half of your fee will be deposited."

As Chase walked away, Lolo teasingly added, "Nice doing business with you. Good hunting."

Lolo wondered what kind of man Chase Chandler was. Was he as cool under fire as he acted? Lolo hoped Chase would lose his temper, and in a fit of jealousy, end Diego's life. How sweet it would be if someone else took care of his problem.

Chase left the lobby of the hotel, knowing he would have to do this one on his own. He couldn't enlist Emiliano to shake down a man who was his hero. He remembered how Emiliano raved about Diego Sanchez and his accomplishments in the fencing world.

Chase spent the rest of the day trying to devise the best way to confront Sanchez. Without Emiliano's assistance, it would be impossible to replay the method they used on the inexperienced Lolo. The other problem with which he had to contend was that Sanchez was celebrity; and any funny business in public would almost certainly cause problems with the authorities. After hours of mulling it over, Chase gave up on any kind of covert action and decided to deal with Sanchez *mano a mano*. He would go to his apartment and ask straight out about the affair with Lorena. Chase knew he was a good judge of character and was positive Sanchez was the kind of man who wouldn't lie straight to a man's face. This was a man who had too much pride to dishonor himself.

It was seven o'clock in the evening when Chase knocked on Sanchez's apartment door. He thought about calling ahead to make sure Sanchez was home but decided to take his chances, and catch him off guard. The element of surprise had always worked in the past.

Diego heard the rapping on his door. He wasn't expecting any visitors, and he hoped he hadn't forgotten one of his many appointments. He peered through the small peephole.

Diego lurched backward, having instantly recognized the person standing on the other side of the door. Somewhere in the back of his mind, he had always suspected he would come face to face with Lorena's husband. He knew Chase could be here for only one thing. Diego heaved a deep sigh, opened the door slowly, and stood directly in Chase's line of fire.

Chase knew his premonition was right; there was no backing down in

Diego Sanchez.

"Señor Sanchez, you don't know me but I think you know my wife?" Chase's voice was strained, but composed. Seeing the man he had come to hate over the last few hours standing only four feet in front of him turned his guts inside out. All his years of learning how to control his emotions evaporated in that instant. His rage re-ignited into jealous fury. Chase was actually relieved he left his 9mm Beretta at his hotel. He might have been tempted to use it on the unwary Diego at this very moment.

"Please come in, Mr. Chandler."

Even though Chase could sense Diego suspected why he was here, he was still surprised to hear the man speak his name in such a calm fashion. Diego's steely blue eyes hardly blinked at knowing he was facing the man who could be there to end his life.

"I suppose you....?"

Diego interrupted his guest. "I would apologize for my past behavior, but that's not why you're really here, is it?"

"No, I am not interested in your apology. I want answers. How did it happen?" Chase was gritting his teeth as he spat out his angry question.

"The details are unimportant.... I take full responsibility for this unfortunate situation. There was no intention by either one of us to get involved in the way we did."

"Some excuse. You fucked my wife but you didn't intend to! Is that how you rationalize it?"

"I didn't seduce your wife, Mr. Chandler. We both let our guard down, and we made a terrible mistake. Lorena never intended to hurt you."

Diego, at hearing himself explain what happened between them as a *terrible mistake*, felt as though he was degrading everything he and had Lorena shared—their consoling words, the healing of their open wounds, the tenderness of their lovemaking.

Chase could no longer contain his temper. "So, Lorena was the innocent victim?" His voice roared with anger.

"No one is completely innocent in a situation like this. As for me, I don't expect you to forgive my actions. Nonetheless, I'm sorry I caused you this pain and hopefully you can forgive Lorena for her part."

The veins on Chase's neck bulged as inflamed rivers of vengeance coursed through them. He clinched his fists dangling by his side. Every muscle in his body was a loaded spring, ready to lash out at his enemy.

"Forgive her? She brought this on herself." He edged ever closer to Diego.

"Did she deserve the black eye she was sporting when I found her crying in the church?"

"You fucking asshole! That was an accident!" Chase lunged at Diego, trying to strike him with a tightly spooled fist.

Diego, an expert at avoiding lunges, quickly stepped to the side.

Chase, expecting contact, lost his balance, and stumbled to the floor. As he hit the cold tile, he reached over and snagged the cuff of Diego's pants leg, yanking it as hard as he could.

Diego fell backwards, his left shoulder slamming into the edge of the marble coffee table. He winced in excruciating pain. It felt as though his left arm was dislocated from the rest of his body.

Chase tried to scramble toward the downfallen swordsman, but Diego reared back with his right leg and sent a smashing blow with the heel of his shoe into the left side of Chase's face. His assailant's head violently rotated to right. Chase could hear the sound of his upper jawbone cracking. He ignored the pain and continued toward Diego.

Diego was able to reach over with his one good arm and grab his leather scabbard leaning in the corner of the fireplace. He quickly drew a razor-thin sword from the leather casing, and pointed it directly at the floundering Chase, who was attempting to commence with another diving charge.

Chase immediately felt the pinpoint tip of the sword on the side of his throat. He was fortunate his adversary was so skilled with a sword, or he might have ended up bleeding to death on the floor of Diego's apartment.

"Mr. Chandler, I thought we could have resolved this like gentlemen, but that's obviously impossible now. I suggest you get the hell out right now!" His voice was stone cold clear and determined.

Diego used use the edge of the nearby sofa to help himself to his feet, all the while keeping Chase at bay with his sword. Chase had seldom been caught off guard in such a compromising position. He wanted to reach up and swat the sword away from his throat, but he had seen for himself how Sanchez could strike an opponent in one thrusting whip-like motion.

Chase cautiously got to his feet. Diego carefully watched Chase's every move, never letting down his guard. He knew from what Lorena had told him that Chase was a highly trained ex-FBI agent, and he wasn't going to take any chances.

Chase backed up slowly toward the door. He reached back with his right hand and turned the doorknob. "Don't think for a minute this is over," Chase fired back in a threatening tone.

"I suggest your life would be better served trying to make Lorena happy, instead of plotting revenge against me. She is a very special woman, and she deserves all the love you can give her."

What would Sanchez know about loving Lorena? He couldn't understand the anguish of knowing that his wife and the daughter belonged to someone else. Chase had not revealed to Diego that Lorena had borne his child. If Chase had to suffer with the reality of knowing Christina was really Diego's daughter, then Sanchez could live his life without knowing the result of his adulterous affair. Chase made a solemn pact with himself as he stared angrily at his enemy. He would take this secret to his grave.

He threatened Diego one last time before leaving. "You may have had the upper hand this time, but you're a dead man."

"I'm sorry you feel that way," Diego said, as he gently poked at Chase's chest with the tip of his sword.

Chase stepped through the portal of the door and Diego slammed it shut. Diego wasn't positive whether he would have actually impaled Chase with his sword, but he was glad Chase had the sense to back down. In all the excitement, Diego temporarily forgot about the stabbing pain in his shoulder. He slumped over, trying to catch his breath. He knew his shoulder was separated by his glancing fall against the table. He wasn't thinking about how it could affect his final performance next Sunday; all he could think about right now was Lorena.

Was she safe? Diego had seen firsthand the results of Chase's uncontrolled anger.

Chase was not in much better shape as he started down the long flight of stairs from Diego's apartment. His upper jaw was already starting to swell. He could barely spit out his vile rumblings through his fractured jaw. With each downward step, it felt as though someone was shoving a hot needle into it. By the time he reached the street below, he was sweating profusely. As he stepped out into the cool night air, he looked up and reaffirmed his commitment to get even with Sanchez. He would pay Diego back for destroying his life, for stealing the affections of his wife, for erasing his devotion to his daughter Christina. It was just a matter of how and when.

The next morning, Chase called Lolo Nieto and asked him to meet at a nearby park. He had spent the entire evening devising a plan to rid his world of Diego Sanchez. Unfortunately, he would have to once again enlist Lolo Nieto's help.

Chase was sitting on a bench under the umbrella of a large oak when Lolo approached.

Lolo spotted Chase's swollen, discolored left jaw.

"Have a bad night?" Lolo guardedly inquired, as he sat down.

"We're not here to talk about my social life." He could barely open his mouth wide enough to vent the angry words. Every time he uttered a word, he felt the stinging blow from the heel of Diego's shoe.

Lolo assumed Chase had received his injury from Diego Sanchez. Lolo hoped that the gringo got the upper hand of the skirmish.

"Why did you call me?" Lolo inquired with a certain curiosity.

"I have another situation and I need your help. My offer involves significantly more than our previous arrangement. The question is, are you a man of your word?"

"It depends on how much money we are talking about."

"One hundred thousand U.S. for starters, and another fifty when the job is completed. Is that enough to buy your so-called *word*?"

Lolo had never heard that large sum of money discussed so casually. Even as a top-level competitor on the exhibition circuit, it would be difficult to earn that much money in three years. Lolo started to quickly calculate what he could do with such a sum. It could change his whole life. Not only would he have the fame, he also would have the riches to live a lifestyle he had only dreamed of as a young boy.

Lolo tried to contain his excitement. "What exactly are we talking about here?" he asked suspiciously.

Chase had spent the night hatching a plan that would eliminate Diego forever. If there was one thing Chase prided himself on, it was his ability to create ironclad plans. He knew any scheme involving the death of a prominent celebrity had to appear as an accident. He couldn't take the chance of raising any suspicion with the police when it came to someone with Diego's stature.

The plan's second critical aspect was that it needed to be untraceable. It was important to pay Lolo enough to keep his mouth shut, to keep his *word* as Lolo had promised. Chase knew he was taking a significant risk, but without Lolo's help, he could not exact his revenge on Diego Sanchez.

"I understand that there have been situations in the past when the tools of your trade have broken in competition and a swordsman has been mortally wounded. Is that true?"

"Yes, it's true....we lost one of our great champions last year in Italy. There have been others, but it is rare."

Chase recalled his brief tutorial from Señor Fernando at the tournament in Ciudad Hidalgo. He remembered the old master explaining how through poor workmanship or a flaw in the casting of the blade, it could cause the sword to break.

"Tell me more."

"Let's say that if a foil was purposely altered or constructed improperly then someone could be seriously injured. Have you ever seen a man run through with a sword, Mr. Chandler?"

Chase shook his head from side to side.

"Well, it's not a pretty sight. A broken blade can go right through facial bone like a hot knife through butter. It's not a scene for the faint of heart."

Chase didn't miss a beat. "What if one of these blades happened to *accidentally* end up in the hands of an unknowing opponent? Would it matter who they were opposing?"

"Probably not."

"With the right kind of money, could someone arrange to have one of these defective foils end up in a tournament?"

"You wouldn't happen to be talking about Diego Sanchez being at the wrong end of such a sword?"

"Let's stop playing games! I want Sanchez dead for what he did to my wife. Are you in or out?"

Lolo couldn't believe he was even considering such a scheme, but the temptation was too great. Getting rich while at the same time eliminating Diego Sanchez was just too good to be true. Even though Diego was retiring, Lolo knew he would have to live with constant comparisons to the great master. If Diego were to fail in his last performance, or even die, it would be indelibly etched in the public's mind—their beloved Diego Sanchez struck down in his last battle.

"I'm in, but I'll need a little more cash to pay off certain individuals."

"That'll have to come out of your share. Take it or leave it."

Lolo was hoping to eke out a few more dollars from Chase, but he could see Chase wasn't going to budge.

"Agreed, but I only have a short amount of time to make this happen. Diego Sanchez's last tournament is at next week's championship. That doesn't leave me much time."

"That's your problem. I'll deposit the money in the bank by close of business tomorrow. I'll want updates throughout the week. Here is my office number in Texas. Use the code name Mano when you call." Chase handed him a slip of paper with his telephone number.

"What if, for some reason, there are complications?"

"I'm confident you will be able to deal with them. For this kind of money, I won't accept anything but positive results," Chase snapped, glaring at Lolo with a threatening glare.

"Don't worry; you'll get your money's worth. By the way, where did you get this?" Lolo asked, pointing to Chase's black and blue jaw.

Chase grabbed Lolo by the shirt and pulled him until their faces were only an inch apart. "Are you through asking questions, because I'm finished answering them!"

Chase let loose of his tight hold.

"Kind of sensitive, aren't we?" Lolo said, as he attempted to brush the wrinkles out of his finely pressed shirt.

Chase stood up and snarled, "Call me when you have something to report." He walked away with second thoughts about having involved an amateur in his deadly plot, but he was so anxious to payback Sanchez that he was willing to sacrifice everything. His hope for a future with Lorena was shattered when she chose to have an affair, and come hell or high water, he was going to make sure Sanchez never had the chance to hold her in his arms again.

CHAPTER 30

Lorena had just put Christina down for her afternoon nap when the phone rang.

"Mrs. Chandler?"

The voice was unfamiliar. "Yes. Can I help you?"

"This is Jane from Dr. Blaze's office. We just wanted to call to let you know that your husband left his jacket here last week. He seemed a little rushed when he left."

Dr. Blaze? Lorena didn't recall the name. Was he Chase's new dentist? She knew he had been looking for a new one, since his dentist retired a few months ago.

"My husband has a tendency to be forgetful when he is anywhere near a dentist."

The woman on the other end of the line chuckled through the receiver, "Dr. Blaze is not your husband's dentist; he's his urologist."

His urologist? Why was Chase seeing a urologist? She didn't recall his complaining about any physical problems. Could there be something seriously wrong with him? Maybe this explained his bizarre behavior over the last couple of weeks. Her thoughts started to meander through every possible theory. She had heard terrible stories of spouses hiding serious illnesses to protect their loved ones.

"What time does your office close?" Lorena inquired.

"Dr. Blaze's last appointment is five o'clock, but I could have the jacket delivered to Mr. Chandler's office."

Lorena rushed her response. "No, that won't be necessary. I'm going to be in town today, and I'll drop by and pick it up. My husband is out of town on business. I'm sure he'll be looking for it when he returns."

Lorena thanked the woman and hung up. Her mind was cluttered with the possibilities as she dialed Rebecca Chandler's number to ask if her mother-in-law would watch Christina while she ran some errands in Pecos.

"Of course, my dear," Rebecca said, in her syrupy drawl. "I'll be right over."

"Thanks, I always feel so much better when Christina is with you."

Lorena felt guilty patronizing Rebecca, but her curiosity about Chase seeing a urologist overwhelmed her normal candor.

Lorena arrived at Dr. Blaze's office at three o'clock. She walked into the plush office and informed the receptionist that she was picking up her husband's jacket.

"Oh, yes," The receptionist said, casually smiling. "Jane told me you were coming in today."

The receptionist disappeared behind a partition, and she returned a moment later holding a jacket. It was Chase's favorite, leather aviator jacket with an Eagle Squadron patch Dutch Evans had given him that was sewn into the left breast pocket.

"Thank you. I know I don't have an appointment, but would it be possible to speak with the doctor for a few minutes?" Lorena asked in a soft, pleading tone.

The receptionist looked through the appointment book, fingering her way down the list of appointments. "Dr. Blaze's 3:30 appointment canceled. Let me check and see if he is available."

Lorena sat down across from a young couple whose conversation was obviously strained. The wife was almost in tears over their emotional discussion. Lorena tried not to invade their private conversation, but it was impossible not to overhear the woman's plea to her anxious husband in the close confines of the waiting room.

"Doug, you have to have the test. How will we ever know what the problem is?" The distraught woman paused, waiting for a reaction from her reluctant husband. "Don't you want children?"

"Yes, of course I do," Doug exclaimed, standing up for himself, "but I'm positive there is nothing wrong with me."

"Then take the test," his wife insisted.

The couple's tension-filled conversation immediately brought back the same discussion she and Chase had had before the birth of their daughter. What was her husband doing seeing a urologist, when they both knew for certain that they could have children? Then Lorena remembered that just before she told Chase she was pregnant, Chase had made an appointment with Dr. Livens to make sure their earlier problems with fertility were not related to any medical problem with him. She couldn't recall whether he had ever told her the results of the test.

The receptionist returned and leaned over the counter calling out to Lorena, who was still engrossed in trying to recall if Chase had ever received his test results.

"Mrs. Chandler, please come back into Dr. Blaze's office. He can see you now."

Lorena followed the receptionist back to his office.

"Just have a seat, and Dr. Blaze will be right in."

A few minutes later, Dr. Blaze rushed into the office. It was clear he only had a few minutes to spend with her. Lorena knew she would have to deceive Dr. Blaze and act as if Chase had told her about his previous appointment.

"Thank you for seeing me, Dr. Blaze. My husband told me about his problems, but I was wondering if you could explain it to me in layman's terms." Lorena acted nonchalant, hoping Dr. Blaze would not pick up on her ruse. "Chase has a tendency to be too clinical in his explanations."

"Well, it's pretty simple, Mrs. Chandler." His tone suddenly turned sober. "Your husband is infertile. He has been this way since he was a young child. I know it must be disappointing to both of you, but there is really nothing we can do in his particular case." Dr. Blaze's words shot through Lorena like a searing knife blade.

Chase infertile? She wanted to scream out and deny every vile word Dr. Blaze had uttered. Her thoughts immediately went to their beautiful daughter. How could this be happening after they worked so hard to reconcile their relationship? Lorena felt desperate to escape the situation. Her chest was constricting; she was struggling for air. She wasn't absolutely sure she could stand without collapsing to the floor in a heap.

Dr. Blaze noticed her ashen color. "Are you all right, Mrs. Chandler?"

"Yes, I'm fine." Lorena's hands were quivering in her lap. "Thank you so much for seeing me."

"I just wish there was something we could do from a medical standpoint. I know it sounds like the end of the world, but there are alternatives, adoption, and so forth." His tone was softening with each word. "I wanted to discuss this with Chase the other day, but he seemed quite upset after I told him his test results. Please don't hesitate to call if you would like to discuss your options."

Lorena thanked Dr. Blaze again and scrambled for the exit.

She left the office building feeling as if she had become trapped in a raging forest fire. Her entire world was burning around her. The answers to all earlier suspicions were being laid out before her like cards in a poker deck, and she was being dealt a losing hand. The stakes were simple and straightforward; her comfortable life was dissolving right before her eyes.

Chase must have assumed his earlier test results were positive when he heard she was pregnant. Why would *he* have cared about the results from Dr. Livens? He was going to have the child he so much yearned to have in his life. No wonder his recent behavior seemed so abnormal. He had a justifiable reason to be short-tempered and angry. She couldn't imagine the depth of his agony, having found out Christina was not his child. What must he have felt when he heard Dr. Blaze confirm his worst fears? The weight of the truth had to be suffocating.

Lorena sat in the parking lot, oblivious to the scorching sun, and suddenly feeling sick to her stomach. She opened the car door and vomited onto the scorched blacktop. Tears were streaking down her hot cheeks. It took several minutes for her to regain composure. The name of Diego Sanchez slowly inched its way into her knotted mind. How was it possible that her one night affair resulted in such a destructive outcome? All the positive feelings she had about having a child suddenly felt tarnished. All the joy of the past few months was replaced by overpowering guilt. It wasn't that she despised Diego Sanchez— quite the contrary. She had often thought about how he had helped her make the right decision the morning after their passionate tryst. Any other man would have tried to use the opportunity of her despondent condition to better his own position, but not Diego. It never crossed her mind the day Dr. Kittles informed her of her pregnancy that Diego could be the father. She would never have put the pieces together considering the circumstances of their brief affair. After all, she and Chase had been lax about using contraceptives after they reconciled. It was only reasonable to think Chase was the father of her child.

Diego Sanchez had rarely come up on her radar screen over the past ten months. She was totally preoccupied with trying to reclaim her relationship with Chase, acclimating herself to being pregnant and starting a family. She never tried to deny she had feelings for Diego, but she had quietly buried them once she decided to resume her life with Chase. Lorena's thoughts were churning, as she tried to sort through what Chase had figured out after his meeting with Dr. Blaze. Did Chase know she had had an affair with Diego? How could he have found out? She tried to imagine the betrayal he must have felt when he finally put the puzzle together. He must have thought she was the devil incarnate, to have so nonchalantly carried on without any sign of remorse.

Breathlessly, she called out to him, "Chase, I didn't know. I swear, please forgive me!"

Lorena tried to imagine what Chase was doing at the very moment. Knowing his background in undercover work, it wasn't much of a leap to realize his trip to Mexico wasn't related to Lone Star business. He must have quickly done the math and figured out when she had the affair. She knew Chase would never forget the date when she informed him that she was pregnant. He was probably hot on the trail, trying to discover who her lover was, who really was Christina's father? She wracked her brain trying to think of any way Chase could connect her with Mexico's most famous swordsman. Surely Felix, Diego's faithful housekeeper, would not have betrayed his master. No one else had seen them together. They were alone at Diego's secluded ranch the entire time.

"Damn it!" she suddenly screamed out, pounding the steering wheel with clenched fists; it was Lolo Nieto. He had seen her getting out of Diego's car the morning after she decided to go back to Chase. She remembered how he had made a sly reference to her "long night," and how hard he had tried to get a glimpse of Diego as he drove away. Why would Lolo betray her? Then she remembered how much Lolo despised Diego. The day they had taken a ride together in the country, Diego's name had come up several times. Lolo revealed his spiteful feelings toward Diego and how he couldn't wait until the old master retired. He complained about how Diego was destroying his rising career, and told her that he would be the first in line pay Diego back for being a spoiler. Lorena remembered being shocked at the genuine hatred Lolo had for Diego. At the time, she just chalked it up as idle jealousy, but now it was apparent her former lover was serious. She didn't want to think of a Chase and Lolo plot against the man who was the true father of her child. She could only hope that all her suspicions were based on her mind running wild with fear and that Chase really was down in Mexico on Lone Star business.

Chase arrived back in Pecos the morning after cutting his deal with Lolo. He went directly to his downtown office. He was still uneasy about relying on Lolo to help him finish off Sanchez, but it was his only reasonable option. If his plan didn't work, then he was committed to taking care of business personally. As for Lorena, Chase wanted her to suffer the way he had suffered, the way he *was* suffering; and maybe ending her lover's life would let her feel some of his pain. Once he was finished with Diego, then and only then would he reveal his knowledge of her seedy affair. He could only imagine the satisfaction of watching her face as he told her about Diego's tragic demise. He relished how she would react to his using all the power his money could buy to obtain full custody of Christina. Even though he wasn't the biological father, Chase was not about to give up his daughter to be raised by her whoring mother.

Chase knew he would have to play the naïve husband if he were going to pull off the charade when he faced Lorena that evening. How much sweeter would the revenge be if he acted like everything was fine? After all, hadn't he been the devoted husband and loving father?

Chase picked up the phone and dialed his home.

Lorena answered, "Hello?"

In his most candy-coated tone, he greeted his wife. "Hi sweetie, I got back early this morning." Each tender word he uttered cut him like a dull knife. "I didn't want to wake you, so I stopped by the office to finish up a few things from my trip."

Lorena decided to play along with Chase, to see where it was leading. "How was your trip? Everything all right?" She almost stumbled over her words.

"It's all straightened out. Everything I needed to put into place is taken care of."

"When can I expect you home?"

"I still have a couple of hours in front of me," he said, "but I should be home by late afternoon."

Lorena let the silence invade their conversation. Resentment over Chase's past lies came cascading home. Her sympathy for having betrayed Chase mutated into the same anger and distrust she had had before their blowup in Ciudad Hidalgo. Chase was up to something. She was positive Chase was unaware that she had found out about his sterility. As much as Chase was willing to carry on this sick charade, Lorena had reached her emotional limit.

"Chase....let's stop this insanity before it goes any further," she pleaded in a firm tone.

"What are you talking about?" His manner suddenly turned cold. "I told you, everything is all right."

"I know, Chase," she announced with as much compassion as she could muster. "I spoke with Dr. Blaze yesterday." She waited for his response. Nothing came. "I'm so sorry, Chase. I didn't mean to hurt you."

"Fuck you!" His ferocious words resounded through the earpiece. "You think an apology is going to erase all your lies?" She could feel his pain reverberating over the line.

"Chase, I need to see you," she demanded, trying to prod him into a more rational state of mind, "This isn't going to work over the phone."

She heard the plastic thud of the phone receiver slamming into its cradle. Lorena couldn't believe their conversation had disintegrated so fast. She called out his name to make sure he hadn't accidentally dropped the phone. "Chase...... Chase!"

There was no answer.

She set the handset down, realizing she had to take the initiative if there was any hope of defusing the situation. She wasn't about to let Chase ignore a crisis that could destroy both of their lives. Even if they couldn't resolve the problems with their marriage, they had Christina to think about. She knew he was furious about her affair with Diego, but she couldn't believe he would simply walk away from the little girl he had doted on since the day that she was born.

Lorena grabbed the bassinet on her way out of the kitchen and went upstairs to retrieve Christina. She carefully swaddled her sleeping daughter in a blanket and transferred her to the bassinet. She looked down at the tranquil face of her daughter, who was beginning to wake up. She felt fortunate Christina was oblivious to the turmoil.

She continued staring at her daughter, trying to discern any resemblance she might have to Diego. She saw nothing at first; then as Christina's cerulean eyes fluttered open. The veiled fog lifted from Lorena's hazy recollection of Diego's features. Those piercing blue eyes Lorena and Chase had discounted as common to newborn babies innocently stared back at her. It was as if she was directly peering into Diego's riveting gaze. Lorena vividly remembered how Diego's eyes poured over her body while they were in the throes of ecstasy. She could never forget the spark of salvation flickering from behind those deep blue pools as he thanked her for saving him from his loneliness.

"*Yes, Chase, Diego Sanchez is the father of our child,*" she whispered. How could she ever utter these excruciatingly destructive words to her estranged husband? She wondered if she had the strength. Lorena knew she would have to reach deep into that place where her inner fortitude resided to survive the next few hours of her free-falling life.

Lorena arrived at Chase's office hoping he hadn't left for the day. His secretary was down the hall making copies. Lorena looked at the secretary's phone console and saw that Chase's personal line was lit up. His office door was cracked open, and Lorena could hear his voice ranting in dissatisfaction to some poor victim on the other end of the line. In their brief marriage Lorena couldn't recall ever having heard Chase sound so aggressive in his business dealings.

She transferred the bassinet holding Christina to her other hand so she could step closer to the open door.

"I don't give a rat's ass what kind of problems you're having in making the arrangements. We had a deal, and I expect you to abide by it. You said it would be no problem." Chase's voice was so stressed that it sounded as if it might crack at any moment.

Lorena could not discern who was on the other end of the line, but the muffled voice was stuttering to make a point.

"Look, Lolo, if you don't take care of Mr. Sanchez, I can promise you, I'll use all the power my money can buy to destroy your career. I hope you're clear on this point." Chase's gruff tone left no doubt about the determination his threat.

Lorena stepped back, shocked over hearing the words coming out of her husband's mouth. If it were not for the fact she was holding her baby daughter, she would have reached up and covered her ears. She stepped back farther from the door, not wanting to hear any more about his plot against Diego, but his voice was so loud she could not escape it.

"So we are still on track for next Sunday, right? The next call I expect to get from you is a confirmation that everything is a go."

These were the last words Lorena could tolerate hearing. She grabbed the bassinet and turned to leave.

Just then, Chase's secretary returned. "Mrs. Chandler, how nice to see you."

The woman's voice was loud enough that even with the office door partially closed, Lorena was sure Chase had heard her name being announced. She waited, holding her breath, hoping somehow she was wrong. Lorena was two steps away from the open elevator when the door to Chase's office swung open, and he nonchalantly walked over to greet his wife and baby.

"Sweetheart, you're not leaving so soon are you?" he said with a smirk.

Lorena was petrified. The coldness of his expression frightened her. Her lips felt numb, and she was unable to return his sinister greeting.

He put his arm around her rigid body and guided her into his office.

"You don't look well, darling. Come into my office and sit down." He looked over his shoulder at his secretary and smiled as he shut the door behind him.

As soon as they were in the office, Lorena twisted violently away from Chase. Her erratic swiveling motion awakened Christina, who started crying.

"What the hell are you up to, Chase?" she charged, tired of playing the lamb ready for slaughter. "Please, tell me you're not working with Lolo Nieto to get back at Diego."

Lorena set the bassinet containing Christina on the leather sofa. Christina's tearful wails only heightened the tension in the room.

"Chase, it was my mistake."

"Your mistake?" Chase snarled as he stepped around his desk. "I believe it takes two to tango."

"Chase, I seduced him. I know that may surprise you, but it's true." Her voice curled back as if it was going to break.

"Shut your filthy mouth!" He took a step toward her. His forceful motion caught her off-guard. She had seen this side of him before and she wasn't going to take any chances. Just as she was stepping away from him, he turned and went over to his desk. Lorena was hoping this was a sign he was gaining control of himself. Then there was a resounding violent thud.

Chase slammed both hands down so hard on the desk that she felt the vibrations from where she stood in the middle of his large office.

"What the fuck were you thinking? Did you think you could shack up with one of your hot-blooded Latin lovers and get away with it?"

Lorena ignored his derogatory reference to Latin lovers. "I was confused and hurt. I wasn't sure what was happening between us," she said, pleading for Chase to understand. "I needed to feel safe after what happened between you and me in the hotel room. Diego just happened to be a victim of our marital crisis." Lorena's words were picking up velocity with each string of words.

"Marital crisis? Is that what you call fucking another man? A marital crisis!" His face pulled into a deep rutted frown.

"Chase, I'm begging you to call off this foolish revenge plot. Haven't enough people been hurt by my actions? I'm the one who is to blame, not Diego."

He stepped closer. "You want me to forget about it so you can sneak off and fuck your famous hero and live happily ever after?"

He inched ever closer as Christina sobbed in the background.

"Chase, you have totally lost control of reality. You need to...."

Before she could utter the next word, Chase's hand rose to slap Lorena across the face, but she raised both of her hands, braced herself and backed up against his desk. Despite a momentary spasm of panic, Lorena was determined to use all of her physical powers to avoid becoming the victim of another one of Chase's angry outbursts. This time, there was no mistaking his uncontrolled temper for an *accident*. His intent was clear; he meant to harm her.

His jolting slap struck her upright hands, grazing her right cheek and it took everything she could muster to stay on her feet. The searing pain from Chase's hand raking across her face was familiar as the first time she felt it in Ciudad Hidalgo. But Lorena was determined to stand her ground this time; to send a message that she wasn't backing down. The force of his blow caused her torso to twist downward toward the top of the desk. Instinctively, she grabbed a pen and pencil holder, recoiled her arm, and slammed the highly polished stone base into the side of Chase's head. He flinched from Lorena's surprise reprisal but quickly regained his composure. Chase reached up and touched the superficial wound. There was blood on his fingers. He stared across at the hunched-over Lorena with a sickening calm expression as thought he was enjoying inflicting pain on his once -beloved wife.

Lorena looked back at Chase with complete disdain. Her expression left no doubt; it was over between them. Their dream of an idyllic life together disappeared like sea-smoke on a blistering tropical horizon.

Lorena anguished over her next thought. *How could the walls of the love they built so quickly collapse into the rubble of such hatred?* Lorena coolly turned away from Chase, walked over to the sofa and picked up the bassinet containing their daughter.

From behind, she could hear Chase making a motion toward her. She swiveled around and courageously snarled at Chase, "Don't even think about it, you son of a bitch."

The boldness of her stance stunned Chase. He froze in his steps.

Lorena was still holding the piece of agate, and her hand trembled with anger. "I'm walking out that door, and if you try and stop me, I swear to God...."

She didn't finish her sentence.

Before Chase could react, Lorena was out the door. She dropped her makeshift weapon just before reaching the outside lobby of his office, calmly walked over to the elevator, and pushed the button for the first floor.

Chase burst out from the inner confines of his office. His bleach-white shirt had several drops of fresh blood on the shoulder. His secretary had a look of shock and fear. It was impossible for her not to have heard the commotion.

Chase started after Lorena, who was entering the elevator, but stopped himself when he heard his frightened secretary calling out to him, "Mr.

Chandler.....is everything all right?" The innocent bystanders' voice shuddered with alarm.

Chase turned to her. "Yes, everything is just fine," he murmured resentfully. He turned back around, just in time to see the outline of Lorena disappearing behind the thin opening of the closing elevator doors. He stood there, staring blankly at his own distorted reflection in the polished stainless steel doors, listening to the rumbling sound from the elevator shaft as it carried away Lorena and Christina. The ill-omened echo carried the last remnants of their life together. Their love had splintered into so many fragments, not even Chase could recognize the pieces.

CHAPTER 31

Diego Sanchez drove up the winding road to Cesar Alvarez's home, hoping he would find the letters he had written to Celaya back in late 1963. If Alvarez had kept them, Diego assumed the maestro had also hoarded the love letters he had written.

Fortunately for Diego, Cesar Alvarez was willing to let him rummage through his father's belongings. If it hadn't been for Diego's reputation and the fact that Cesar knew his father had been devoted to him, Diego might have lost his only chance to find the definitive proof he needed to substantiate his devotion to Celaya.

Nunez, his manager, went ballistic when he heard that Diego had run off in search of some old love letters. It was less than four days before Mexico's Championship Tournament and Nunez couldn't imagine what Diego was thinking.

Diego had told no one about his recent discovery. He wanted to keep it a secret until he had a chance to personally break the news to Lolo. Nunez begged him not to go on his insane wild goose chase. What about all the publicity and hours spent making arrangements for his final battle at the Plaza Quitzal? Diego apologized to his manager, but wasn't about to pass up such an important opportunity to prove his innocence.

Diego pulled up in front of a colonial house and was greeted by a man with a strong resemblance to his old mentor. "It's a pleasure to meet you in person, Señor Sanchez. My father often spoke about you," Cesar Alvarez said, welcoming his guest.

"Thank you. The pleasure is mine." Diego reached out and shook his host's hand. "I appreciate you letting me look through your father's private papers."

Cesar led Diego into his father's cluttered private study. "Well, here it is. As you can see, my father was not exactly organized. I've tried my best to sort out as much as possible, but it's been an impossible chore. I don't envy you."

Diego looked about the chaotic office, wondering where he should start.

There were boxes stacked to the ceiling along the far wall. The shelves were a jumble of loose papers, magazines, and photographs. Alvarez's desk was piled with stacks of letters and books. He imagined his old teacher sitting behind his desk; reminiscing about the students he had taught, his wrinkled, arthritic hands shuffling through the mess, looking for a letter requesting his services to teach the next great Mexican fencing champion.

Although he knew it was going to be a daunting task to find the letters, Diego felt excited about the possibility of bringing an end to his search.

"I promise not to be any trouble," Diego said gratefully.

"No problem. It feels right that you're here where my father spent the last years of his life. Of all his students, just the mention of your name brightened his day. Please don't hesitate to ask for anything."

"Thank you," Diego said, as he removed his coat.

He started on the pillar of boxes stacked against the far wall, hoping he might get lucky on the first try. He reached up above his head and retrieved the first box; the weight almost made him lose his balance. He opened it, eager to find out if his intuition was right. It was filled to the brim with stacks of loose papers and folders. Looking around once more at the disorganized office, he sighed in frustration, and started meticulously sorting through each piece of paper. It was going to be a long next couple of days, he thought.

Lorena arrived in Mexico City exhausted.

After the episode in Chase's office, all Lorena wanted to do was go home to Mexico, and to get there as soon as possible. It was the only place where she felt completely protected from Chase. More importantly, she needed to warn Diego about her husband's plot against his life. She felt personally responsible for driving Chase into the depths of fanatical revenge. Already she had played a major role in dismantling three lives; she wasn't about to let Diego become a fourth casualty.

Her first call after arriving at the train station in Mexico was to an old friend to see if she could stay at her place for the weekend. She hadn't even thought about where she was going to go when she hurriedly left Texas. She could only take one step at a time right now.

As she stared out impassively over the small plaza below her friend's apartment, she could feel the awkward tension dissipating. She was home again. She began to consider the events of the past few days. After leaving Chase's office, she had rushed home and gathered as much as she could pack in a couple hours. She didn't want to take any chances with him so close on her heels. She had seen the sadistic look in his eyes burning through the slit in the elevator door. Even if he hadn't followed her back to the ranch, she was positive he was up to something to pay her back for destroying their lives.

It was a bizarre experience sorting through all the material objects representing their marriage; from pictures of them posing as a happy couple that sat on their dresser, to separate his and hers shoe closets to the engraved pillow cases with their separate initials. Every detail, all the way down to which side of the bed each one of them preferred, spoke of their shared lives. As she rifled through the dresser, she came across her wedding dress in the bottom drawer and paused. How could it have dissolved so quickly into such a quagmire of distrust and anger? For just a brief moment, she felt deep remorse for her part in destroying their relationship. Her guilt didn't last long; she could still hear Chase talking to Lolo over the phone about plans to kill Diego. She could still feel the rough chafing from the back of his hand striking her on her cheek. Her left wrist was still swollen from having stopped his vicious blow. Yes, she was guilty of infidelity, but nothing warranted such hateful physical abuse toward her.

As Lorena finished packing her two, small suitcases, she passed over most of the expensive presents Chase had given her, including several pieces of valuable jewelry. She wasn't only leaving all of her feelings for him behind; she was saying good-bye to everything that symbolized their lives together. The only thing she took that had any connection to Chase was a simple, gold necklace from which the initials *CC* dangled. Chase had given it to her in the hospital after Christina was born; it was her first mother's day gift.

She gathered all the things she needed to survive, and then picked up the bassinet where Christina lay sleeping, walked out the door, and never looked back.

The only unexpected mishap on her trip back to Mexico City occurred on the short drive out to the main highway from the ranch. As she approached the highway a car turned down the dirt road. Lorena panicked at first, thinking it was Chase coming after her. As the approaching vehicle came closer, she saw that is was her mother-in-law.

Lorena hadn't thought about the impact of their break-up on Chase's parents, particularly Rebecca. Lorena deeply regretted taking Christina away from her grandmother. Rebecca would be crushed when Chase told her that he was not the father of her grandchild. She wondered if Rebecca would denounce her granddaughter, knowing Christina didn't have one drop of Chandler blood flowing through her veins.

Lorena was a few hundred yards away when she blinked her headlights several times, signaling Rebecca to stop. Lorena was taking a chance. She knew her crazed husband could have called his mother to ask her to try stopping Lorena from leaving ranch. It was a risk Lorena was willing to take. Rebecca deserved at least one final glimpse of Christina. As the two cars came to a stop, Rebecca opened her window and called out to her.

"Where are you headed?"

Lorena couldn't tell from the noise of the car engines whether it was a threat or a simple innocent question. "Just heading to town to run some errands," she lied in her most convincing tone.

Both women shut off their cars, and Rebecca stepped out. Strangely, she was dressed in a red and white cotton plaid shirt and Levis. In all the time Lorena had been around Rebecca, she had never seen her dressed so casually. It was ironic now that she was leaving her mother-in-law was letting down her Southern Belle composure. Lorena was prepared for the worst.

"Why don't you let me take care of our little doll while you're in town?"

"Thanks, Rebecca, but I'm meeting a friend at the park, and we're going to take the girls for a walk around the lake."

"Sounds wonderful. Can I hold her for just a minute?" Rebecca's voice pleaded. "I promise not to make you late." It was obvious she was not here to stop her, but only to get her daily Christina "fix."

"Of course," Lorena said, in a sympathetic tone, "She's asleep in the back seat."

Rebecca opened the rear door of the car, pulled the bassinet in her direction, and gently wrapped her arms around Christina. She brought the sleeping child up against her breast and cooed Christina's name tenderly.

"Isn't she the sweetest thing you ever saw?" Rebecca's drawl purred out between her pursed lips.

"Yes, she is." It was all Lorena could bring herself to say, as she watched Rebecca cuddle her grandchild.

She felt as though her chest was being split open, that someone had reached inside and squeezed her heart so tightly that it could stop beating. Watching Rebecca stand out in the middle of that dirt road with the backdrop of the cobalt blue Texas skyline made Lorena feel like an invader, marching through her mother's-in-law life and plundering her most prized treasure. Rebecca had been her stalwart supporter from the very first day she showed up at the ranch bedraggled and beaten up. Chase's mother was with her every step of the way, through her difficult adaptation to life on the ranch, through her long pregnancy. She could only hope Rebecca would understand once she knew the truth.

"Well, I guess I'd better let you get on your way," Rebecca said reluctantly.

She lovingly gazed one more time at Christina's chubby pink face, kissed her gently on her forehead, and started to put her back into her bassinet. Lorena stepped over to Rebecca and warmly hugged both of them.

"I love you, Rebecca," Lorena whispered with deep remorse in her voice. Lorena stepped back from Rebecca and tears were trickling down her cheek.

"Of course you do, my dear." Rebecca reached up, gently brushing her hand on Lorena's cheek. "Now, let's not have any more tears. We'll see each other this weekend." Rebecca laid Christina back into the bassinet in the back seat.

The two women hugged one more time and Lorena drove off, straining to hold the fading image of Rebecca in her mind. She stared at the rear view mirror until Rebecca completely disappeared.

Lorena was snapped out of her dark nostalgic journey by a hungry, demanding Christina. After feeding her daughter, she made her first attempt to call Diego at his rancho outside of Ciudad Hidalgo. She didn't know that he had left for Mexico City the day before she left Texas.

Felix answered the phone and she was told that Diego was staying at his apartment in Mexico City in preparation for his final duel in the ring. Lorena realized how fortunate it was that he was there. She wasn't looking forward to a four-hour trip to Ciudad Hidalgo.

"Could I please have his number where he is staying? It is very important that I speak with him as soon as possible." Lorena pleaded.

In his most polite voice, Felix said, "Sorry, Señora, but Señor Sanchez is currently not in Mexico City. He informed me yesterday that he would be out of town for a couple of days on some personal business." Felix explained to her that as far as he knew, Diego was not planning on returning until the night before the tournament on Sunday. Felix gave her Diego's phone number in Mexico City and wished her well in her effort to reach him.

Lorena desperately needed to share what she had learned about Chase's plot against Diego. She didn't have much detail except that Lolo was involved and was making arrangements to fatally bring down Diego. She knew it would be almost impossible to stop Diego from competing in the tournament given its importance, but she had to try.

Lorena didn't know when she planned to reveal to Diego that he was the father of her child. She didn't want to foist this shocking news on him without some kind of warning, but if it was her only alternative, she wouldn't hesitate laying that emotional card at the feet of the determined swordsman. She could only hope that whatever reason she gave, Diego would consider retiring before the tournament. Maybe, just maybe, she could gain some redemption from all her past mistakes by trying to save Diego.

Lorena hadn't really thought about Diego since she said good-bye to him on the curb in Ciudad Hidalgo. But what happened between them that night couldn't be completely ignored. All the memories and feelings she had so easily stowed away were starting to inch their way back into her thoughts. Knowing Diego was the father of her child created a strong emotional bridge. She was still reeling from her break with Chase, but at the same time, she felt drawn toward Diego.

Diego had spent the entire first day and part of the next morning sorting through boxes, file cabinets, and desk drawers, searching for any sign of his letters to Celaya. He took only a few necessary breaks, enough to eat a few bites of food and sleep briefly. Then he was back at it. It was obvious to Cesar Alvarez that the man living in his father's library was obsessed with finding something.

By Saturday morning, Diego was left with only a few hours before he had to leave for Mexico City. Time seemed to stand still, although he was aware of it slipping away. He could feel himself losing hope as each piece of paper passed through his hands. Diego had already meticulously searched through the obvious places where Alvarez might have hidden the letters. He had only a few more small boxes to sort through. The false hope of thinking that at any moment the letters would magically appear had taken its toll on his nerves.

He opened yet another box. It was filled with loosely stacked papers, and decided to stop being cautious in sorting. He poured the entire contents onto the floor. The paper splashed out like a scattered deck of cards. He saw nothing and began pushing papers to the side. Suddenly, he felt something bulky hidden within the pile. He pushed a few more papers aside and exposed a set of envelopes, bound together with the same twine as the letters he had found in his father's office. Diego was hesitant to pick up the age-stained letters, afraid his hopes would be dashed again, but as soon as they were close enough for him to read the inscription on the outside of the envelope, he recognized his own handwriting. They were his letters to Celaya.

Diego's hands trembled as he unraveled the twine around the letters. Every letter he had written over the first four months of his life in France was laid out before him. Celaya had not received one word of his encouragement, of his devotion to her! As emotional as he had been about finding Celaya's letters in his father's office, discovering these letters brought him to the brink of an emotional cliff. How abandoned she must have felt to have never heard from him. There she was, pregnant with his child, bearing the full weight of being ostracized by her friends and society while he was furthering his career. What agony must she have been feeling? No wonder she almost gave up hope.

The vision of Celaya lying in her hospital bed, and calling out his name in the hope that he would magically appear to save her slammed into his brain.

He doubled over in pain as though being stabbed by someone who was turning the knife slowly. Diego never felt as hopeless as he did at this very moment. He rocked back and forth, tightly clutching his unread letters. He started calling out her name, softly at first, then building to a crescendo until it was a debilitating chorus, Celaya ... Celaya!..... Celaya!

Cesar, who was busy working in the adjoining room, overheard his pathetic wail. He rushed into his father's study to see Diego crumpled on the floor in an embryonic position, tightly hugging the letters. Cesar rushed over to the fallen man, suspecting that he might be having a heart attack.

"Señor Sanchez, are you all right?" Cesar's voice was frantic.

It seemed like forever before the contorted figure on the floor responded. Diego finally squeaked out a feeble answer, "Yes. Thank you. I'm sorry to have caused you so much concern."

Cesar was relieved to see that Diego was not in physical pain. Seeing one of Mexico's valiant competitors lying in a crumpled heap on his floor with tears streaming down his face left him feeling helpless.

Diego sat up slowly and apologized. "I'm so sorry for making a scene. If you don't mind, I would like a few minutes alone."

Cesar obliged his guest and left the room.

Diego appeared a few moments later in the foyer. He was carrying the small bundle of letters. "I have one more favor to ask of you, Cesar. Would it be asking too much if I took these letters?"

As difficult as it was for Cesar to understand his unusual request, he could see they were what Diego had been consumed with for the past two days. He was not about to deny Diego's request. From the look on Diego's beleaguered face, it would have been like denying the last request of a dying man.

"Of course, Señor."

"I can't promise you I'll return them."

"I understand." Cesar knew the letters probably had something in common with the letters he had sent to Diego's father.

Diego drove back to his apartment in Mexico City. After all this time, he had the final pieces to the puzzle that had been haunting him for over a year.

What seemed like an endless search had finally come to an end, and now he was struggling over what to do with his letters. For the first time, he knew he would have to confront the reality of facing Lolo with the truth about himself and his mother. Walking through this emotional minefield with Lolo was one thing, but he also knew he would have to tackle his own fears about being a father to a grown man, to a man who despised him. All of these thoughts terrified him, but he was ready to take on the challenge. He felt a sense of duty to carry on the proud heritage of his family name, to let Lolo know that he was not alone in the world.

CHAPTER 32

Diego's final day of reckoning in a major tournament had finally arrived. As soon as he laid down his sword and protective mask in the center of the *piste* to signify the end of his career, he would tell Lolo the truth about his mother and him. Not only was he starting a new life in retirement but he would have a new role to play as Lolo's "father". It still sounded awkward as he whispered the word under his breath.

Diego had a strange sense of uneasiness and pride as he looked across the small dressing room, watching his son preparing to do battle in Mexico's most prestigious championship. He tried to avoid staring as Lolo put on his fencing garb but it was too hard to resist. He watched as Lolo flexed the blade of his foil and adjusted his protective mask. In all his years of observing this sacred process, it never had seemed so important to Diego. He was watching his own son prepare for the classic encounter between a man and the limits of his own ability. There was a sense of pride intermingled with real concern for how Lolo would accept the news that he was his father.

Typically, Lolo ignored Diego when they were competing in the same tournament, but today he seemed even more distant. Diego attempted to make eye contact with him, but Lolo immediately turned his head away. Lolo did notice the former champion staring at him in a peculiar way, and wondered if Diego somehow had found out about his role in the plot. Lolo felt a sudden shudder of guilt. He actually had had second thoughts about assisting Chase Chandler in seeking revenge against Diego. The day after Chase returned to his Pecos office, Lolo had called and tried to convince Chase to forget about his plot against Diego. Chase was furious and threatened to do everything in his power to ruin Lolo's career if he didn't fulfill his part of the bargain. Given Chase's threat, Lolo felt he had no option other than to close the deal. There was no turning back now and there could be no regrets on his part. Besides, he would rid Diego Sanchez from his life forever.

Lolo had found a sword maker in Monterrey. Benny Huerta, who was suspected of making low quality blades, had been reprimanded by the Fencing Federation and essentially run out of the business of making competition weaponry. He knew Huerta was hurting for cash, so it had been an effortless negotiation to convince him to forge a blade with faulty steel. Huerta had asked only one question of Lolo. "How exactly are you going to get this in the hands of the right swordsman? "You leave that to me," Lolo had confidently replied, as if he had made arrangements similar to this in the past.

In fact, Lolo *had* already made the appropriate arrangements. Lolo had deceived an up-and-coming swordsman, Jaime Valle, under the guise that he was giving him one of the highest quality foils made as a gift to celebrate Valle qualifying for Mexico's Fencing Championship. At first, the unsuspecting contestant was reluctant to accept Lolo's offer, but when told that he was matched up against Diego Sanchez, Valle gladly accepted the generous offer, and hoped that it would give him an edge against Mexico's greatest fencing champion.

As Lolo nervously sat a few feet away from Diego, he was confident the stage was set for the former champion's final battle. If everything went as Lolo had planned, Diego's first match would be the last of his life. Everyone in the dressing room could sense the tension between Diego and Lolo. There was always animosity on Lolo's behalf toward Diego, but today was different. Diego's retirement would almost come as a relief to most of his colleagues. After today, they wouldn't have to face the fireworks that occurred at every tournament between these heated two combatants.

Diego continued to glance in Lolo's direction during the pre-tournament preparation. He particularly noticed the cream-colored scarf Lolo had tucked under his *lame*. Lolo wore his mother's scarf in every tournament since the day, a few months ago, that his grandmother had given it to him. Diego instantly recognized the scarf as the one he had worn for over twenty years. He was pleased to see that the tradition of wearing Celaya's scarf continued. She would have been pleased, he thought.

Lolo finished checking his equipment one last time, and started toward the tunnel entrance of the Plaza Quitzal along with his fellow contestants. Diego stood up and walked over to Lolo.

"I wish you the best of luck. You have the potential for becoming the next great fencing champion of Mexico. Carry that responsibility with pride and respect."

Diego stared into Lolo's blue eyes and was struck by the strong family resemblance. The high cheekbones and the dimpled chin from Celaya, combined with the sandy blond hair, were all the physical signs Diego needed to know. He was standing shoulder to shoulder with his own son, and they were a perfect match in physical stature and form. *How could he have not noticed it before?*

Lolo turned to him, curtly replied, "Luck has nothing to do with it," then turned away abruptly and opened the door leading to the entrance tunnel of the *salle d'armes*.

A few minutes later, Diego joined Lolo, who was standing with the other contestants, waiting for their names to be announced in the order of the day's matches. Each competitor was accompanied by his coach, and Manuel Carbajal stood faithfully at Lolo's side hoping this would be a breakthrough day for Lolo

The promoters of the event could not have squeezed another person into the Plaza Quitzal. Every seat was taken by fencing fans and luminaries wanting to see Diego Sanchez's final match. The front row seats were filled with notable fencing aficionados. Interspersed among them were top Mexican film stars political dignitaries, and a few family members of the competitors. The fervor for this tournament was beyond anything Mexico had seen in its history. Diego Sanchez was already destined to be a legend; after today, there would be no question of his place in history.

Before the first match got underway, Lolo turned to Carbajal and proclaimed "After today, we won't have to worry about Diego Sanchez anymore."

"Of course," Carbajal said, affirming Lolo's obvious point. "He's retiring today."

"Well, we shall see if Señor Diego Sanchez leaves the court of honor on his feet or on his back," Lolo sarcastically exclaimed.

Before Carbajal could ask what he meant by his caustic remark the announcer barked out the contestants of the first bout. Carbajal had noticed that Lolo had been acting edgy the last couple of days but assumed it was in anticipation of having to possibly battle Diego in the final match. He wondered whether his young prospect was actually nervous about accepting the full brunt of the spotlight once Diego was no longer distracting fans from his performance. Carbajal was waiting until Diego retired to reveal the secret he had learned from the dying lips of Diego's former maestro, Señor Alvarez. He couldn't fathom how Lolo was going to react upon hearing the news that Diego Sanchez was his father. Carbajal was actually tempted at this very moment to reveal his secret, but he held himself back. Carbajal and Lolo were both aware that the baton was being transferred from Diego to Lolo today. Of all days, Carbajal knew it was critical that Lolo be at the top of his game and not be distracted by personal issues. Lolo had to demonstrate unequivocally to everyone in the stadium that he was worthy of the prestigious honor of replacing Mexico's greatest fencing champion.

Silence came over the audience when it caught sight of Diego. He didn't know what to make of it at first. Then he heard the dull hum of the crowd starting to chant, "Diego! Diego! Diego!" as everyone stood up, clapping their hands in a punctuated rhythmic pattern. Diego thought the ovation would never end. He valiantly tried to stop the persistent outpouring, but the crowd ignored his plea. It was his fans' last chance to show their appreciation for all that he had accomplished.

In the second row, center stage, sat a lone figure. The tall, slender gringo was the only person in the entire stadium not on his feet applauding. The enthusiastic crowd smothered Chase Chandler, and his view of the man he had come to watch die was completely obstructed. All the better, he thought; even the sight of Diego Sanchez turned his blood into scalding acid; eating at any last remnants of civility he had had toward the man who had ruined his life.

Chase had flown down in the morning to make sure Lolo fulfilled his part of the bargain. He had no idea Lorena was in Mexico City, staying only a few blocks away. At this point, he didn't care where his estranged wife was or whom she was fucking. All in due time, he thought.

Before leaving Pecos to attend Mexico's Fencing Championship, he had contacted his lawyer to start proceedings for custody of Christina. If he couldn't have the love Lorena had promised him on their wedding day, then she was not about to live happily ever after with her illegitimate daughter. He knew she would eventually return to Mexico, thinking she was safe from his vengeance, but she was naïve regarding his determination to inflict revenge. He knew it would be no easy task convincing the Mexican courts to give him custody of Christina, but he also knew that with enough money and persistence, almost anything could be accomplished within the corrupt Mexican legal system. First things first, he thought—Diego today, Lorena tomorrow.

Lolo stood next to his manager throughout the entire epic scene honoring Diego. Whatever remorse he had for his part in the plot against Diego evaporated upon hearing the enthusiastic affection the fans had for his archrival. Carbajal could see by Lolo's wounded expression that his protégé was at the flash point ready to explode. To break the tension, he asked Lolo what he meant by his comment in the tunnel about Diego not leaving the tournament on his feet.

Lolo sharply responded, "We'll get a chance to see how truly talented Diego Sanchez is today."

"Lolo, what are you up to?" Carbajal challenged, recalling their conversation in his office over a year ago when Lolo angrily threatened to take things into his own hands.

"You'll just wait and see." There was a spark of sinister joy in his voice.

Carbajal didn't like the direction in which the conversation was going. He had watched Lolo become more obsessed over the past year with all the attention Diego was receiving. Lolo became more bitter and aggravated with each tournament and each newspaper story regaling Diego's feats with the sword. Carbajal grabbed Lolo's arm and turned Lolo's attention away from what was happening in preparation for the first contest.

"What the hell have you done?" Carbajal demanded. "You'd better tell me now before it is too late."

"It's none of your business."

Just then, the first two competitors stepped onto the fighting strip and began their match.

The bout order for the day's tournament was based upon previous rankings.

The highest ranked swordsman would battle the lowest ranked and so on down the line. Lolo's bout was just before Diego's.

Carbajal, still curious about Lolo's reference about Diego going out on his backside, started toward his protégé. Lolo could see that Carbajal was furious and stepped away from him. He would deal with his manager later.

The first bouts went as planned. They were well fought but not spectacular. As expected, both winners dedicated their performances to Diego Sanchez. When it came time for Lolo's bout, he ignored tradition and dedicated the fight to the beautiful young woman with whom he had been shacking up over the last couple of weeks. The insult was obvious to Diego, but he politely ignored Lolo's indignation. He could already feel parental compassion setting in for Lolo.

Lolo fought brilliantly, and it was apparent to everyone in the arena that they were seeing the next great fencing talent. His work with the foil left no doubt that he was following in the footsteps of Diego Sanchez. Although he was not a crowd favorite due to his arrogant attitude, fans couldn't deny his dedication and skill.

Diego watched in wonder at the expertise Lolo demonstrated with each point scored. His brash, upright stance, egging his competitor into making mistakes, left no doubt in his mind that his son was one of the best he had ever seen. For the first time in his life, Diego knew the true meaning of the words, "A father's pride has no boundaries." He smiled confidently, knowing he was a part of Lolo. Diego had experienced the power of love's captivating grip only twice in his life, once with Celaya, and more recently, with Lorena. But now he felt a different sense of that emotion as he looked at his son battling in all his glory. It was the legacy of the family bloodline, that special bond between father and son. He realized that his familial legacy would not end with him. He knew it was going to be a difficult journey, but at least, he now saw the chance for a new beginning with Lolo. Finally, he could become part of something called a family, even if it was without Celaya.

Diego was locked in a trance when a light tap on the shoulder suddenly awakened him. It was his manager, Roberto Nunez.

"Diego, someone is here to see you," Roberto said, with an intense look of concern.

"What do you mean?" he demanded, irritated that he was being distracted from Lolo's performance. "I'm about to go into my bout."

"I think this is someone you need to talk to before you go out there."

"Are you crazy? This is my last tournament." Diego fought off yelling at his manager for his ridiculous request.

"It's Lorena Santoya."

Diego couldn't believe what he was hearing. *Lorena Santoya! What was she doing here?* He never expected to see her again. Could her sudden appearance be the reason Chase Chandler had burst into his apartment a few days before in an attempt to throttle the very life out of him?

"She's waiting for you in the entry tunnel." Nunez's voice trailed off into silence.

Diego looked back at Lolo and could see he was preparing to finish off his opponent. It would only be a few minutes before he himself was beckoned onto center stage. *Lorena Santoya!* Her name rang out again in his head. He still couldn't fathom why she had appeared at this moment demanding to see him. Was she on the run from her estranged husband? Had she changed her mind about their one night affair? Whatever the reason, he was irresistibly drawn to her. It was one of the most inopportune times, but he felt compelled to honor her unusual request.

"All right, I'll go meet with her, but you need to let me know as soon as Lolo's bout is finished," he insisted, as he nervously glanced one more time at Lolo. Diego slowly walked toward the entrance tunnel, not wanting to attract any attention. All he could think about was how he would react to seeing Lorena again, particularly after what had happened between him and her enraged husband.

Diego couldn't believe Lorena was at the Plaza Quitzal. As he approached the entrance tunnel all the emotions he felt about their one night together came rushing back. He entered the long passageway, his eyes struggling to adjust to the darkness. The only source of light came from the arched portal at the far end of the tunnel that led to the dressing rooms. He could barely make out the silhouette standing about halfway down the tunnel as he walked cautiously in the lone figure's direction. The harder he tried to concentrate on the image he was approaching, the more he was distracted by the increasing volume of the crowd's cheering. The sustained applause signified that Lolo was about to finish off the match.

Diego was being pulled in two directions. He wanted to see Lorena but didn't want to miss his son winning his bout. His thoughts rolled around in his head like scattering ball bearings on a clay-tiled floor. As hard as he tried to gather them up, the more they escaped his grasp.

Diego was only a few steps away when he heard her soft voice spill down the empty passageway. "I'm so sorry. I didn't mean to cause such a scene, but I need to talk to you."

"Lorena, what are you doing here?" he said, knowing his tone of voice probably sounded somewhat annoyed.

"I tried to call your apartment last night, but you never answered." Her tone of voice had a low, pleading urgency to it, "You have to listen to me."

Diego remembered hearing the phone ring, but he was so exhausted that he thought it was dreaming. He could see from her expression that Lorena was carrying a terrible burden. She had dark shadows under her eyes, and her skin appeared ashen from lack of sleep.

"I'm sorry, but I don't have a lot of time," Diego offered, as his voice became more consoling.

"It's not what *has* happened; it's what *could* happen if you go back out there. Your life is in danger."

"What are you talking about?" he asked, stunned by her conviction.

"Diego, it's over between Chase and me. He found out about our affair."

"I'm so sorry, Lorena," Diego said sympathetically, and suddenly feeling guilty for his curt reaction to her sudden appearance.

"Chase is in a jealous rage; all he wants is revenge. Lolo is involved somehow. I overheard the two of them discussing something about making sure you ended up dead. You can't fight in this bout. You can't go out there, Diego." Her voice was strained from the desperation of her plea.

Another roar echoed down the tunnel. Lolo had won his bout. The next cheer would be when they announced Diego's name.

"It can't be true. I know Lolo can sometimes be an angry young man, but

I can't believe he would stoop to this level," Diego said, refusing to face the possibility that his own son would plot to end his life. "Lorena, I have no choice I won't dishonor everything I've lived for in my entire life. I know you know what this means to me. Of all people, you must understand the importance of finishing what you started. Besides, I'm not just doing this for me."

"Would you do it for me, if I asked you not to go out there? Would you change your mind?" She was practically begging Diego.

"Lorena, when I lost Celaya, I thought I lost any chance at falling in love. I never thought I would be so fortunate to feel that kind of love again, but then I met you. As much as I would like to say yes, I'm sorry; I can't. You wouldn't want me, if I walked away from this. I couldn't live with myself. I'm sorry."

Lorena was prepared to do anything to stop the father of her child from potentially facing his own death. "What if I asked you to do it for your daughter?

"What are you talking about?" Diego's face was quizzical and pained at the same time. In all the confusion, Diego had not noticed the small bassinet of rumpled cloth sitting directly behind Lorena.

Lorena reached down into the bassinet, gently lifting the small bundle while exposing the angelic face of Christina. "I want to introduce you to Christina Sanchez Santoya," she proudly whispered. She hoped that by using Christina's traditional Mexican name, which included Diego's, it would create the affect she needed to stop the stubborn, proud champion.

Diego stood dumbfounded, reeling from Lorena's bold proclamation. *His daughter?*

"You're the only man I've been with besides Chase." Her honesty was unquestionable. "Chase found out two weeks ago that he was infertile. That's when he started planning his revenge against you."

Diego was suddenly overwrought with emotion. Within the matter of two days he had found out not only about his son's identity, but now that he had a baby daughter as well.

Lorena handed Christina to Diego. He gingerly accepted her. Christina looked up at him with her sparkling eyes. He instantly recognized the resemblance; the same crystal blue eyes of a father, a son, and now a daughter.

"Diego, I'm begging for your daughter's sake, don't go back out there."

Diego was mesmerized by Christina's innocent pink, chubby face. He was holding the one thing he thought he would never have in his life, the pure innocence of his offspring. He thought of all the years he had missed out with Lolo and the memories he could never share with him as a child. The thought of having this opportunity with Christina left him feeling excited and overwhelmed at the same time.

While Diego was learning about his new daughter, Lolo stood in the middle of the tournament accepting the crowd's applause. There was no question in the minds of the fans and officials that if he kept performing with such skill he would be the next potential Olympic fencing champion from Mexico.

When Lolo returned to the sidelines to accept congratulations from his colleagues, Carbajal made another attempt to jar the truth out of his young upstart. His demonstrative pleading was of no consequence; Lolo was standing firm through his silence, and moved a few steps away from his manager to avoid any further confrontation. How ironically sweet would it be to have performed so brilliantly while Diego failed? He finally would have his retribution against the great Diego Sanchez.

Out of desperation Carbajal decided that it was time to reveal the secret he had long held about Diego being Lolo's father. He knew Diego was up next and he needed time to warn him. If in fact, Lolo was planning something underhanded as he suspected, there was no time to waste. Carbajal walked directly over to Lolo, grabbed his right shoulder, and spun Lolo in his direction until they were face to face.

"What did you think of that performance? That should go a long way in shutting up the critics," Lolo boastfully stated.

"Lolo, whatever you have up your sleeve, you need to stop it now!"

Lolo had never seen his manager so furious before. "What are you talking about?" he coyly asked.

"I'm going to tell you something you will have a difficult time believing, but I swear on my mother's grave, it's the truth."

Lolo knew Carbajal well enough to know that he would never swear on his mother's grave unless he was dead serious. "What is it, Manuel?" Lolo's voice for the first time had a tone of concern.

Carbajal paused, and then he slowly murmured, "Diego Sanchez is your father."

There was no hesitation as Lolo slapped his manager hard across the face. He needed to strike something to stop the vicious lie that was being foisted upon him. Carbajal reached up and wiped away the trickle of blood from the corner of his lip. He stared directly into Lolo's eyes, making sure there was no doubt about what he had just conveyed.

Lolo yelled out, grabbing his manager by the front of his shirt. "Who told you this lie?"

Carbajal quickly recapped everything he knew about Diego and his relationship with Celaya. Carbajal told Lolo how Diego never knew that Celaya had borne him a son. He even told Lolo about bribing Pepe, the night watchman, to keep his mouth shut. Carbajal could see the anger dissipating from Lolo's face as he explained how Señor Alvarez had confided in him on his deathbed, and how Diego's old maestro had kept his secret from Diego for all those years.

Lolo listened in disbelief; shock slowly being replaced with clear-eyed fear. In the background, he could hear the next bout being announced, and a look of panic began to race across his face. As Diego's opponent flexed the defective foil provided by Lolo, the realization that the man who was moments away from stepping onto the fighting strip to face his death was his own father. Lolo didn't have time to ask all the questions he needed answered from his manager about Diego. His mind was reeling. *What have I done? Conspired in my own father's death?*

Lolo quickly told Carbajal about the plot against Diego and how he had arranged to have a defective foil put into Jamie Valle's hands.

"We have to warn Diego," Lolo blurted out to Carbajal. He wasn't quite ready to use the words "my father" in reference to Diego Sanchez.

Carbajal's expression suddenly turned pale with alarm. "We have to do more than warn Diego. We have to stop this!" Carbajal shouted, as he turned searching for Diego.

Diego was still standing in the tunnel holding Christina. He had yet to answer Lorena's plea to not enter the bout. Finally, he spoke in a low, solemn whisper, "I'm sorry, but I have to finish this."

"Diego you have a daughter to live for. You can't risk it all for your foolish macho pride!" She was practically screaming at him. Her anxious cries reverberating down the long tunnel.

"I wish you could understand. I love you, Lorena, and you've given me so much." He now had the strength to look her straight in the eyes. "But my reasons are so much more complicated than I have time to explain right now." He knew trying to explain that her ex-lover was actually his son would take more time than the few minutes he had left before his bout.

She begged him to reconsider, but it was clear there would be no stopping him. Diego gently handed Christina back to Lorena and kissed her on the cheek. He turned and started back toward the entrance of the stadium.

Lorena made one more desperate plea. "Diego, please no!"

Diego so much wanted to turn around and rush back into her arms, but he knew he had to finish what he had come to do. Diego was only a few paces from the archway leading back to the *salle d'armes*, when he heard an unexpected roar. He rushed into the stadium to see two men squaring off on the fighting strip. Initially Diego was confused, sure that he was supposed to be in the next bout. He recognized Jamie Valle by his slightly stocky stature, but who the hell was preparing to do battle in his place?

Carbajal ran over to Diego, pleading with him to stop Lolo, and stumbling over words as he tried to explain about the defective foil.

"What the hell are you talking about?" Diego pleaded, hoping for a different answer but before Carbajal could reply, Diego felt the cutting edge of truth. It was the same warning Lorena had just tried to give him in the tunnel. Her accusations about Lolo conspiring with Chase were coming true right before his eyes. Valle's foil was intended for *him*.

Diego was snapped out of his stupor by an all too familiar sound of steel on steel. The sharp rattle of the foils resonated across the *salle d'armes* as both men fought for an early advantage. Diego stood watching from the sidelines, not knowing when or how to step in and stop the bout. He prayed that his son could weather the first stages of the bout.

Lolo made several brilliant lunges and was outscoring his opponent with every move. Caught up in the heat of battle, he momentarily forgot about the danger he was in. He could see Diego out of the corner of his eye, and he wanted to prove to him that even with the potential danger of the defective sword snapping in two, he was skilled enough to win the bout.

Diego, on the other hand, knew the imminent danger his son faced having seen the great Russian champion viciously skewered in the eye by a broken foil in Rome. Diego couldn't stand it any longer and started to step onto the *piste*, but Lolo adamantly motioned him away. Diego recognized the unflinching gesture of fierce determination in his son's gesture, and stepped back to the sidelines. As much as he wanted to rescue Lolo, he realized the humiliation for Lolo would be almost as damaging to his son's ego as suffering a major injury. This was Lolo's chance to prove to the world—and now to his father—that he was worthy of carrying on the tradition of a great fencing champion.

In preparation for his next move and in a bold demonstration of his fearlessness, Lolo backed away from his opponent, openly inviting Valle to charge. His opponent, already humiliated by Lolo's dominance in the bout, answered the challenge. Valle aggressively lunged forward, brought his foil high above his head and viciously sliced it downward onto Lolo's. The foil snapped a quarter of the way down; the jagged sharp tip of raw steel glimmered in the bright lights.

Diego watching the steel fragment soar skyward, frantically screamed at Lolo in an attempt to warn him. Lolo, hearing Diego's warning, turned to see his father's contorted face. Without hesitation and unaware his foil had broken, Valle thrust his foil forward and struck Lolo just below the heart. The sound of steel striking one of Lolo's rib bones sounded like grating metal on a sharpening stone. Lolo did not move; it was as if time and space were suspended. He couldn't hear the gasps of the crowd, nor the panic in his father's voice screaming from the sidelines. Realizing what had happened, Valle quickly withdrew his bloodied foil from Lolo's chest. Lolo, barely aware he had been stabbed by the razor-thin blade, look down at the blood that was starting to stain his bleach-white lame. He slowly dropped to his knees with a look of complete astonishment. Diego and several of the other competitors rushed to Lolo's side. Lolo lay on his back staring at the ceiling. His eyes tried to follow the sun as it peaked over the crown of the tainted glass ceiling.

Diego stood momentarily over Lolo in a paralytic trance, not believing what he was seeing. When his eyes finally met Lolo's, Diego expected to see a terrified look of fear on his son's anguished face; but what he saw was a blank, calm expression. Lolo tried to form words but he was unable to utter a sound. Blood was spurting violently from his wound, flowing as if from a broken garden hose. Diego placed his hand over Lolo's lethal wound and pressed down hard. The purple-red fluid poured up through his fingers and stained his sleeve.

"Lolo, why....why did you take my place?" Tears were streaming down Diego's face.

Lolo was barely able to suck in enough air into his lungs to utter the words he had waited his entire life to speak. "For you....my father."

"Hold on, son, the stretcher is on the way." Diego was frantically trying to stop the flow of life pouring out of Lolo. He looked around the room but everything was just a blur of bodies and motion.

Lolo gurgled, struggling for another breath. The insides of his mouth were soaked entirely in crimson. "Just hold me, father." His eyes were begging for Diego's affection.

Diego gently placed his bloodied hands under Lolo's head and held him in his arms.

"Father, I have only........one.........request." There were long, painful spaces between each of his barely audible words.

"Ask anything." The pain on Diego's face was as if he were the one with the piercing wounds and not his fallen son.

"Make sure I'm with my mother." Lolo took a deep, heaving breath and then his chest went still.

Diego lifted Lolo up and embraced him tightly, trying to squeeze life back into his son. He rocked Lolo's limp body back and forth. The tears flooding his eyes splashed on his son's ashen face.

Lorena, having heard the sickening sound of the crowd, rushed into the stadium to see Diego clutching Lolo. She had no idea why Diego was suffering so much, but seeing the father of their child in such pain left her aching with compassion. She realized that her feelings for Diego were genuine and not a passing infatuation. The slow, burning flame she had conveniently hidden when she reconciled with Chase had never really been completely extinguished. She wanted to hand Christina to someone and run to Diego to console him, to comfort him as he had comforted her.

They had to pry Lolo from Diego's arms. He was not about to relinquish the only connection that still linked him to Celaya without a major struggle. It took two of his fellow swordsmen to finally extract Lolo from Diego's unwavering grip.

"Wait!" Diego cried. He looked down at his son's lifeless body. Lolo had a peaceful expression of content on his face. Diego reached over and unbuttoned Lolo's fencing jacket and removed the blood-stained scarf from his son's neck. As the stretcher-bearers carried Lolo's lifeless body away, Diego thoughtfully placed Celaya's scarf around his neck and tucked it into his fencing jacket.

Juan Guzman walked over and attempted to help Diego to his feet. "You must finish the bout, Diego."

"No, I can't," he mumbled despondently.

"You must. It is the only way you can honor his death. It's your obligation," Juan petitioned.

Diego looked at his son's foil lying on the fighting strip. With the backdrop of the tragic sighs resonating across the broad expanse of the stadium, Diego stood up and signaled to the judges that he wanted to resume the bout. The judges hurriedly discussed Diego's request and out of respect for the great champion, signaled for the two opponents to resume the bout. At first, a devastated Jaime Valle refused to engage, but when Diego pleadingly motioned to him to fight, the young man assumed an *en garde* position. Diego took one heaving breath, trying to exhale all his sorrow, and then stepped forward with Lolo's foil in hand.

Diego fought with such single-mindedness and motivation that he surpassed even the brilliance of his early career. Diego could feel Lolo's spirit, floating somewhere above the arena, watching the whole procession. It was as if Diego could see every move his opponent was going to make before it happened. *"Yes, father; a brilliant move, father,"* Lolo's voice resounded in Diego's head.

Near the last stage of the bout, Diego contemplated laying his sword onto the *piste* and simply walking away. Suddenly, he had grown tired of all the rivalry of competition. But he knew in his heart that it was time for him to bring his last battle to its natural end, and with lightening speed, Diego lunged forward, making two pinpoint-accurate *coup doubles*, scoring the final points against his outmatched opponent.

The entire arena became eerily silent as Diego walked to the center of the *piste* and placed his son's foil next to his own protective mask. The crowd slowly rose to their feet giving him a standing ovation. Oblivious to the applause of the crowd, Diego walked over to the bloodstained mat where Lolo had been struck down, collapsed to his knees, and began crying uncontrollably; his hands rested in his lap, tightly clutching Lolo's bloodied scarf.

EPILOGUE

Six months had passed since Diego's epic bout triumphantly signaled his retirement from fencing competition. He knelt at the foot of Celaya's gravestone at her parent's rancho. Lolo's more recently dug grave lay only a few feet away from his mother's. If Diego let himself fall forward with outstretched his arms he could embrace the two people he had hopelessly loved but never had a chance to really know. Diego bowed his head toward Celaya's gravestone and removed the freshly laundered scarf from around his neck. He carefully draped it around the angel adorning her headstone; he was returning it to its rightful owner. He stared at the finely engraved stone as if Celaya were peering back at him with her piercing emerald eyes, and tenderly whispered, "Mi Amada." He paused, almost suffocating on his own words, and repeated them again.

Diego stood up and brought his fingers to his lips just as Celaya had gestured when she said farewell to him at the train station over twenty years ago. He touched his heart, pressed his cupped hand against her cool tombstone, then stepped away and walked down the long slope of the hill to join Lorena, who was waiting under the shadows of a Jacaranda tree. The tree's purple flowers were in full, radiant bloom, and the sweet bouquet wafted around them as they strolled down the path with their arms wrapped around each other. Diego was tempted to look back one more time in the direction of the gravesite, but resisted. As much as he wanted to linger in the memories of Celaya and Lolo, he had more than enough reason to move on with his life. Lorena and Christina had moved in with him at his rancho outside of Ciudad Hidalgo, and Diego and Lorena were planning on getting married in the springtime. Healing for both of them was slow and difficult at times, but their devotion to each other was slowly erasing the disillusionment and pain of the past few months. As they made their way down the knoll, they could feel their newfound hope steadily melding into the present, filling their future with the liberation that comes with redemption.

The winter of 1985 ended as it had begun for Chase Chandler. He was a bitter, solitary man. He had failed in his attempt to end Diego Sanchez's life, but when he read that Lolo Nieto was Diego's son, he felt some sense of retribution against the man who had destroyed his world. Chase made several attempts to persuade his lawyer to begin legal proceedings in Mexico, hoping to gain temporary custody of Christina, but he ultimately gave up the fight when his lawyer convinced him it was doomed to failure. Chase even asked Emiliano to help him in his effort to exact revenge against Lorena. Emiliano, recognizing the sickness consuming his longtime friend, suspected Chase had something to do with Lolo's death. He refused his former partner's desperate request and told Chase he needed to move on. In fact, Emiliano made it clear to Chase that if he ever made an attempt to insert himself into Lorena and Diego's life that he would make sure to reveal the secrets of Chase's illegal missions in Mexico to the authorities.

In his obsession to inflict suffering on his ex-wife, Chase lost even the support of his devoted mother. Lorena had extended an olive branch to Rebecca and made arrangements for her to see Christina in Mexico City later that year. Even though Rebecca knew Christina wasn't part of the Chandler bloodline, she couldn't relinquish the love she had for her "granddaughter." Chase, having heard this news, became furious at his mother and threatened never to speak to her again. Rebecca tried to console her son, but made it clear she was not about to be a party to his ill feelings toward Lorena and Christina. Chase, stubborn and true to his word, never again uttered another word to his mother.

In the spring of 1986, Chase returned to the only thing that had given meaning to his life before meeting Lorena Santoya. He resumed his work as a contract agent for the FBI. Eight months later, on assignment in Colombia, he was gunned down on the backstreets of a remote jungle village. Ironically, the head of the drug ring he was attempting to infiltrate was said to have ties to another drug lord in Mexico. It was never determined that Chase's death was directly associated with retribution for Fermin Lorca, but the coincidence even raised eyebrows among the hardcore agents at the Bureau. Of course, the FBI denied any knowledge of

Chase Chandler. The only reference to his death was a back-page story in the local newspapers in Bogotá, reporting the unfortunate death of an American businessman caught in the crossfire of drug-related activities.

Wes Chandler retrieved his son's body and laid him to rest next to his Uncle Chas at the family cemetery. As the funeral party whispered their last parting prayers, the relentless winds that crisscrossed the west Texas plains seemed to echo the words of the his late Uncle Chas, "*You don't ever beat down this God-forsaken land; you just try to survive it.*"

ABOUT THE AUTHOR

 MICHAEL HAGER was born and raised in California and graduated from the University of California. His credits include essays, short stories, poetry and a theatrical play ("The Last Ride", August 2008 Production). He lives with his wife in Mexico. This is his first novel. Visit his website at www.michaelhager.net.

Breinigsville, PA USA
27 September 2010
246141BV00002B/1/P